4447 5431 ✓

EREC REX

THE THREE FURIES

EREC REX

THE THREE FURIES

KAZA KINGSLEY

Illustrations by Peter Mohrbacher

Simon & Schuster Books for Young Readers
New York   London   Toronto   Sydney

ALSO BY KAZA KINGSLEY

Check out all the books
in the Erec Rex series

Book 1: The Dragon's Eye
Book 2: The Monsters of Otherness
Book 3: The Search for Truth

EREC REX

THE THREE FURIES

SIMON & SCHUSTER BOOKS FOR YOUNG READERS
An imprint of Simon & Schuster Children's Publishing Division
1230 Avenue of the Americas, New York, New York 10020

SIMON & SCHUSTER BOOKS FOR YOUNG READERS
is a trademark of Simon & Schuster, Inc.
For information about special discounts for bulk purchases, please contact Simon & Schuster Special Sales at 1-866-506-1949 or business@simonandschuster.com.
The Simon & Schuster Speakers Bureau can bring authors to your live event. For more information or to book an event, contact the Simon & Schuster Speakers Bureau at 1-866-248-3049 or visit our website at www.simonspeakers.com.
Book design by Lucy Ruth Cummins
The text for this book is set in Adobe Caslon.
The illustrations for this book are rendered digitally.
Manufactured in the United States of America
2 4 6 8 10 9 7 5 3 1
Library of Congress Cataloging-in-Publication Data
Kingsley, Kaza.
The three Furies / Kaza Kingsley. — 1st ed.
p. cm. — (Erec Rex ; [bk. 4])
Summary: Twelve-year-old Erec Rex must meet the terrifying Nightmare King as he struggles to save his best friend Bethany from the evil Baskania.
ISBN 978-1-4169-7990-6
[1. Fantasy. 2. Dragons—Fiction.] I. Title.
PZ7.K6153Th 2010
[Fic]—dc22
2009036404
ISBN 978-1-4169-8559-4 (eBook)
erecrex.com

To Jennifer, the best sister in the world

CONTENTS

BOOK ONE
Alecto the Angry   1

PROLOGUE
3

CHAPTER ONE
Letters in Pie   5

CHAPTER TWO
The Dumpling Invasion   20

CHAPTER THREE
King Piter in Chains   30

CHAPTER FOUR
A Surprise Visit   46

CHAPTER FIVE
A Green House Investigation   64

CHAPTER SIX
A Sister's Help   74

CHAPTER SEVEN
Magnet Mountain   83

CHAPTER EIGHT
Cinnalim   97

CHAPTER NINE
Danen Nomad   107

CHAPTER TEN
Little Erec   116

CHAPTER ELEVEN
Paper Can't Be Fooled   128

CHAPTER TWELVE
The Nightmare King   140

CHAPTER THIRTEEN
Love and Sand Crabs   151

CHAPTER FOURTEEN
Finger Magic 164

CHAPTER FIFTEEN
A Final Birthday Party 177

CHAPTER SIXTEEN
Wandabelle 192

CHAPTER SEVENTEEN
The Beauty of Dreams 208

CHAPTER EIGHTEEN
The Best Present 223

BOOK TWO
Tisiphone the Vengeful 237

CHAPTER NINETEEN
Doubts 239

CHAPTER TWENTY
*One Impossible Thing
Before Breakfast* 256

CHAPTER TWENTY-ONE
Kilroy's Cuddles 269

CHAPTER TWENTY-TWO
An Even Trade 284

CHAPTER TWENTY-THREE
Windows to the Soul 302

CHAPTER TWENTY-FOUR
Lalalalal's Flight 317

CHAPTER TWENTY-FIVE
Mind Reader Extraordinaire 331

CHAPTER TWENTY-SIX
Blind Followers 347

CHAPTER TWENTY-SEVEN
Special Delivery 364

CHAPTER TWENTY-EIGHT
An Interesting Crowd 382

CHAPTER TWENTY-NINE
Your Sworn Enemy 400

CHAPTER THIRTY
The One 417

CHAPTER THIRTY-ONE
Schmaltzberry Pies 436

BOOK THREE
Megaera the Jealous 450

CHAPTER THIRTY-TWO
A Productive Swim 452

CHAPTER THIRTY-THREE
Noble Revenge 472

CHAPTER THIRTY-FOUR
The Fate of Bobby Kroc 487

CHAPTER THIRTY-FIVE
*Love, Chocolate, Conversation,
and Massive Death* 503

CHAPTER THIRTY-SIX
Tartarus 519

CHAPTER THIRTY-SEVEN
534

CHAPTER THIRTY-EIGHT
The Boy 536

CHAPTER THIRTY-NINE
Cookies and a Charm 540

EPILOGUE ONE
Three Days Later 556

EPILOGUE TWO
Two Weeks Later 558

EPILOGUE THREE
Five Hundred Years Earlier 560

BOOK ONE

Alecto the Angry

*L*ET US GET *one thing straight. I don't care how nice you act. I don't care how many wonderful things you think you have done in your life. I don't even want to hear about how much you admire me, or watch you kiss the ground that I have walked on. No matter how much you try to appeal to me, I will always, completely and irrevocably, hate your very existence.*

I want to make that fact very clear. I cannot stand you. I despise you. And I cannot wait until the day when I can sink my sharp claws into your flesh and rip all of you to shreds.

I won't ask you to understand me. Nobody does. The burdens I bear are far beyond your simple human comprehension. But let it suffice to say that I am miserable, and that is making me furious. Which makes me even more upset. Because I've been so head-splittingly angry for so long that the mere thought of my anger just enrages me even more.

I have been locked away here for an eternity. I have been mistreated. My very own sisters have made my life more of a misery than you could ever imagine. So, if you have any sense at all, when I finally do get out of here and come after you, don't try to run, or think you'll get away. Oh, and don't try to feel good about it, like your death is helping things somehow. Beyond that first moment of satisfaction for me, it will just be a meaningless waste.

That's the way life is. Get used to it.

Now, pardon me while I go and scream.

FOR JUST A fraction of a second, Bethany Cleary's head bobbed from exhaustion. But before sleep could sneak one pajamaed toe into the bedsheets of her consciousness, an electric shock jolted her painfully into alertness. If she had a voice, she would have screamed. But that had been stolen—along with her freedom.

So, instead, she settled on watching the screen. Before her, her entire life was being played like a movie in fast motion. Little things that she had long forgotten—stubbed toes, birthday parties—were dredged out for all to see.

Every part of her body ached from sitting still at this desk for so long. She couldn't move, though, because her hands were chained tightly to the chair arms. Her head throbbed from exhaustion, and from the strange metal clamps that dug into her scalp. How long had she been a prisoner here? Weeks? Months? With her mind controlled by someone else, her thoughts projected on a screen, it was impossible to say.

Her captor wanted her uncomfortable. She was freezing, starving, and the little sleep she was allowed was spent chained to this desk. That gave more incentive for her to talk if she was holding anything back—as if she wouldn't have told him whatever he wanted just to get out of here.

Well, *almost* anything. There was one person whom she would die to protect.

How old was she on the screen now? About eight years? That left only six more years of her life for her captor to sift through and then he'd be done. But that was the worst part of all. Because if he didn't find what he was looking for by then, she would not be set free.

No, unfortunately, it was quite the opposite.

CHAPTER ONE

Letters in Pie

T HERE ARE TERRIFYING monsters in our world, like the Grumbleswitch of Alexia and the frightful Minotaur. There are beautiful places, too, like Smoolie in Otherness, which is so delightful you can feel the butterflies of disbelief fluttering in your stomach when you first arrive. There are sweet things, like the Valkyries in Lerna who spend their lives happily serving the families who grew them from seeds.

But there is nothing in the universe that is more annoying than being teased again and again by a sibling. And again. And again. And again.

Except maybe being teased by two siblings.

Erec Ulysses Rex should have been having a wonderful time at home in New Jersey. It was like having a vacation in his own house. He had been away for months doing quests to become the next king of Alypium. That was the hidden land where he had been born, where magic was still known and practiced. Now he was enjoying a well-earned break. His adoptive mother, June, had been cooking his favorite meals since he came home last month. And he didn't even have to go to school, like his five siblings did. When he returned to Alypium he would meet with a tutor instead—a tutor who taught magic. Really, he should have been enjoying himself now, in every way.

But Erec had no such luck. When his five siblings were in school he was bored beyond belief. With his mother working, there was nobody for him to talk to. And when his brothers and sisters did come home, things only seemed to get worse. Danny and Sammy, his twin brother and sister who were adopted like the rest of the kids, seemed to know exactly the wrong things to say. Or, more like, the right things to make him furious. And when Erec's face turned red it was just an invitation for Danny to dish out some more.

They teased him about being "special," becoming a king, and getting spoiled at home. But those things weren't a big deal to Erec. It was the *other* thing that they kept bringing up that tormented him—a thing that was already torturing him inside. It was the very reason he was staying in New Jersey, bored and teased, instead of returning to Alypium to finish more of his quests.

That thing was Bethany, his best friend in the world. She had traveled with him from New York into wild unknown places that they had never thought existed. She was smart and funny and a lot of fun. Beyond that, she really understood him. She knew what it was like to be different. In fact, she was the only other person Erec knew who had grown up in Upper Earth but later learned that she had been born in Alypium.

The problem was, right before he came home, he had done something to completely ruin their friendship. Well, *maybe* he had ruined it. Erec still wasn't sure from all the snail mail letters she was sending to him.

He had kissed her.

Really, it wasn't as bad as it sounded. He *had* to kiss her to save her from a deathly enchantment that Baskania, the evil Sorcerer Prince, had put on her. But he had liked kissing her. A lot. So much that it was really starting to bother him. Kissing was not what he had in mind, not as far as his best friend was concerned.

Bethany seemed to be handling their kiss better than he was. At first her letters seemed totally normal, just chatting about Erec's dog, Wolfboy, that she was watching in Alypium for him. Then she started asking when Erec was coming back, then why he wasn't returning her letters. Erec wanted to write back. He was just confused about what to say. And the longer he had waited, the harder it seemed to pick up a pen. How would he explain why he had been ignoring her?

Part of Erec wanted things to be just like they were, when they were only good friends. And another part was terribly afraid that things really *were* the same, and they were still only friends, and nothing more. If he could just sort out his own head about things, and if the twins would leave him alone about it, maybe he could find a way to write her back and explain.

It had not seemed this bad right after, when Bethany and he were together, in person. Just a little embarrassing, but no big deal. But being away from her and dealing with his crazy, mixed-up thoughts was making it worse.

Erec shrank back into the overstuffed chair in the living room of their small apartment and dug his chin into his fist. He'd have to write her back soon. He didn't want her to think that he was mad at her. If he only knew what *she* thought about the whole kiss thing, it would help. . . .

The family's coat rack had been watching him and decided it was time to try cheering him up. The coat rack was, in nearly every sense, alive—as were the alarm clock, toaster, and toothbrush that Erec's mother had bought from a magical store called Vulcan. The coat rack skipped on its short legs into the middle of the room juggling four winter hats and a mitten. The act was surprisingly good, but Erec just crossed his arms. He had seen this performance so many times this winter that even the coat rack's best efforts couldn't make him smile anymore. The thing tried to toss the hats farther and skip higher, until it finally tripped, crashing into the couch and throwing hats all over the room.

From the hallway came the sounds of feet running and the apartment door slamming. Erec quickly grabbed a book that he had already finished and pretended that he was reading.

Danny burst into the room first, running a hand through his sandy brown hair. He was getting taller by the day, and he towered over Erec even though they were both almost fourteen.

"Woo-hoo!" Danny shouted, and plopped himself on the arm of Erec's chair. He tossed a frightened-looking snail into Erec's lap. "You got another snail mail thing. It was sitting outside near the front step. Looks like it's from lover girl again. Let's see it, dude."

Sammy came in after him, a slender girl-version of her twin, with long hair pulled into a bow in back.

Erec stuffed the snail into his pocket. "As if. The last time I was stupid enough to open one of these in front of you, I heard about it for weeks." He was relieved that the snails gave their letters only to the people they were sent to. The only problem was that Danny and Sammy seemed to be experts at finding his letters no matter where he put them.

Danny winked at him. "I understand. It's obviously true love, or you wouldn't need to hide anything." He grinned. "Ah, the secrets you two must have. . . ."

Erec bit his lip, trying to keep himself from whipping the letter out of the snail just to prove Danny wrong—which, of course, was exactly what Danny wanted. Danny would find *something* in the letter to make fun of. Something small that Erec wouldn't have even noticed. And then Erec would start to wonder what that little thing meant. Which Danny probably knew would happen. Which was making everything going on in Erec's head worse and worse.

Sammy walked over, swinging her backpack around before dropping it on a chair. She bowed low to Erec, nearly touching her head to her knees. "King Erec," she said when she stood. "I understand your queen has sent you another love letter."

Erec scowled at her. "Give it a rest, Sammy. Just because you don't have a boyfriend, you don't need to be all over my case."

Sammy's face lit up. "Did you hear that, Danny? He admitted it! That's the first time he admitted he was Bethany's boyfriend." She smiled at him. "We're making progress."

"Ugh!" Erec dropped his head into his hands. "I didn't say that at all."

There was only one thing he could do to get rid of them. It was a cheap trick, but it worked every time. He looked up at the twins with a grin, and played with his eyes.

Erec had once had a dragon friend named Aoquesth. The dragon had given him both of his eyes before he died saving Erec in a battle. They had been attached to the back of Erec's own eyes by a magician-surgeon. In the beginning it had been hard for Erec to swivel his eyes in their sockets so that his dragon eyes faced out, but after practicing at home, rotating his eyes had now become second nature.

Sammy backed away, knowing what was coming. She hid her face with her hand. "Oh, no . . ."

But Danny wasn't expecting it. Erec rolled his eyes up and up until he saw all the way into the darkness of their sockets. Seconds later his dragon eyes emerged into view. The room looked bright green as he looked up through the slitlike pupils. He rolled them slowly to the left until he was looking into darkness again, and then from the right his normal eyes appeared.

Danny watched him a moment, trembling. Then he walked away with a queasy look on his face.

Erec smiled. It was a cool thing to be able to do. And a darn shame that he had to hide it from the other kids in New Jersey. Wouldn't it be fun to get a reaction from someone that had never seen magic?

Heck, even people who knew all about magic would probably scream if they saw him do that. He was the only one ever to have a dragon eye, let alone two.

The only person who didn't seem to mind watching him roll his eyes around was his adopted brother Trevor. Redheaded Trevor, nine years old, sat down by Erec's feet on the floor and looked up, watching with a quiet reverence. Trevor had his own way of looking at the world. He didn't speak much, and most people thought he didn't understand what was going on. But every now and then he would pop up with some amazing statement that showed he not only got it, but he was quite brilliant.

Once Danny and Sammy went into the kitchen, Erec pulled the snail out of his pocket and slid out a long slip of white paper. Bethany's handwriting was scrawled on it. It looked like she wrote it in a hurry.

Erec,

I hope you are okay. I'm really starting to get worried that something is wrong. Are you angry at me? I hope you don't mind that I e-mailed your mother. I thought that maybe you were missing or that something horrible happened to you. But she said you were fine.

So why aren't you writing me back? Did I do something wrong? If so, please tell me so we can get over this. I really don't understand.

Like I said before, you should come back here soon. I've been getting these weird ideas in my head. Something is telling me that I need to leave this house and go find Baskania. I know it sounds crazy, but I'm having a harder time resisting it. Something is making me want to go, bad. I have a feeling that if I do go, I'll find him easily, too.

But what will I do if I _do_ find him? I mean, I'm supposed to be hiding from him. I know that. Maybe if I found him, I could talk to him and that would make everything better. Oh, I don't know. None of it makes sense.

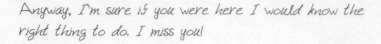

Anyway, I'm sure if you were here I would know the right thing to do. I miss you!

Your friend,

Bethany

Erec's heart sank when he read the letter. He had not been a good friend at all. Now was the time to write her back. So what if he was confused about things and didn't know what he wanted? He could just keep that all to himself.

He stuffed the paper back into his pocket when the twins walked back into the room. What was she talking about, though? Wanting to find Baskania? That was crazy. The evil Shadow Prince, Baskania, wanted to capture her. He was convinced, from a prophecy he had heard, that Bethany held the secret that would let him learn the Final Magic. With that power he would have ultimate control over life and death. Just what Baskania didn't need.

Erec's father, King Piter of Alypium, had assured him that Bethany would be safe in his house, as long as she didn't leave. Her older brother, Pi Cleary, would be there too, to watch over her. But Bethany knew better than to leave. What was coming over her? She wasn't making this up just to get him to come back, was she? She was probably beyond frustrated that Erec never answered her letters. But no . . . Bethany would never make things up like this.

Danny pulled a paper out of his pocket and read it, a funny look on his face. "Weird. Check this out, guys."

Sammy looked at the letter, then sat down on the couch and stared at it harder. "I've never seen anything like this. It looks like it's written in . . . *pie.*"

"That's what I was thinking," Danny said. He sat next to her and stared at the paper. "Blueberry pie, actually."

"Uh-huh." Sammy nodded. "I thought it was boysenberry, but you're right. It's blueberry. How did it get in your pocket?"

"No clue. Someone must have slipped it in without me noticing."

Erec's curiosity got the better of him. "What are you guys talking about?" He sat on the other side of Sammy and looked. Symbols covered the page, and they seemed sloppily drawn in a purplish mess, as if someone actually had dipped a stick into a pie and wrote with it. "Maybe this was drawn with some kind of dye . . . or a falling-apart marker, maybe."

Both Danny and Sammy looked at him like he was crazy. "It's pie," Danny said. "That's pretty obvious. But what worries me is what it says." He leaned the note toward Erec, a concerned look on his face.

Sammy nodded, but Erec only stared harder at the page. He had no idea why they thought it was obvious that this was written in pie—and no clue what it said. The symbols made no sense at all. "You guys understand this?"

"You don't?" Sammy said. "It's pretty clear. I'm hoping it's a sick joke."

Danny raised an eyebrow. "What's not to understand here? Maybe true love has finally gotten to your brain."

Erec grabbed the paper and studied it. The smudges looked like a thick, messy exclamation point, followed by a pattern of small smears and then an upside-down rainbow and a small handprint. After that was a box completely filled in with blueberry pie filling, or whatever the note was made with.

"Guys, I'm thinking this is just a bunch of stains. Someone probably used this paper instead of a napkin."

Danny lowered his eyebrows at Erec. "Don't be a dope. This is as simple as a message with an eye, a heart, and the letter *U*. I love you.

You know, like your girlfriend writes you in her letters."

Erec swallowed down the anger brought up by that comment. "All right, then. What does this thing say?"

Sammy looked at him strangely, as if he really should know already. She pointed at each blotch in order. "This footprint is smudged, showing that someone was running. It says we must run away. Then the splattered pie after it says 'Be careful,' like someone got a pie in their face."

"What?" Erec was incredulous. "How can you tell that is pie in someone's face? It looks like rain to me."

"Rain?" Danny looked as amazed as Erec. "This is totally obvious. The frowns and the handprint say there are bad men coming to capture us. And the dark box says go hide, right away."

"Eeew—kay." Erec raised his eyebrows, but the twins were too caught up in the letter to notice.

"This isn't funny," Sammy said. "Is someone trying to scare us?"

"I don't know." Danny went to look out of a window. When he didn't see anything unusual he sat back down. "There's nothing we can do. Just keep an eye out for other strange things, I guess."

Neither of them looked happy. In a moment the door opened and Nell came in with her walker. "Hey, Erec. I found a snail mail for you outside by the front step."

Another one? Erec went and got it from her. Who could this be from? He was too curious to wait to open it this time. Could Bethany have written back so soon?

Erec,

Something is really wrong with me. It's getting harder and harder for me to stay in the house. I'm really fighting it, but I have to go out and try to find

Baskania. I don't know what's making me do it, but I don't think I can control it anymore.

If I do go, I'm going to take a bunch of snails and paper with me so I can let you know where I am.

Don't worry, I have a feeling everything will be okay.

Bethany

Erec gulped. Everything would *not* be okay. Had she gone crazy? He grabbed some paper and wrote her back.

Bethany,

Do not, I repeat, <u>do not</u> go out of the house. You would be in terrible danger. I don't know why you want to go find Baskania. He'd capture you right away.

Just talk to King Piter about it. I'll try to come soon.

And sorry for not writing back sooner. I was just being stupid.

Erec

If he only had his mother's magical Seeing Eyeglasses. They let the wearer see and talk to the person they missed the most, so he could get in touch with Bethany right away.

He had no sooner given the letter to the snail when a crash resounded. Bits of sparkling glass shot through the room. A silver baton with glittering blue ends had been thrown through the window and hit the wall not far from where Erec stood.

"What's this?" Danny picked up the baton. A paper was tied to it with string. He unfolded it and grew pale.

"What is it?" Sammy took it from his hand. Erec saw more smudges on the paper, like the one before, except this time they were brown. "It says, 'Get away now. You are in danger.' This one is written in chocolate cream pie."

"Are you sure that's what it says?" Erec asked.

Sammy shot him an annoyed glance. "Of course. I think we should call Mom. *Someone* threw this in here, and they must still be outside."

Danny and Erec looked out the broken window, but they saw nobody on the lawn. Trevor appeared behind them and pointed. "Look."

"What?" Erec didn't see anything.

"It's another snail. I bet it's for you."

Erec rushed out and scooped the small creature up. In a flash he pulled a crumpled paper from its thin, flat shell.

Erec,

I had to go out. I'm being careful, don't worry. I just wanted to let you know.

I have more snails with me. If anything happens I'll let you know.

Bethany

Erec smacked his head. *No!* He had to get to Alypium fast and find her. As he ran back inside, though, there was another crash.

A red ball shattered another window. Everyone looked afraid to pick it up. Finally, Danny went over to it and pulled a note off of the ball. "It says, 'Get away from your apartment immediately, or you will be captured. Run.'" He closed his eyes a moment. "I'm not sure if we should believe this note. At least Zoey is safe at day care until Mom picks her up."

Danny picked up the phone and called their adoptive mother, June, on her cell phone, and told her what happened. She told them to call the local police station, which was a few blocks away, and see if an officer would come pick them up. She would meet them at the station.

Trevor tapped Erec on the shoulder and pointed out the window. There, unmistakably, was another snail shell sitting on the grass.

Erec gasped. Whether or not crazy people were throwing things into their apartment, nothing was going to keep him away from this letter. Trembling, he ran outside to pick it up.

Erec,

Sorry. I must be worrying you. I know I'm being an idiot. I just have to let you know I decided to go to the Green House, where President Inkle lives. I don't know why, but I'm sure Baskania is there, and he is waiting for me.

I wanted to let you know where I was in case anything happened.

If it does, I am forever sorry.

Your best friend,

Bethany

Erec ran back inside, torn between fear and anger. How could she do this? She knew better. It was like walking into sure death. How could he stop her?

Then, all of a sudden, he stumbled across the floor. The room was spinning. He grabbed onto a wall to steady himself.

A scene flashed through his mind like a short movie:

Bethany wandered in through the front doors of the Green House, a blank look on her face. Five paces into the building a tall man grabbed her by the arm and pulled her forward. She did not resist.

Thanatos Baskania stood at the other end of the room, laughing. Tall and imposing in his flowing black pin-striped cloak, he smirked at Bethany. Three eyes glared from his forehead and one from each cheek. "Let her go, Mauvis. She'll come to me on her own — won't you, my dear? I see you are right on time."

Mauvis let go, and Bethany continued straight toward Baskania, looking confused.

Baskania pointed at her slowly, eyes narrowing. A puff of smoke shot from his finger, and . . .

The vision faded.

Erec looked down at his hands, where dragon scales had appeared. They were now fading away. It had happened to him again. He had just had another cloudy thought.

CHAPTER TWO

The Dumpling Invasion

VER SINCE HE could remember, strange commands, which Erec called cloudy thoughts, would come over him in times of crisis. They forced him to do what they said. Even if he tried to resist, he could not. Everybody from the Kingdoms of the Keepers had some type of unusual gift, and this was his.

After the eyes of Aoquesth the dragon had been attached to the back of his own, Erec's cloudy thoughts had changed. They became more intense. He would get visions first, before the commands. They were like movies showing him what would happen next if he did not change things. This was because the dragon eyes could show him the future.

What also happened now when he got cloudy thoughts was even stranger. His whole body changed. Scales appeared on his skin, and he turned green. He had even breathed fire before and sprouted wings and flown into the sky. It was weird, and a little scary, like he was actually turning into a dragon. He hoped it would not keep getting worse.

But never, ever, had he experienced anything like the vision he had just seen. His chest tightened as he thought about it until it was hard to breathe. Bethany had been captured by Baskania! Before this time, his cloudy thoughts had always told him how to stop the bad things he saw from happening. But this time the vision ended abruptly. The image of Bethany had flashed into his head and then it was gone like a puff of smoke. There were no commands. How was he supposed to fix things?

Danny, Sammy, Trevor, and Nell were staring at him.

Danny was the first to come out of his shock. "Dude, that was really freaky. You know that?"

Erec nodded, unable to talk. All he could think of was Bethany. He slumped down against the wall and sat on the floor, then dropped his head into his hands.

"Are you okay?" Sammy sat next to him and put her arm around him.

Nell came closer with her walker and leaned over it toward him. "Did changing like that scare you?"

"No." Erec's voice sounded squeaky. "It's Bethany. She . . ." He had to bite on his tongue to keep from losing it, but it didn't work for long. Hot tears overflowed his lids and spilled down his cheeks. He couldn't say it. Bethany was in terrible danger. Or maybe even dead.

Now everyone looked more worried. "What happened?" Sammy said. "Did you get a vision of Bethany? What did your cloudy thought tell you to do?"

Erec sniffed and wiped his face with his sleeve. "There is nothing I can do. It's too late." He put his head into his arm so that nobody could see him crying. How could he have let this happen? She was his best friend. He was such an idiot. He hadn't even answered her letters. Why was he so completely stupid?

He could tell from the short vision he had that Baskania must have bewitched her to come to him. If he had just gone back earlier, like Bethany had wanted him to, he could have stopped this from happening somehow.

But he had been too worried about his idiotic feelings to be there protecting her.

Something crashed through the window and hit him on the head. It was gloppy and sticky, sliding down his check like a slug. He peeled it off and wiped his face on his sleeve. The thing in his hand looked and smelled like a big, oily dumpling. It had another note tied on to it.

Danny unwrapped the note and showed it to Sammy. "Look, it's the same symbol language. This one is saying that our old babysitter will meet us and help us hide. We just have to go outside and she'll take care of us."

"Old babysitter? I wonder who that could be. But thank goodness someone is helping," Sammy said. "Let's go find her."

Erec's mind was spinning, but he could still process what Sammy just said. "Are you crazy? Has everyone gone completely nuts? First Bethany is walking into mortal danger on purpose, and now you!" He immediately felt bad that he had blamed Bethany for going to Baskania. She had obviously been put under a spell. But what was Sammy's excuse? "Don't you realize these people are trying to tempt us to go outside? They are probably the ones after us to begin with.

Which old babysitter is it, anyway? If it was someone trustworthy, they would come knock like a normal person."

Sammy looked at the paper, frowning. "It's really strange, though. I can tell by this writing that this person *is* trustworthy. Don't you think so, Danny? I think that it's our old sitter, Mrs. Smith. Even though she was a bit odd, she must be trying to help us."

Danny nodded. "I know. It's weird to me, too. I remember her as being awful. But there's something about these symbols. It seems like I can read more into them than just what they say. This person is telling us the truth."

Erec almost screamed. "Has it ever occurred to you this is just a trap? A spell put on those notes to make you think that way? I can't even read them. Maybe they're just bewitching the two of you." He grabbed the note from Sammy's hand and handed it to Nell. "Do you understand this?"

Nell shook her head and giggled nervously. "Uh, it just looks like a bunch of scribbles written in . . . is this written in blood?"

"No," Danny rolled his eyes. "It's in strawberry rhubarb pie. Can't you tell?"

"Um . . . no." Nell handed the paper back to Erec with an eyebrow raised.

Erec held the paper before Trevor. "What about you? Any luck with this?"

Trevor studied it a minute. It looked like he was making calculations in his head. In fact, it seemed sure that he would soon come up with an interpretation, but then he shook his head. "It's a language. See the patterns? But I don't know what it says."

"Okay, guys," Erec said, "let's call the police. It's too dangerous to go outside. Someone is waiting for us out there."

"Erec," Sammy explained patiently. "Of course someone is waiting. It's our old babysitter Mrs. Smith out there. Don't you remember her? She was a little weird, but not a maniac or anything. She just wants to help us."

Erec remembered Mrs. Smith very well. The only time he had seen her before was the morning after his mother had been kidnapped by Baskania's servants. She was probably one of them.

He felt dazed. Part of him wanted to run as fast as he could to Alypium and try to find Bethany, but it had to be too late. He had to keep everyone safe here. Danny and Sammy were affected by those notes somehow. It was up to Erec to make sure they didn't do anything crazy. If he could only ignore his heart tearing to pieces over Bethany . . .

"Look." He got up and started to pace near the door. "Let's just think things over logically. Okay? We can't leave this place with crazy people outside that are throwing rocks through our windows. Mrs. Smith is the least trustworthy person I can think of. Okay?"

Danny and Sammy looked at one another, exasperated. "It's not safe in here," Sammy said. "Those letters were clear. We have help out there. We need to go now." She linked her arm around Trevor's and tried to wave Nell toward the door. Trevor and Nell didn't look excited about leaving.

Erec blocked the doorway. "Nobody is going anywhere." Reasoning with them wasn't going to work. He would have to use force. But Danny might overpower him.

Everyone stood still, watching one another. Tension surged through the room. Nell slowly walked next to Erec, swinging her walker around to face the room. She might not have been strong, but it felt good to have something big and metal blocking the door.

Loud knocks pounded on the door at his back. The vibrations hammered through his spine. A familiar voice, like a rake scraping through gravel, called out, "Open up, Sorry. Danny and Sammy, are you okay in there?"

Erec remembered that Mrs. Smith had thought his name was Sorry. It was obviously her.

Sammy shouted, "We're fine. We'll come out in a second," and hurried to the door.

Nell held up her walker, and Trevor stood at her side. The door started to shake behind them. Danny was trying to reach for the doorknob.

Erec shoved Trevor in front of the doorknob instead. "Hold on to it for dear life, Trev. I'll be right back."

Erec ran into his mother's room and madly fished through her drawers. He found what he was looking for under a blanket. It looked like a small silver ring, but it was the Substance Channel, an item his mother had bought from that magical store called Vulcan. It could transport people anywhere. All they had to do was concentrate on where they wanted to go.

He took the Substance Channel out of its box and rubbed it in his hands like he had seen his mother do. Soon it glowed with a greenish light. More rattling and shouts came from the front door. He had to hurry.

How had his mother made this ring big enough to climb through? She had pulled it somehow. Erec latched his fingers around the ring and tugged—it grew wide. The metal was soft and sparkly now, and stretched easily in his hands. It opened into a huge hoop. Sparks of electricity shot from it, jolting him so that he had to pull his hands away. Still, it hung in the air on its own.

The commotion in the living room was growing louder. Stomping and urgent shouts carried down the hall. Mrs. Smith sounded like she was coming inside.

Erec took a breath. The Substance Channel started to spin so fast that the air whirling around it blew his hair back. He had to get everyone in here fast before it was too late.

He ran into the living room but stopped short. Mrs. Smith's round frame filled the entryway. A sickly white powder made her look ghostly, and her generous cheeks were decorated with sharp circles of bright red makeup. Black hair was slicked tightly down each side of her face, meeting under her fourth chin and giving her face the shape of a wobbly heart. Thick layers of toothpaste-blue eye shadow encased her narrow eyes. She was eating a handful of what looked like the same greasy dumplings that had been thrown through their window.

After polishing off the last dumpling, she wiped her slick hands on her bright yellow overcoat, stepped forward, and grabbed Sammy's and Danny's wrists in her thick paws. Erec was amazed to see that neither of them struggled. Trevor, however, began to kick at one of her staunch legs. Mrs. Smith did not seem to notice.

Also in the room were two other very unusual-looking people. A skinny man who looked about seven feet tall was juggling some small balls—at least they looked small compared to his hands. Half of his shocking red hair was slicked down onto his head with thick grease. The other half had escaped its oiled jail, standing a foot above his head and sprouting wild curls in all directions.

The other man was short and normal-looking—except for the tall top hat on his head and the huge wooden barrel that he wore, hanging with thick straps over his shoulders so only his head, arms, and feet were poking out.

Erec had to get his siblings away from them. He hooked Nell's arm over his shoulder and grabbed her waist, picking up her and her walker. "C'mon, Trevor. And Danny? Sammy? Could you come here a minute?"

"Not now, Erec." Danny sounded annoyed. "It's dangerous here. Okay?"

"That's right, Sorry," Mrs. Smith snapped. "It's time you got the message, and scrambled like an egg."

The man in the barrel nodded. "Tha's right, kid. You best listen to Dumpling here, if you knows what's best for ya."

Dumpling? Mrs. Smith's name was Dumpling? Well, it did seem to fit. "You guys," Erec said, smiling like their best brother, "this will just take one minute. Please, come into Mom's room. We need to take some things with us before we go."

Danny and Sammy didn't answer, but just stood there as if they were unsure what to do. Nell and Trevor, however, jumped toward him, wanting to get away from the visitors. He helped Nell down the hall into his mother's room, and Trevor followed. The Substance Channel had stopped spinning. Now it hung still, suspended in the air. A green light pulsed from it. Nell and Trevor looked into the blackness inside, eyes wide.

But he had to get Danny and Sammy. Erec could hear them explaining to Dumpling Smith that they couldn't leave without Erec, Trevor, and Nell. She was arguing with them. So Dumpling only wanted the twins? Erec panicked. He had to get them away from her. Trevor helped steady Nell in front of the Substance Channel, and Erec sped back into the room, just as Mrs. Dumpling Smith was trying to drag the twins out the door.

This time they were struggling, trying to make her understand. Sammy pulled back against the door frame. "We can't leave our brothers and sister here. We have to protect them, too!"

"There is no time for them," Mrs. Smith said. "We must get you to safety quickly."

The huge woman and her two friends could easily overpower Erec. He glanced at the coat rack for help, giving it a shrug. "C'mon, guys. Please. You left all your important stuff in Mom's room. You can come right back, okay?"

"All right." Danny yanked his arm out of Mrs. Smith's grip. "We'll be right back."

Mrs. Smith looked suspicious as she watched the twins walk away. "What is that Sorry up to? We better check." She got up to follow them and nodded to her friends to come along. Her girth filled the hallway in front of the tall man, and the man in the barrel closed in behind him, leaving little room for his wide strides.

"Hurry up, guys!" Erec tore ahead to his mother's room, and Danny and Sammy followed him. He was amazed at how fast Mrs. Smith was. She would never let them climb into the Substance Channel.

Dumpling Smith was closing in on them. But right when it seemed hopeless, the coat rack threw itself down across the entrance to the hallway, right in front of the shorter man's feet. The third man had too much momentum to stop himself, and he tripped over the coat rack and started rolling in his barrel down the hall. A bowling ball in motion, he knocked the tall man over like a pin, sending both of them flying into Mrs. Smith's back end.

Shaped a bit like a ball herself, Mrs. Smith tumbled forward. The two men spilled over her, rolling and tangling more until they resembled a pile of spaghetti and meatballs.

Erec lifted Nell up to the Substance Channel. "Climb in and I'll give you your walker. Here." He grabbed Trevor. "Hold Trev's hand. We should all hold hands in there so we don't get separated."

Erec helped them both in quickly. Sammy took Trevor's hand and climbed in after, pulling Danny in after her. Erec grabbed Danny's hand and Nell's walker and dove into the ring after them.

An unseen force seemed to pull him through the hoop. He looked back and saw Mrs. Smith and her strange friends flopping over one another, trying to stand up. Then he sank into the blackness around him.

Danny's hand and the walker were the only things he was sure were there. It felt like he was floating in space.

He heard Nell's voice. "Erec? Where are you?"

"I got him," Danny said. "What is this thing? Don't you think we should have just listened to Mrs. Smith?"

"I don't like this place," Trevor said.

"Listen, guys, I've been here before," Erec replied calmly. "I'm taking us somewhere safe. Just let your minds go blank and hold on tight."

Erec shut his eyes and concentrated on the home of his father, King Piter. It was hard not to think about Bethany, but he closed her out of his mind. If he did concentrate on her, even by accident, the Substance Channel would take him to her and, at the same time, right to Baskania.

King Piter's home. His castle no longer existed. It had been destroyed. But his father's home would be safe. They could stay there until he figured out what to do next. Maybe his mother could even come stay with them.

Take me to my father's home.

If only he knew what he would find waiting there.

CHAPTER THREE

King Piter in Chains

T HE SUBSTANCE CHANNEL worked. In moments, Erec and his siblings were whizzing through space. Erec could feel a tunnel forming around him, opening and shutting as he went through almost as if he was being swallowed. The warm material around them was the Substance itself: the network of magic that filled the world. Without it, life could not exist. But in our everyday world of Upper

Earth it had thinned so much that magic was no longer possible.

He was having trouble holding onto Nell's walker, which kept wanting to yank out of his grip, and keeping Danny's hand in his. Then, with a sharp jerk to his left, Erec was spit out through the ring of light. His siblings toppled onto the floor after him. The ring glimmered a moment in the air and then disappeared.

Erec sat up and gasped. A shocked face stared straight back at him. After a moment he came to his senses and recognized that it was his old friend and butler, Jam Crinklecut. Gray-green eyes twinkling, Jam sported his usual black butler suit with tails, gray vest, and white gloves.

"Young sir? I was . . . not expecting you." He looked around. "Danny and Sammy, I presume? And Trevor and Nell? I remember you from my wonderful visit at your home. What a pleasure. Welcome, sirs. Modoms." He bowed low.

"Jam!" Erec sprang to his feet and threw an arm around the butler.

At first Jam looked surprised, but he quickly smiled. "And how is young sir doing?"

That question brought everything home for Erec. He had not had time to process what had happened to his best friend, and now he found himself choking on his words as he tried to speak them. "Is . . . Bethany . . ."

"Bethany?" Jam smiled. "She must be in her suites. Shall I ring her?"

A ray of hope lit within him, but he was afraid to believe it. Had his vision been wrong? Maybe nothing had happened yet . . . and he still had time to stop her.

But the phone rang and rang in Bethany's suites. Jam frowned. "I don't know where else she could be. I thought she had been working on her book. That's mostly what she's been doing since she's been stuck inside here."

Erec's stomach turned over, and his last hopes blew out in a long sigh. It was no use. He knew exactly what had happened to her. How could he tell Jam? And worse, her brother Pi?

Even the air felt thick and heavy. It seemed to drip sadness. Then he remembered that there was another reason it was hard to breathe here. Each time he returned to the Kingdom of the Keepers after being away awhile, he would notice this feeling. The Substance here was thicker, and it gave off a depressing aura that he grew used to after a day or two.

Trying to ignore it, Erec glanced out the window, as if Bethany might be outside walking with her pink kitten, Cutie Pie. Of course she wasn't there. What if he never saw her again? Why hadn't he just come back a month earlier when she wanted him to?

Something caught his eye on the grass. It looked like a growing drop of blood. In a moment it started wiggling, and Erec recognized it as a snail. Bethany was writing! He ran outside and grabbed it off the ground.

But the snail letter was from a friend of Erec's, Oscar. At first, his heart sank—but he had been worried about Oscar for a while now. What had happened to him was awful. Oscar's old tutor, Rosco, had somehow learned how to read his mind. That might not have been so bad—except that Rosco was one of Baskania's favorite assistants. So everything that Oscar knew was reported straight to their worst enemy. If Oscar saw Erec somewhere, Baskania would know where Erec was and try to capture him.

Dear Erec,

I've decided that things have to change for me, so I want to let you know what's been going on. It feels like I've been alone forever now. I thought that if I just hid and spied on people I would learn how to get back at Rosco, and maybe also find a new magic tutor. But it was so hard being away from everyone that I care about, with no friends. That was driving me crazy.

Well, I just can't do it anymore. I mean, I still am trying to stay hidden. I don't want to run into you by accident—we both know how horrible it would be if Baskania found you. But a new idea finally hit me, and I have some big plans. Revenge. After everything that Rosco has put me through, it's all I can think about. So don't even think about trying to talk me out of it. If somebody was reading your mind and telling everything you thought to your worst enemy, and if that somebody had killed your father, you would feel the same way. This is all I've been thinking about for months.

I spent time in Aorth tracking down where Rosco lives and spying on his house. He was never there. The guy travels all the time. So I snuck into his house and used his Port-O-Door once to see where he just went, and it was the Green House in Alypium. I need to go there, spend time there, and really see what's going on.

You should know that I'll be in Alypium. I'll make sure to wear sunglasses and a big floppy hat to stop me from looking around at things. Also I've gotten really good at watching my feet when I walk, so hopefully I won't see you. Hopefully with the hat and dark glasses Rosco and Baskania won't recognize me, either.

I'll stay in touch to let you know everything I see when I spy on them. It's the least I can do for you. One thing I've found out is that Balor, Damon, and Dollick Stain had crowns made for themselves, along with thrones. They have days set aside for people to come meet them and take their pictures with the three kings-to-be. It's enough to make you throw up.

I hope you're okay. Don't feel like you have to write back. If you do, remember not to tell me anything important. I'm sure Rosco would appear and grab the snail letter right after I read it again.

Your friend forever,

Oscar

So the Stain triplets were posing as the next rulers of the three Kingdoms of the Keepers? Erec cringed. Balor, Damon, and Dollick Stain, kids his age, had been cloned from Baskania himself. They were doing everything they could to really become the next three kings, but if they did they would rule with greed, malice, and violence. On top of that, they would hand over their royal scepters to Baskania. According to King Piter that would cause mass destruction.

If only Bethany were here, she could reason with Oscar, get him to move on and forget about revenge on Rosco. She was good at that kind of thing. Oscar had nobody to hang out with now and nothing else to think about except for what Rosco had done to him.

Erec found some paper and wrote back to him.

Dear Oscar,

Bethany has been captured, and I don't even know
if she's alive. I don't care if Rosco sees this letter
and tells Baskania—he's the one who took her, so it's
no news to him. I'm worried sick. If you're . . . around
anyone who might know, tell me if you overhear where
they are keeping her, or anything at all that could help.

It sounds like Baskania is trying to make everyone
excited about Balor, Damon, and Dollick becoming kings.
How could people fall for that? Can't they see that
the Stain triplets are rotten to the core? It's such
a joke. If they really became the three new rulers
of Alypium, Ashona, and Aorth, they would hand their
scepters to Baskania, and he would go mad with power
and destroy the world. Try to tell people that, though,
and they think you're crazy.

I'm glad you're okay. I really miss hanging out with
you and Jack. I haven't seen him in a while. You should
forget about revenge, though. It's only going to make
things worse for you, I think.

Your friend always,

Erec

Erec put the letter into the snail's shell, then looked out the window. Rosco would take the letter from Oscar and trace it minutes

after he got it. Unless he wanted Baskania paying him a visit, Erec thought he had better send it from somewhere else.

Cutie Pie, Bethany's fluffy pink kitten, pounced onto the window sill and looked at him suspiciously.

"Have you seen Bethany, Cutie Pie? Do you know where she went?"

The cat put a paw on the window and looked outside.

"She was captured by Baskania, kitty. We have to save her." Erec felt dumb talking to a cat, but Cutie Pie was pretty smart. Maybe she would help in some way.

Cutie Pie stared at Erec for a second and then darted through the open window. In a moment she was tearing toward Alypium. For a moment, Erec considered following her. But chasing a cat didn't seem promising, so he wished her luck instead.

Erec found the Port-O-Door in his father's house and randomly picked a city called Clalm, the first place he saw on the map of Otherness. He tossed the snail that held his letter to Oscar onto the red soil of Clalm and watched it disappear into the earth.

What would he do about Bethany? He could not face the reality that he was probably too late. Was he just going to sit here and accept that she was captured and dead? No. He had to do something....

Maybe his father would know what to do. He found Jam and asked, "Is my dad here?" It still sounded strange referring to King Piter as his father. That truth had been hidden from him since he was too young to remember.

Jam cleared his throat and whispered, "It's best you go alone, sir. He has been having a bit of a tough time. I'll make some snacks for your brothers and sisters."

The king sat on his throne in a smaller version of Castle Alypium's throne room. A few tapestries hung on the walls, and ornate leaded windows made the room sparkle. The throne itself was immense. Solid gold, it must have been fifteen feet high, studded with gems. Pearl inlays and carvings decorated the sides and back in what looked like strange languages, and a huge diamond, the size of a bicycle wheel, was embedded in the center of its high back.

A big, rough stone, the Lia Fail, sat at the base of the throne. This magical chunk of rock was said to scream in the presence of the true king during a coronation. Erec, in fact, had seen it happen. During a coronation ceremony, the thing had once screamed for him.

Chains hung loosely around the king, holding him in his seat. His hair had grown a pale yellow, and his skin hung loose off of his frame. The king looked so sickly and frail that Erec almost didn't recognize him. Distracted, he stared in wonder at something in the long arm of the chair. Erec saw the king's scepter there, resting in a slot that had been created for it. The chains held King Piter's arms back from the scepter, just allowing one of his fingers to graze against its edge.

For a moment, Erec forgot all about the king. His entire being was drawn to the scepter. Its ornate gems and patterned, carved gold called to him, waking all of his old desires for it. The scepter's powerful magic had felt so amazing when he had used it before. It had sent jolts of electricity and power through him, leaving him with deep cravings for that feeling to happen again. His mouth watered, looking at the thing. It did not help that it was *his* now, officially.

Erec walked slowly toward the scepter, reaching out for it. His need for the thing seemed to grow the closer he got to it. He was silly to have left it here. King Piter had insisted that he guard the scepter for Erec, that Erec was not yet ready to use it. But that was just silly. He would be *fine* feeling its power again. It was the most wonderful thing he had ever experienced. It gave him the strength and purpose he needed.

Chains were around the king's arms . . . maybe they would keep him from grabbing the scepter before Erec could. In a moment Erec trembled with excitement and hope. He could take the scepter now—just reach for it and snatch it—and the king wouldn't be able to stop him!

He was breathing faster. But then he looked at his father's glazed eyes and a chill raced through him. Was that what Erec looked like now? Haunted, possessed by this magic, ready to do anything for it?

Erec took a breath. A small voice in his mind reminded him that his father was right. He wasn't ready. The scepter haunted him, filling his days with longing and his nights with vivid dreams. It didn't matter if he told himself that he would use it only for good, to help right the wrongs of the world. Deep inside he knew what would happen if it was his. His own dreams had showed him. He would only crave more and more power. There was no way he would be able to resist its pull.

He forced himself to step back away from it. Why was he here? He was confused now . . . Bethany! How could he have been so distracted by the scepter that he could forget her? The idea made him sick, and he backed away from it more.

"Dad? How are you doing? Dad . . . ? Hey, it's me, Erec."

The king's eyes were glazed. He ran his finger along the gold scepter as though he hadn't heard a thing. Erec noticed how thin and sickly he looked.

Erec spoke louder. "Dad? King Piter?"

Erec touched his father's shoulder. There was still no response, so he shook the king. "Are you okay? What's going on with those chains?"

King Piter startled a bit, then turned toward Erec. Recognition lit his face and he sighed. "Erec. You're back." He shrugged in embarrassment. "It's easier for me with these chains here. I can take them off if I need to. They're just a . . . reminder to hold back." He cleared his throat, looking awkward. "How was your trip home?"

"Fine. Dad, Bethany is—" Erec's throat tightened and he could not speak. Those words could not be said, or they would make her danger more real somehow. Everything might shatter around those words.

The king's forehead wrinkled with concern. "What's wrong with Bethany? Can I help?" But then he looked back at his scepter and immediately was lost.

Erec could not imagine how hard this must be for his father. If Erec had been near the scepter for more than a month, like the king had, he would never have kept himself away from it. No, he would have become a power-mad psycho trying to rule the world with it.

For a moment everything seemed to glimmer. Erec felt his knees buckle. This was all his fault. The king *used* to be able to use his scepter with no problem at all. The power of his castle had given him that stregnth. Erec had ruined that. He had found out, against the king's wishes, that King Piter was his father. Which led to the castle being destroyed. Worse yet, the king himself was destroyed.

He had wrecked his own father.

And now he had let his best friend die.

Erec felt like falling through the floor and never seeing anyone again, never doing more harm . . . but he couldn't even do that. If only the scepter was gone . . . That horrid thing had brought out the worst in him, and now it was doing the same to his father. He grabbed it to fling it anywhere, through a window, wish it to explode and never come back.

But the second the warm gold was in his hand, everything changed. Calmness filled him, and control. It was all okay. He would help his father get better. He could make everything better. With this power there was nothing that would stop him.

In the distance he heard "Erec, *no*." And a second later the scepter was knocked from his hands.

With tremendous effort, King Piter pushed the thing away from both of them.

"You aren't ready." He panted, hair drooping into his face. "Please, Erec. Please. Just leave it here with me. It's all I can stand to be with it now, not using it. But I've gotten good at it. You see I just sit here and look . . ." His voice trailed away as he stooped down and gazed into the scepter on the ground. He sighed deeply. "Without my castle to protect me, I can actually see it more clearly now. It's dizzying." He looked at Erec pleadingly. "I don't think either of us should touch it. It's best we leave it where it is."

Erec looked at his hands in shock. The moment he touched the scepter it had changed his mind completely. He had been determined to get rid of it. But it felt so good in his hands. . . .

Erec grabbed the king's shoulder and told him everything that had happened.

King Piter's weak eyes widened and he looked like he might faint. "I . . . I didn't even know she was gone. Erec, I should have been there with her. I don't even know when I saw her last. I've been . . ."

Erec knew what the king had been doing. He'd been sitting here entranced by the scepter. Erec sat next to him on the ground. "It's my fault, Dad. I wasn't there for her."

Of course. It was so obvious, and it was right there in front of them. He pointed at the scepter. "Could that bring Bethany back?"

The king sniffed, voice hoarse. "It's possible. If she's still . . ." He looked at Erec, wary, as if afraid of what might be said next.

On cue, Erec said, "Well, then, could you bring her body back, if she didn't make it? We can bury her." He felt sick thinking about it.

King Piter nodded. "Yes, but . . . I'm afraid. If I use it one more time, I'll be gone, I think."

"Have you been using it, then, since I left?" Erec was afraid to hear the answer.

The king nodded. "Just little bits. It's so hard to resist." He stared at it. "I suppose it is for the best, though, using it one more time. Right? It is for Bethany." His eyes hardened as he reached for the scepter.

As the king closed his eyes, Erec could feel a surge in the room. The king's lids flashed open, wide. "She's alive. I'm bringing her back."

Erec jumped to his feet. Alive? Baskania let her live this long? It seemed impossible.

King Piter's hands shook on the scepter. They looked bonier than Erec remembered. Flashes appeared in the room in front of them, sparkling like a thousand tiny stars. Erec bit his lip. *Please let Bethany be okay. Please let her come back.*

Something glimmered in the room. It formed into a shape, and then an image of Bethany appeared before them. She didn't look solid, though, more like a ghost. Erec could see a stained glass window right through her. Something odd and shiny was around her head, like small metal funnels coming from her scalp. She was sitting on a wooden chair, her arms chained down to it at her sides, and she was looking around in surprise.

Erec could see a glimpse of what looked like a desk in front of her and some books. Her feet were chained to something too, but he could not see what. When Bethany looked at him, her eyes bugged out as if she were seeing a ghost as well. She was talking. . . . It looked like she was calling to him, but he could not hear a word.

The king shook, straining from the effort of trying to save her. Then his breath caught, and her image vanished. The scepter fell from his hand. "I couldn't do it. Baskania has a Draw on her. That's how he must have captured her." He hung his head. "I don't know how he got such a thing. *Something* needs to be explained here."

Erec was confused. "What's a Draw?"

"Baskania fixed it so nobody can save Bethany. A Draw is an

earth enchantment that cannot be removed by any magic. But the odd thing is that there are no Draws in our world. There is no way Baskania could have attained one, unless . . ." He rubbed his head, stunned. "I shudder to think how he got it."

"Where do Draws come from?"

"Tartarus. The only living beings who possess Draws are the three Furies that live there. And they don't just hand them out to people."

"Wait a minute." Erec wasn't sure whether to be celebrating that Bethany was okay or losing all hope again. "What are the Furies? What is Tartarus?"

The king started to gaze at the scepter again, but Erec pulled him around to face the other way. "Ever since the dawn of time, six powerful sisters have helped weave the fabric of our universe. Two sets of triplets. Like all siblings, there were rivalries, jealousies. The older sisters, Decima, Nona, and Morta, became who you now know as the three Fates. As you are aware, they are kind, just, and very wise. But they are no-nonsense, too. They like things to follow rules, orders. Life goes according to plan under their watch. Everyone has a chance, gets a choice.

"Their younger sisters were a little different from them. If the cup was half full for the older triplets, it was half empty for Alecto, Tisiphone, and Megaera. Those three have been angry since birth. They wanted the same powers that their older sisters had. And when they realized that they could never be as strong, would never have the responsibilities, they instead set about destroying things. Their actions earned them the name the three Furies, for they were truly terrifying and ferocious.

"At first the Fates tried to put the Furies to work for them, harnessing their natural aggression for good. The Furies became the police of humanity, judging individuals and punishing those who were not pure of heart. But this quickly became a problem. The Furies were not fair in their judgments, and they were very harsh. They enjoyed causing trouble even more than scaring people with their violent ways.

"In the end, the only way to save humankind was for the Fates to lock their sisters into a prison land called Tartarus. It is deep within the earth, far below Aorth. There is only one way in and out, and that is at the base of the Nether Volcano, past the Waters of Oblivion. Some of the creatures that live in Tartarus can pass freely back and forth through its entrance. But the Furies are stuck there, and they cannot exert their powers on humanity from inside.

"They say that there is only one way that the Furies will ever escape. If each of the Furies is able to collect a thousand human souls in Tartarus, they may be able to split themselves into these souls, leave their prison in tiny fragments, and reassemble themselves outside again. Of course, if that ever did happen, eternal chaos would be the best we could hope for. With the eons of anger those three have built up, not even the Fates may be able to save themselves from their wrath.

"That is why the Furies use Draws. Only they know how to make them. Once a Draw is set on someone, they will come to you, no matter what. And once they come, they will stay with you. That is their only way to draw humans into Tartarus—their only hope for eventual escape." He rubbed his head. "I don't know what Thanatos Baskania is getting himself into here. If he's dealing with the Furies now, we're all done for."

"And the scepter can't overpower the Draws?"

"The scepter is powerless against the Furies, the Fates, and the deep magic of the universe. But Baskania is defenseless against these things as well. He must think he is far beyond human if he's trying to deal with them. It's ridiculous."

They sat in silence awhile. Then Erec asked, "If the Furies can pull humans into Tartarus with their Draws, won't they be able to get three thousand souls soon?"

"Luckily, no," the king said. "In order to place a Draw on someone, they would have to see them directly. Any unfortunate person wandering within sight of the entrance to Tartarus would have a Draw placed on them right away. But this is the first time I have ever heard of a human owning or using one."

Erec still could not believe their bad luck. "Are you sure that is what Baskania used on Bethany?"

The king nodded. "The scepter confirmed it."

Reality started to sink in. "So *nothing* can get rid of a Draw?"

"Not when the Furies use one." The king looked thoughtful. "But we should talk to the Fates and see what they say. Baskania's Draw may not be as strong."

Erec jumped up. "Let's go to the Oracle now and ask them. We can't afford to wait any longer. Something terrible could happen to Bethany."

The king glanced back at the scepter, shaking. He didn't say anything, but Erec could see the longing in his face. His father must not think he could walk away from it . . . or pick it up.

This was ridiculous. They couldn't just sit around and wait. Erec would wish the scepter away, make it disappear. He dove upon it so quickly that the king could not grab it out of his way.

But the minute he touched it, he lost all his willpower to get rid of it. He could do anything with it. The scepter was the solution, not the problem.

Then a voice spoke to him, from the scepter itself. "I can help you, you know. That's what I'm here for, mate. Just use me as you will. We'll make it all better. What can I do for you, now?"

Erec relaxed. It *was* okay. The scepter could save Bethany—

Then he shrank back. What was he thinking? The scepter could *not* rescue Bethany. He had just seen that with his own eyes. *He* had to save Bethany. The thought of her was stronger than the power of the scepter. This thing was just in his way.

Against every fiber of his being, he made a decision. *Scepter, I want you to get lost. Stay far away from human beings, and don't come back to me until* someone else *tells me that I am ready for you.*

Suddenly, in a golden flash, the scepter was gone. Emptiness seemed to resound in its place.

CHAPTER FOUR

A Surprise Visit

EREC FELT LIKE he was going to be sick.

King Piter curled into a ball. "Is it gone forever?"

"No." Erec was afraid to tell him the instructions that he had given to the scepter. In a moment of weakness, if the king wanted it badly enough he would know how to bring it back. "We'll see it again someday."

The king nodded. "Good." He huddled awhile in silence,

then with great effort said, "We should go talk to the Fates about Baskania's Draw on Bethany."

Erec agreed. But it was a long while before they made it out of the room.

Jam and the remaining servants had made a multicourse meal for Danny, Sammy, Trevor, and Nell. They were all looking a little rocky, adjusting to the heavy feeling in the air from the Substance.

Erec could not eat at all. Bethany was in incredible danger, and he had to get her back. The Fates had to know a way to beat this Draw that Baskania put on her.

Erec got up and paced, watching his siblings eat. He had to leave now, find out what he could do about Bethany. He knew his father needed rest, but how could they wait when Bethany was in Baskania's claws?

"Dad, should we go to the Oracle now? If you're too tired, I can go by myself."

The Oracle was in Delphi, Greece. It was the only place where Erec could speak directly to the three Fates. The waters in its deep well were one of the few connections to their home.

The king nodded. "You are right. I should go with you." He looked down at his shaking hands. "I'll . . . try. It would do me good to get away from here and clear my head. If I only hadn't been so caught up with that scepter, this whole thing wouldn't have happened." His voice broke.

Erec shook his head. "No. It's my fault, Dad. I should have come back sooner."

Danny looked back and forth between them. "I can't say you guys look a lot alike, but I can tell you're related. You both have the guilt thing down really well."

Erec shot him a fierce look.

Danny leaned back and put his hands up. "Settle down, bro. The way I see it, it's Baskania's fault, not yours."

Somehow that did make Erec feel a little better. Danny was right, in a way.

"Hey," Sammy said, trying to change the conversation. "There's a big metal plaque in the floor with an eye carved into it down the hall."

"That sounds like the cover over Hecate Jekyll's old storerooms." Erec remembered some of the amazing things that she kept there. "I'll show you sometime—"

A loud shriek boomed through the room, making everyone jump. "They're *here!*" a gravelly voice boomed. "Where am I . . . ? I can see them. Look! The kids! Danny and Sammy! Come on, you two. We need to go—"

Then the voice was cut off abruptly. Erec looked around the room, but nobody else had come in.

"What was that?" Sammy looked confused.

A moment later the same voice returned, mid-sentence. "—when I took these off. But look! Now I can see them again! They're in someone's house. And . . . there's King Piter! I knew it. These glasses are magical."

In a flash Erec knew what was going on—someone had his mother's Seeing Eyeglasses. When a person put them on, they felt like they were right in the very room with the person that they missed the most in the world. They could see and hear that person and any people around them. The one wearing the glasses could be heard, but not seen in return.

So who was wearing them? Someone who missed them—and who obviously had no clue how the Seeing Eyeglasses worked. The voice sounded familiar, but he couldn't place it. "Someone's looking through Mom's glasses, guys. Who could it be? I know that voice. . . ."

The person had mentioned Danny and Sammy first. Was she looking for them? Who would miss them more than anyone else? It didn't make sense.

Danny and Sammy came to a realization at the same time. Sammy hugged herself tightly. "Mrs. Smith."

Danny nodded. "Dumpling Smith. She got Mom's glasses."

A wild cackle echoed from the walls. "Very good. You recognized my voice, children. I'm so honored. What a lucky day this is for me! These two noble kids, this . . . Danny and Sammy, as they are called, know me *that* well." She gave a deep, grating laugh. "Well, you might as well tell me where you are. I'll figure it out soon enough myself. And then we'll find you, don't worry. It's time for you two to come with us."

Sammy's voice shook. "You . . . you just want me and Danny, then? Not everyone else?"

"Yes, that's right," Dumpling's gravelly voice answered. "Let's drop the pretenses. I thought you two might come along easier if you thought we were saving all of you. But there's no reason for that. If I take just the two of you, that will be perfect. I promise you, we will leave your siblings and mother alone if the two of you will meet me somewhere, right now."

Their mother! Erec gasped. What had happened to her? Dumpling had her glasses—that must mean that his mother had come home to find Dumpling and her crew waiting in the house. Was she okay? Was Zoey safe?

Danny looked terrified. He murmured to Erec, "Can she grab us with those glasses on? Should we run?"

Erec shook his head and murmured back, "No, we're safe for now. She'll be able to see you wherever you are, though. If you go somewhere that she can recognize, she can use the glasses to find you. We'll have to hide you guys somewhere safe, in a place she's not familiar with. As long as she can't figure out where you are you should be okay."

"You were right," Danny whispered. "She must be up to no good. There must have been a spell on those letters from her to make us think she was safe." He scratched his head. "I still don't get it, though. I was sure from that writing that she meant well. . . ."

"*No secrets!*" Dumpling's gravelly voice thundered. "Let's make this easy. Tell me where you are, and I'll come get you two. You need our protection, you see. We'll take care of you. And we'll leave your mother alone."

That sounded like a threat to their mother. "Is she okay?" Erec asked.

"She is fine." Dumpling's voice became sickeningly sweet. "I'm sure we'll all keep it that way. Now, where are you?"

Sammy blurted, "Um . . . we can't say right now. But please, don't hurt our mom. We'll come with you, okay?" She looked at Danny desperately. "Meet us in Alypium in one hour. In front of Medea's magic shop. Okay?"

"Very good." Dumpling sounded satisfied. "Kookles, stay here with June and Zoey until we get back."

She must have taken the glasses off, because the room fell silent. Everybody sat, frozen, afraid to move.

"Hey, Sammy, not bad," Danny said. "I know you're not thinking we're going to meet that maniac. But you bought us an hour. Now we better figure out what to do."

"Will Mom be okay?" Trevor looked white as a ghost.

"Yes." Erec was suddenly confident. "As soon as Dumpling and that guy in the barrel go to meet Danny and Sammy, Mom and Zoey will be alone in the apartment with just the tall guy. We can take him out and rescue them."

"But how can we get back there fast enough?" Sammy looked

confused. "We don't have the Substance Channel here anymore."

"I know. But we have something better." Erec smiled. This world had all sorts of magical ways. "This house has a Port-O-Door."

"What's that?" Nell sat straighter in her chair, hopeful.

"It's a door that you can tell to open anywhere. It lets you travel there immediately. Let's go. Dumpling Smith has probably left by now. I'm sure she'll hurry so she doesn't miss you guys." He led them to a thin wooden door in the hall by King Piter's bedroom. The kids and Jam crowded into the small room inside. The king stayed at the kitchen table. He looked like he could barely hold his head up.

Once the door shut, a screen lit up. It was divided into four squares: a white one marked ALYPIUM, a blue one marked ASHONA, a red AORTH square, and a yellow OTHERNESS one. Underneath lay a thin orange stripe saying OTHER. When Erec poked it, a world map appeared. He touched North America, then New Jersey. Each map grew bigger as he zoomed in—right to the apartment where they lived.

"Wow," Trevor said, impressed, when Erec touched the apartment in the building, and a room plan sprang onto the screen.

"The bathroom, guys?" he asked. "I think that's the best place if we don't want that Kookles guy to see us come in." After they agreed, he opened the Port-O-Door right into their bathroom at home.

"Cool!" Trevor grinned.

"Shhh." Sammy looked frantic. "You guys stay here. I'll go try to find Mom and Zoey. If we all come out, it might take too long to get back in."

"No, wait," Erec said. "Let me go. I think it's safer. It's you they're after, not me."

Sammy nodded reluctantly.

Erec twisted the bathroom doorknob slowly, hoping it wouldn't squeak. Nobody was in sight in the hallway, but he could hear Zoey crying in the kitchen. "I don't *like* that funny guy, Mom. Make him go away. I want Trevor and Nell!"

He could barely hear his mother soothing her. Then he saw movement at the end of the hallway. He jumped, almost slamming the door shut, but luckily he stopped short before making a loud noise.

It was the coat rack. The thing was sad, pacing the floors, limbs drooping.

Erec waved toward it, staying silent. The coat rack stiffened, then waved a thin arm back at him. Erec held a finger up and motioned for it to come closer. It swung its top from side to side, as if making sure the coast was clear. Then it hopped down the hall.

Erec whispered to it, "Can you get Zoey and Mom to come here—to the bathroom? We're going to save them."

In a matter of minutes, Zoey was following the coat rack down the hall, laughing. They were playing a version of their favorite game, the hat toss. The coat rack was using the hats as lures, tossing them closer to the bathroom.

Zoey was distracted by the game, forgetting about her other problems. Erec wished his mother had come along too, but a minute later June popped a head around the corner. "Stay with me, Zoey," she said.

Erec waved at her frantically. When their eyes caught, June's jaw dropped. She clasped a hand over her heart and walked quickly down the hallway toward him.

Everything would have been perfect if Zoey had not shouted, "Erec! Yeah! You're here!"

"Huh?" Erec heard a deep voice from the other room.

"Come on, quick!" He waved his mother and Zoey into the bathroom. Just before he locked the door behind them, he caught sight of the tall man, Kookles, peering around the corner. His long strides carried him down the hall. He pounded on the locked door. "Open up! I said, open up!"

Erec yanked his mother and Zoey into the Port-O-Door and slammed it shut just as the bathroom door burst open with a loud thud. He wondered if Kookles saw a flash of the Port-O-Door in the wall before it disappeared.

After June had finished bowing to King Piter for what seemed like the hundredth time, Jam fixed her a pot of cocoa and a warm meal.

"I don't understand," Erec said to her. "Why do they just want Danny and Sammy, and not the rest of us? Who *are* those people?"

"I wish I knew." June shrugged nervously. "They must know something about the twins." She picked at her food, upset.

"Know something? What is there to know?"

June shrugged. It seemed strange to Erec. Usually he was the one that everyone was after. He was the known heir to the throne of Alypium. He was one of King Piter's triplets—the other two were still missing. Even though most people thought they were dead, Erec knew that they were alive. One day the three of them would claim their thrones in the Kingdoms of the Keepers. So that made Erec an obvious target.

Of course, if the other two missing triplets were found, then they would be targets too. But they were safe somewhere, according to King Piter, unknown probably to even themselves.

An idea occurred to Erec. What if . . . No. It couldn't be.

But the truth was plain as day. No matter how much he tried to deny it.

Danny and Sammy might be the other missing triplets.

That would explain why people were after them now. It all made perfect sense. They *were* Erec's age—now that Erec had learned he was really thirteen, almost fourteen. He didn't know his real birthday, but maybe it was their birthday, in March, and not April eighteenth, like he thought. That would explain why June was taking care of all of them. Erec had found out who he was. But they didn't know yet, so they were still safe.

That meant that Mrs. Dumpling Smith and her friends must be working for Baskania. He had found out who the other triplets were and wanted them killed. But why didn't they want to take Erec, too?

Then Erec had a chilling thought. Maybe Baskania had other plans for him. He needed Erec for the twelve quests that were needed to become rulers of the Kingdoms of the Keepers. Only Erec could draw the next quest from Al's Well. Baskania gave the quests to the Stain triplets. Even though they didn't finish Erec's quests, if everyone thought they did, those three could become the next kings.

So Baskania wasn't done with him yet. But Erec was not about to let him get Danny and Sammy.

So they were his missing triplets? Erec stared at them for a long moment. The two of them looked so much alike. Hadn't June changed their looks like she had changed his? Is that what he would have looked like now, if he grew up the way he was supposed to?

But he could not ask. Danny and Sammy were only safe because they did not know they were the heirs to the thrones of Ashona and Aorth, and he would not put them in danger by telling them.

"Hey, look." Danny pointed out of the window. "There's a red snail sitting out there. Looks like you got another letter."

Erec went outside and picked it up off the ground.

Dear Erec,

I had no idea about Bethany. I can't believe it. Baskania and Rosco will pay for this. You mark my words. It wasn't enough to ruin my life. Now they're destroying hers too. And yours.

I've been spying in the Green House as much as I can.
It was hard to tell what was going on, though. So I got a
job there. I gave them a fake name, and I'm working for
the custodian now, doing things like cleaning up messes. I
water all the plants, which lets me walk all over and listen in
to conversations. I haven't heard anyone talk about Bethany
yet, but I found out where Baskania's offices are. Rosco
goes there a lot—I've seen him. I'm going to spend the
most time there, spying on them.

Balor, Damon, and Dollick Stain come around all the time.
Those jerks are cheating even more, but I guess that's
no surprise. They wear phony amulets that make it look like
they did the quests. And their friends, Rock Rayson and
Ward Gamin, follow them around. They have eye patches
now. You know what that means—Baskania took an eye
from them. Yikes!

Your Friend,

Oscar

Erec dropped the empty snail into his pocket. He walked inside, clutching the letter in his hand so tightly it was nearly wrinkled into a ball. This was all too much. Baskania was after his sister and brother. Bethany was captured—alive at the moment, but probably not for long. Oscar was in hiding, seeking revenge on Rosco and spying on Baskania. And the Stain triplets were well on their way to taking over the Kingdoms of the Keepers . . . which would destroy the world.

A loud voice made everyone jump. June dropped her spoon into her soup with a big plop. "I see you're all still there," Dumpling Smith growled. She raised the pitch of her gravelly voice and tried to sound sweet. "Very clever. But you two have it all wrong, dearies. I only want to help you. There are bad people about, you know. You need to trust me, no?" Then she became angry. "Don't think you can stay hidden away for long, you two. I'll keep watch with these nice glasses here. The time has come." Erec could hear her heavy breathing. "Interesting house. Is it King Piter's? There he is. I believe this must be his house, now that his castle is gone."

Everyone in the room looked at one another, afraid to talk.

"Okay, then. Excellent. We'll be seeing you there very soon." Dumpling's laugh ended abruptly, midstream, as she must have pulled off the glasses.

June spoke in a hushed voice. "We need to get out of here, to somewhere she doesn't recognize. This house should stay empty until they are sure that none of us are coming back to it." She lowered her face. "I'm so sorry, dear King, to have brought intruders to your home. I'm sure you'll be safe here—nobody would dare to bother you. But I should take my family away."

The king's voice sounded hollow. "I'm afraid I'm as vulnerable as anybody else right now. I don't have my scepter. I should probably go with you." His hair looked wispier than it did this morning, his face more sunken. Erec hoped that the scepter being gone would help the king regain his strength, but he guessed that might take a while.

Jam cleared his throat. "Modoms, sirs. If you don't mind me making a suggestion, I have an aunt who lives in Americorth North. She has a simple house, nothing in it that stands out as unusual that I can think of. And I am sure she would be delighted for us to visit for as long as necessary."

"I didn't know you were from Aorth, Jam," Erec said. "I thought you were from Alypium."

A despondent look flashed across Jam's face. "I am pretty sure that my parents were from Alypium, but they both died a long time ago, and I have no siblings. Once I tried to research my family history, and see if there was anyone else left. I did find some long-lost relatives in Aorth—at least I think they might be relatives. They weren't exactly sure either. But they took me in immediately, accepting me as family."

The king nodded silently, looking too weak to speak.

June said, "Thank you, Jam. We should go there. As long as Dumpling doesn't put on my Seeing Eyeglasses right as we go through the Port-O-Door, she won't know where we went."

"How did she get your glasses?" Nell asked.

"It was terrible." June shuddered. "They kept asking where you went. Not that I would have told them if I knew. The tall one—Kookles, I think his name was—grabbed Zoey. He started throwing her into the air, and then he was *juggling* her with a bunch of balls."

"That was fun!" Zoey looked excited. "I went all the way to the ceiling."

June looked sick. "I panicked. Kookles was walking closer and closer to the window. I was afraid he would throw her out." She didn't look sure. "I told them they could have anything they wanted—anything. Dumpling told me to give her my magical glasses. Next thing Dumpling put on my glasses, and you know the rest."

Jam handed out shiny silver suits that they slipped over their clothing. "This is UnderWear," he explained. "It will keep you cool when you're deep under the Earth's surface, in Aorth." The fabric was slippery and stretched easily over everyone, expanding to their sizes.

Erec pulled his UnderWear on fast and scrawled a quick letter to Oscar while Jam helped the king into his silver pull-on outfit.

Dear Oscar,

Be careful working in the Green House, okay? I was
thinking—if Rosco can read your mind, he must know
that you're there, right? He probably knows you are
spying on him. Don't do anything to make him angry. He'll
show up wherever you are, and he's really powerful.

Thanks for trying to find out about Bethany.

Your Friend,

Erec

"Hurry, guys," said Sammy. "I'll feel better when we leave this place."

"I'll go there with you," Erec said. "But I can't stay. King Piter and I have to go to the Oracle and find out how to get Bethany back."

The king breathed heavily. "Erec, I would like to go. But I'm afraid I'm just too weak. I'm sorry to let you down. Will you let me know what you find out there? I need to rest with your family, if that's okay."

Jam cleared his throat. "I would be more than happy to accompany young sir to the Oracle. Would you like some company?"

Erec grinned. "Sure, Jam. That would be great."

Jam bowed his head. "At your disposal."

June sighed. "Come right back, Erec. And let me know what you find out, okay?"

Erec nodded. The king was right about not being able to go along. Erec and Jam helped him walk down the hallway after the rest of his family.

Jam dismissed the remaining servants, then pressed a few spots on the Port-O-Door maps and opened the door into an unexplored spot in Otherness so that Erec could toss his snail letter through. "Now to Aunt Salsa's. Hoods on, everyone." He pushed the red AORTH square. "Eight Anodyne Road."

A furnacelike blast of heat hit Erec in the face when Jam opened the door.

"Sorry, sire." Jam bowed his head to King Piter. "Do you think you can handle the heat while I ring her doorbell? I would have ushered you straight into her home but I haven't spoken to her yet."

The king nodded, and they all dragged themselves outside. The heat was like nothing Erec had experienced. His hair felt like it was melting and might explode into flames. He tried to speak, but his breath would not carry into the ovenlike temperature. But then his silver UnderWear suit puffed with cool air, blowing a steady stream up onto his face. He still felt warm but was amazingly comfortable.

"How hot is it here?" he asked Jam.

Jam's hair was blowing straight up from the cool breeze flowing from his UnderWear. "Probably a good hundred and seventy-five degrees, young sir. It can get up above two hundred in the summer."

Erec looked around. "So, this is Aorth." He had never seen anything like it. Tall spires of a city rose all around him. He had expected Jam's aunt Salsa to live in a quiet village, but this place seemed packed with more skyscrapers than New York City. The buildings looked sharper, too. Most were pointed on top, with barbed spires projecting from their sides. When Erec looked closer, he could see that each building was one solid slab of stone stretching from the ground to what must have been a thousand feet in the air. Small gaps in the stones served as windows, which most of the rooms in the buildings did not have. The stone towers sloped just a little from the bottom to the tops, ending in long, narrow funnels. They looked like gigantic stalagmites in a cave.

All the giant rock formations along the busy, clustered streets would have given the city a Stone Age look, Erec thought, if not for the crowds of immense neon signs and glittering computerized advertisements hanging from all of the buildings. They made the billboards in New York's Times Square look dull. Sophisticated computer graphics flashed movie ads onto stone walls, strobe light images of products sparkled in the air, and holographic visions of celebrities danced down the streets, selling products to pedestrians.

His siblings and mother were gazing around in wonder. The spectacle was almost too much to take in. Erec wondered why Alypium was so quaint compared to this. This must be King Pluto's taste, he thought, in contrast to King Piter's. In fact, this city did seem to fit King Pluto's brash, fast-talking personality.

"Are all the parts of Aorth like this?" Erec asked Jam, remembering that there were cities under each of the continents of Earth.

Jam nodded. "Quite. Well, Antarticorth is quieter. It is busy here. Not to my taste, exactly, but it's all what you're used to." He pushed one of the hundreds of buttons on a tall brass plaque attached to the entrance to a skyscraper, and a woman's voice called out.

"It is Jam Crinklecut," he said. Erec wondered how many other people were named Jam, so that he had to use his last name too. "I've come for a stay with some friends, if it is okay with you, Aunt Salsa."

A squeal issued from the speaker, then a loud buzzer made everyone jump. Jam opened the door and ushered Erec's family upstairs to his aunt's apartment. Cold air from the building rushed over them like a soothing lotion. The UnderWear suits stopped blowing air and flattened against their clothing again.

Aunt Salsa looked nothing like Jam, making Erec wonder if they truly were related. She was round and comfy in a bright red sweater dress, with black spiky hair. But what caught his eye the most was her love of jewelry. From her sparkling tiara all the way down to her jeweled shoes, Aunt Salsa was covered with pins, brooches, and necklaces of all sizes. The gems must have been fake, or they would have been too expensive for any one person to own.

Jam's aunt scooped him up in her arms, squeezed him, and spun in a circle. Jam's face reddened, but Erec could tell he was pleased.

"Oh, Jam dear. I'm so delighted that you could visit! If I only knew in advance, I would have cooked up a storm. But don't worry, I'll whip something together now. You don't know how much this means to me, visiting when it's not even a holiday! Your poor aunt gets so bored nowadays. And you brought your friends!" She surveyed the haggard crowd, then gasped when she noticed the king. "King . . . is this really the king . . ." She rushed to help him into a chair, then bowed to the floor. "Oh, forgive me, your majesty. I have only a very plain apartment, nothing compared to what you are used to." She bowed a few more times and then rushed into her kitchen, talking about preparing snacks. Jam followed her, and Erec could hear them happily arguing that the other should sit and rest, and let them do the cooking.

Aunt Salsa won the argument at last, and Jam emerged from the kitchen with a sheepish grin. "I explained the situation to her, of course offering that we all stay in a hotel if she preferred. As I expected, she was delighted to have us stay here with her." He nodded to Erec. "Young sir, I suppose we should go right away and speak to the Fates? I know you are in a hurry."

Nodding, Erec said good-bye to his mother and siblings. They headed out into the heat of Americorth North again, and then Jam pressed code numbers into their Port-O-Door, which had stuck itself on a stone wall nearby. The lighting seemed odd, somehow, glowing with a warm but almost fluorescent feel. Erec looked up and shuddered, seeing that the sun was amazingly close to them. Something else was different about it too. A large face was filling it.

Jam saw Erec shielding his eyes while trying to get a glimpse. "Don't worry, young sir. This sun will not hurt your eyes like the one we are used to. It's just a light source, really."

As Erec relaxed, he realized that it was the face of King Pluto himself lighting the city. That struck him as funny, and he laughed.

"Shh." Jam looked around. "Don't let anyone see you do that. The laws are fairly loose here, but anyone who disrespects the king can be punished by death."

They climbed into the vestibule of the Port-O-Door. Could King Piter's brother have gotten this crazy from using his scepter so much? Or was it Baskania's influence on him that warped him more? "That sun is so close. Is that what is making the city so hot?"

"No, sir. The cities of Aorth are a mile and a half under the ground. The earth's core heat does it." They closed the vestibule, opened the other door, and appeared back in King Piter's house. It felt great to be under the dome of the controlled, perfect weather of Alypium after that roasting blast. Jam and Erec took off their UnderWear suits.

Jam went to pack some snacks for their quick trip. For a moment Erec worried that Mrs. Dumpling Smith might peek in on them, but then he remembered that she was only missing Danny and Sammy. She would only see the twins in Americorth North.

Soon Jam came back. "Are you ready to go meet the Fates, young sir?"

Light flashed outside, then flashed again. Erec looked out the window and saw a tall man taking pictures of the house and trying to spy inside. Slick strands of dark hair were badly combed over most of his bald head, and a monocle squeezed into one eye. He spotted Erec looking at him, and waved to him wildly, shouting, "Come out here right now, young man!"

Erec knew he had seen the man before, and he had a bad feeling about him. Going outside didn't seem like a good idea, but he raised the window a crack. "What do you want?"

The man snapped a photograph of Erec through the window. "You hoodlum. This house is under investigation. It will soon be deemed illegal under the new rules of the Green House administration. There was no building warrant made for it, and there are rules about houses being built on castle property."

"Castle property?" Erec was confused. "King Piter's castle is gone."

The man sneered. "A new castle is being built very soon, right where the old one was. So your presence here is against the law, which makes you a criminal as well."

A bad feeling crept over Erec. This house would not be safe for long. The Shadow Prince was pulling the strings of the government of Alypium, and they could cause a lot of trouble.

CHAPTER FIVE

A Green House Investigation

INSIDE THE PORT-O-DOOR, Jam poked the picture of the Temple of Apollo on the map of Delphi. Erec remembered a safe spot to put the door, in a grove of trees just a little ways off the path. Delphi might be a mystical place, but it was still a part of Upper Earth. If someone saw a door appear, and people walk out of it, they would probably call the police.

The sun shone down on them from a vivid blue sky, but a cool breeze hit their faces. Erec was glad Jam had insisted they wear jackets.

It was in the low fifties, and after the furnaces of Aorth it felt even colder. They casually strolled away from the Port-O-Door onto the paths that wound up the hill. On top the Temple of Apollo had once stood in its full glory.

Jam stuffed his hands into his pockets. "It's earlier here than in Alypium, young sir. Time change. Lucky it's not dark yet. And not too crowded today."

Erec nodded. A few people walked near them toward the ruins— gleaming white columns and parts of ancient stone walls that were scattered around the paths. Cliffs dropped in deep reds and browns from trails that wound through stately olive groves.

A hawk plummeted toward the ground in the distance, probably toward an unsuspecting field mouse. For a moment it made Erec nervous, like a warning to keep his eyes open. He reminded himself that he would soon be speaking directly to the three Fates. Could they tell him how to save Bethany?

There were so many other things that he wanted to find out from the Fates. Maybe he'd get more information from them now. The only other time he had spoken to them, they had seemed willing to tell him anything he wanted to know. But, then again, King Piter had said they could be vague, too. Maybe he could find out where his birth mother was now. He had met Queen Hesti once when he traveled into his past and knew she was supposed to still be alive. He was relieved to know who his father was now, but it would be so nice to find his mother, too.

He felt a pang of guilt. Was he wrong to want to find his birth mother? His adoptive mother, June, would always be his true mother. She had raised him. Would that make her feel pushed aside?

Maybe he'd ask June when he saw her. She probably would understand. June had worked as one of his mother's nursemaids. Maybe June would like to see her again too. And his two missing siblings—the other triplets.

Erec almost stopped in his tracks. He had forgotten for a moment. Now he was sure who those other missing triplets were. No doubt they were Danny and Sammy. He strained to remember the little girl and boy he had met that time he traveled into his past. The girl had looked so familiar. It must have been Sammy.

"Jam, do you think Danny and Sammy are my missing brother and sister?"

Jam smiled. "I've been wondering that myself, young sir. It would seem likely."

"And that's why Dumpling Smith is after them," Erec said. "Baskania must have found out about them, and he's sending people out to capture them."

Jam thought a moment. "But, young sir, in that case, why are they not after you, as well?"

"I don't know. Maybe he has other plans for me." Erec shuddered.

"Possibly he expects you to come after Bethany, young sir."

Erec shook off that thought. He had to rescue Bethany. Even if he was walking into a trap, how could he leave her in Baskania's clutches? He shuddered, remembering how she had looked in his vision, chained to a desk. He pictured that black band with little metal funnels around her head. He had to save her as fast as he could.

For a moment, he almost laughed, thinking about the twelve quests he had been doing to become king. How insignificant they seemed now that Bethany was in danger. Who cared about being king, anyway? Let the Stain triplets have the stupid crowns. So what if they destroyed the Kingdoms of the Keepers? If Bethany was gone, Erec would walk away from it all anyway.

They wandered off the paths and into the woods at the edge of the mountainside. Soon Erec found the bubbling Castilian Spring and followed it to the stone well that was the Oracle of Delphi.

Down below glimmered the smooth, dark waters. He squeezed his eyes shut. A wave of fear came over him. What if the Fates told him he was too late? What would he do?

"How does young sir speak to the Fates here?" Jam glanced into the well, clutching his arms. Erec realized he was probably afraid as well.

"I have to concentrate and bring out my dragon eyes." Erec raised an eyebrow. "So you might not want to look at me, if that creeps you out."

"I think I can handle it, sir."

Erec paused, looking into the well. He had forgotten what this would involve. It wasn't just rolling his dragon eyes forward that let him talk to the Fates. He had to use them in a way that he had not done in a long time.

Only a medium or a psychic could conjure the Fates at this well. He had learned how to use his dragon eyes to see into the future, which classified him as a medium. That was exactly what he had to do now, in order to call the Fates to come to him. Looking into the future wasn't so hard for him, but the problem was that he could not control what he saw there. What if he saw something that he couldn't face? What if his vision showed Bethany dead?

Every ounce of him wanted to walk away, to avoid seeing what lay ahead. But he couldn't do that. Instead Erec leaned over the well so the Fates would sense when he looked into the future. Only then would they come talk to him. He closed his eyes and concentrated on using the eyes of Aoquesth the dragon.

Please, he asked himself, *just this once, show me something good. I can't handle seeing terrible things happen now. Nothing bad about Bethany, especially. Just show me a happy time ahead.*

As he had been trained, he pictured himself walking into a small, dark room in his mind. After he adjusted to the feeling, a calmness came over him. He visualized another room, blacker and smaller, within this first one, and he entered it, relaxing even more. Deep inside his own mind, he saw a small box set on a table. He was partly imagining it and partly feeling it as a real thing next to him. He could sense its presence more than see it. This box held all the knowledge of the universe that was inside him. Soon it would show him a piece of his future. It felt like a movie projector playing a random, surprise film. And he asked it to show him a happy ending.

His fingers touched the box. It was humming, vibrant. Two windows hung on a wall before him, their shades pulled shut. They would be his eyes once he was ready to see what the box would show him. He felt for the small, soft cord that hung between them, took a breath, and pulled it.

Wild applause and cheers shook the walls, and the floors vibrated from the dancing and celebration. On two tall thrones before him, his brother and sister, Danny and Sammy, sat glowing. They wore tall, pointed crowns of gold, with diamonds and emeralds capping each tip. Sammy giggled, waving at the masses celebrating behind Erec.

June stood next to him and could not wipe the grin off of her face. "Isn't this wonderful? I thought this would never happen. Now everybody knows!"

Erec crossed his arms and nodded. "Now we all know." And he knew everything would be better now.

Overwhelmed, Erec backed out from the dark rooms in his mind. He could feel his eyes swivel in their sockets, sliding his dragon eyes back into the darkness and bringing his normal blue eyes out. When he opened them, everything seemed so bright. He was looking down into the well, yet still processing what he had just seen.

So, there was no doubt, then. Danny and Sammy were definitely the missing triplets, the other two slated to be king and queen. They would live, unharmed. They would be crowned king and queen. Maybe not at the same time that he was, but soon enough. When he thought about it, they didn't look much older than they were now. Sammy was wearing more makeup, he remembered, and her nose looked bigger, so maybe it was a few years from now. But they still were young.

They had looked so happy. In Erec's vision, he had been filled with the feeling of everything being right. Maybe soon he would have companions on his quests. What a relief that would be.

If Bethany was okay, that is. He wouldn't do any quests if she wasn't.

Could that have been why only Danny and Sammy were sitting on the thrones? Did Erec drop out and stop doing quests, because something bad had happened to Bethany?

No, he couldn't think about that. The thought flew out of his mind anyway, for the waters below him began to swirl. A rainbow of colors raced around the whirlpool. Hues Erec had never even seen before flashed through the water. Then, all at once, the water rose toward him, bubbling like a boiling stew. A moment later it was quiet again—dark like glass looking through into night.

Erec gazed into the well. Would he have to call for the Fates? Did they know he was there? Feeling a little awkward, he spoke into the still waters. "Fates? Are you there? This is me . . . uh, Erec Rex." He glanced nervously at Jam and made a face.

Wild shrieks issued from the well, turning into fits of giggles. They sounded like girls at a slumber party that had stayed up too late. "Look, you guys—no way! Erec's here!" "Oh, whoopee!" "I mean, like, what a perfect way to end our gossip hour. Unh!" "It's our favorite hero." There was so much laughter, clapping, and hooting that Erec wondered if he would ever get a word in.

He shouted over the noise. "Fates? I have to ask you something."

The laughter after he spoke seemed to triple in volume, so they must have heard him.

The voice that followed sounded ageless, warm, and yet just like a Valley girl. "Get that, Nona! Like, he like has to ask us something. Like we don't like *know* that, duh-uh."

"Oh, sa-weet! I love this stuff, Decima. Let's shush up and hear him ask."

The giggles piped down a bit, so Erec said, "My friend Bethany—I'm sure you know she's captured by Baskania. Is she going to be okay? She won't . . . ?" He felt his breath stop. This was the question he couldn't bear an answer to.

A voice called out, "Well, like du-uh, of course she is going to die. I mean, come o-on. You have to know that, like, isn't it obvious?"

Erec felt his heart stop. His hands froze onto the cold stones rimming the water. Their laughter seemed to grow stronger for some reason, but he couldn't think past what he had just heard.

"You are *so* bad, Morta! I love it!" a voice cackled. "Oh, go on, tell him more."

They were enjoying this, to Erec's disbelief. He could barely process what one of them said next.

"Okay. Like, Bethany will die, your whole family will die, everyone you ever knew will die, you will die. Oh, yeah, and the whole world will die." She chuckled.

The words entered Erec's mind like army ants, unstoppable regardless of the damage were doing. Why were the Fates so gleeful? Everyone would die? What would happen? This was too awful to think about.

A voice said, "Oh, stop it, girls. Look, we've made him all like upset and everything. Listen, kiddo. As if. Your friend Bethany, she isn't going to die, like, *now*. Well, that is, if you *save* her she totally won't. You do have a chance. And your family is fine. But, like, everyone dies eventually, right? I mean, like, you have to watch what you're asking us. We just told you the truth. Unh. Nobody lives forever."

The haze of sorrow dropped from Erec's mind. So, everyone would be okay? Bethany would not die—at least now—if he was able to save her? A sense of purpose filled him again, along with a spark of anger. "So . . . you were just saying all that to upset me?"

"Just having a little fun, worry wart. Stop taking everything so seriously. Blah, blah, blah. What a bore." The Fates sounded quieter, like they were fading away.

"Wait! Sorry. How can I save Bethany from Baskania? He has a Draw on her. I heard those are unbreakable. Is his Draw as strong as the ones that the Furies use?"

All sound stopped. Erec feared that the Fates had gone, but then he heard a solemn voice.

"We don't like to think about our sisters locked away in Tartarus."

Erec looked into the well, panicked that they would not help him. "S-sorry I brought it up. Can you help me? Please? How I can save Bethany with that Draw on her?"

The voice that answered echoed quietly, no longer sounding like a chirpy teen. "I shall tell him." There was a pause. "Of the many things you could do, only one will work. In this order: You must first find the man with the magnet and ask him to use it on Bethany. Second, you must do most of your next quest. Only then must you find Bethany. Feed her a sip of dragon blood. That will break the Draw. Baskania is not able to make it as strong as our sisters could. Good luck, Erec Rex."

Erec recited the steps in his head, frantic to remember until he saw Jam jotting in a notebook.

"*Most* of my next quest? Not all of it?"

One of the Fates giggled. "You'll understand later."

Relieved, Erec sighed. "Thank you so much. I'll do those things right away."

"If you love Bethany, you'll do them as soon as you can." The voice began to giggle and chirp. "But, like, if you love your father, then you won't."

"What?" Erec was tired of being confused, but he was so grateful for their help, he didn't dare to complain. "My father wants Bethany safe too. He wants me to rescue her."

"Like, fer sure. But he also wants to stay alive, like, a little while longer. Totally up to you. Whatever."

"What? My dad is in danger?"

"Oh, like, only if you call *dying* being in danger."

This was the last thing Erec expected to hear. "Why is he dying? What can I do?"

"I mean, like, isn't it obvious? I mean, totally. What was keeping him alive for five hundred years? A good diet?"

The answer was obvious to Erec immediately. The magic of King Piter's scepter gave him a life much longer than normal mortals. It even gave the people near to him longer lives. When the king had been put under a spell, hypnotized for ten years, the scepter must have been near enough to him to keep him alive—even though not in the best condition. But now it was gone. Erec had sent it away, and he could not bring it back by himself. How long would the king last without it? His age was probably catching up with him by the moment.

He had to get back to his father and figure out how to save him—and fast. "Bye. Uh, thanks!"

"Good luck!" The Fates' voices were fading into the distance.

"Wait, come back!" Erec shouted into the well. "How do I save my father? How much time do I have? How long will Bethany be okay?"

A few more murmurs bubbled up before the water grew quiet. Erec thought he heard one of the Fates complaining, ". . . wants us to tell him, like, everything. As if. He is *so* not using his head today."

CHAPTER SIX
A Sister's Help

J AM'S HANDS TREMBLED. He looked as shaken up as Erec felt. "Young sir. I . . . we should go back to the king. What can we do? I should know—I'm supposed to be prepared." Jam dropped his face into his hands. Even though his magical gift was being prepared, Erec knew that some things were impossible to be ready for.

Jam paused. "Unless young sir feels it more important to help Bethany than the king?" He looked terrified to hear the answer.

"No, we need to help him first. He looked really bad. And it sounds like Bethany will be okay for a little longer." Erec hoped he was right. "But what can we do?"

There was one obvious solution to the problem. Jam could say to him, "You are ready to use the scepter once again," and it would appear in his hands. He would just have to hand it over to the king again. Simple.

Or maybe not so simple. He wasn't sure. The more Erec thought about it, though, the more appealing it began to seem. Maybe he could put a spell on the king and keep him alive forever. If he just held it again, and could feel its warmth, its strength. He could use its power to become strong and take care of everything.

"Young sir?" Jam looked relieved. "I know what we need to do. He must go stay with Queen Poscy. Being near her scepter, in her castle, should keep him young and strong. At least until he is able to be with his own scepter again."

Erec wanted to argue. His way was better! He could fix it all if he just held the scepter once again. The king would never get it back. It was Erec's now.

Then, like a slap in the face, he realized that his cravings were taking over his mind again. Jam was perfectly right. The king's sister would be glad to help, and Piter would enjoy the visit.

"Thanks, Jam. Great advice—as usual."

Jam grabbed Erec's sleeve and yanked him along the path. "Please hurry, young sir. We don't know how much time is left."

Erec sprinted behind Jam back down the path toward the Port-O-Door. Sunny-faced tourists wandered past them, happily admiring the scenery, unaware of the terrible danger. Erec was amazed how fast Jam's fingers flew over the Port-O-Door maps in the vestibule, directing the door right into the living room of his Aunt Salsa's apartment in Americorth North.

After a quick rap for politeness, Jam opened the door to his aunt's heavily air-conditioned apartment. It felt so strange to Erec that in just a few steps he had moved from Europe to a land far underneath the earth's surface. Everyone shouted hellos, and little Zoey threw her arms around his legs, almost tripping him.

Aunt Salsa was bustling about, serving homemade cookies to Danny, Sammy, Nell, Trevor, and Zoey while talking to June. King Piter was asleep in a chair. He looked crumpled, as if his bones had shrunk. "There you two are!" she called out. "Come have some cinnaberry cookies. It's my mother's recipe."

Jam raced to King Piter's side. In another minute the king was stretched out on the couch, surrounded by pillows. "He's so light now, young sir." Erec pulled a blanket over the king.

"Is everything okay?" June looked concerned. "I didn't want to wake him. It seemed like he needed a nap." She put a hand on Erec's head and whispered, "Did you find out about Bethany?"

He nodded, but pointed at the king. "He's in danger without the scepter here. He has to go stay with Queen Posey right away."

June's face turned pale. "I never thought about that. He's so old. . . . I know what you're saying."

Jam rested a hand on the king's shoulder and gently shook it. "Wake up, sire."

The king's eyes fluttered, but only opened a trace. "Yes, Jam?" His voice was like a wisp of smoke.

"We must call your sister, sire. Right away. It's urgent—for your life."

King Piter did not seem to understand.

"Sire. Call Queen Posey, now. She must come get you."

The king barely nodded, then shuffled under the blanket Erec had placed on him. Jam helped him draw an arm out, and the king made some motions in the air with his finger. He gestured a few more times before his hand sank back down. "I can't, Jam." He panted for breath. "I'm too weak. My powers seem . . . gone. . . ." The king's eyes began to close.

In a flash, Jam was speaking into his own finger, then putting it in his ear.

"That looks funny." Zoey giggled. "Is Jam pretending to talk on the phone?"

"No," Erec explained. "He has a tiny cell phone in his finger."

Jam was murmuring urgently. ". . . don't understand. I need Queen Posey immediately, for King Piter. I can not leave a message. . . . No, her closest attendant would be best. The matter is highly urgent. . . . I see. Well, the king is right here. We will wait until the queen herself may speak to us. And remember, I would not want to be the servant who took too long and caused something terrible to happen to the queen's brother."

In a few moments, Jam fell to his knees. Erec worried that he was hurt, but then he heard him say, "Yes, my Queen. He is quite sick without his scepter. We spoke to the Fates at the Oracle in Delphi, and they said you must take him with you. Your scepter will keep him alive. Thank you. We will see you there, in one minute."

Jam shook his hand and announced, "The queen will take care of King Piter. She will come through her Port-O-Door to meet him in his home. That will be quicker than explaining where Aunt Salsa lives, or for us to try to find her in her castle." He easily lifted the king into his arms, the blanket still covering him. "He's getting lighter and lighter."

The king shuffled a tiny bit, then gave up. His head hung straight back, chin up, and an arm hung loosely to the floor.

Erec followed them into the Port-O-Door vestibule. "We'll be back soon."

"Do you two need help?" June said.

"No, we're okay. You can stay here with Danny and Sammy."

Jam's Aunt Salsa shuffled over and slid a cinna-berry cookie in Erec's hand. "Take this with you, dear."

Erec took a bite of the amazingly good cookie. "Thanks." He pulled the door shut and opened the other door that led straight back into the king's home in Alypium. Jam rested the king on a soft couch—the same one where Bethany had lain a few months ago when she was caught in one of Baskania's spells. Erec reddened slightly as he remembered how his kiss had woken her.

A few seconds later, a thin wooden door appeared in the wall. Out of it strode a tall, beautiful woman with dark, flowing hair. Her dress was almost scalelike: a shimmering aqua that draped her slender figure with greens and shadows that seemed to slink through the material. On her head sat a gleaming silver crown, and she held her scepter, which looked very much like the king's, in her hand.

Erec noticed the three dark, thin lines under each of her eyes. They made her look tired, but he recognized them as the same Instagills he had in his own wrists. With them he could breathe underwater. He and Bethany had won them in Queen Posey's Sea Search contest.

At the same moment, a crowd of people appeared at the window. A hand was pointing in, then waving, and people were peering in. Some huge objects whizzed through the sky toward the window—at first they looked like humongous birds. As they landed in the grass, Erec could see that they were people flying, likely with the aid of magical heli powder.

The queen rushed to her brother's side and put a hand on his forehead. "Oh, dear Piter. Look at you." She hugged him and rested her scepter over his blanket.

The king's eyes slowly opened. "I'm feeling much better already, Posey. Thank you for coming."

The queen smiled. "You just needed a sister's help." She startled when fists began to pound on the window. "Who is that?"

"I think they work with President Inkle at the Green House," Erec said. "One of those guys was looking in the windows earlier today. He wanted to arrest me for just being here."

"Maybe he recognized you, young sir." Jam frowned. "That could be why he's back—to hand you over to Baskania."

Queen Posey looked at the men through the window. "Have they no respect? I'll take care of them for you."

Her chin made a quick jerk and they disappeared. Then she tapped her scepter on the floor once.

"What happened?" Erec looked out of the window. The men were standing fifty yards away now.

"I put a water wall around the house and gardens," she said calmly. "It will keep everyone away."

Erec could not see the thin stream of water until one of the men tried to step over it. A huge wave shot up from the earth, knocking him up into the air, then flat on his back.

The queen eyed Erec up and down. She slowly said, "Erec Rex. I just can't believe it's really you. I'm so glad you're alive."

Suddenly Erec made a strange connection: Queen Posey was his aunt. He had a real aunt, and she was here right now. He bit his lip, wondering if he should give her a hug, or shake her hand.

They stared at each other until finally Queen Posey grabbed Erec and gave him a huge squeeze. "Erec. I'm sorry I didn't recognize you before."

"Thanks, Queen Posey. Should I call you . . . Queen Posey, then?"

"Nonsense. Call me Aunt Posey. Just like you once did." She asked the king, "Do you want me to move your house into Ashona?"

"No, dear. It needs to stay where it is for now. I'm afraid I won't be able to guard it myself, however. If I'm here without the scepter much longer, I'll just fade away." He chuckled sadly.

"Well, let's take care of you," Posey said firmly. "No worries. The house can be dealt with later. I'll take you to visit with me awhile. Erec, would you like to come too? And you . . ."

"Jam Crinklecut, your highness." Jam bowed low. "Thank you so graciously for coming to help so soon."

"Of course. Jam, you saved my brother's life. You are welcome in my kingdom anytime. And Erec, why don't you come spend time with us? I'd love to get to know my nephew better."

Erec tried to smile. "That would be great, but we need to help my friend Bethany. She's been captured."

The king raised his eyebrows, and Erec told him what had happened with the Fates.

King Piter sat up on the couch, puzzled. "The man with the magnet? I have no idea who that could be. Maybe I should come with you. If I had my old scepter back . . ." His voice trailed off and he looked sheepish. "Look at me, letting my desires speak for me. My place is to stay in Ashona until either you or I am able to be near my old scepter safely. If I feel I am ready, I'll let you know. Tell me, of course, when it returns to you." He smiled.

"I wish I knew who this man with a magnet was." Queen Posey crossed her arms. "I'll ask everyone at home. If he lives in Ashona, you will soon know." She looked at her brother. "Are you ready?"

"As ever."

Jam helped the king up. He looped an arm around his sister, they walked to her Port-O-Door, and with a slight splash it disappeared.

***

Erec looked out the window. The sun was setting, leaving a hazy pink aura over the open field behind his father's house. The men had gone away, but they would probably be back with reinforcements. Erec wondered if Baskania would figure out a way through the water wall. At the least it would show the Alypian people that the king still had some power—unless they realized the water wall was Queen Posey's trademark.

A red smudge in the grass caught his eye. It looked like the snail Oscar had been using. Erec went to pick it up.

Dear Erec,

I heard some news about Bethany, but I'm not sure that you'll like it. At least she is alive. She's a prisoner in Baskania's fortress in Jakarta, in Upper Earth. It's his top-security complex, where he keeps the people and things that are most important to him. That place is totally locked up with spells and armed guards.

I don't know, Erec. I'm sure you want to rush in there and save her, but it sounds like if you did you'd just be locked right up alongside her. I know Bethany would rather have you free than be a prisoner next to her.

This next part is really hard to write. Baskania is scanning through Bethany's brain. He's trying to find out where the key is to teach him about the Final Magic. He's already given her a bunch of tests, but they didn't turn up anything. If he runs out of other ideas, he's going to take her brain out and see if his scientists can figure out where the message is hidden.

I was thinking about going there myself, but there's no way
I could get to her. I don't know what to do. If you need
me for anything at all, though, I'm here for you.

Your pal,

Oscar

It felt like rocks filled the inside of Erec's stomach. The enormity
of what he had to do hit him like a bullet. Bethany had been captured
by their worst enemy. Even if Erec did everything that the Fates
told him to do, in the right order, how would he ever get her out of
Baskania's prison?

He silently thanked the Fates for telling him how to go about
saving her, but he was still terrified that he wouldn't succeed. What if
there was more he had to get right and he didn't figure it out? If he
had to climb the steepest, ice-covered cliff, if he had to swim through
boiling tar pits, Erec was ready to do whatever lay ahead.

With his blood boiling and no clue what to do next, he felt frantic. What he wanted the most was to find Bethany immediately, to
go straight into Baskania's fortress in Jakarta and demand to see her.

Just what Baskania would want him to do, of course. The only
reason he was still keeping Bethany alive at all might be to capture
Erec.

CHAPTER SEVEN

Magnet Mountain

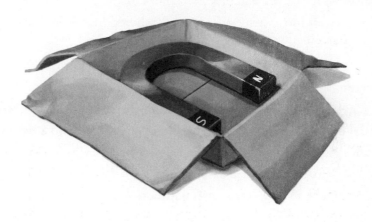

THINK. *FIND THE man with the magnet. Find the man with the magnet.*

King Piter had no clue who it could be. Queen Posey was going to ask around Ashona, but she had never heard of him. Could it be someone in Aorth? Or in Otherness—the wilds where untamed magical creatures roamed?

Jam stared at the notes he had jotted down as if he were wondering the same thing. He sighed. "Should we perchance look for a magnet store? Not sure if there even is such a thing. Maybe a magic shop would know if there was a magnet specialist." He looked doubtful.

"We can look on the MagicNet. I'll search for 'magnet man' or 'man with magnet' and see what comes up."

"Great idea, young sir," Jam said, relieved. "Let's do that straight-away."

Jam led him to King Piter's MagicNet screen in a large sitting room. "Search, please. Eight on one."

A woman's face appeared, lighting the screen. Her left eyebrow and the hair on her left side was blond and pulled into a tight pony-tail along with the black hair on her right side. "May I help you, sirs?"

"Quite." Jam looked at Erec.

"We're looking for a man with a magnet. Or *the* man with *the* magnet. Whatever that is." Erec hoped that made sense.

The woman nodded briskly. Eight boxes appeared on the screen, each with a merchant inside. Seven were men, and in the bottom right corner was a woman in a black pointed hat and a crooked nose. Erec had bought something from her before online, he remembered, for a blasting potion he once made. They all looked at him attentively. He was surprised none of them were shouting out, hawking their wares, but then again his request had been pretty strange.

"We need to find a man with a magnet," Erec said.

Several of the vendors immediately waved magnets in front of their screens. "Nice magnet here. This one's a food magnet. It has a special attraction for sweets and snacks. Whisks 'em right off the tables when you walk by at restaurants—well worth your money. Only five Bils."

"This one's the best you can find. It's a health magnet—good for whatever ails you. Sucks the health right away from people around you. You can live a long time with this beaut. Um . . . three gold rings, of course."

Another man waved a thick gray block. "I've a strong magnet. And for you it's only one Bil. *Very* unique—this one picks up metal objects. Isn't that interesting?"

"Five gold rings here for this money magnet. Bring it to a bank and you'll make your money back in one day."

Other vendors waved their products around, excited. But the woman in the corner narrowed her eyes. "And you only want to buy this from a man? Because I assure you, my wares are top of the line. Only the best magnets in my bunch. Any kind you want."

"No, no." Erec held his hand up. "I don't want to buy a magnet. I want the man *with* the magnet."

Silence fell over the vendors as they processed this. "Aha!" The woman grinned so hard that a wart on her cheek touched the one on her eyelid. "I've got it." She reached out of her window and pointed into the screen next to her where a man held a magnet in his hand. "Here's a man with a magnet for you. Just one silver shire and there he is." She rubbed her hands together.

The man looked over at her with a groan. The other vendors started pointing at each other, trying to both outbid their neighbors and sell them at the same time.

"Wait! Stop. I don't just want some man with a magnet." Erec thought hard, trying to narrow down his question. "Do any of you know a man who makes magnets . . . or sells only magnets? Like someone who owns a magnet shop?"

One of the vendors disappeared, leaving a blank screen in his place. He must have thought it was not worth wasting his time, and Erec didn't blame him.

"Well," a man in a tall hat said cautiously, "I bought this jewelry magnet from a factory that specializes in magnets. You'll find it works very well."

"Where is that?" Erec said. "Is that factory owned by a man?"

Another screen went blank.

"Listen, sonny," the woman said. "We've all had a terrible week here. Everything that's happened with the clowns is really hurting our business. So if I were you, I'd buy a big bag of magnets now before all of our shops close down for good." She smiled. "Can I help you, then?"

"What happened with the clowns?" Erec had been to a clown colony once. He had no idea how they could have any impact on the MagicNet shops.

She rolled her eyes. "Don't you know anything, boy? The clowns in Otherness supply most of our magical herbs and about half of our other supplies as well. And now they're all in chaos. The Clown Fairy is gone. Vanished, they say. Maybe dead. And without her they won't last long, they won't. Nothing is keeping the clowns under control any more. They're just wandering wild. So, no more herbs, potions, or much else unless she reappears."

Jam looked pale. "That's impossible. The Clown Fairy is immortal. She can't be dead."

"That's what I thought," the woman said. "But if she was alive, she'd be reigning over her people now, wouldn't she?"

This story was interesting, but not what Erec needed to find out. "Thanks for the info. Look, I'll pay for information from anyone who can help me. I'm supposed to find 'the man with the magnet.' I don't know who it is, but someone who owns a really powerful magnet, I think, that can attract people to him. Or maybe just any kind of super-strong magnet. Any ideas?"

The remaining vendors leaned forward, scratching chins and ears and muttering to themselves.

"You must be looking for Magnet Mountain," the man in the tall hat said grudgingly. "That place has the strongest magnets I know. I get some there myself."

Of course, Erec thought. The vendor wouldn't have told him about his competitor unless he was getting paid for it. Magnet Mountain sounded like exactly where he needed to go. "Thanks. That's perfect."

Jam pulled some silver coins from one of the many pockets in his vest.

"Wait!" the woman shrieked. "That's not it. I've heard of a man who has a magnet. A really powerful one. He lives in . . . um, Cinnalim. Yeah, that's it." She held her hand out for money triumphantly.

"I don't think so," the man with the hat said. "I know who you're talking about. That's just some guy who bought a magnet. And guess where he bought it from? Magnet Mountain. That's the place you want." He tapped his open palm for payment.

"Well, that 'guy' is a man," the woman fired back. "And he has a magnet. That's what you are looking for, right?" She signaled to her hand for money.

"So, I'm a man, and I have a magnet too." The man's voice rose. "I gave you the best advice here. Magnet Mountain is the only place that makes strong magnets. She knows that too."

"Kind sir, modom." Jam put a handful of silver coins in each of their hands. "Thank you both so much for your help. Could you please tell us the locations of these places?"

Peace and satisfaction took over the expressions of both vendors. The man said, "Magnet Mountain is in the Outskirts of Alypium, right by the Citadel of Clouds on the north border. Ask around—people will know where it is. They hire a lot of folks down there."

The woman nodded. "And the man is in Cinnalim. I've heard he's made quite a nice place for himself there."

"What is his name?" Erec said.

She scrunched her nose. "Damon, I think? Something like that. I can't remember exactly."

Erec immediately thought of Damon Stain, one of Baskania's cloned triplets, but he knew that it must be someone else. "Thanks."

Jam shook his head after they left the room. "I just can't believe the Clown Fairy is missing. It doesn't make sense."

"Is she the ruler of the clowns?"

"More like their guardian protector. But she's been their ruler, too, for the last ten years. So this is a catastrophe for them."

"Why was she their ruler for ten years?"

Jam hesitated. "Baskania's followers killed their old rulers. It was terrible. That happened at the same time so many people were murdered here in Alypium, in King Piter's castle. Baskania was hoping to take over everywhere at once." He clucked. "It makes me worry that Baskania did something to the Clown Fairy. But I thought that was impossible. She is not only immortal, but unholdable. That is, even if he did catch her by surprise, there is no place he could keep her where she could not escape."

Baskania, Erec thought. *Always the cause of every problem.* He took a breath and said, "We have no time to waste."

Jam stopped Erec from running straight to the Port-O-Door. "Young sir, it's getting late, and you haven't eaten a thing. Shall we go to Magnet Mountain or Cinnalim in the morning?"

"We can't wait that long. Bethany is in danger."

Jam looked out the window and said quietly, "I'm not sure that the man with the magnet will want to see us at nighttime. And where would we sleep? I think Bethany will be all right for a day or two more. After all, this is the path the Fates told us that we should take."

Erec mulled over that thought. Jam offered to pack backpacks for their trip now, so that they could leave immediately when they woke up. "You never know how long we might be gone, young sir. Best to be prepared."

Erec followed Jam to the kitchen, where he weighed an identical silver tray in each hand. Erec immediately recognized his favorite magical object—Jam's Serving Tray. It conjured delicious versions of any food that someone asked for, the perfect thing to take on a trip. The other one was a gift Bethany had received from some fun-loving druids. It was also a Serving Tray, only it made spoiled, disgusting versions of foods.

"Bethany had these both out, and I'm not sure which is which." Jam turned them over and found them identical. "Let's see. Give me an apple, please." On one tray appeared a red ripe apple that gleamed in the light shining in from the window. On the other was a pile of brown sludge with worms and black beetles in it. "Right." Jam threw out the rotten apple, wiped that tray clean, and taped a label onto it. "I don't see why Bethany would want to keep this."

"I think it's pretty cool, actually. Never know when it could come in handy." Erec laughed. "It can make food that looks just as good as the real thing if you want it to."

Sniffing, Jam stuffed the good Serving Tray into his pocket. He fished two large pink erasers from a drawer. "I'll put a food eraser and a taste-erase by this other tray, just in case someone uses it by accident and gets an unpleasant surprise."

Erec wondered if this place would stop amazing him. "A taste-erase. I could have used that when I was little."

They ate a huge meal, courtesy of the Serving Tray, although Erec could tell that Jam was slightly uncomfortable not having prepared it himself. Erec chose spaghetti with meatballs, pizza slices with mushrooms, green peppers, and more meatballs, sweet potato with marshmallow on top, and chocolate cream pie. Jam had salad and some kind of fish. Erec caught Jam eyeing his mounds of food. "Do you want some?"

Jam turned slightly pink. "Oh—no, sir. No. But thank you."

Erec had not realized how hungry he was. Before, he hadn't been able to eat a thing. But now that he was on a mission, with some direction about how to save Bethany, he felt so much better. Thank goodness she was alive—even though the Fates had scared him there for a while.

With a full stomach and high hopes, Erec went to sleep.

Backpacks on, in the Port-O-Door, they stared at the map choices.

"Which should we try first, Jam? Magnet Mountain?"

"I do think so, young sir. The unknown man in Cinnalim sounds . . ."

"Random?"

"Yes, sir. Random." Jam smiled.

After traveling such great distances, it felt almost strange to be going somewhere close, right outside Alypium. When Jam pushed the white square on the screen, a map popped up with the Outskirts surrounding Alypium on all sides, just outside the Citadel of Clouds—the tall wall of cloud that surrounded and protected Alypium proper. Jam pointed to the northern border and Erec saw a square building labeled MAGNET MOUNTAIN, which looked nothing like a mountain at all.

"That was easy to find." Erec parked the Port-O-Door in an outside wall of the building. They stepped out into a crisp day. Light streamed over imposing cliffs and gleamed through fir trees onto the run-down streets and buildings around them. The magnificent surroundings only made the Outskirts look more shabby. Hunched figures walked in front of boarded-up windows, throwing shifty glances in their direction.

Jam stood a little closer to Erec. In a hushed voice he said, "We should be careful, here, young sir. I've heard of countless crimes committed in the Outskirts. Not a choice location."

A block away, a white wall of cloud extended high into the sky and ran in both directions as far as the eye could see. White vapors swirled within it, but they did not float away.

"Can people walk through the Citadel of Clouds?"

"No, young sir. You go through passageways, but those have checkpoints. Buses can go through, and people with permits. Otherwise it's impenetrable."

Unlike its name, the Magnet Mountain looked like a skinny, run-down factory with tarry blue-black smoke sputtering from several chimneys. Tall doors filled a narrow arch at the front. Erec glanced at Jam hopefully, then pulled one of the heavy, creaky doors open.

A rancid odor rose to meet them as they walked into the dimly lit front room. People walked past, carrying boxes on their backs and chests. One of them spit on the floor when he saw Erec, then walked on.

"Do you think he knows who I am?" Erec said.

"I doubt it, young sir. Probably just his way of saying hello."

Their eyes adjusted to the dark interior of the factory. Boxes were stacked on shelves that seemed to stretch up to the tall ceilings. This appeared to be the warehouse part of the building. Erec guessed the magnets were made in the back.

They wandered around until Jam pointed at an open door leading into a brighter lit room. At first Erec was relieved to hear voices coming from the room, but when he got closer he was sorry that he did. Someone was getting fired, or at least screamed at for doing something wrong.

Erec peeked into the open doorway and saw a small man shaped like a jiggly beach ball with stick limbs and a sour face screaming at a filthy factory worker.

"And that wasn't all, was it? I *told* you never to bring the magnet magnets into the storage rooms. *How* many times did I tell you, Billy? *How many?* More than the number of brain cells in that stupid head of yours. Of course that's not too many at all, is it? Since the day I brought your sorry hide into my factory, I've been telling you that the magnet magnets can *never* come in here. They go straight into their silver cases. And what do you do the minute I step away for one second? You bring a box of them in here.

"Now maybe you finally understand why you need to listen to me. You made a huge mess. All of our new assortments flew straight into the magnet magnets. Brilliant. You think *I'm* going to pay to clean up this mess? To order and replace all these mixed-up magnets? Oh, no, Billy. Your pay is being docked. You'll have to work for free for five months to make up what you owe now."

"B-but I can't afford that," Billy stammered.

"You know my friends on the street?" The short man kicked his feet up onto his desk. "Unless you want to get to know them better, you'll shut up and do what I say. Now get out of here." He spit over his shoulder.

Billy, tears in his eyes, shoved past Erec, almost knocking him over. Once he was gone, the short man at the desk noticed the new-comers. His eyes narrowed. "Get in here, you two. And who would you be?"

Jam elbowed Erec's side in warning, but the last thing Erec was going to do was tell this guy his real name. He would probably call for Baskania in a heartbeat if he thought he could collect a reward for catching Erec Rex. "Just shoppers," he said. "Do you have any really strong magnets?"

The man relaxed in his chair. A sick grin spread over his face like an infection. "You've come to the right place. We don't usually get customers in the factory. You can find our deluxe magnets in many fine stores. But I'm happy to help you right here." He rubbed his hands together. "Any certain type of magnet you'd like?"

"Well . . ." Erec wasn't sure how to explain, as the clue did not make sense to him. "I'd be curious if you had any people magnets. To attract people. Or if you know a man that has one."

"I see." The man's grin grew until his pointed teeth showed. "You want to attract a certain person, eh? A girl, maybe? Or is it a lost friend? An enemy?

No, Erec thought. I don't want to attract someone with the magnet. I just want someone who has the magnet. "I don't have a plan for it. Actually, I'm more interested in who you've sold one to. Are there many magnets like that floating around?"

The man's smile crumpled. "I see," he growled. "You're not here to *buy*, you're here to *spy*. Is that it? Afraid one of your enemies bought a person magnet here?"

Jam pulled a gold ring out of his pocket and the man gulped, staring at it. "Not at all, kind sir. Nothing like that at all. We're here to buy. Either a magnet or your advice, that is all."

"But of *co-ourse*." The man's voice sounded snakelike. "Call me Bill, by the way. I'm so pleased to give you any advice you want. And if you have two of those"—he pointed toward the gold ring coin— "I'll be able to give you the best advice I have."

"Of course, Bill, sir." Jam produced another gold ring coin, making Bill nearly drool.

A dirt-crusted worker stuck his head into the room. "Excuse me, sir, but there's a problem down in the—"

"*Shut it, Billy,*" Bill roared. "Can't you see that I'm busy here? Use your eyes, since you don't have a brain. Now get out of here."

Erec could not help but point. "His name was Billy? Wasn't the other guy in here named Billy . . . ?"

"Yes." The sick smile spread over Bill's cheeks. "All of my workers are called Billy when they are here—after me, of course. They're all like parts of me, you see, running around, doing what I want them to do."

Erec shuddered. He could not wait to get out of this awful place.

Jam seemed to understand. "Sir. Please, for these coins. Who has bought the most powerful person magnet that you've sold?"

Bill put a finger on his chin and pursed his lips. "Well, recently there was a young woman in love with a man who couldn't stand her. I gave her one of my specials." He raised his eyebrows as if that might be good enough.

"Well, sir, we were looking for a man who bought a person magnet. Do they come in different strengths, maybe?"

"No. I get all my complicated magnets imported from the clowns. Of course, the recent clown problems have driven prices up quite a bit."

"Have you ever ordered a stronger person magnet from somewhere else?"

"No." Bill was beginning to look angry again. "I think it's time to pay me those ring coins now. My advice is done."

Jam dropped the coins in Bill's chunky palm and produced one more. "Think hard for me, sir. Do you know anyone, anywhere, who has an especially strong person magnet?"

Bill's eyes lit up again, staring at the new gold coin. "Of course, mister. There is that one guy. You know. He's famous for that magnet—at least in my circles. He won't sell it, though, so don't even try. It works too well for him."

Erec caught Jam with a glance. "What's his name?"

"Oh, man. What was it? I used to just call him 'the man with the magnet.' Oh, yeah. Danen Nomad is his name. Moved to Cinnalim recently, I heard."

Jam dropped the coin into Bill's hand and thanked him.

"Come back soon. I've got a lot more advice where that came

from." Bill jangled his coins greedily. Then he flicked an eyebrow up. "Hey, how much more money you got with you?"

"That was about it, kind sir. We really must be leaving now."

"No, wait. You can't leave without buying a magnet. They're real cheap. One more gold ring and you can have any you want in the whole place."

Erec knew he could get magnets for a few Bils online, or at most some silver shires. "I don't think so."

Bill jumped up and blocked the door, determined to get their last coin before they left. "I'll be insulted. You came all the way here, bothered me for my help. Now buy a stinkin' magnet, all right?"

Jam held up a hand. "I only have a few shires left, sir. Is there a magnet you recommend?"

"Yeah, sure." Bill held his fat fist out. "Get a luck magnet. You might need it." He yelled into the storeroom to a young man walking by in a yellow hard hat. "Hey, Billy. Get this gentleman a luck magnet. Our very *best*." He chuckled as if sharing an inside joke with himself.

Billy came back holding a box out far in front of him. He turned it over and dumped a silver horseshoe-shape magnet into Jam's hands like he couldn't get rid of it fast enough.

"All right," Bill said. "You can leave now. You know where to come if you need any more help." He sat back in his chair and crossed his arms over his beach ball stomach, a look of amusement on his face.

A black bat screeched out of nowhere and straight into Jam's face, knocking him onto his back. Erec could not believe how many things rolled out of Jam's pockets, including several more gold rings.

"Well, look at that," Bill said. "Let me help you pick those up."

Jam winced and struggled to sit while Bill rooted through his things on the floor. They were disappearing before Erec's eyes.

"Cut that out." Erec grabbed the Serving Tray and handed it to Jam, and he picked the silver luck magnet off the floor. In a moment Jam seemed better and stuffed the other things back into his pockets.

Bill squinted at Erec and grinned. "Well, well. I don't know why I didn't recognize you before. It's Erec Rex. Right here in my very own shop. What a prize for me, eh? I'm sure I can get quite a reward out for turning you in—everyone knows that the Shadow Prince is after you. Heh heh heh." He shook his index finger, put it to his mouth, and spoke in the cell phone planted there. "Green House, please. This is Bill at Magnet Mountain. I've got a fugitive here. Yup, you heard me right. His name is Erec Rex."

CHAPTER EIGHT
Cinnalim

EREC AND JAM took one look at each other and then ran from the room.

"Stop them!" Bill screamed at several workers. He stabbed a button on his desk. "Two fugitives are trying to escape the warehouse. A boy and a . . . a butler. Stop them *now*!"

They had a clear shot to the front doors, but men trotted out of the warehouse aisles and blocked them. Erec slowed down, darting a bit to his left, then right to find a path through. Just as he saw a gap, a huge metal beam dropped from the ceiling and landed right in front of him. Before he could stop himself, he tripped over the thing. His pants leg caught fast on one of its bolts.

"Come on, young sir!" Jam grabbed him under the arms and yanked, but Erec remained stuck.

Men formed a circle around them. "Got him. Go get the boss," someone said.

Jam pulled a scissors from his pocket and snipped Erec's pants to free him. With a little struggling, and Jam's help, he soon popped back on his feet. "Um, excuse me, guys." He tried to squeeze past a row of men, but they only shoved him back into the middle of their circle. For a moment Erec almost gave in to them, but then he thought about Bethany. He wasn't going to let her down. With a roar, he threw himself into the knees of one of the men in his way. The man fell back, but another dove on top of him, hitting him square in the back. He felt like an elephant had sat on him. The doors were so close. If only Erec could just get a cloudy thought now, he would know how to save himself, he thought. But he had no such luck.

Erec tried again, ramming himself into someone's knees. When they fell out of the way, he made it only a few feet before a worker drove by in a cart, colliding into Erec and grabbing his arms.

"The magnet," Jam shouted. "Erec, get rid of it. It's bringing you bad luck."

As soon as Jam said that, it seemed obvious. Erec stuffed the magnet into the shirt of the man that was holding him.

"Ugh." The man yanked back his hands and grabbed the wheel of his cart. "My head is pounding. I can't see anything. I can't believe I got my migraines back again." He made some funny noises, then threw up all over his overalls. The cart sparked a few times, then shut off, and smoke poured out of its engine. With a hiss, two of the tires went flat, sinking into dark puddles on the floor. The man tried to get out, but banged his head hard against the door frame and fell back into the cart.

In the confusion, Erec and Jam ran toward the front doors. "Get that magnet out of Billy's shirt," Erec heard Bill scream. "Throw it back to them before they escape!"

The luck magnet clattered near Erec's feet as they approached the doors. With a deep crunch, the tops of the doors slid toward each other with a bang.

Erec pulled, but they were stuck shut. "Two of the hinges popped," Jam pointed out. Erec threw the magnet hard back into the crowd of men that were closing in behind them.

"Ouch!" He heard Bill's unmistakable voice.

"Um, boss? I got your magnet for you right here. Were you looking for this?"

"No!" Bill screamed. "Get that away from me, you moron!"

The weight of the heavy wood doors became too much for their frames to support. With sharp pings, three more hinges popped. Jam yanked Erec back before both doors tilted over and slammed flat onto the warehouse floor, leaving the entrance wide open.

As they ran out, they could hear Bill scream, "Get this magnet off me. You, Billy, go bury it by the stream down the hill. Get out of here!"

"You smell something funny?" Jam said as he punched in the code to open their Port-O-Door.

Erec nodded and looked up. A small fire had started on the roof of Magnet Mountain. "We better go."

"Good idea, sir. I'll call a fire squad for them once we're safe in Cinnalim."

* * *

After a few taps on the Port-O-Door map, Cinnalim appeared on the screen. It was in a section of Otherness that overlapped with the outer reaches of the Philippine islands.

Jam smiled. "Cinnalim is rather famous. An explorer from Alypium discovered that Otherness extended all the way out to some of these uninhabited islands. They were incredibly beautiful, and they soon became resort towns for the wealthy and famous in the Kingdoms of the Keepers. They used to have typhoons and tropical storms, but with all of the money around, someone was able to work out a little weather adjustment. Now that's all under control." He tapped on Cinnalim, a larger sickle-shape island.

Hot, humid air instantly wrapped itself around Erec, blowing in rhythm with the soothing sound of rushing waves. Tall palm trees waved in the mild ocean breezes. It felt like they had walked onto another planet after the worn-down Outskirts of Alypium. Erec dragged his feet across the smooth white sand beach, resisting the urge to pull his shoes off and wade into the sparkling water. This wasn't the time to get distracted.

The image of Bethany chained to a desk with that strange thing wrapped around her head filled his mind. It wasn't fair that he could be surrounded by such beauty and she was a prisoner of Baskania's. Someday, if—no, *when*—she was safe, he would bring her here. But until then, there was no time to stop.

Jam made a call on his cell phone, reporting the fire at Magnet Mountain. It seemed impossible that they had been there so recently. "You haven't eaten yet today, young sir. Would you like a snack from the Serving Tray?"

Erec nodded. "Good idea, Jam. It won't slow us down if we eat when we walk."

Jam pulled the silver oval tray from his jacket.

Erec said, "I'll have a cheeseburger with ketchup and tomato. And a brownie."

A burger and a brownie immediately appeared. Jam produced a salad and fork for himself, and they walked toward a small strip of shops along the beach.

Surfboards lined the walls of a juice shack. Calypso music hung ten over the crash of the waves. The kid behind the counter looked as laid-back as the music. Long dreadlocks dangled around his deeply tanned shoulders. "Hey, dudes! What can I do you for?" He grinned. "We got a carrot-wheatgrass special today, with a shot of jumbly juice if you want an extra kick."

"Um, no thanks." Erec's nerves ground together when a thought came to him. What if nobody here had heard of this magnet man? What if they were in the wrong place? If he couldn't get to Bethany in time . . .

"Kind sir. Have you heard of 'the man with the magnet'? We were told he resided here in Cinnalim."

"Whoa, dudes." The young man grinned. "Of course I've heard of him. That's Danen Nomad, man. He's famous around here. I mean, if you haven't been 'called up' by Danen you're, like, nobody."

Erec was filled with relief. "So, you were called up by him, then?"

The man looked embarrassed. "Uh, no. I guess I'm nobody." Then he laughed. "But that's the way I like it, man. Hey, call me Jo Jo."

Jam nodded. "Quite wise, Jo Jo, sir. What exactly does it mean to be 'called up' by Danen Nomad?"

"Well, you know, man. It's his magnet. It's like a person magnet or something. He can use it on anyone he wants to come to him. So, it's like a big party over there all the time, they say."

"Where does he live?"

"The big place by the North Beach. It's not too far from here.

But good luck getting in to see him. He's called some of the best security guards to live with him, and they keep all the riffraff out." He chuckled and stuck a hand up. "Not that I'm saying anything, dudes. You know."

"Quite." Jam pulled out the Serving Tray. "May we repay you by giving you a bite to eat, Jo Jo? Anything you like at all and it's yours. Name your favorite, sir."

"Whoa." Jo Jo looked appreciatively at the silver tray. "Awesome, dudes. This will give me anything I want?"

"Just name it, sir."

After stroking the few hairs that jutted from his chin, Jo Jo cried, "Ooh, I made this for myself once when I had the munchies. I'll have an extra giant sushi kelp roll with tuna, mayonnaise, banana, and chocolate sauce. Oh, yeah, and put some bran sprinkles on top, man."

When the messy roll appeared, he scooped it off the tray with both hands. "Wow, thanks, dudes. This is totally awesome." Erec looked away while Jo Jo took a bite of his sushi roll. It looked like something from the *other* Serving Tray. "Hey, I have an idea, you guys. Maybe I could help you out. Danen Nomad's secretaries are always calling me for juice and snack trays. Why don't I give you a few to take along when you go up to his complex? You can just tell them you're working for Jo Jo's Juice Bar, and I'll bet they'll let you right in."

"Thank you so much. You don't know how important this is—" Erec's words caught in his throat. He wanted to do something for Jo Jo, but then he remembered that Jam already had.

They each left the shop with flimsy trays covered in plastic wrap. Erec walked slow, trying not to spill the cups of green juice. "Did you give him that snack so he would help us?"

Jam winked at Erec. "Of course not, young sir. But it never hurts to make friends, does it?"

"That's true, Jam."

Hot sand wormed its way into Erec's shoes and socks. He was dying to kick them off and walk barefoot along the beach, but he needed both hands to carry the big juice tray without spilling it. Soon a huge villa appeared on a cliff before them, overlooking the sea. Steep steps carved into the hillside led up toward a sprawling collection of mansions, gardens, gazebos, and tennis courts. Erec counted five pools and figured there were probably a lot more that he couldn't see.

"Guess this is the place." They had a hard time climbing the uneven rocky steps without spilling the juice glasses. Erec was glad they were still at least half full.

The humongous house loomed over them like a crystalline giant. Glass walls and beams reflected rainbows in all directions, mirrored back by steel doors and rails. Amidst all of the sparkle, white painted wood porches and window frames added a feel of peacefulness.

Two large men appeared in front of Jam and Erec, blocking them from taking another step. "And who would you two be?" one asked with a smile.

Jam bowed his head. "Kind sirs. We are making a delivery from Jo Jo's Juice Bar for Danen Nomad." He smiled. "If you don't mind."

The man frowned at the other one. "I don't know, Mike. Jo Jo isn't exactly the kind to hire a butler." He looked at Erec. "Or a kid."

"Well, maybe a kid." Mike squinted at Jam. "But not a butler. You're right. I think a phone call is in order." He shook his finger, then put it to his mouth. "Jo Jo's Juice Bar, please. Thanks . . . Yeah, is this Jo Jo? I'm calling from Mr. Nomad's complex. Did you hire a kid and a . . . butler recently . . . ? Oh, you did?" He looked Jam and Erec up and down. "I see. Okay, thanks, Jo Jo." Mike shrugged and stuck his hands in his pocket. "Says he did. Says the butler was out of a job and is bringing his kid along to help him." Mike looked just as suspicious as before, and not about to let them go anywhere.

"Doesn't explain why you'd still be wearing that butler suit, though. Or why your kid isn't at school."

Jam's mouth opened, but he couldn't think of a thing to explain.

Erec coughed a few times. "I had a day off today. I was sick." His weak coughs sounded as pathetic as his excuse.

Mike nodded. "I see. I think you two better stay right here with me for a while. Zeke, why don't you bring those trays in for them? Have a good look at them too, before you serve anything."

Zeke looked annoyed. "Of course. I always do. Any other orders?"

Mike laughed. "Sorry. Just making sure. I'll take care of these two for now."

Zeke walked away with their trays, their only tickets into the mansion.

"You two sit here." Mike led them to a lawn table and chairs. "I need to find out a few details about you before I can let you go. Just formalities, of course." He pulled out a small computer touch pad. "Names?"

Erec looked at Jam. Was it worth the risk of telling his real name? He had no idea how this guard would respond. Maybe it could help somehow. "I'm Erec Rex."

Mike looked at him with wry amusement on his face. "Very funny, kid."

An alarm issued from his handheld device and he jumped to his feet. His voice grew tense. "Uh-oh. This is big. I'm sorry, the two of you are going to have to stay here until I get back. We've got something major going on right now."

Erec's eyes widened. He'd been worried that they would never get inside. But if Mike had to go somewhere, they could just sneak in—

Before Erec knew what happened, Mike clapped each of their wrists into a set of handcuffs. He led them down a few steps to a door in the basement of the house, then into a wine cellar, locking

THE THREE FURIES

their cuffs onto a steel bar that was part of an uncorking shelf. "I'm sorry to leave you guys here. I really wouldn't do this normally. Just can't take any risks today. I promise I'll be back soon, get you two on your way." He waved apologetically and ran out. The heavy steel door slammed behind him.

"Oh, my." Jam looked around, distraught. "This is a bit of a problem."

"I hope he does come back." It occurred to Erec that if something happened to Mike, nobody else would know that they were locked down there. At least they had one hand free each, so they could use the serving platter and not starve to death. But they didn't have time to waste.

Jam leaned against the counter that they were stuck to. "I'm sorry, young sir. I am usually prepared for anything. I should have been ready with an excuse to get us out of this mess."

Typical Jam, Erec thought. Taking responsibility for everything that went wrong, and no credit for things that he did right. "No, there was nothing you could have done. I got us into this mess. I should have come back to Alypium sooner." He wanted to kick himself.

"What should we do?" Erec could see no way to break free. "Did you bring a remote control?"

Jam, whose magical gift was always to be prepared with everything, produced a magical remote filled with buttons. He handed it to Erec with a doubtful look on his face. "Can you use it, sir?"

Erec looked at the buttons. "I wish. The only thing I know how to do is move things, and I haven't done that forever. I'd be surprised if I could move a feather." He glanced down. "I guess I can try to move our handcuffs."

"No, no." Jam whisked the remote back. "Sorry, young sir. We could lose our hands that way. I think something other than moving things would be in order. Maybe melting the metal."

"Can you do it, Jam?"

"I wish. I've no idea how to use one of these. I would like to learn someday." He turned the remote over in his hand. "I think we're stuck here, sir."

An hour ticked by, according to Jam's watch, but it felt more like ten. All Erec could think about was Bethany: the way she was when he saw her last, and the way she looked now. The good times, and now. The kiss . . . and now. His best friend was gone.

Finally there was a shuffle at the door and Mike walked in. He unlocked their handcuffs without speaking. Erec noticed he looked pale and shaken.

"You said your name is Erec Rex?" Mike glanced at him with a new respect. "And you're a butler." He looked Jam over as if this was not obvious. "I suppose you two came to the right place, then. Mr. Danen wants to meet you two."

"What happened?" Erec said. "Did you tell him we were here?"

"Uh, no. You think I would've bothered Mr. Danen about two strangers on the property? Something . . . funny went on. We got a surprise visit from a friend. The Shadow Prince."

CHAPTER NINE
Danen Nomad

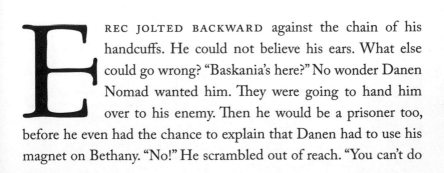

EREC JOLTED BACKWARD against the chain of his handcuffs. He could not believe his ears. What else could go wrong? "Baskania's here?" No wonder Danen Nomad wanted him. They were going to hand him over to his enemy. Then he would be a prisoner too, before he even had the chance to explain that Danen had to use his magnet on Bethany. "No!" He scrambled out of reach. "You can't do this. Don't turn us in to him. People will die. I have to see Danen in private."

"Whoa, kid." Mike looked over the counter. "Baskania's gone. He might come back, but you're safe here for now. In fact, if Baskania hadn't shown up looking for you here, you wouldn't be getting to see Mr. Danen at all. So calm down, okay?"

Erec's breathing calmed down a bit, but he still wasn't sure if he could trust Mike. Why was Baskania here looking for him? How did he know?

"Bill," Jam said breathlessly. "He knew where we were going."

Then it all clicked. Bill from Magnet Mountain knew they were coming to Cinnalim to find Danen Nomad. He must have called the Green House to report having seen Erec Rex. Of course he'd have told them where Erec was headed.

Erec's head dropped to his chest. He should have realized this might happen. Coming here after talking to Bill was a huge risk. He was lucky that he and Jam weren't with Danen when Baskania appeared.

"Does Baskania . . . know we're here?"

"Nah. Danen's not the type to help that guy. I mean, he treats the man nice, you know. The Shadow Prince has a lot of power, and it's best to be on his good side. But he's a real jerk. We don't like him a lot around here."

"Couldn't Baskania have read his mind and seen that we were down here?"

"Yeah, he could have," Mike said. "If Mr. Danen had known anything about you two then. I didn't tell him a word until the Shadow Prince was gone." He chuckled. "Of course I'd have never believed that you were really Erec Rex until Baskania showed up out of the blue looking for you 'and a butler.' But then I thought I should keep my mouth shut. It would be best not to burden Danen with that information yet. Baskania wasn't going to read *my* mind; I'm just one of the hundred people milling around here."

"Thanks, Mike." Erec looked at him with new appreciation. "You saved our lives."

"Eh, it's in the job description." He shrugged. "We better get you two in to Mr. Danen and then on your way before the Shadow Prince decides to pay another visit."

Jam looked around suspiciously. "Isn't he going to keep an eye out for us here?"

The thought made Erec shudder. In Baskania's case that was literally what he might do. He had taken the eyes of many of his followers and used them to see out of their remaining eyes, whenever he wanted. If one of Baskania's henchmen did see Erec, it would be the same as Baskania seeing Erec himself.

"No. You're safe now," Mike said. "Zeke and I keep tabs on everyone on this property. They're all our staff and guests who have been here quite a while. But the Shadow Prince *will* want to send one of his men here to keep a watch if he doesn't hear back from us soon. He trusts Mr. Danen, I think, to let him know if you show up. Big egos like that expect that people will do as they say." He laughed. "Like Mr. Danen takes orders." He led them out through hallways in the basement, and then up steps to an immense white room with pillars that stretched to a soaring ceiling.

Party music blared through the room. People from wall to wall were laughing, playing cards, and talking. Erec was immediately struck by how beautiful and intense the crowd was. He searched for Danen Nomad, but quickly realized he had no clue what the man looked like. A tall woman with long straight blond hair did look familiar, though. She had to be Meg Lorent, a wildly famous movie actress from America. And not far from her was a short, bouncy, dark-haired young woman with a turned-up nose. It was Sophie

Tacket, who had just won the Academy Awards for her latest movie. Erec would know her anywhere.

Mike led them through the crowds to a tall chair set up from a pedestal in the center of the room. The cushions sewn onto its back, seat, and arms were an odd forest green and dirty white, but their pattern caught Erec's eye. Not until he was right in front of it did he realize that they were made of money stitched together. Thousand-dollar bills.

"Like it?" A tall man with dark brown hair plopped onto the seat. "Go ahead. You can touch it. They're stuffed with hundreds. But this is my real gem." He pointed at the headrest on the chair. "These are the good ones. Five-hundred-dollar bills with McKinley on them. Five-thousand-dollar bills with James Madison. And look here, front and center." He pointed at a black-colored bill with GOLD CERTIFICATE printed on it, in a denomination that seemed too high to be real. "Yup. It's a hundred-thousand-dollar bill with Woodrow Wilson on it. These are rare, kid. None have been printed since 1945. Here's the back." He pointed at an orange bill sewn right above it, with ONE HUNDRED THOUSAND DOLLARS printed on it.

The man, who Erec supposed must be Danen Nomad, snuggled against the headrest cushion. "Best to enjoy the good things in life, right? Live well. That's my motto."

A dozen animals raced through the room between people's legs, and all of them jumped up onto Danen's lap. He laughed, nuzzled one of the dogs, shoved away a rabbit who was doggedly trying to climb up to his face, and petted a cat all at the same time. Everything about Danen seemed strange and remarkable. Erec noticed the man's shirt was odd. He leaned closer without meaning to.

"Yeah." Danen fingered his collar. "This one's sewn from Euros. But you should see my underwear. . . ."

"Uh, no thanks." Erec stepped away.

Danen chuckled. "I'm sorry. I get a little carried away. I'll send you guys with a bunch of this stuff if you like. Wear it and impress your friends."

Erec could not help but like the man. "Mr. Nomad? We need your help. Is it true that you have some kind of people magnet?"

Danen's eyes widened and then he burst out in side-splitting laughter. "Do I have a magnet? A person magnet?" His face reddened and his eyes watered, and it seemed like he would never catch his breath. Danen poked a man lounging nearby and said, laughing, "This kid wants to know if I have a person magnet."

The man chuckled in response, raising his eyebrows at Erec. "How did he get in here?"

Danen quieted down and coughed a few times. "Never mind." He waved the man away and leaned toward Erec. "Yeah, I have a magnet. How else do you think I get all this money? People love me. The richest families in the world are my best friends. They insist on giving me more than I ever wanted. How else would I get the best and the brightest to hang out with me all the time? My parties here are wild." He cleared his throat. "See her over there?" Danen pointed to a slender woman in a long purple gown and a tiara. "It's Princess Vicki. She faked her own death in order to live here with me. That's how strong my magnet is. A lot of others have done that too." He waved around the room, pointing at Nobel Prize laureates and famous artists.

Erec was glad the magnet was that strong. It would have to be in order to help pull Bethany away from Baskania's Draw. "I guess you know who I am. Thanks for talking to me, and for not handing us over to Baskania."

Danen nodded. "Anytime. That guy is trouble. I've never liked him. Of course, with all my famous guests and money he feels he has to make me a friend, I guess. So, what can I do for you?"

"Could you use your magnet on a friend of mine? She's trapped, and the Fates told me you were the only one who could help her."

Danen paused, lips pursed. "I don't know, kid. It's not that I don't want to help you. But I have to have a policy. Word spreads, you know. If I do a favor for one person, soon the whole world is begging me nonstop to bring their lost loves back, find the guys who owe them money. I'd get no peace." He thought a moment. "But you are Erec Rex, though. King Piter's son. And the Fates sent you here, you say?" After going back and forth a while between scratching his head and rubbing his chin, he said, "Well, okay. I guess just this time I can make an exception."

A grin broke over Erec's face. "Thank you! Her name is Bethany Cleary. And she's being held prisoner by Baskania in one of his fortresses—"

Danen went pale and held a hand up. "Whoa. Wait just a minute, young man. Did you say she's a prisoner of Baskania's? Because that changes the picture. I mean, I may not like him, but I'm not stupid enough to go completely against him like that. He'll take this magnet off me in a heartbeat. And then what would I do? Of course, after he's through with me I'd be lucky to even be alive, let alone worry about the magnet." He crossed his arms resolutely. "I'm sorry. I can't help you. You better get going before he comes back here looking for you."

Erec and Jam exchanged shocked looks. "But wait!" Erec grabbed Danen's arm. "You have to help us. If you don't, she's going to *die*. The Fates said you were our only hope." Danen did not look convinced.

"Please, kind sir." Jam clasped his white gloved hands together. "This is the request of a future king. He would not come to you for this unless he had to. Don't let Baskania win."

Danen slapped himself on the forehead. "Stop. Enough!" He sighed. "I don't know. If anyone, *anyone*, finds out about this I'll be dead. You understand me? I can't believe I'm even thinking about

THE THREE FURIES

this." Danen grabbed Erec's shirt. "If I use the magnet on this girl, you have to understand that she's going to do anything she can to get out of where she is and come to me. Anything. That could kill her too. It might make her do something stupid."

"I doubt she'll get too far," Erec said. "Baskania put a Draw on her to keep her there."

Danen's mouth hung open. "A Draw? From the three Furies? How did he get that? And . . . you want me to turn the magnet on her too? What do you want to do, rip the poor girl in half?"

"No. Please listen. I know it's dangerous, but it's the only way. The Fates told us that you have to use your magnet on her, then I have to draw my next quest from Al's Well, and then I can find her and give her some dragon blood to break the Draw. It's the only way."

"Kind sir, if Baskania was to find out that you did this, could you simply tell him you were trying to help locate Bethany for him? That you heard he wanted to find her?"

"Oh, yeah. Right. Like he's going to buy that. He reads minds, remember? If this backfires, which it might, I'll be dead, you'll both be dead, and your girlfriend will be dead." Danen's face sank. "Ugh. Problem. Baskania will send someone back here soon. I doubt he'll come himself again, but if he does, he's going to know about all of this when he sees me next. I'm guessing he'll read my mind." He hung his head in his hands. "I'm going to have to turn you both in. . . ." He looked Erec over warily. "I'm sorry. It's all I can do. Unless you both were to hold me at knifepoint, or if I was in danger and *had* to do what you said." Danen stared at them, as if waiting for them to take the hint.

Jam was searching his many-pocketed vest. He was prepared for almost anything, Erec thought. Could he be carrying a weapon?

In a moment Jam shakily held a pocket knife before him. He looked far more afraid of it than Danen was, but he still held it, trembling, close to Danen's throat. "Kind sir, would you please use your magnet for us now?"

Some laughter filled the air—people who saw Jam seemed not to think that he amounted to any danger at all. Erec almost laughed thinking of Jam at large. Nonetheless, Mike and Zeke arrived in a moment and Jam was disarmed.

Erec saw Danen make a signal to Mike, and then the knife was back in Jam's hand. A space was cleared around Danen, and they all moved slowly toward through the crowds and down a long hallway.

Two guards stood against a tall carved wooden door, long spearlike pikes and machine guns crossed in front of their chests. "I get the best soldiers and guards from all over the world," Danen whispered. He nodded to the guards, and then said, as if he were reciting from a boring textbook, "Stand aside, men. I am in danger of being killed if I don't listen to these hoodlums." Erec was sure he saw him wink, and Mike was shaking his head.

The guards looked confused, and Danen had to repeat himself, this time with an edge of warning in his voice. Mike motioned the guards to step away from the door, and they finally did. Erec and Jam followed Danen through. "I can't believe I'm doing this," he whispered. "If Baskania ends up finding out, I'll have to hand the girl straight back to him when she gets here. I'm not going to die for this, guys."

"If Baskania does show up here again, sir, he might know about this whole conversation."

"I know. If he gets suspicious, then he could read more heavily into my mind and see this whole ruse. But he trusts me. I should be able to get away with thinking about your knife at my throat. Of course, my cooperating with him will be the final proof in the end."

Danen opened a large safe, then two smaller ones inside it. He removed a rusty metal bar about the size of a finger and then nodded for Jam to bring the knife closer to him. "Tell me the girl's name, and her parents' names if you know them. Also one distinguishing feature that makes her stand out."

"Okay. Her name is Bethany Cleary. Her parents were Ruth and Tre Cleary, and they died . . ."

"Her parents died ten years ago," Jam said.

"She is really good at math."

"Good at math?" Danen raised an eyebrow. "Can't you think of anything better than that?"

"No, she's *really* good at math. It's her magical gift. She could be a seer someday because of it."

"Okay." Danen closed his eyes and concentrated. "Bring to me Bethany Cleary, daughter of the late Ruth and Tre Cleary, who is magically gifted with math skills." He waggled his eyebrows at Erec and Jam. "Get a load of this. It's pretty awesome. Watch out, now. Oh, you better put the knife away."

The room seemed to ripple. Suddenly, Erec was yanked off his feet by a force so strong that it slammed him into Danen. Jam, Mike, and Zeke followed, crashing into them at full force. The magnet seemed to be sucking them in like a black hole in space. Just when Erec thought that the magnet was pulling the wrong people to it, a spark shot out of the small piece of rusted metal and sailed out of the window and into the sky. The five of them were released, tripping backward across the floor.

"I forgot how that happens when there are other people in the room with me." Danen laughed. "Usually I just stick to the thing for a minute. Well," he said louder, "I've done what you asked, so please release me and let me live." He put the back of his hand dramatically to his forehead, and Erec and Jam darted out of the room.

CHAPTER TEN

Little Erec

MIKE FOLLOWED THEM down the hall. "You two better go find your princess now."

"She's not a princess, actually," Erec explained. "She's just my friend."

"Okay, your girlfriend, whatever." Mike pushed them through the crowded atrium, where the party continued as if nothing had happened. "I'm not going to call you, give you our number, or anything else that might implicate Mr. Danen more. If your girlfriend shows up here, I'm sure he'll take the magnet off her and she'll be free to go find you. Unless he gets in trouble for this, and then all bets are off."

"Thank you so much, kind sir."

Mike winked. "You better scram out of here quick. It's supposed to rain soon, so everyone will be going outside. You don't want to be conspicuous." He led them back through the huge party room.

"People go outside in the rain?" Erec said. "Why would they do that?"

Jam smiled. "Cinnalim is famous for it, young sir. It rains chocolate drops here. Quite good ones too. They sell them all over the Kingdoms of the Keepers."

People were squealing and pointing out the windows. Servants showed up with trays full of empty bags, which guests grabbed by the handful on their way out. The party was starting to spill through the doors.

Mike handed Erec an empty bag. "You might want to catch some rain on your way out." He winked. "Just be careful of the bugs."

The chocolate raindrops were light and delicious, with just a hint of cinnamon flavor. Erec found out the hard way, though, that Mike was right about bugs. After a few handfuls he ended up spitting out a chewy, wormlike thing.

Step one was done, and Erec was overwhelmed with relief. This part had seemed like it would be impossible: finding the right man who had the right magnet. But he had done it. The magnet was turned on to attract Bethany, just like the Fates said had to be done. Now all that was left was to complete most of his next quest, find Bethany, and make her drink dragon blood.

Erec's feet slowed in the sand as he and Jam crossed the beautiful beach of Cinnalim. The rainstorm was nearly over now, and only a few pieces of chocolate were sprinkling down. He picked up the Amulet of Virtues, which hung around his neck. Four of the twelve segments on its circular front glowed with colors for each of the four quests he had done so far. Although he had managed to complete them, they had been nearly impossible. And, if anything, the quests seemed to be getting harder and harder.

But this one would have to be easier. The Fates wouldn't let Bethany sit too long chained to that desk, would they?

But then Erec remembered. They didn't make all of the decisions. The Fates knew what might happen. They knew what his choices would be. But it was up to him and every person to decide their own course.

Jam studied his face and said little. He followed Erec to where their Port-O-Door was parked.

Erec said, "We have to go straight to Al's Well. I need to find out what this next quest is."

"Young sir, should we stop at my Aunt Salsa's on the way and let your family know your plans?"

"Let's go there afterward. I need to get this done." He remembered how he used to be worried about getting killed doing dangerous quests. What a luxury that seemed now. With Bethany in danger he only cared how long it would take him to get done so he could save her.

"And who will you take with you this time on your quest, may I ask?"

Erec remembered that he could bring two people along on his quests. He had been thinking that he would do this one by himself. Jam had gone with him on a quest before, as had Bethany and his good friend Jack. Maybe this time he would take his siblings Danny and Sammy. Since they were his siblings by birth, the true successors to the throne, they probably should go with him. The quests were meant for King Piter's three triplets to do together. Erec was so relieved that he had finally figured out who his real brother and sister were. How great to be a part of a team, and not the only one responsible anymore.

But then again, he thought, Danny and Sammy had never been in the Kingdoms of the Keepers before. He wondered if they would slow him down. Normally he wouldn't mind that, but with Bethany stuck . . . Or maybe Jack could go with him. He knew what Bethany would say if she was here—that he should let other people help him, and not try to do everything himself as usual.

Jam pressed the code into the Port-O-Door, and instantly they found themselves back inside King Piter's house. A wild barking echoed outside. Erec immediately recognized it as Wolfboy, his dog.

"Oh, dear. I'm sorry, sir. It looks like Ms. Frinley hasn't been able to come feed and train your dog today. Queen Posey's water wall must have kept her away. I never thought about that. I will take care of him and be right back."

"No, Jam. Let me do it." It had been too long since Erec had seen his pet wenwolf—a dog who changed into a huge wolflike creature when there was a full moon.

When he walked outside, a red shell poked through the grass. Erec picked up the snail and took a letter out.

Dear Erec,

I don't know what to think about this, but I don't like it. I was dusting and watering plants, my job in the Green House, and I was just outside the Inner Sanctum—that's Baskania's area. It has the biggest offices, right in the middle of the building. When President Inkle is in there it's obvious that Baskania is completely in charge of him.

Anyway, I was eavesdropping on their conversations, and they started talking about me! Baskania was telling Rosco how great he was, and Rosco said, really loud, "Did you catch that, Oscar?" And they all laughed. Baskania said that my spying on them was good training, and they could start using me for missions soon. As if I'd even begin to help them!

I can't believe that they knew I was there all along. You were right about that. Rosco knows everything. Don't think that will stop me from my revenge, though. I'll get him if it's the last thing I do.

Your friend,

Oscar

Erec shook his head. If only Oscar could move on and let things go. He was going to get into big trouble if everyone knew he was spying on them. How far would they let that go?

He wished Oscar was able go on his quest with him. He wanted to go on a quest with Erec more than anyone else. Of course, that was impossible now.

As soon as Erec was in sight, Wolfboy yelped and dove on him, knocking him flat on the ground and licking huge drooly kisses all over his face. The dog's tail wagged so hard that it smacked into his own sides with thuds echoing against his ribs, but he didn't seem to mind.

"Down, boy." Erec laughed. "Let's find some food for you."

The dog's house was more of a mansion, he thought. There were rooms of toys, a kitchen full of dog food. Its walls were lined with a thick rubber padding for times when the moon became full, so he didn't hurt himself.

On his way back into the house he heard someone calling from a distance. A woman in a long skirt waved from the other side of the water wall. That must be Ms. Frinley. Around her were more people milling around the water wall, staring at his house. He was sure some of them had come from the Green House and were just waiting to arrest him. How would he get past them all to go to Al's Well? It was located in the middle of Alypium, attached to the Labor Society building. Even when he did get to the well, pulling his next quest out would not be easy. It was guarded by flying Harpies on the lookout for him.

Erec found Jam inside. "It's too bad Oscar can't come to do my quest with me. I really miss him."

"Are you sure Oscar is still . . . unsafe?"

"Positive. I'll probably never see him again. It's really sad."

"I'm afraid you may be right, young sir." He cleared his throat, pointing at the crowds gaping at them through the window. A few of the people waved from behind the water wall. "Word may get back to Baskania that we are here. We should hurry. And next time we're here, we'll have to stay away from the windows. Right, young sir?"

"Right," Erec agreed. "Then nobody will know we're back. I'll bring Wolfboy into the house so we don't have to go out and feed him." A possible problem came to his mind. "Is it close to a full moon?" He hoped not, thinking about how his dog could destroy a room.

"We have a week or two, sir."

Erec brought the dog inside along with giant bags of dog food. Wolfboy sniffed around for a few minutes, then found a cozy spot to curl up on a couch.

"I don't think these people outside the water wall are going to let me just walk past them and go get my quest. They're probably waiting to arrest us." He jabbed a thumb toward the window. "Could you think of a way we could sneak past them? Maybe if I throw a cape on with a big hood they might not know who I am."

"I'm afraid they would probably guess. I don't think it's safe for you to cross through Alypium on foot."

Erec smiled with relief. "The Port-O-Door! That can take us right where we need to go."

"Yes, young sir." Jam refilled his vest pockets with a few more items, and the two of them entered the Port-O-Door vestibule again. In moments Erec found a tree on a map of the Labor Society's lawn that was a few feet away from the side door that led to Al's Well. Perfect.

But when he opened the door and stepped outside, a branch exploded next to him. Fiery splinters drifted through the air in front of his face. Erec froze, confused.

"There he is!" A group of Alypium army soldiers standing with saber rifles in front of the Labor Society raced toward him. A few shots rang out, and Erec tripped backward. He fell on top of Jam back in the vestibule and slammed the Port-O-Door shut. Erec stumbled back into the hallway of King Piter's house, panting. Discouraged, he slid down the wall until he was sitting with his head between his knees.

"Are you okay, young sir?" Jam pulled out a water bottle and a handkerchief from his vest pocket.

No. Erec was not okay. His voice was gone and he was shaking. He managed to nod to Jam and wave away the water bottle. How would he get that quest? He didn't know how much time he had, but it couldn't be too long. After Baskania had sorted through all of Bethany's memories he was going to kill her. Erec thought about the way Bethany looked, chained to that chair with little metal cones in her head, and hoped it was not too late already.

What had he been thinking? That he could just waltz into the

Labor Society, somehow get through the locked side door, and draw another quest without any interference? But how could he get a quest if he couldn't get into the Labor Society? How would he ever save Bethany?

Jam cleared his throat. "Sir? I have an idea." His voice sounded weak. "I'll go through the Port-O-Door close to where we were, but a bit farther back. I'll distract the guards, shout that I'm Erec Rex. If I wear a cloak they won't see who I am, and they'll assume it's you. Then you can take the Port-O-Door to the back side of the lawn and sneak through the door when they're coming after me."

Erec's jaw dropped. "Jam, that's crazy. Those soldiers would shoot you on the spot." He realized from Jam's expression that Jam was fully aware of that. He was willing to sacrifice himself to help Erec get his quest and save Bethany.

Erec put a hand on Jam's trembling shoulder. "Jam, that's the craziest, most ridiculous idea I've ever heard in my life. I can't believe you would die to help me."

Jam looked like he couldn't believe it either, but he shook his head. "It's the only way I can think of. I'll go find a cloak, sir."

"No! Look, even if I did make it to that door, it would be locked, and I'd be dead a second after you were." He started to pace the hallway. "Is there a way to make the Port-O-Door go underground? Maybe I could dig my way up into the Labor Society."

"Not into the ground, no, sir. Only underground to Aorth."

"That won't help. Could it put me on the roof?"

"I don't believe so. The only options I've seen on the maps are at ground height." Jam frowned. "It's too bad that it won't put us high up in the tree."

"If we bring a ladder and climb up into a tree out of the guards' sight, we could swing from branch to branch, then drop onto the roof."

"Like monkeys?" Jam looked skeptical. Erec almost laughed. Jam was right, it was another crazy idea. The trees were too far apart anyway, and probably none were close to the roof of the Labor Society building.

Erec paced some more, then stopped. "I know. A bomb. We could blast our way into the building."

Jam looked at him blankly, saying nothing.

Erec closed his eyes. "Yeah, I know. How would we even get a bomb? How would we get it close enough to blow up the Labor Society? And after we blew it up, we'd be arrested before I drew a quest."

"Should I go get the cloak, then, sir?"

"No! Jam, we'll find another way." *Think*. How could he get up high, or around the guards somehow? If only he could fly. . . .

That was it! He knew what he could do.

A smile lit up his face. "Jam, I just remembered some friends who might be able to help." He leaned against a windowsill that faced away from the gathering crowds from Alypium and looked across the fields where the castle gardens once stood. He could picture the entrance to the castle maze, the rows of perfect roses, the daisies with the huge spinning tops whirling into the air. He remembered running through the flagpoles that sported flags from more countries than he ever knew existed.

Erec hadn't done a Dragon Call in a while. He closed his eyes and turned them around in their sockets, bringing his dragon eyes forward. He could do it so easily now, accessing the right feelings he needed to make his eyes change. Thinking about Bethany in danger was more than enough. As usual, everything around him looked bright green once his dragon eyes were out. Big clumps of white hung in the air—the Substance that carried all the magic in the world. It looked beautiful beyond imagination.

He gazed into the skies and sent a message with his eyes. *Dragons! I need your help to save Bethany. Please come quickly!* His thoughts beamed upward into the clouds, along with the pure ray of love that would send it through. He tried to focus on his Dragon Call, sending its message far and wide.

Within moments, two flecks appeared on the horizon. They bobbed up and down through the wind and grew into graceful creatures, long tails arcing behind them. Erec went out a side door, careful to keep his dragon eyes out so that the incoming dragons would recognize him right away. When dragons saw each other's eyes, they were able to read the other's mind and know immediately what was going on.

But when the two dragons landed, Erec let his regular eyes come back out again. The big dragon, Patchouli, would know him anywhere. Her bloodred spines glowed against her reddish scales, and her black jointed wings were massive. The other dragon was small and green, only about eight feet tall and fifteen feet long. It gave Patchouli a questioning look when they landed.

Rushing forward, Erec threw his arms around Patchouli's long neck. She lifted her head and he dangled for a moment in the air before he slid back down along her scales.

"Thank you so much for coming," he cried. "Bethany has been captured by Baskania. The only way I can save her is by doing my next quest, and the Labor Society building is guarded by an army. I can't get in. Can you fly me over the building, straight to Al's Well in back?"

"Of course, Erec. As I've said, I'm at your service. You once rescued my babies. Here I have someone I'd like you to meet." She nodded toward the smaller dragon, who looked away shyly. "This is my son, Little Erec. I named him after you, since you saved his life."

Erec could not believe his eyes. This could not possibly be the tiny dragon who once had fit in the palm of his hand. It had been injured, with a bent neck, and Erec had pulled it out from where it was trapped and fed it until its mother returned. "But he was so tiny. . . ."

"Dragons grow fast." Patchouli snorted a gust of steam into the air. "All of my children owe you their lives, but Little Erec does the most. He insisted on coming with me to help you."

The small green dragon blinked its large eyes. Erec came closer to pet its smooth scales and then it smiled.

"Why don't you climb on Little Erec's back and we'll fly you over Alypium? We can find the best spot to land from the air." Patchouli sighed a blast of heat. "It's still dangerous for us to be here, though. The army is on alert for dragons, by order of Baskania. As soon as they see us, they'll try to shoot us down."

"That won't give us much time." Erec climbed his namesake's green spines up its tail and onto its back. He frowned. "Maybe you shouldn't come, Little Erec." He petted its snout. "One dragon will be enough to fly me there. It doesn't make sense to put you both in danger."

Patchouli hesitated. "I would rather go by myself and keep Little Erec safe. But on the other hand, he owes you a blood debt. It is his destiny to be at your side when you need him."

Little Erec looked around at him and nodded, not a trace of fear in his eyes. Erec put an arm around his neck. "Wow, thanks, guy. We better be careful, then. I have to return you back here safely."

Patchouli agreed. "I'll wait for you both here."

Erec looked around for the Alypium crowd. They were out of sight, but they had probably seen the dragons landing. Patchouli might not be safe here for long. "All right. Let's go, then, Little Erec."

He stepped onto the green spikes that stuck from the dragon's back and wedged himself between two of them. Little Erec soared straight upward into the sky. Cold wind blasted Erec's hair back, and blue sky surrounded him. Erec squeezed his arms around its neck, holding on for dear life. The small spines around him weren't enough to hold him, and the one in front of him wagged dangerously from one side to the other. Without warning, Little Erec turned sharply in the air, and Erec slid off its back, dangling from the dragon's green scaly neck. He grabbed as hard as he could as they shot straight into a fluffy white cloud.

CHAPTER ELEVEN

Paper Can't Be Fooled

SWIRLS OF CLOUD spun around Erec as he held on tight to the young dragon's neck. As soon as he caught his breath, he screamed, then finally was able to shout, "I'm falling! I'm falling off! Help!"

In one curling motion, little Erec dipped down and up again to catch Erec on his back. He floated evenly in the air until Erec was able to adjust himself between the spines again. "That's good. Thanks."

They soared lower until Alypium grew from a tiny patch into a village. Erec pointed out the looming silver spires and flags of the Labor Society to Little Erec. From high up, Erec could see the walled-in back gardens and the hill where Al's Well sat. He smiled at the ease of flying. Why bother trying to break into his usual side entrance when he could go straight to the well itself?

The guards shouted and fired off a few gunshots as Little Erec soared over the turrets and into the field behind the building. Yet there was no passageway for the guards to get through to them here. Little Erec landed at the top of the small hill, outside the large round stone wall.

A door opened and Al, the keeper of the well, appeared. He looked like a plumber, with a rubber plunger in his hands and a tool belt weighing down his sagging overalls. AL was embroidered on the front pocket. "Heeey, yer back again. Clever," he said, nodding at the dragon. He ran a hand through his hair, a big grin on his face. "Now you've got dis guy to take you around. Nice. I was wondering if I'd ever see ya out here again. Dey got this place locked down pretty tight." He rubbed his hands together. "Da Fates have been ready ta give ya your next quest for a while now, but I had no way ta get the message to ya."

"Yeah, I'm just glad I got here in one piece. It's good to see you, too. I better hurry and get the quest before Baskania shows up. He'll probably find out that I'm here soon from the guards out there."

"Or dose Harpies will tell 'im when dey come back. Dey're always flying around looking for you." Al looked up at the sky. "One problem, though. You're supposed ta sign Janus's paper pad inside before ya draw yer quest, or the Labor Society will say it don't count. Not dat it matters, I say. The Fates are giving you your quests, not them. Up to you, though."

"I'll just get the quest, thanks."

Al led Erec and Little Erec through the door into the small

grassy enclosure where several of the well's servants were polishing gleaming wrenches and pliers. The stench of the place hit Erec immediately. Al took a deep whiff. "Ahh. Ya can never get enough of the smell of life. No?"

In the center of the enclosure hung a round shower curtain. Al pulled the cord and it slid open to reveal Al's Well, which looked like a large white toilet. Green smoke wafted from its bowl.

At once the servants around Erec fell to their knees and bowed repeatedly toward the toilet. Erec kneeled in front of it. The water looked black, going down into what seemed like a bottomless pit. He took a breath and stuck his hand deep inside. The water was freezing and hot at the same time. What would this quest make him do? It better not keep him away from Bethany too long.

A thick paper was in the water and he pulled it out. For a moment he was afraid to look at it, but then he read, "No quest will be given until Janus's pad is signed."

A flash of feathers flapped in front of his face and Erec gasped. The dripping note was snatched from his fingers by a claw. He looked up with shock as a Harpy sailed away with it. A few more were coming toward him—sharp, sneering, beaklike women's faces on vulture bodies.

Erec climbed Little Erec's scales onto his back. "Hurry. Down the hill there's a back door into the building. I know how to find Janus from there."

Several more Harpies circled in the sky as Erec and the dragon flew over the stone wall to the bottom of the hill. Erec shook and jiggled the door but it was locked. "Ugh! What are we going to do?" He gave the dragon a long look. "Can you breathe fire yet? Maybe you can blow the door down."

Little Erec took a breath and blew hot steam onto the doorknob. Other than making Erec feel like he was visiting the equator, though, the smoke had no effect at all. The dragon turned its head and looked at Erec sheepishly.

"Come on, guy. You can do it! Haven't you breathed fire before?"

It shook its head.

"Try again, okay?"

Erec looked up nervously. Some of the Harpies were flying closer. Once enough of them gathered together to lift him, they would grab him with their claws and fly him to Baskania.

Little Erec panted in and out deeply and then took a big breath. He held it a while, then blew at the door as hard as he could. A thin flame, like a blowtorch, burned a small hole above the doorknob.

"Good job, little guy!" It felt funny calling a creature much bigger than he was "little." Erec stuck his arm through the hole and unlocked the door, and they ran inside. "This way!" They ran to the elevators up in the building lobby. Little Erec could barely fit inside the elevator. It had to wind around so that his body lined the walls.

Just a few steps out of the elevator, Erec froze. Armed guards filled the lobby.

"Hey, there he is!" Guns were pointed at him from all over the room.

Erec's head spun in a blind spasm of rage. He started to fall, and for a moment he thought he had been shot. His shirt started to tear. Dragon spines rose from his back, ripping through the cloth. He was growing, stretching. Claws popped from his fingertips. Green scales rose on his skin, and everything around him turned green.

A cloudy thought vision filled his head:

A guard stepped forward with his gun pointed at Erec. He looked around nervously, hesitating. Then another guard behind him rushed forward with a wild grin, as if to claim the glory for himself. Shots rang through the air. Erec crumpled to the ground, dead. Bullets continued to fly at Little Erec. At first they bounced off his scales, but one eventually found a softer spot. A moment later, the dragon fell to the floor, face first.

Erec trembled. No, not Little Erec. He had told his mother that he would bring him home safely. Anger surged through him as his arms rippled with new muscles. His breath was hot and steamy. No. He couldn't let this happen. He had to get that quest for Bethany.

A guard stepped forward with his gun pointing at Erec. This was first one that Erec had seen in his vision. It was happening now. The guard looked around nervously, hesitating.

No! Erec stepped forward, and his roar echoed through the huge glass and chrome lobby. Everyone stopped and stared. He had to stop the second guard from shooting. Erec took a deep breath and felt something hot burst from his mouth. Fire spread everywhere in a huge gush.

The guards stepped back, confused. Curtains and plants were burning, and charred ash drifted through the air.

"Get him!" A guard rushed toward Erec, gun out, and fired.

Duck.

The command of his cloudy thought was loud in his head. He fell to the ground and rolled as bullets sailed over his head.

Leap.

His legs were stronger than ever before. Dragon muscles running through them let him sail over the guards, leaving Little Erec behind.

Roll.

He knocked over ten soldiers like bowling pins.

The door to the side room where Janus kept the paper pad was locked. Men behind him picked up their guns, and a stray shot whizzed over his shoulder, lodging in the wooden door.

Breathe fire.

Erec focused his anger and desperation on the door that was blocking him from where he had to go. With a deep breath, he blasted an immense hole in the wood. He stepped through it into the little room that looked like an old curio shop. Looking up in surprise was Janus.

Ashes and dirt whirled around him like a miniature cyclone, but even the wind was not enough to remove the piles of dust on Janus himself. Scrawny limbs with knobby joints jutted from under his dingy gray smock, making him look like a prisoner who had been locked in a dungeon for all time.

Janus looked Erec up and down with admiration and amusement. "Well, good fellow. What an interesting way to pay a visit."

Erec ran to Janus's desk, trying to slow his breathing. "I'm Erec Rex. I need to sign the paper so I can draw a quest."

Footsteps scrambled behind him, and guards appeared at the doorway. One reached through the hole, unlocked the door, and swung it open. But then he froze, shouting, "Whoaaaa . . . !"

The man, along with others behind him, screamed, looking up the hallway. Then they all disappeared, thrown to the floor as Little Erec butted his horns into them like an enormous ram.

Janus shook his head. "I'm sorry, Mr. . . . . whoever you are. But I know Erec Rex personally. He's a boy, not a scaly creature. Whatever you may be." He tapped the pad in front of him. "Besides, the paper can't be fooled. It knows who the real Erec Rex is. And"—he pointed at the door—"you won't be able to go back through that door unless you are Erec Rex. So I'm afraid you're trapped in here now."

Erec saw the shimmering bubble that filled the far doorway. It would only let him go through if Janus's paper pad recognized him. But would it, now that he had become part-dragon? For the first time he realized he might be trapped in this small room.

"Listen, Janus. I know I look funny. But it's really me. Let me sign it, okay?"

Janus seemed quite pleased at how odd this all was. "Well, there's nothing to lose, I suppose. You can't fool the paper."

Erec took the pen, though he had a hard time holding it between his claws. He had to turn his hand upside down to write, which made his signature look completely different than usual. If this wasn't his real signature, the paper really might not recognize him. He bit his lip, hoping . . .

The letters he had scrawled onto the page turned dark, then fissured deep into the writing pad. Each letter cracked open, and beams of light shone from them.

"Well, look at that." Janus regarded Erec in wonder. "It really is you. What an . . . interesting new look." He shook his head and smiled. "Good luck on your quest, Erec."

"Thanks."

Erec ran through the bubble material in the doorway and called for Little Erec. "C'mon." He wasn't able to fit onto the other dragon's back now, but he put an arm around its neck. "Straight through the windows, out back there. Let's go!"

Erec leaped alongside Little Erec, and the two of them crashed through a giant window onto the grass. Guards scrambled after them, guns firing.

Fly.

With an itchy feeling, wings sprouted from his shoulder blades. He leaped into the air, Little Erec at his side. They soared over the stone wall.

A slew of Harpies buzzed through the air around Al's Well like an overgrown mosquito convention. Their black hair was pulled so tightly into buns that their huge noses stuck out like beaks. They snapped at Erec with their sharp claws, spewing insults and threats.

"We'll get him, won't we, girls?"

"Yeah, we'll shred him."

"Don't forget to leave him a little bit alive. I know the Shadow Prince wants his eyes intact."

Erec breathed torrents of fire into the air, making them back off. Al watched, amazed. "Is dat really you in dere, Erec? Looks like you changed a bit."

"It's me. Let me try to get a quest, quick. Okay?"

Al gestured toward the toilet. Erec sprinted over, grabbed it, and reached deep inside. He couldn't feel the water through his scales, but in a moment he noticed a warm slip of paper and pulled it out.

"Let's go, Little Erec." He squeezed the dripping paper in his hand, afraid to look at it. What would it make him do? He hoped it would say something like "Save Bethany." That would be perfect.

Fly.

A few breaths of fire scared the Harpies back. Erec stretched his wings and lifted from the ground beside the dragon. The wind felt good on his face. He was putting his troubles behind him. He couldn't climb fast enough into the air, the higher the better.

He made it. Got the quest. Now he could relax. Whatever it was, at least he and Little Erec were out of danger.

Erec felt his dragon eyes slide back into his head. The sky around him became a beautiful blue, no longer the vivid green that his dragon eyes imparted to everything. His flying felt a little jagged, like his wings weren't working right. For some reason they seemed too small. He saw the scales disappearing from his skin in time to realize that his cloudy thought was over. He wasn't part-dragon anymore—how would he be able to fly?

"Whoa—help! Little Erec—I'm falling!" Erec tumbled straight down through a cloud toward the ground. Moments before he hit, the small dragon grabbed him with its claws and yanked him back into the air. He felt like a mouse caught by a hawk, watching the ground go by right under his hanging limbs, but he held tight to the quest paper.

They landed next to King Piter's house, where Patchouli was waiting. Little Erec set him down, and he collapsed onto the ground.

After he caught his breath, Erec smiled. "You saved my life, bud. Now you don't owe me anymore."

Patchouli breathed hot steam at Little Erec. It seemed like that would fry him, but the little dragon seemed to like it. "That is not our way, Erec," she told him. "My son will owe you his life forever."

"Really, it's okay. I'm calling it even now."

Patchouli shrugged. "Is there anything else we can do before we go?"

"No ... Wait. There is one more thing." Erec hesitated, not wanting to ask. But he had to. "When I find Bethany, I am supposed to make her drink dragon blood. The Fates said that that would break the Draw that Baskania put on her to keep her prisoner."

"He put a Draw on her?" Patchouli said, upset. "There is only one place he could have gotten that."

"I know. The Three Furies. My father told me about them."

Patchouli nodded. "I can't imagine how he persuaded them to give him one of their Draws. This is very troubling. He must be doing something terrible to gain their favor." She shook her head. "Of course you can have my blood. If you get a container from the house I'll give it to you."

Erec found Jam inside, who produced a vial the size of a large test tube with a screw top. Erec brought it out back to Patchouli.

"Little Erec insists on giving you his own blood, if that's okay."

"No, he's done enough for me. He already saved me a few times today."

"It would make him happy, and it won't hurt him one bit." She reminded him, "You used your own blood to feed him when he needed it."

"All right, then," Erec said. "As long as it doesn't hurt him."

Patchouli brandished a claw and stuck it into the scales on Little Erec's shoulder. She scraped until a small stream of blood appeared. Erec quickly filled his vial. Patchouli breathed more steam onto her son, and the bleeding stopped.

"Thank you so much." Erec petted the small dragon on the head. "Listen, you've more than paid me back, okay? We're just friends now. No more owing anyone."

The dragon did not seem to listen. Instead it flew away with its mother into the sunset.

"Young sir, would you like some new clothing?"

Erec had forgotten how terrible he must look. His shirt had been shredded, and only a few patches of fabric remained around his cuffs. His pants were on, luckily, but the lower legs were torn.

"Yeah, good idea, Jam." He looked at the quest paper in his hand. How much longer could he put off knowing?

Jam seemed to know what Erec was thinking. "Do you want me to read it for you, young sir?"

"Okay." Erec handed the paper to Jam and sat on a couch.

"Hmm." Jam turned the paper over and inspected it. Then he turned pale.

"What does it say?" Now that Jam knew what it said, Erec suddenly couldn't wait to find out. He snatched the paper back, sure it would say something horrible like "Kill the entire Alypian army in five minutes."

His hand shook as he read. "Visit King Augeas and introduce yourself."

That was it? Visit a king? He laughed with relief. This was perfect. Who better than a king to help him? His own father was out of commission, but another king would have some power at his command. That made sense—the king would have what Erec needed to free Bethany. Maybe he would send a whole army with Erec to Baskania's compound so he could set her free easily. All Erec would have to do was show this King Augeas how awful Baskania was, what he would do if he succeeded in taking over the world.

"Hey, Jam. This isn't so bad, after all. Is it? A king is just what I need."

For some reason, Jam was having a hard time responding. He looked sick.

"What's wrong? Are you feeling okay?"

Jam shook his head. "Young sir. You cannot follow this quest. I know you need to free Bethany, but this is not the way. It's not possible."

"I don't understand."

"I know, sir. You see . . . King Augeas is . . . not someone you want to meet."

"Why not?"

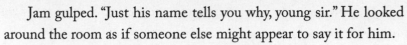

Jam gulped. "Just his name tells you why, young sir." He looked around the room as if someone else might appear to say it for him.

"What do you mean? Isn't his name King Augeus?"

"Well, yes. But . . . he is called something else."

"What is he called?"

Jam gulped again. "King Augeas is the Nightmare King."

CHAPTER TWELVE

The Nightmare King

ELICIOUS SMELLS OF waffles, cookies, and hot chocolate wafted through Aunt Salsa's apartment. Erec didn't realize how hungry he was until she handed him a plate stacked with sandwiches and chips.

It was good to see his family safe. Erec found that he kept staring at his adopted twin siblings, Danny and Sammy. He kept wondering how he would look if he had their sandy brown hair and their height. If his looks had not been changed.

Luckily, they didn't seem to notice. "You should have heard her!" Sammy squealed. "The last time Dumpling Smith used Mom's Seeing Eyeglasses on us, she was almost crying, demanding we tell her where we were. As if! She keeps coming back every hour or so."

"She's persistent." Danny shook his head in amazement. "I mean, she says things like she needs to get us all to safety—which is really lame, since we're all safe and sound right now. But she can 'take better care of us.' I can't imagine what that means. But I don't understand why she still wants only me and Sammy."

Erec knew just why that was. He'd seen with his own eyes a vision of them becoming king and queen—his corulers of the three Kingdoms of the Keepers. Erec knew from his father that he was destined to rule Alypium. Maybe Sammy would take over Ashona from Queen Posey, and Danny would inherit Aorth from King Pluto. It was hard not telling them right now—they would be so excited. But after what happened to King Piter's castle when Erec learned who he was, he wasn't about to say anything. Who knew what other spells were in place, what other awful things might happen if they found out too soon?

But, on the other hand, who better to come along on his quest than the very two who were supposed to go with him? If they all went together, the three triplets destined for the crown would grow stronger and tackle evil.

The only problem was the Seeing Eyeglasses. If Dumpling Smith could tell where Danny and Sammy were, she'd come and snatch them up—or tell Baskania, who she must be working for. If he could just get those glasses back—

"What's wrong, Erec? Do I have snot on my nose? A pimple or something? You can just tell me. You don't have to stare me down all day."

"Sorry, Danny. No, you're fine. I've just been . . . spaced out after getting run down by Harpies and having armed guards shoot at me."

June's hand flew to her heart and she gasped. "If I hear that one more time, you'll never be allowed out again. In fact, I don't think you should go anywhere. It's far too dangerous out there with people looking for you, hunting you down." She sat down and crossed her arms.

"I'm so sorry, modom," Jam said. "It was completely my fault. I should have been supervising him. It was wrong of me to let him go alone."

Erec did not say a word. Jam had not let him go alone, he just had gone without asking Jam. Which was what he would do again, if anyone tried to stop him. He had a quest to complete. He had to save Bethany. The dragon blood was in his pocket, ready. Everything was lined up as it should be. The only question was if Danny and Sammy should join him.

Little Zoey plopped on his lap, and Trevor lay on the floor next to him, his red hair flopping over his dark brown eyes. Trevor set down his Super A Team action figures and said, "Tell us about your next quest."

Everyone in the room looked at Trevor. He spoke so rarely that people were usually surprised when he did. Erec often wondered what was going on in Trevor's mind. He had a feeling the thought process was probably pretty complicated.

"Okay, Trevor. It doesn't seem too bad, really. I just have to go visit this King Augeas guy and introduce myself. Pretty boring, huh?" This seemed like a good time to play up how safe it was, for his mother's sake. "I'll say hi, then he'll say hi. I'll say, 'I'd like to introduce myself, your highness. My name is Erec Rex.' And he'll say, 'Well, hello there, young man. It's nice to meet you. Is there anything I can do for you before you go on your way?' I might ask him for a snack, then I'll be off." He smiled. "It's cake."

Zoey giggled. "Cake. I want some cake." Aunt Salsa rushed over with a slice of cake on a plate for her, making her laugh more.

"One thing I don't understand," Erec said. "The Fates said I had to do most of the quest before saving Bethany. How can I do most of introducing myself? Should I say, 'Hello there, nice to meet you King Aug—'" He laughed. "And then later I'll come back and say, '—eas. My name is Erec Rex.'"

Aunt Salsa handed Erec a plate of cake and cookies. Zoey scooped a handful from his plate, getting more crumbs on Erec's lap than into her own mouth.

Jam cleared his throat. Clearly he wanted to say something about King Augeas, but was holding back to avoid being rude.

Erec did not want Jam to scare his mother with whatever terrible story he had about the king. But, at the same time, he was burning with curiosity. The Fates wouldn't give him as simple a quest as just saying hello to somebody, would they? He hoped they would, this time, because they knew he had to hurry for Bethany's sake. They were on his side, weren't they?

This quest sounded so simple, how bad could it be? Then again, he remembered some of the other quests he'd had. "Open Patchouli's eggs in Nemea" had sounded like opening Easter eggs, but it turned out that he had to hatch baby dragon eggs without getting attacked by their protective mother. He smiled, remembering that that was when he had saved Little Erec's life. And the quest, "Get behind and set it free," hadn't sounded bad at all, only a little confusing. It ended up being one of the most gut-wrenching ordeals he had ever gone through.

Finally, Erec's desire to know outweighed his worry about what his mother thought. It didn't matter, anyway. Nobody would be able to stop him from going. Not now.

"Jam, what do you know about this King Augeas? What's his story?"

Jam looked relieved. "It's best that you know, young sir, before you go anywhere." To prepare for his story, he arranged a few pillows around himself on the couch. Erec and his siblings sat on chairs and the floor, ready to listen.

"Sirs and modoms, the story of King Augeas is told as a fable. I had myself believed that, like most tales, it was not true. That is, until I learned it was one of Erec's quests.

"Legend says that King Augeas was born wanting more. As a baby, he wailed each time he looked at his parents, as if disappointed that they were not good enough for him. As he grew up, as an only child and prince, he was spoiled by the entire court, demanding one thing after the next. He was never satisfied. The prince did not care for anybody but himself, so most people tried to steer clear of him. But he ordered the children of his servants to play with him, making them fetch things and obey his commands.

"So the other children did not really like him. Only one boy treated the young Prince Augeas as a true friend, sharing secrets with him and inviting him on adventures. His name was Hector. Somehow, Hector was able to see through the prince's spoiled behavior, and his royalty, and glimpse the lonely child inside. So, over the years, the two became close. As long as Hector was serving the prince in some way, and the prince was able to brag to him about all of the cooks, servants, horses, and toys that he had—things that Hector could never afford—he was glad to have Hector at his side.

"Of course, if Hector was lucky enough to be given anything, Prince Augeas had to have the same thing, only better. When Hector got a book that he loved from his mother, Prince Augeas had to have an ornate copy of the same book, handwritten by the author. When Hector was given a cake and a celebration on his birthday, Prince Augeas demanded a feast in his own honor on Hector's birthday.

"But Hector did not seem to mind. He accepted that was the

way it was with princes and servants. One day, as they approached twenty years old, Hector told everyone in the castle about his beautiful bride-to-be. She was a village girl named Arachne, and she had long golden hair with curls like spun silk. But, as Hector said, more important than her beauty, Arachne was kind. She always had gentle words and cookies for the children in the village, helped the elderly with their tasks, and sung sweetly if anyone needed cheering up.

"Prince Augeas immediately decided that he could not be outdone. He had the palace courtiers scour the surrounding countries for the finest and most educated princesses. Augeas wanted to find the most beautiful and graceful girl in the world, someone who would put Arachne to shame.

"For nearly a year, princesses were brought to his court for him to judge. Most were immediately sent away, but some were kept on. He held sewing tests, poise tests, races, cooking tests. Even if his future queen would never cook an egg for the rest of her life, he wanted to be able to say that she was the best. Each had to demonstrate hobbies, which were rated by the prince and his judges.

"Hector and Arachne were not allowed to marry until the prince had found his wife. Augeas said it would not be fitting for Hector to marry first, but they both knew the real reason. The prince would have been jealous. Finally, Augeas found a bride who was fitting in every way. Princess Lito had mastered seven languages, wrote poetry, wore clothing that she designed herself, and was as rich as she was beautiful.

"Prince Augeas arranged a simple dinner with his bride-to-be, Hector, and Hector's bride. He was sure that when they were all together, Hector would realize how foolish he had been to think that he could ever have anything half as good as the prince.

"But Prince Augeas was in for a surprise that evening. Princess Lito was gorgeous, poised, and well spoken. But when Arachne walked in, hand in hand with Hector, to meet the prince for the first time, she seemed to glow. She wore only a simple peasant dress. She was not worldly or sophisticated. But her kindness made her sparkle, and Hector only had eyes for her. He bowed to Princess Lito and wished his best to Prince Augeas, but it was clear that he would never want anyone more than his own Arachne. Even the prince had a hard time taking his eyes off her.

"Blushing, Arachne handed Augeas a wedding gift that she had made for him and Princess Lito. It was a woven silk tapestry that was more skillfully made than any Augeas had ever seen. Boiling with anger, the prince stormed out of the room. The next day he called the wedding off. Now he knew whom he had to marry, and it was not a princess after all. Only one girl was good enough now—the beautiful peasant who was engaged to Hector. So he sent word to her family that she would be his queen.

"You might think that Hector fought the prince, or that Arachne refused to marry him. But that is not the way kings and servants acted back then. For Augeas was no longer just a prince. His father had decided that the wedding would be the perfect time for him to step down and hand over his throne to his son. And if Hector gave Augeas problems it would have meant death.

"As Augeas stood in the chapel before the wedding started, a bedraggled old woman approached him. She told him that he would make a strong king and that his just rewards would come to him someday. Augeas had her thrown out, as he did not approve of beggars in his castle. But before she was dragged away, she told him that he would see her again in his dreams.

"It seemed that Augeas enjoyed the sad looks that his friend threw to his bride during the wedding. In fact, he gave Hector the task of carrying both rings down the long aisle of the castle chapel and handing them to Augeas and Arachne. After the wedding, King Augeas often would spend time with Hector, with Arachne right at his side.

"King Augeas did eventually grow tired, though, of the sad longing in his bride when she was around Hector. Even though he didn't like seeing him go, he decided to send Hector away. A regiment of soldiers was heading south into the dreaded Sludge Lands of Nequid. Each of the soldiers had been chosen because they had made mistakes in the past, or their commanders did not like them for one reason or another. It was a highly dangerous mission, and they were sent as punishment more than any real threat to Nequid. Hector was made the commanding leader of the troops. Soon after they marched south, word came back that they had been quickly overpowered. None of them returned.

"Augeas never forgot that first night he had met Arachne. He enjoyed bragging about his wife's weaving skills. After hearing about Hector's death, she spent most of her time at the loom. King Augeas told anyone who would listen that Arachne could weave better than Minerva herself. Minerva was the most powerful sorceress of her day. People thought of her as a goddess. One of her special skills was that she could weave the finest fabrics from her loom.

"Before long, Minerva showed up at the palace, wanting to see Arachne's work for herself. Arachne tried to make light of her skills. But King Augeas kept building her up, goading Minerva into a challenge between them. Minerva was only too happy to agree—for a price. She was sure she would win more land from the king.

"So Arachne and Minerva sat at their looms for a day, and at the end their work was inspected. Even the sorceress had to admit that Arachne's cloth was perfect and the artwork devastatingly beautiful. Arachne had woven a scene of the sun setting over a castle, with a lone soldier trudging into the woods in the distance.

"Like King Augeas, Minerva did not take losing lightly. She congratulated Arachne, then bestowed her own gift upon her, which would let her spend the rest of her days weaving silk. The witch turned her into a spider, and then vanished before the king could retaliate.

"King Augeas fell into despair. His only friend was gone, and his wife nothing more than a web spinner in the corner of his chamber. But then one day the king had a great surprise. His old friend Hector returned. Hector was dressed in finery. Amazingly, he did not bow before him when King Augeas demanded it. After being taken captive, Hector had befriended the king of Nequid and become his best advisor. When the king fell ill, with no sons of his own, he passed his crown on to Hector. He was now king of an even larger land than Augeas. Hector's beautiful wife and queen had traveled with him to meet his old friend.

"Augeas was beside himself. How could Hector have more than he did? He had more money, a larger, more bountiful kingdom, and a wife instead of a spider on the wall. And worse, there was nothing that Augeas could do about it.

"That night, the old woman whom he had thrown out of his wedding came to him in his dreams. She offered a way to lord over King Hector once again. More than that, he could rule over everybody, even kings and sorcerers. He would be the king of kings. Augeas agreed, glad to take whatever power he was offered. So, in his dreams, he took the official oath to become the Nightmare King.

"They say that he vanished that night from his bed. He was sent to rule alone in the dark shadow lands that form the border between our world and the realm of dreams. Under his command are hordes of restless-thought monsters and unsatisfied dark-vision hounds that can break into our world through our nightmares. The unlucky few in his dominion are the only humans unlucky enough to meet King Augeas where he lives now. They are enslaved in a nightmare in his lands forever."

A rapt silence followed the end of Jam's story.

Erec's eyes widened as he remembered his quest. *"What?"*

"I'm sorry, young sir. Did you not hear—"

"No. I heard, Jam. I just . . . There must be *another* King Augeas somewhere, right?"

Jam cleared his throat politely. "Not that I've heard."

Everyone was quiet during dinner until Mrs. Smith's gravelly voice boomed through the room. "Still there, I see? I have people *all over* looking for you two, Danny and Sammy. This hiding out is a bad idea. I need to find you." Her voice became wheedling. "Do you two know that you're making life very hard for your dear friend Dumpling? How am I going to do all the nice things I planned for you children if you don't come to me? You need to *trust* me. I'm your friend. Right?"

The twins looked at each other in horror, neither wanting to answer.

"Well," Mrs. Smith roared, "if that's the way you want it, then *fine*. My job's not an easy one, I'll tell you that. But I will find you two, if it's the last thing I do. The Shadow Prince is on the move, and I want to be ready."

"You hear that?" Erec sat up straighter. "She's admitted it. She works for Baskania, and she wants to capture the twins because—" He stopped himself, not wanting to explain his logic that Danny and Sammy were King Piter's missing triplets.

"Garbage!" Mrs. Smith's fury resounded through the room before she made her voice sickeningly sweet. "I do not work for the Shadow Prince. I would do no such thing, dear children. I only want to protect you from him. Do you understand? Will you at least talk to me about it?"

Erec caught Sammy exchanging a glance with Danny. They couldn't actually be thinking about talking to Dumpling Smith, could they? He shot Sammy a warning look and shook his head firmly.

"Well, then, children. It's good-bye for now. But don't worry. I'll be checking back soon, wherever you go." Laughter that sounded like a rusty hinge scraping open echoed around them, ending mid-chuckle as Mrs. Smith pulled the Seeing Eyeglasses off.

"You can't believe what she's saying is true," Erec said to Sammy.

"No . . . I mean, I don't know. She sounds so earnest. I understand her better than you do, I think."

"You're being put under a spell. Believe me, she's up to no good."

Well, this was beyond ridiculous. He was supposed to become enslaved in a nightmare for eternity in order to rescue Bethany as soon as possible? It was the only way she would escape? Was this the Fates' idea of a joke?

Erec's eyes were open and glued to the clock on Aunt Salsa's wall. His family was asleep. He had been offered a bed to share with Trevor, but insisted on taking the couch instead. Not that he minded sharing. But tonight he wanted some freedom.

His mother had spent the rest of the evening insisting that the quests were getting out of hand. With both King Piter and his castle gone, no one knew how the kingdoms would be passed down any-way. She insisted—which made logical sense—that Bethany would never be saved if Erec was trapped in a nightmare. She probably couldn't be saved by Erec at all. Queen Posey seemed to be the best person to rescue Bethany, and they would talk to her tomorrow.

Erec did not argue. He didn't want to raise his mother's suspicions that he might sneak away. Which, of course, was exactly what he was planning to do.

THE THREE FURIES

CHAPTER THIRTEEN

Love and Sand Crabs

FORGET TAKING DANNY and Sammy with him. Forget taking anyone else. This quest would be dangerous, and he would not put anyone else's life in jeopardy. The only person that he would let join him was the Hermit. Erec's tutor was a bit unusual, but he was wiser than anyone Erec had ever met. King Piter had assigned him to watch Erec when he did his quests. He always would show up then, out of the blue. Erec was doing a quest now, and he hoped the

Hermit would appear. He could use all the help he could get.

But maybe Jam was wrong. This still might all be a mistake. There was probably another King Augeas in Otherness somewhere who would be a good friend and happy to meet him. The first thing he would do when he got out of here would be to check the MagicNet and find out.

Once the clock struck two in the morning Erec put his shoes on and threw a few brownies into a bag for a snack later. A metal object was leaning against the Port-O-Door. Erec picked it up and saw that it was Jam's Serving Tray. He smiled. Jam knew him pretty well, he thought. He left it here just in case Erec did sneak off on his own.

Once back in his father's house, Erec turned on the MagicNet. A dark-skinned woman's face filled the screen. Her hair was mussed as if she'd just woken up. She yawned and looked slightly annoyed. "Can I help you?"

"Yes, I need to find out if there is more than one King Augeas. I don't want to buy anything, just get information."

The woman was trying to fix her hair, pushing it out of her face. "Is four on one okay?"

"Sure."

She nodded and the screen was replaced by four boxes, each with a person inside. In the upper right, a middle-aged man yawned and leaned over a podium with books stacked upon it. In the box to his left, a woman sat at a desk filled with papers, filing, jotting notes, and organizing them. A sign on her desk said ALECTICON MUSEUM OF ANCIENT CULTURES. In the box below her was a bed. A person in it snored, the covers over their head. In the final box a young man with very thick glasses was blowing his nose into a red handkerchief.

"Um, do any of you know about King Augeas?"

The three awake people on screen began to answer at once.

Then two of them turned politely to the man with the glasses.

His voice was nasal. "I've specialized in King Augeas studies throughout grad school. The myth came from ancient Greek culture from Upper Earth, before the formation of the Kingdoms of the Keepers. It's been changed over the years, and embellished, of course. But as far as I've guessed from my research, the story was a way for ancients to understand the significance of dreams and to explain why nightmares happened. King Augeas was probably made up based on the Greek god Apollo and King Nestor—"

"I beg to differ," the woman at the desk said. "Augeas was a very real ruler of old. He reigned in ancient Elis in the Peloponnese peninsula during the time of Hercules."

"Another myth!" the man in glasses shouted. "These fables have been disproven more than once. Augeas was constructed out of several stories that date back into the Archaic Period."

The man at the podium began to snore, his head bobbing.

"Excuse me," Erec said. "Assuming that he was alive, where would the nightmare realm that he was sent to rule be located?"

The man with the glasses laughed so loud he woke up the man at the podium. The figure in bed stirred and then was still.

The woman looked at Erec over her glasses. "I'm sorry. You must understand that even if King Augeas was a real person at some point, the story is still fictional. Nobody was made the King of Nightmares." Her mouth twisted, trying to suppress a laugh.

Erec tried another tack. "Were there other kings named Augeas? Are there any now somewhere?"

"No, I would think not," the woman answered. "Who would give a child such an infamous name? Especially one who was in line to become a king?"

The man with the glasses shook his head. "There's only one King Augeas I've ever heard of." He thought a moment. "I guess you could make sure by asking a listing specialist." He looked around at the neighboring boxes, then pointed at the screen where someone slept in a bed. "Isn't that one right there?"

Erec noticed a sign in the corner of the box with the bed that said LISTING. "What does that mean?"

"He's programmed with a listing of everyone living in the Kingdoms of the Keepers, Otherness, and Upper Earth."

"Like a living phone directory?" Erec looked at the bundle in the bed in awe. How could one person remember all that? Magic, he was sure, but still . . . "He's asleep, though."

"Wake him up. They're used to it. Throw pebbles at him, or rice, whatever you can find."

Erec looked around and found a drawer with some money in it. If he was going to wake the poor guy up, he might as well give him some change. He tossed a few bronze gands into the box. Several bounced off the figure until one finally hit him in the head. The man sat up groggily. "What? Huh?"

"Is there a King Augeas living today?"

Erec could almost see the listings run through the man's head. "No." He fell back onto his bed and threw the covers over himself.

Erec knew he had to set out before daylight, or his family would find him in King Piter's house and try to stop him from leaving. He filled a backpack with a few extra clothes, the Serving Platter, some money, the vial of dragon blood, and his MagicLight, a prize he had won that left light hanging in the air when it was dark.

He had no idea which direction to go, or where he would sleep on the way. His only hope was that the Hermit would show up soon and direct him.

Erec thought about using his dragon eyes to show him a bit of the future. Maybe that would give him a clue. But he realized that he couldn't do it. What if he found out that he wouldn't be able to save Bethany? He could not deal with that possibility. He had to believe this would work or everything would fall apart.

There was nobody standing outside the water wall around King Piter's house, but walking through his yard into town made no sense at all. He wasn't headed into Alypium, he knew that for certain. This land that bordered between reality and dreams would be far away, on the far reaches of Otherness maybe. He had to go another way.

He headed for the Port-O-Door and was almost surprised when the Hermit was there holding the door open for him.

Wiry, dark, and bald, wearing a long white toga-style outfit, the Hermit wasn't laughing and acting silly as he normally did. Even though his mood seemed fitting—as Erec was sure he was insanely walking straight to his death—the Hermit's silence managed to scare him more. The Hermit gazed at him with calm eyes that seemed to see right through him.

"You have a choice, Erec Rex. Do you pick the big box on the right, or do you prefer to go for what's behind the curtain?"

Erec looked at him blankly.

The Hermit waited, patient.

"I don't understand. What box?"

The Hermit pointed at the Port-O-Door screen, tapping the yellow box marked OTHERNESS.

"So, we can go to Otherness? What is the other choice? What curtain?"

The Hermit waved in the direction of one of King Piter's windows.

"You mean the curtains here?" Erec asked. "Alypium is behind those curtains.

The Hermit giggled. "Okay, then. You can choose to stay in Alypium or go to Otherness."

Erec was confused. What could be in Alypium that he would need now? "I don't know. Can you tell me why I should want to go to Otherness or Alypium?"

The Hermit put a hand against his own cheek and dropped his jaw in mock shock. "You mean you actually want to know why you are going somewhere before you rush off? You want to know where you're supposed to be going? To have a bit of knowledge about your situation? Not to just wander off aimlessly?" He shook his head. "This is revolutionary."

"Hey." Erec crossed his arms. "Don't make fun of me. I tried to find out where the Nightmare King lives, and nobody seems to know. Most people don't even think he's real."

A pleased smile stole over the Hermit's face. "You really tried to find out what you need to know?"

"I think so. I could look through King Piter's books, but that could take a long time. Jam didn't know any details, and nobody else does that I know."

"*No*body else? Think hard, Erec Rex. Think hard."

In a flash, Erec realized. "*You* know. You can tell me where to go."

"Tsk, tsk." The Hermit shook his head condescendingly. "How many times have I told you that the answers lie within yourself?"

"Um, none?"

"Never mind that. If the answers lie within, I shouldn't have to tell you."

"C'mon. Just tell me what I need to know."

"No, Erec. Only you can tell yourself what you need to know. When is the last time you visited the room in your head?"

Erec immediately thought of the dark room in his mind, using his dragon eyes to show the future. But that was the last thing he wanted to do now. "I can't do it."

"Scared of what the future brings, are you?"

Erec nodded. "I don't want to know. If something goes wrong and I can't get Bethany . . . I need to believe that the future will turn out right so I can try my best."

The Hermit pursed his lips. "So, this is a logical decision, then. You're not just afraid to see. You're only doing what is right for Bethany."

"Exactly." For some reason, Erec was not as sure of himself as he felt a minute ago.

"Isn't that funny? I had thought it was more logical to see what is coming so that you know how to face it. I thought you might want to do things differently and change the future if it did not work out the way you wanted." He scratched his chin. "I guess you can't trust yourself to show you what you need to see."

That all made perfect sense, and Erec groaned. His fear was stopping him. Everything he needed to know was at his fingertips. It was his own self, at some level, that decided what he should see when he used the dragon eyes. With more practice he could control it.

He had to face his fears and use his dragon eyes. The Hermit was right—if he saw something terrible happen, that didn't mean that it *had* to happen. He would just figure out a way to change things, that was all. Maybe he could try to see what he needed to do for this next quest.

"Okay," he said. "I'll do it. Should I look into the future now?"

The Hermit scratched his bald head. "Not yet. There is more you need to know. Let's go someplace quiet. If you're interested in learning what to do, then I'll bring you with me to a nice cave in Otherness. Do you have the Serving Tray with you?"

Erec nodded and pointed at his backpack. The Hermit touched the screen in the Port-O-Door a few times, and they walked out onto a warm beach. Ocean waves lapped the shore in the darkness, reminding Erec how tired he was. Balmy breezes tossed his hair. As he walked beside the Hermit, he had no idea where he was headed, but was sure it was the right way.

When the Hermit pointed out a hammock to Erec, he climbed in and was asleep before his shoes hit the ground.

He was searching for something. Searching. What did he need to find? He had a sneaking suspicion that it was his own self that was missing. What if he never found himself? Would he be lost forever?

Then something glistened in a pile of mud. It looked like a bubble, but he knew it was important.

It was a key. Of course! He felt so stupid. This key was all he ever needed. He used it to open a locked door and behind it was ...

Bethany. She had been sitting at a desk. They were in Baskania's complex, but Erec wasn't afraid of him. Bethany rose to her feet and gave him a hug, so happy to be saved. "You're my hero. Can I kiss my hero?"

His knees almost buckled from the kiss.

Her big eyes blinked up into his. "I love you, hero."

She loved him. His head spun.

He reached toward her, but for some reason she scratched him. Her claws were sharp. She turned into a tarantula, and scuttled across his face—

Erec awoke from something spiky moving on his face. A big bug? He brushed it away, sending a sand crab spinning to the cave floor.

The Hermit giggled. When Erec focused, he saw the Hermit was holding another crab in his hand. "Was that a nice addition to your dream, Erec Rex?"

Erec groaned and put an arm over his eyes. What a crazy, annoying thing for the Hermit to do—and so typical for him. Erec tried to remember what his dream had been about. Bethany was in it, he was pretty sure.

Well, that was better than his usual dream about his "father," who was not really his father at all. Erec had gotten a memory implant when he was three—and it had turned out to be Bethany's memory. In his dreams, he would relive a scene of Earl Evirly, abandoning him in the streets at night.

Erec had wanted to get rid of the annoying memory—but now he felt like keeping it. It was the only part of Bethany that he had now. Was she still alive? Why did this have to happen to her? She did nothing to deserve being captured. This was all the fault of that dumb prophecy: *The secret of the Final Magic is hidden in the mind of the smallest child of the greatest seer of the first king of Alypium.* The first king of Alypium was Piter—he was the only king of Alypium so far. And his greatest seer, everyone knew, was Ruth Cleary, Bethany's mother. Bethany's brother Pi was older than her, and bigger than her as well, so in both senses she was the "smallest child."

It wasn't fair that she had this happen to her. She was just an innocent kid. Bethany didn't ask to be born with amazing math skills. She could speak and understand math like it was her first language. For fun, in her spare time, she disproved theories that had taken math geniuses their whole lives to come up with. It didn't surprise Erec that she had it in her to solve Baskania's problem.

Part of him wanted her to tell Baskania anything he wanted, so he would let her go safely. But he also knew what that would mean to the rest of the world. Baskania wanted more power than even he could handle. King Piter had said that if Baskania mastered the Final Magic, he would end up destroying the world in a fit of madness.

The Hermit watched with amusement as Erec sat up and rubbed his eyes. The sun was bright outside the cave. Erec wondered how long he had slept. "Where is King Augeas's castle? Is it nearby?"

"Just steps away, yet further than you can imagine."

Erec shivered at the thought. Why was it close to a small deserted cave in a rocky bed near a peaceful beach? "Does this cave lead back into it?"

"No, silly prince. This cave is a dead end."

Prince? Erec was distracted for a moment, thinking of what the Hermit had just called him. His father *was* a king. He *was* destined to be king himself someday. Did that really make him a prince? He supposed it did, but it still sounded awfully strange. He was just a regular kid, and he always would be.

How would Danny and Sammy react when they learned that they were a prince and princess? Danny would love it, he supposed. He always liked lording over people in his own funny way. Sammy would get a kick out of it too, he thought.

A red blob appeared in the sand by his feet. It was a snail. Erec picked up the snail and took a letter out.

Dear Erec,

I was spying on Baskania, and all of a sudden an invisible force pulled me right in front of his huge desk in the Inner Sanctum. It was really creepy. He had about a million candles lit, and all the furniture was gold, so everything was sparkling. Baskania said I was doing great work—which really made me angry, since I was against him, not for him. He said it was time I had a promotion. So he offered me a real job, with money and a nice place to live in Alypium.

I guess he was reading my mind about all the things I really wanted the most, because in front of me was this table full of great food. I've been hungry a lot lately. It's not good, I know, but the only way I can eat is by using spells to steal food. I don't like to do it much, but I don't have any money. And it's not fun sleeping on benches all the time.

Baskania also said to keep your friends close and your enemies closer. I don't know if he was saying I was his enemy, or if he meant that I should keep Rosco close by. Maybe he meant both. But why he would want me to spy on Rosco is beyond me.

I was going to tell him no way, but then I realized that it might actually help me. Don't worry—I won't be swayed by him in any way. I'm just going to use him and his money—let them all start to trust me. When I can get back at Rosco for everything, then I'll strike.

I'm not sure what the job is yet that Baskania wants me to do. I know I'll be meeting with him and the Stain triplets, though. So that will give me an inside scoop for you.

Your friend,

Oscar

Baskania's job offer sounded like bad news, but Erec was afraid to write Oscar back. He wasn't near a Port-O-Door, and he didn't want anyone able to find where he was now.

The Hermit was watching him expectantly.

"I guess I'll look into the future now." A wave of fear washed over him. What if he were to see something terrible happen to Bethany?

But if it was going to happen, the least he could do was try to prevent it. "Then we can go."

Erec made himself comfortable on the hammock, crossing his legs.

"Remember," the Hermit said, "you watch what your eyes show you. But somewhere inside you, you know what part of the future you need to see. The more you use your dragon eyes, the better you will get at it."

The Hermit was good at saying things that made sense but were confusing at the same time. Erec closed his eyes and relaxed. It was time to face what was coming head-on.

He imagined himself entering a small, dark room in his mind. It was a place of peace. Everything seemed right. Another door inside led into a smaller room within the first room. If possible, this room was darker, cozier. He could sense two big windows in the front of the room, and he knew that they would look out through his dragon eyes into his future.

A warm box sat upon a table beside him. It did not exactly glow, but the energy radiating from it filled the room. It was a great feeling, being so close to so much knowledge. His fears seemed to drain away, leaving only excitement. Yes, what he saw might be horrible, but he could face it.

Erec rested a hand on the box and felt it pulsing with life. Everything he didn't know that he knew was locked inside there.

He was ready. A warm cord dangled between the windows, and Erec grabbed it and pulled. The window shades flew open.

A wall of water raced toward him, towering over him like a tsunami. In a second he was immersed, whipped around in gusts and torrents until he didn't know which way was up.

THE THREE FURIES

It was impossible to tell which way the surface of the water was, but it was so far away he might never reach it before he ran out of breath. He shot forward like a bullet along with the rushing waves.

Amazingly, even though he was sore, frightened, and aching for breath, he was happy. No, that wasn't a strong enough word. Gleeful. Ecstatic. This was the best thing ever.

The vision started to fade. Erec pulled the shades and left the room. That was not at all what he had expected to see. Where was Bethany? What about his quest? King Augeas? Nothing about this vision told him what would happen.

Then another thought came to him. Did this mean that Bethany would die? Maybe he was trying to drown himself. Why else would he be so happy to be wiped out by a tidal wave? The only reason he could think of was that he had failed and decided to end it all, glad to see the world go away.

He pushed that thought out of his head. Whatever the vision foretold, it didn't matter. He would try to do his best anyway.

It was time to meet King Augeas.

CHAPTER FOURTEEN

Finger Magic

"**O**KAY. LET'S GO." Erec did not want to waste another minute.

The Hermit raised an eyebrow. "You're ready?"

"Yes." He gulped deeply.

"Ah, impetuous youth. Always ready to rush in unprepared, make a complete mess of things. Strike fast and straight into the jaws of death, right? No looking ahead, coming prepared?"

"What do you mean?" Erec was exasperated. "I just saw into my future, and I got drowned by huge waves of water."

The Hermit giggled. "Brilliant. You have a very creative mind."

Erec wasn't so amused. "Creative? I didn't make this up. It's just what happens to me."

"Very creative," the Hermit repeated. "So, do you choose to go now, or would you like me to prepare you for your voyage?"

"Prepare me. But we better hurry. I don't know how long Bethany has."

"Make a cup of tea for me with the Serving Tray. Not too hot."

Slightly annoyed, Erec pulled the silver Serving Tray out of his backpack and asked it for a warm cup of tea. It appeared in an instant, and he handed it to the Hermit. Didn't he know they had to hurry?

The Hermit smelled the tea and smiled. Then he turned the cup and tossed the tea straight into Erec's face.

"Wha—" Erec wiped off his wet face. "What was that for?"

The Hermit laughed. "Nothing. I saw a movie where a Zen guru taught the most important lesson to his student by tossing a cup of tea into his face. This was not exactly a lesson, but I thought it looked like fun."

"Fun?" A spark of anger kicked Erec in the stomach. "Do you think Bethany is having fun right now?"

The Hermit smiled mysteriously. "I hope so."

"You hope so? How can she have fun chained to a desk, about to die?"

"That could be fun." The Hermit frowned, in thought. "If it were viewed in the right way."

"Viewed in the right way?"

"That's all there is to life, you know. Fun things. We just need to remember to enjoy them or we waste it all."

Erec calmed down. It wasn't worth getting upset at the

Hermit. He had a screw loose. "Okay, then. How can I get ready?"

"You must learn to control your dreams. It is the only way you will return from the Nightmare King's realm. He is not used to people being ready for him. So he won't expect you to find a way out. But you can. That is your quest, of course."

Erec sat straighter. So, he could meet the Nightmare King and return again? Now that he understood his quest, a wave of hope rushed over him. If there was a way out, he would find it. "And his realm is right here, near this cave?"

"It is the cave."

Erec looked around. "But I thought you said this cave was a dead end."

"It is. Look out onto the beach. His realm is there. And in your father's house, it is there, too. The Nightmare King rules everywhere. All over the world people fall asleep."

"I don't get it. If I'm in his realm when I sleep, then why haven't I met him already?"

The Hermit shook his head. "That is not where you can meet him. When you sleep, you may sometimes meet his restless-thought monsters and dark-vision hounds. Most nights we resist following them, but when they catch us off guard we can find ourselves peeking into the Nightmare Realm."

"I must be off guard every night, then." Erec thought about his recurrent nightmare of Bethany's father.

"Yes, having a memory chip insert can throw you off. But that also can work to our advantage now, help us practice." He smiled. "You must fall asleep and practice controlling your dreams. Because when you are a slave of the Nightmare King's dominion, you will be completely helpless otherwise. It can be done, but it is not easy. It takes strength and determination. If you are not ready, your life will be over."

"Do I have to wait until night to practice? I'm not sure I can go back to sleep now."

"No. Ask the Serving Tray for a sleeping potion, one that will let you dream."

Erec asked, and a glass of steaming red liquid appeared on the tray.

The Hermit produced a sand dollar, a starfish, and a smooth stone. "Feel these. Remember that they are near you. When you sleep, you will have each of these objects at your command. Use them." He took the glass off the tray, handed it to Erec, and put the tray alongside the odd assortment of items. "Think of these before and during your sleep. Keep your hand near them.

"Before you drink, remember when you once were near the Awen of Knowledge. It made you forget everything you ever knew. You had to repeat to yourself again and again what you had to do, or you would have been lost."

Erec's hand touched the empty vial, shaped like a small boar, that still hung around his neck. It was a souvenir from his experience with the five Awen. Five tiny colored balls had been attached to it—four were now left. He had used one of them to save Bethany and Pi from Baskania. When he had used that little ball that was from the Awen of Sight, everyone around him was blinded while he could see better than normal. He wondered if the other balls from the Awen of Knowledge, Beauty, Creation, and Harmony would have the same effect.

"This will feel the same, at first, as when you were near the Awen of Knowledge. You must say to yourself, again and again as you fall asleep, that you will change your dreams. Think about your usual nightmare. How would you end it differently?"

The red liquid burned his throat when he drank it. How would he change his usual nightmare? With the objects the Hermit put down next to him, somehow? He laid his head on a pile of sand and picked up the starfish. What could a starfish do? Maybe it could be a weapon, a throwing star. Maybe a star in the sky. Maybe the sand dollar could be a silver dollar, or a plate. . . .

The room became hazy. He felt sleep pulling him in. *Change your dreams. Change your dreams.* He kept the chant going in his head as he went under.

The Hermit laughed and laughed. Erec wondered why, then saw that he was sinking in quicksand. . . .

He was flying. He was a dragon, flying with Little Erec. They soared above the mountains of Otherness, over the great dragon reserves of Nemea. Clouds whizzed past his face as he spiraled toward the sun. . . .

Change your dreams . . . change your dreams . . .

Everything was dark. He was alone, cold, and very small. It was night and Erec did not know where he was. A big leafy bush looked like a good hiding place. There might be big dogs around, or scary monsters. He better hide there.

The world seemed huge, and he felt as tiny as one of the leaves on the bush. Nobody wanted him. His father had ditched him on the streets.

After he was hidden, huddled into a ball, he heard a deep voice cut through the blackness. "There's the child, you moron." His bitter voice sounded familiar. It was his father's boss—Baskania, looming tall over him in his dark cape. He had found Erec under the bush. Baskania grabbed his father by the collar. "You're a useless idiot. The one thing I asked you to do, you botched. Can't you even babysit a child?"

His father stammered, "Sorry. I—I didn't think it was important. This kid's useless. Believe me."

Baskania slowly lowered his open palm toward the ground. As he did, Erec's father fell to his knees, crumpled in the dirt. "I'll determine what's useless and what's not. This child very well might serve me in some way. Think who the mother was—only the best of King Piter's AdviSeers."

A voice was echoing in the distance. "Change your dreams. Change your dreams."

Something rough was in his hand. He looked down. One of the branches of the bush had broken off. Spokes radiated from it like a star. Erec pictured it changing, and it became metal. It was a studded silver throwing star.

He eyed Baskania. This man was his enemy. He was insulting his father. Erec's hand was small, but he made it grow enough to hold the weapon firmly. Not sure how to use it, Erec held a blade between his finger and thumb, then threw it level like a Frisbee. It sailed through the air toward Baskania. When the metal hit him, Baskania exploded in a burst of white smoke.

Erec looked at his own hands, elated. They were growing, aging. Soon they looked like his own almost-fourteen-year-old hands. He had done it. Something was different now. Good. He had conquered a bad thing, put himself in control of it.

A realization hit him. This wasn't real. It was a dream.

Or was it? He was a dragon again, soaring away. Someone was shooting at him from Alypium, below. He dodged the bullets. "Change your dream" chimed in the distance. He had things to protect himself. He could use them. What did he have? A star. A circle. The circle was a shield. He wore it over his chest, deflecting all of the bullets.

Erec was unstoppable. Nothing could touch him now. He was more alive than ever. What else did he have? A shiny metal tray. It was his flying carpet. He rested on it, sailing through the breeze. . . .

A splash on his face jolted him and he opened his eyes. How long had he been asleep? The sun was setting outside the cave. Ugh. He had wasted an entire day.

He wiped off his face and saw the Hermit holding an empty teacup. "I see the caffeine has woken you up."

Erec sat up groggily. "I don't think that's how caffeine works."

"If you say so." The Hermit studied his cup, frowning. "Looks like it worked to me."

"I did it," Erec announced happily. "I changed my dreams like you said." It felt great to have controlled what happened in his sleep. He remembered exploding Baskania with a throwing star and flying on a shining tray. No longer would he have to live with that awful nightmare. From now on he would change it every time. "Is that all I'll have to do when I'm stuck in the Nightmare Realm? Just change my dream and leave?"

"Not so simple. You will have to practice controlling your dreams here, so when you go there, you'll have a fighting chance. Here it's just a dream. There you'll be living it. Very different."

Erec yawned. "I just don't want to waste all this time sleeping. I have things to do."

"You'll have to get used to it. You'll be asleep the whole time you're with the Nightmare King."

It was hard to imagine what the Hermit was describing. He would be asleep, yet living in his dreams in reality? He was tired now, and even though he had slept all day he found his eyes closing. It must have been a strong sleeping potion.

"Find a few things to put in your hammock next to you before you sleep. You should practice changing your dreams more."

Erec put his MagicLight next to him, along with a cookie in a napkin that he produced from his Serving Tray, and a few silver coins. He touched them all as he fell asleep, thinking all the while: *Change your dreams. Change your dreams.*

The morning sun's rays stretched into the small cave, waking Erec. He remembered his dreams much better than usual, because he had been somewhat awake during them. He had used the money that he had put next to him to pay for Bethany's return home. He had eaten the cookie, and it had made him invincible. The napkin was a paper map that showed him the way to King Augeas. And he had used the MagicLight to shine his way through dark tunnels and find his way home.

His usual nightmare had returned as well. But this time Erec had turned into a dragon and breathed fire on Baskania, turning him into a starfish.

The Hermit was meditating in a lotus position on the floor. He opened one eye at Erec, then closed it again. "All right. Time to get ready, then." The Hermit rose on one foot, the other still crossed in the air. One of his eyes stayed closed.

"Are we going to meet King Augeas?"

"I think you are forgetting something." The Hermit was talking out of only one side of his mouth, as if the entire other half of his body was still meditating.

"What?"

"Your father asked me to be your magic tutor as well as watch over you during your quests. Remember that?"

"Yes," Erec said, perking up. He had hoped that he might finally learn some magic from the Hermit at some point.

"Well, it's time for a lesson."

"Now?"

"'No time better than the present,' I always say. Or was that, 'Nothing is better than a present'? I forget." The Hermit slapped the side of his face with the closed eye. It opened and he set that foot down.

"Can this wait until I get back?"

"Not if you want to come back."

"But I don't even have my remote control."

The Hermit tossed something into the air, and Erec caught a

remote control. "Thanks." It was the one that Rosco Kroc had given him a long time ago. "How did you get this?"

"I found it for you. What can you do with it?"

"Barely anything," Erec admitted. "If I put it on level one and really concentrate, I can move small objects. If I say the word . . . what was it . . . ?"

"Phero?" The Hermit chuckled. "Lame crutches, these words. Just as this remote is. Your friend Oscar can do magic without words or remote controls." The Hermit tapped the remote control lightly. "First I'll teach you the secret of using the remote, what the words do. Then we'll forget all about them and concentrate on the magic inside you."

"Will this help me save Bethany?" Erec asked, impatient.

"It may . . . or it may not. But I am your tutor now. So let me tute you. You'll never know when you'll be glad you were tuted." He pretended to play a trumpet for a moment, then burst out laughing. "Toot, toot."

"Ooh-kay . . ." Erec grinned despite himself. He had been dying to learn magic, and had no luck with his old tutor, Pimster Peebles. Maybe now he'd actually learn something. Magic tricks could only help him with whatever obstacles lay ahead.

"First, learn a word or two. *Phero* means to move something. Make it more specific. Aeiro levitates, lifts things upward. Anastrepho turns them upside down. Simple. You set your remote on level one. That's the easiest level. See what you can do."

Erec pressed the button in the lower right corner of his remote control until it read 1. He pointed it at the starfish lying on the sand and pushed the glowing green button on the device. "Phero." The starfish budged a little as if a wind had blown it. Erec was disappointed that it had not moved more.

"Now, picture where you want it to go, and try it again."

Erec imagined the starfish sailing into his lap and pressed again. "Phero." The creature whizzed through the air and dropped straight onto his legs as if the Hermit had tossed it. "Wow. That was easy."

"Very easy for you. Not always for others. You're very absorbent, like a good paper towel." The Hermit giggled. "That means the Substance fills you up easily. Lets you use it. That is why you can do magic and others cannot. The more absorbent you are, the easier it is for you to do.

"You have seen the Substance with your dragon eyes. You know how beautiful it is. The reason it is so perfect, so glorious, is the magic that runs through it. Think back to when you looked at it closely, so close that you cut a hole in it with your own eyes. It was molecules, atoms, neutrinos. It was stars, galaxies, universes. The same Substance that fills you up fills all of these things. Every molecule is a universe to its particles. Every person is a star, pulling people in with their gravity. You can feel that more than most, because you are open to it.

"A remote control takes any magic that people have inside and concentrates it so that even the weakest can use the Substance. It takes no thought, no effort. You don't need it. Use it just for a tool, so it can teach you how to do magic without it. Turn it up to level two and try moving the starfish again."

Erec pushed the button to read 2. This time when he said "Phero" and pressed the green button, the starfish shot into his stomach so hard it hurt.

"Now try to make it happen slower. Same thing."

"Phero." The starfish moved just as fast onto his legs. "Ow."

"Concentrate. Slow."

Erec pictured the starfish moving in slow motion. He focused on the thought as he pushed the button and said, "Phero." This time it lifted into the air and gradually spun toward him, dropping onto his lap. "It worked!"

"You can do more things when you turn it up to level three. That is the level that can teach you how to move on. That is where you will start to feel it."

Erec pushed the small button to read 3, then tapped the large glowing green one. "Phero." He willed the starfish to spin slowly up toward the roof of the cave, make a figure eight, then drift back down to the floor. Doing it was as easy as wanting it to happen. All it took was a little imagination.

"Did you feel it? Feel where the power is coming from inside you when you do it? Think this time."

Erec tried another command. "Anastrepho." He pushed the green button and the starfish plopped hard onto its back.

"That was a weak command. Be specific. Use your mind's eye."

"Anastrepho." Erec concentrated and this time the starfish floated up gracefully and turned in the air, just as Erec wanted it to. He could tell that the remote was pulling his power from deep within him. It felt like its source came up through his heart into his head—like it was his very will itself, running through a spot deep inside his mind where his ideas came from.

"Can you feel it? Pay attention."

Erec had felt it. But the magic was not what he had imagined it would be like. It was more a part of his imagination than a command. He had to try it again.

He pushed the green button. "Phero." The starfish lifted into the air, first one side rising higher and then the other, until it settled delicately upon the Hermit's bald head. Interesting. Erec felt a definite pull when he was doing it. A concentration of his energies. The remote control brought the power out of him easily, but he could tell that the feeling was what he must imitate in order to do magic on his own.

"Bravo!" The Hermit clapped his hands. "You can do the simple things that any little baby can do. Very good!"

That seemed like a backhanded compliment. Erec pointed the remote control at the Hermit's head and pushed the button. "Phero." The starfish spun atop his bald pate. The Hermit looked like he was wearing a propeller beanie hat. Erec laughed.

"Now you've got it."

The more he played with the remote control, the better he could identify the feeling of where the magic was coming from. Now he understood how others could reproduce this same feeling and do magic without one.

"Try it." As if the Hermit had read his mind, he grabbed Erec's remote away from him and crossed his arms.

Erec stared hard at the starfish and tried to make it spin up into the air. He could imagine the feeling he needed to pull out to make it work, but for some reason it would not budge.

"You need to use a motion. That will act as a gateway for your power."

Erec focused again, imagining the starfish rising, spinning. He pointed at it, tapping his finger in the air. The movement triggered a response deep inside him. A rush of power blasted through him along the same channel where the remote had pulled his magic from. He could feel it racing inside his body and leaving through his finger. The starfish shot into the air so fast that it hit the roof of the cave.

"Control now. Control. Finger magic takes practice."

Erec almost didn't hear what the Hermit said. He was so happy that he had created magic on his own, without a remote. It never seemed possible, but it had been so easy!

He pointed down at the sand and crooked a finger at it. A column whirled into the air like a mini sandstorm. *Control,* he told himself. He made the particles spin slower and then faster. The more he did it, the more natural it felt. "What else can I do? This is level-one magic, right?"

The Hermit seemed bored. "Some people describe magic as being in levels. 'Level one is manipulating objects, level two is causing sensations, level three is flying, changing chemistry.' Putting magic into levels is a way to rate people, put them down when they can't do as much as someone else: 'You're a level one. You're a level three.'

"Magic should not be competitive. You will learn more going by feel, trying out new techniques as they hit you. Practice is your friend. Don't worry about levels."

Erec nodded, but the levels still sounded interesting. Could he start a fire? That was level-three magic, he was pretty sure. He concentrated and wiggled a finger. A flash of burning pain seared his finger, leaving a bright red mark on his skin. "Ow!" He blew on it and shook it in the air to cool it.

"That happens when you learn. It's okay." The Hermit touched Erec's finger and the pain disappeared.

"Thanks."

The Hermit tossed Erec's remote control back to him. "Spend the rest of the day practicing both with and without this to help you. You'll catch on fast. Tonight you can work on controlling your dreams again. Then tomorrow you will visit the Nightmare King."

CHAPTER FIFTEEN

A Final Birthday Party

ERECT SPENT THE day making sand crabs fly, sending stones crashing into each other, and levitating himself. He tried to make the Hermit feel like he was being tickled, but that didn't seem to work.

A thought occurred to him while he was practicing. Maybe now he had a better chance of rescuing Bethany. Learning magic had to have improved his chances. If he looked into his future now, through his dragon eyes, he might be able to see more. Maybe his vision wouldn't show him drowning in torrents of water. Instead he might see himself holding hands with Bethany somewhere safe, like his home in New Jersey.

Erec sat on the sand and let the waves wash over his bare feet. He closed his eyes. The sun shone warmly on his back. Confidence ran through him, and his spirits soared. He could do anything now.

First he imagined going into the small dark room deep inside his mind. It was inviting and peaceful. He pushed open the other door and went into the darker room inside the first one.

The table still held the warm box thrumming on top of it.

He found the warm silky cord and pulled it, opening the windows, and looked through them.

A mountain crashed toward him, flecks flying as it sped closer. It moved so fast that it almost looked solid until it was close enough to see the frothing foam and rushing waves.

Water raced toward him, towering over him like a tsunami. In a second he was immersed, whipped around in gusts and torrents until he didn't know which way was up. It was impossible to tell which way the surface was, but it was so far away he might never reach it before he ran out of breath. He shot forward like a bullet along with the rushing waves.

Erec pulled the cord and shut the windows. This was not at all what he wanted to see. So this would be the end of him still? He would drown?

If that was the case, he would face that now. He pulled the cord again and watched what happened next.

THE THREE FURIES

He crashed into the dirt at the bottom of the flood, then bounced up again into the never-ending deluge. Big clumps of green and brown goo swirled around him, picked up by the rushing river. He could not hold his breath any longer. His head spun, and he choked.

He was so relieved, so excited. It didn't matter if he inhaled the water and all the disgusting things in it. He sputtered and coughed, limbs flailing wildly in an attempt to reach air.

Things were turning gray. He needed oxygen. Just as he was about to pass out, something hit him hard on the head. Did he crash into a wall? It looked like a door. He burst through an opening and was thrown to the side of the flood. Water sloshed around him, spreading out across the fields.

Right before everything turned black he gasped for air.

Erec closed the windows. Was that gasp really his own? He was pretty sure it was. He had felt himself take the breath. Would he survive, then?

He left the dark rooms in his mind and lay back onto the sand. Had he been *trying* to drown? He didn't think so. It wasn't like he jumped off a bridge into the middle of a lake. It seemed more like he was standing in the way of a tidal wave. But the tidal wave had been good, for some reason, even though it had knocked him out. So what was that supposed to mean?

This would be Erec's last chance to work on changing his dreams before meeting the Nightmare King. He hoped that he would learn enough to get him through whatever faced him there.

He put an odd assortment of items next to him on the hammock before he fell asleep.

Change your dreams. Change your dreams.

As his eyes drifted shut, he felt an awareness dawn within him. He would sleep, yet he would be watching.

Sand covered his toes, then rose to his knees. He was buried in quick-sand. Every move he made pulled him in deeper. Then enormous waves rushed over him, freeing him from the sand. He tumbled in the water, banging against walls, confused. . . . But then a surfboard appeared in his hand. He pulled it straight into his dream, conscious that he was still dreaming. Up and up, he became king of the waves, riding them on his board with ease.

Bethany and Erec were prisoners together. An executioner appeared, ready to take one of them to their death. The other could live another month. Erec stood to go first . . . but then his hand grabbed hold of something. It was a remote control. It remained in another world, but his hand could still reach it. He commanded it to come to him. He pointed it at the executioner and pressed a button, and the man vanished in an explosion of light. Erec and Bethany walked away, hand in hand.

In the morning Erec felt tired, like he had been awake all night. In a sense he had. "I still don't know what the Fates meant about getting *most* of my quest done before saving Bethany. If I'm stuck in a nightmare world forever, how will I get anything done at all?" He thought a moment. "Well, they said I'd understand later. We'll see about that."

"Do you know what today is?" The Hermit's eyes twinkled.

"Yup. The day I meet King Augeas." A cold wave of fear washed over him. This might be his last day on Earth as he knew it.

"You're right. But today is a big day for another reason."

Erec shrugged. Nothing else seemed important compared to what was coming. "I give up."

"It's your birthday. Happy birthday! Let's eat some cake before you go."

"My birthday?" For the first time in his life Erec had forgotten his own birthday. Celebrating it seemed like a luxury now, from another time. "It's April eighteenth already?"

"Yes, it is. Prince Erec is growing up." The Hermit spun the Serving Tray on a long finger until it sailed off and hit the cave wall. Chuckling, Erec asked the tray for a birthday cake, and one appeared complete with fourteen lit candles and HAPPY BIRTHDAY EREC beautifully inscribed in frosting.

The Hermit amused himself, singing a squeaky rendition: "Happy Birthday to you. You're smelling like poo. You think you're so big now, but you act like you're two."

"Ha, ha." Erec ate a huge slice of cake. It was light, with just the right amount of sweetness, tasting a bit like lemons and white chocolate. "I guess this is a good send-off."

"The best way to walk into a nightmare is with a smile." The Hermit stuffed nearly a whole slice of cake into his mouth at once.

A red dot in the sand grew until it became a swirl of color. "A snail!" Erec picked it up and pulled a letter out.

Dear Erec,

I had to tell you the news. Baskania is involved in something big. I mean huge.

He's been meeting with the Three Furies—Alecto, Tisiphone, and Megaera. They're the sisters of the Three Fates, and they're locked away in this place called Tartarus. I guess they're really powerful and dangerous. The only way that they can escape their prison is by capturing a thousand humans each and stealing their souls. But they can't get out to find any humans. And they're connected together, so they can escape only when there are enough souls for all three of them.

Baskania is working out a deal with them. He's bringing human captives to them in trade for their powers. They want the best and brightest. The more important the people that Baskania brings to them, the bigger his rewards. So he's already taken some government leaders from Upper Earth, and some sorcerers who've opposed him. He's given them the ex-president of the United Nations.

But the biggest news of all is that Baskania has captured the Clown Fairy. She is ancient and powerful, so it's really hard to hold her captive. I haven't heard where he's keeping her, but no normal jail could hold her. He's going to give her to the Furies in return for some big prize. The clowns in Otherness are in total chaos now. Their king and queen are dead—Baskania's assistants got rid of them ten years ago when they killed half the people in the Castle Alypium and put a spell on King Piter. But at least the clowns could function without their king and queen because the Clown Fairy was around. Now they're totally out of control and will probably all die. Baskania doesn't like them, so he doesn't even care.

I have to give Baskania credit. He has this whole thing planned out to a tee. He's going to give the Furies 2,999

people, just one away from letting them all escape. Then
he'll strike some bargain with them. He'll give them the last
person only if the Furies agree to be his slaves when they
get out.

The guy thinks big. I don't think he's that bright, though.
The job he gave me is to advise him! Can you believe that?
So he lets me in on all of his meetings—when he's here,
which isn't all that often anymore. I hear everything. Like
he doesn't realize I'm just going to report it all straight to
you! And when he's gone I just have to hang around and tell
him what I see.

Well, at least I'm getting paid, and have a roof over my
head. And I stay far away from Rosco. My plans for him
are getting clearer now. He'll pay.

Your friend,

Oscar

Erec's mind reeled at the thought of Baskania releasing the
Furies on the world. And Rosco advising him—how strange was
that? Something was fishy, and Erec had a bad feeling about it.
He hoped Oscar kept his wits about him. But at least he would be
alive . . . which is more than Erec had to look forward to, given
where he was headed.

Erec trudged across the sand, feeling like a prisoner walking to his
execution. He was following the Hermit back to the Port-O-Door.

His backpack was heavy—the Hermit had insisted on throwing shells and the starfish inside, to remind him of the beach. Could he possibly be the only human ever to escape from the Nightmare King?

The Hermit tapped a finger on the map of the far reaches of Otherness where it joined with Upper Earth on tiny Henrietta Island in the East Siberian Sea. The door opened into a blast of freezing air. Erec shivered as he walked out into ice-covered rocks. Frigid winds whipped his arms and legs. If Jam was with them, they would have been cozily wrapped in down parkas, he thought.

He slipped, cutting his hand on a patch of jagged ice, but he picked himself up and followed the Hermit through mounds of snow. A flock of tiny black-and-white penguinlike birds rushed away as they came near. His legs were getting stiff and numb. He forced them to keep moving even though he could barely feel them anymore.

Soon he felt like he couldn't possibly go much farther. Erec hunched over and hugged his legs, trying to rub some feeling back into them. The Hermit turned and waved him forward. Erec could not see his face anymore, only the pale sheet of cloth he wore. It looked like the cloth was moving on its own, with nobody inside it.

That was crazy, though. Was he hallucinating from the cold? If he didn't get indoors soon, he would certainly die out here. The Port-O-Door was well behind them now, or he would have staggered back to it.

The white sheet that seemed to be the Hermit waved for him to follow down a slope. He put one foot in front of the other, stumbling into a tunnel that led under a steep, snowy cliff. It looked like the tunnel ahead was filled with ice-covered water. He would freeze in an instant there. Where was the Hermit? Who was that white sheet ahead?

He pushed onward, afraid that the next time he stopped moving would be his last. He would surely die out here. The sheet was clearly empty now, the Hermit long gone. It waved like a flag, pointing toward the water-filled tunnel.

He didn't have any choice. Erec would never make it back to the Port-O-Door. This was the end of him. He fell forward, stiff, sliding down the slope and straight into the icy tunnel.

His consciousness flickered as he felt his body rushing through waves. The cold no longer bothered him—probably because he was about to die. Was he dead already? It seemed likely. How could he have survived the icy water?

Yet he was still having thoughts. What did that mean?

It was hard to get a sense of what was around him. Everything was white. Not cold, not snowy. Just . . . white. Empty. Vacant like a piece of paper before you decide what to draw or write on it.

Laughter echoed through the tall white chambers. Two huge thrones made of ice stood against the wall, one twice the size of the other. Sitting in the large one was a man with dark hair and a beard, dressed in black. He was doubled over in hysterics. His skin glistened, sparkling like the icicle-coated stalactites that hung around him like crystal chandeliers.

The man pointed at Erec. "You came to visit me. Isn't this rich?" He cackled with glee. "Another king-to-be, eh? It's like a party here. You're not planning to take over my spot, I hope? I'd like to see you try." He wiped tears of mirth from his eyes. "I'm sorry. May I introduce myself? My name is King Augeas. Although you probably know that if you've come this far to find me." He pointed at the smaller throne next to his. "If you thought you'd sit at my side, it's too late for that, too. I have another king-to-be keeping me company for a while. Only he has a special guest pass. Which, unfortunately, you do not."

Erec's jaw dropped when he saw who was sitting next to King Augeas. Wrapped in red ermine and black mink, Balor Stain was shivering in his icy seat. He looked miserable. Balor looked just as shocked to see Erec.

"So, you two know each other? How fun. It's not often I get visitors, you know. If I had any servants left, I'd have them bring out snacks." He tittered. "I personally have lost my taste for food. I'm beyond those crass mortal longings. More power to me, I say, if I'm not subject to the whims of hunger and sleep. Oh, yes. Especially *sleep*." He cackled, waggling his eyebrows with a knowing look.

Erec felt odd, but he couldn't put a finger on why. He wasn't dreaming. Of that he was fairly sure. Things here seemed much clearer than in a dream. Yet at the same time, they did not quite seem real, either. The icy chamber should have been freezing, but Erec felt no sensation of temperature at all. Even though he was standing, he almost felt like he was floating in nothingness. For a moment he wondered if he was dead. Maybe he had fallen into the icy water and didn't make it out again. Was this some kind of final hallucination?

In any case, his quest was to visit King Augeas and introduce himself. Erec bowed like Jam would. "Nice to meet you, King Augeas. My name is Erec Rex."

King Augeas howled with laughter. "Rich. So rich. Did you think I am so mortal that I don't know exactly who you are? I am the king over kings. My realm covers the known world, plus places only recognized in the souls of each person on Earth. The most powerful, the richest, the kings—they are all my subjects, trembling before me and my guards in fear when we approach."

Erec bowed again. He had done what the quest had sent him to do. Time to cut his losses and leave. The guy liked flattery, he thought. Maybe that would work. "Thank you for meeting me, King Augeas. It was an experience I'll never forget. I should go back now, but I'll tell everyone how great you are." He looked around to see which way he had come in. The room looked like a rounded bowl with no exits in sight.

The king laughed even harder. "We have a comedian with us today, Balor. He thinks he can waltz in here, meet me, and leave again. But those aren't the rules, are they?"

Balor sneered at Erec. At least that part about him hadn't changed.

"What are you doing here?" Erec asked Balor.

Balor blinked a few times as if he was trying to remember. "Keeping watch on . . ."

"It's a laugh, isn't it?" King Augeas said. "Like this human boy is going to be able to guard something here in my realm. He's lucky he's awake at all, but that was the deal I struck with his father, the Shadow Prince. The man's got some interesting deals up his sleeve. I get to keep the biggest prize of all here, because I'm the only one who is powerful enough to control her." He rubbed his hands together. "They'll want her back at some point, I assume." He giggled, then whispered to Erec with a hand cupped around his mouth, "It may be harder to get her back than they think, though."

The king pointed toward the small throne and a flash of white electricity shot from his finger. Balor's eyes bugged with fear and his mouth opened into a wide *O*. Then the king put his finger down and sighed. "And *this* is supposed to be guarding my prize from me. Keeping watch, are you?" Suddenly Balor gasped and felt around in the air in front of him as if it was pitch black, even though Erec could see perfectly. "Oh, fine. Have your sight back." The king snapped his fingers and Balor blinked with relief.

Erec felt awful for Balor. He wasn't a nice kid, but he was still a kid. It wasn't his fault he was cloned from Baskania. Not too long ago Balor had been doing the Tribaffleon contest with him. Erec remembered how they had to pull swords out of stone anvils. Balor made his remote control turn into something like a jackhammer, breaking the anvil so he could pull it out easily. Erec had been so angry that Balor had cheated. Now he wondered if he had been too hard on him. It wasn't like the poor guy had anyone teaching him right from wrong.

But then Erec remembered the Stain triplets gleefully killing baby dragons. No, those three definitely had something wrong upstairs. They were probably lost causes.

What kind of prize had Baskania given King Augeas that was so important Balor had to keep watch over it? Something only King Augeas was powerful enough to hold? What did that mean?

"I don't get guests often, but when I do, I have a little habit. I collect dreams. Nightmares, really. My collection is spectacular. I generally demand a donation when I come upon a live person." He smiled. "I'm not asking much, really. Most people are happy to be rid of them. They can't appreciate their beauty like I can." The king gestured toward Balor. "This young king-to-be offered me a nightmare, even though he didn't have to. Balor's not subject to my rules—that's part of our deal. But he kindly offered anyway." The king smiled. "Come close to me, boy. Let me take your best nightmare for my own."

Erec shuddered. What would taking a nightmare involve? He looked around the room again, trying to find a way out.

"That won't work, boy. The only way out is to do as I say." The king cackled.

Erec approached the king, trembling. If this was all he had to do he could handle it.

"Kneel at my feet."

Erec bent onto his knees. Up close, he could see that King Augeas's skin was hard, sparkling like diamonds. His black eyes, empty dead holes, bored down into him. They grew quickly, sucking Erec into the nothingness inside them.

Erec was transfixed. He could not move, could barely breathe. The king's pupils seemed to spin, making a vortex that pulled Erec's soul from his body. He could sense a mist lifting from himself. He was the mist. The body he left behind was cold and abandoned.

"There it is," the king said. "That's a juicy one. And well developed, I see. You use this one quite often. I like it."

Erec knew immediately what nightmare the king had seen. It was the one that stemmed from his memory implant when he was three—the one that had turned out to be Bethany's memory. Something strained and tugged inside of his very essence. It was tearing, pulling away from himself. He heard his own voice screaming . . . and then he fell back onto the floor, back into his own body.

Out of his chest, like a reflection in the mist, stepped a small child. It was nameless, faceless, but it was shivering and afraid. A bush rose from Erec, out of his right arm, and it rolled out onto the icy floor, taking root. The child looked around, shaking and crying, and then it hid underneath the bush.

Erec jumped in shock as a car's horn blasted. The car sailed out of his own body, creating a road under it as it drove near the bush. The child sniffed, clinging onto the small branches.

More cars drove by, some emerging from Erec's body with a gut-wrenching pull, and others weightlessly running him over. A man poked his head out of Erec's stomach and looked around. "There's the child." The man sneered, climbing out of Erec as if he was a manhole. His voice, and soon his face, were unmistakable. It was Thanatos Baskania.

Balor gasped. Erec heard him whisper, "Father . . ."

Earl Evirly climbed out of Erec's stomach after Baskania, hanging his head. "I'm sorry, boss. I didn't know it was that big of a deal."

"Didn't know?" Baskania's voice was controlled, but Erec could tell he was enraged. "There's the child, you moron." He grabbed

Earl's collar. "You're a useless idiot. The one thing I asked you to do, you botched. Can't you even babysit a child?"

"Sorry." Earl talked faster, as if trying to distract him. "I—I didn't think it was important. This kid's useless. Believe me."

Baskania slowly lowered his open palm toward the ground. As he did, Earl fell to his knees, crumpled in the dirt. "*I'll* determine what's useless and what's not," he spat. "This child very well might serve me in some way. Think who the mother was—only the best of King Piter's AdviSeers."

The child watched them, shaking. It looked just as frightened to be found as it was being abandoned.

"I'm sorry. So sorry, sire. Please forgive my stupidity." Earl spoke into the dirt covering his face.

"You'll take this thing." Baskania tapped his toe into the child's side. "And bring it straight to the Memory Mogul. Any memory of all of this"—he waved around—"should be removed. The child will forget you abandoned it, and you'll start fresh as its caretaker."

The figures became hazier as they spoke until they were hard to see. Then the child, the bush, and the two men shrank into tiny plastic statues and whirled through the air into a glass trophy case against a wall. Other small statues lined the shelves. Erec wondered which of them was Balor's nightmare. Suddenly he realized that he was exhausted. Even sitting up seemed to be too much of an effort.

"Care to sleep now?" The king laughed. "I'd advise that you get your instructions first. It would be a shame if you gave up the only chance you had of returning to your world."

"What?" The room was spinning, and Erec forced himself up onto an elbow. "Can't I go home now?"

"Go home? Absolutely not. Our fun is just beginning. You don't have a free pass out of here like this gentleman does." He waved a hand carelessly toward Balor. "You are my subject forever now. As soon as you fall asleep, I will add you to my little village. I so enjoy keeping people here. And I'll give you a job to do there too. Everyone gets a job." He grinned, tapping his chin. "Let's see. What will your job be? Something wonderful, I think! Everyone gets a wonderful job in my Nightmare Realm.

"I know. You'll be the stable boy. The stables are a bit of a mess, I'm afraid. But I'll offer you a deal. Once you finish your job you'll be free to leave. Fair is fair, right? You'll find everything that you need there in order to make them sparkle." A sickening smile spread over his face, but his eyes remained cold.

"Don't worry. You don't have to go quite yet. Not until you fall asleep, anyway. So stay awake and keep us company as long as you can. It looks like your birthday will be the last day you are ever awake. Sorry I couldn't make your final birthday party more . . . fun."

A wave of exhaustion hit Erec and his eyes drooped closed. He forced them open. Not yet. He didn't want it to be over yet. But it was impossible to stay awake.

The room grew black as a wicked cackle filled the air.

CHAPTER SIXTEEN
Wandabelle

EREC SPUN DOWN a huge dark tunnel that led straight into the earth. The walls of the tunnel narrowed, closing around him. As he dropped, little creatures with pincers reached for him from the walls. Red liquid oozed then gushed down the sides of the tunnel, covering the creatures. A few drops splashed onto his clothing, burning holes through his sleeve like a strong acid. He tumbled head over heels, waiting to crash.

Below him, fast approaching, was a bubbling pool of black lava, steam gushing up to meet him. He dropped into it head-on, and it turned into a murky ocean. Heavy weights were tied to his ankles, and he was sinking, fighting for breath. He kicked and struggled to get free. The surface was just feet above him, but he was being pulled farther away.

Laughing mermaids with long, sharp teeth pointed at him as he sank. He reached up in desperation . . . and then he was tied to a huge target. Circles were painted on his chest and on the round board he was stuck to. The water was gone, replaced by a huge man dressed like a pirate with a torn lacy shirt and vest, and billowing knee pants. He glared at Erec, sabers in both of his hands, then raised one high in the air and flung it toward Erec. The blade sank straight into his heart, pinning him to the board.

For some reason he wasn't dying. The man threw some more sabers at him, stabbing him in the stomach and legs. They didn't hurt, but they terrified him.

Why couldn't he feel them? Erec was confused. Was this a dream? He must have fallen asleep. But it didn't feel like a dream. He could remember what happened before he got here—that wasn't normal for a dream. He remembered eating birthday cake with the Hermit, then dropping through an arctic channel into King Augeas's chamber.

No, this wasn't a dream. But he also remembered falling asleep. What did that make this, then?

The Hermit had said that while he was here, he would be living a nightmare. Would it really go on forever, like King Augeas said? Would that be his fate?

Once he realized that the sabers did not hurt, the huge man lost interest in throwing them. "Eh, if only me sabers worked like they should here, I'd be doing ye a favor. Nobody in this place will die." Then he waved at others around, shouting, "Look what we have here, people! Another new peasant. Funny-looking clothing this one has too."

People poured out of buildings until a crowd formed around Erec. They seemed to be from another era. Some of the men were mud-covered, wearing ragged britches and cloaks made from animal skins. Others wore simple tunics, reminding Erec of ancient Greece. One man sported a short dress with shoulder epaulets and tight knee-length pants underneath. A few of the women, with tattered puffy-sleeved dresses and bonnets, looked like they had come out of a picture book of the Middle Ages.

But what struck Erec more than their odd clothing was the look of their faces. All of the villagers wore the same fierce, hateful expressions.

"Well, look what we've got 'ere." A woman walked around him, eyeing him up and down. "Is this some type of clown, I suppose, sent to amuse us? What's your job here, boy?" Erec stared, speechless, and she slapped him in the face. "Answer me, wretch. What job did the king give you?"

Erec tried to remember what the king had said. It seemed like that had been in another world. "I'm a stable boy."

The crowd laughed, jeering. A few people threw things at Erec.

"So, we've got ourselves a stable boy now," the woman said. "Well, don't think we'll let you hang around resting all day. It's work, work, work around here. We're all working our way out again, you know. As soon as I get my job done, I'll be free as a bird, back to me old life."

"What is your job?" Erec asked. He was starting to feel uncomfortable pinned onto the target board. If only he could reach the rope ties, maybe he could free his arms and pull the sabers out. . . .

The woman scowled. "I'm the cook here. I have to hunt the rats with my bare hands and turn them into stew. Eat them before they eat us, that's what I always say. I chop their tails off first while they're biting me. That way I can season it a bit with my own blood."

The image was so atrocious that Erec almost threw up. He would not be eating anything here, that was for sure. "But I thought you said you'll be free when your job is done. When will it be done?"

"As soon as I catch the last rat."

The big man with the sabers laughed. "They multiply by the hundreds each day. There's a million more rats here now than when you arrived."

The woman kicked the man in the shins, but he did not seem to mind. "That's better than what you have to do," she screeched. "At least I'm not a toilet scrubber."

Being a stable boy didn't sound half bad compared to what these people had to do. The crowd was getting restless. People were spitting, cursing. Someone threw a moldy tomato at Erec. Then everyone joined in, throwing things that smelled so awful they must have been rotting for months. He gagged, struggling against the ropes that held him.

A twinkle of light appeared in the corner of his eye. As it came closer, Erec saw a beautiful girl in a long sparkling dress walking toward him. Long, golden hair flowed around her face. Her eyes sparkled in a multitude of colors, like a small child had made them from glitter. The girl looked remarkably clean, even in the filth that seemed to hang in the air. The people throwing things at him cowered in her presence, throwing her disgusted looks. Then they started throwing fistfuls of mud at her white dress.

Erec felt a tug and then his hands were free. The girl had come close enough to untie him, but then the crowd grabbed her, shoving her back where she had come from.

Only a few people stayed around as Erec worked the sabers out of himself and finally stepped off of the target board. A gray-haired man in a tunic flexed his arms and walked closer. Erec cringed, wondering if the man was getting ready to punch him. The man's face changed into that of a horse, then a hideous creature with long, sharp teeth. He shoved Erec roughly down a narrow cobblestone path. "Get thee to the stables. They haven't been cleaned since we've been here, for about two thousand years now. You've got a lot of work to do."

Erec could not leave that creepy guy behind fast enough. Horrid screams filled the air as he walked. Crumbling buildings lined the road and rats raced through the dirt streets. Inside a few open windows Erec saw enormous spiders with webs filling entire rooms. This was a nightmare. It felt like one in every way. Only, he was awake. But then he remembered King Augeas saying that he would stay asleep forever. Which was he, then? Awake or asleep?

Walking seemed to steady him a little. He felt himself shaking from fear, so he tried to ignore the disturbing images, some of which winked in and out along the sides of the road.

A familiar voice called to him. "There you are, you pathetic scoundrel. I've been trying to get rid of you for a long time." Erec was shocked to see Balthazar Ugry pointing his walking stick at him. A blast of smoke sparked from its end—Erec barely jumped out of its way. The rocks behind him exploded.

Erec shrank back in terror. Then he remembered how powerful Ugry was. Maybe he would know a way for them to get home. "Balthazar!" Erec ran toward him. "How did you get here? Are you stuck here too?"

Balthazar Ugry sneered and faded into the air. He was just another of the false visions that haunted this wasteland. This realm was populated with nightmares, drawn from all of its residents. He doubted that anyone else but he knew Balthazar Ugry, so he must have been a new addition.

Out of nowhere, a hissing snake appeared at his feet, ready to strike. Erec dove away in the nick of time. Whose nightmare was the snake from?

And who was that girl who had untied him? She didn't fit into this horrible place at all.

The stable was located at the end of the road, although Erec could smell it long before he could see it. Animal dung, ranging in age from ancient to new, filled the entire huge stable. Only a few animals were inside, because they had barely any room. But masses of oxen, cattle, and goats roamed around the yards surrounding the stable.

A thought occurred to Erec. With so many cattle here, why was the cook making stew every day out of rats?

"Because." Raucous laughter filled the stable. King Augeas's face was projected onto the enormous dung heaps inside. "Those are the rules. And why would the cook waste her time preparing cow meat if her only ticket out of here is to kill all the rats for supper? Rules are rules. This is your stable to tend. You must clean it day and night until every last piece of filth is removed. Once you make room for more animals, you must bring them inside to stay, taking them out and bringing them back in every day."

Erec felt tiny among the mountains of mess surrounding him. "What shall I clean it out with? Where are the shovels?"

The king tittered. "Use what you brought with you, of course. Your hands. You'll find a river behind the stables. You can use it to wash up with. Dump this mess into the water so the grounds outside don't get dirty." King Augeas was loving this plan. "A perfect job for a prince—some good, hard labor will put you in touch with the earth. Once this place is sparkling clean, you'll be free to go." He vanished, leaving only echoing laughter hanging in the air.

Erec put his hands on his hips and looked around. The enormous stable was nearly filled with mud and slop. He tried not to be overwhelmed. If this is what he had to do, then he would do it. Disgusting as it was, there could only be so much filth in this stable. He would scoop every last bit of muck out and go save Bethany.

Holding his breath, Erec grabbed two handfuls off a towering pile. Then he looked around. This was ridiculous, he thought. He dropped the muck back onto the ground. He would take forever to clean this place out if he took such small bits at a time. No—he had to take larger loads somehow. Really blocking his nose, Erec leaned into a smelly stack of sludge, wrapped his arms around it, and pulled, grabbing an armful out. The stuff was mushier than he thought, though, slipping through his arms and down his stomach, leaving him grasping only a small wet mound against his chest. He picked up some of the more solid parts from another pile, loading up as much as he could carry.

With all the piles of manure in front of him, he couldn't see where he was going. After only a few steps he slid in some wet dirt. His feet shot out from under him, and he collapsed, face first, into the dung.

"Eeewww!" The mire was all over him. He tried to get up, but his feet gave way, slipping on more wet slime. In a minute he was covered, swimming in it. Every time he managed to stand and grab an armful of muck, he slipped right back into it.

Finally Erec gave up trying to take an armload and carried two large handfuls down to the river behind the stables. The mindless oxen and cattle nudged him as he wound his way through the hordes that filled the yards.

The river raced cold and clear behind the cattle yards. Erec dove in, letting the water wash the filth off him. After pulling himself out, he lay dripping on the bank and looked back at the enormous stable. Why had the Fates sent him here? At least his other quests did some good for someone. This task wasn't going to help anyone. It was just keeping him away from Bethany. He should never have listened to them. His mother had been right. Queen Posey had a better chance of getting Bethany out of Baskania's fortress than he did. What was he trying to prove, anyway, doing all this himself?

Erec closed his eyes. His mother. He had forgotten how this would affect her, too. She would never see him again. What had he done? This truly was a living nightmare.

Well, as long as he was stuck here, he would never stop trying to get out. He sloshed back into the stable, this time slipping even more since he was drenched from the river. He fit a little more into the crook of his arm this time before sliding back out and going down the hill to the river. Then back again to the stable.

After a few trips, he tried to take his shirt off and use it to carry piles of gunk. But it was stuck to him. His clothing seemed to be part of him now.

This was definitely not reality, he decided. Some weird, crazy version of it was running around inside his head.

At least he wasn't getting tired—probably because he was already asleep. Back and forth, back and forth, Erec trudged from stable to river, bringing small bits of slop out with him. How long had he been doing this? Days? Weeks? Months? Time seemed to blend together. Soon he had cleared out enough space to bring more animals inside. The only problem was that they made a huge mess as soon as they came in.

He needed to find help here. The thought occurred to him that if the entire village worked with him, he just might get the stable cleaned. He rinsed himself off in the river, then set out to see if anyone would lend him a hand.

A small bald man in a worn gray tunic was sweeping the rat-infested, filthy streets. Bugs raced through the dust behind him, and bats flying above left fresh droppings that he sailed into the air with his broom. Thinking he knew how to clean up, Erec approached him. "Excuse me. I was wondering if you could do me a favor. I have to clean out the stable in order to get out of here, and I have a friend who is in trouble, waiting for me. Could you please help me with the stable? If I find a few people to work together, I might be able to get out of here sooner."

The man scowled at him. "Listen, boy. I was one of the first people here. I was a villager in Elis, where Augeas used to be king. He brought me and some others with him two thousand years ago. If anyone should leave first, it's me." He leaned on his broom. "I'm tired, boy. Help me out sweeping, okay? I have only one broom, but if you use your hands, maybe it will help me get out of here. Ask around and find some people to help you. Then when I'm free, I'll work on that stable with you."

As much as he hated not helping the poor old man, Erec could not imagine spending even more time here than he had to already. The man's job seemed impossible. Then what would happen to Bethany? Erec shrugged and ran off.

Strange images popped up and vanished along the craggy roads as he walked. Bats and beasts, zombies lumbering out of haunted houses. Strolling through the Nightmare Realm was worse than digging through the stinking muck at the stable. A scream of frustration came from a decrepit shack by the road. Not sure if it was part of another nightmare segment, Erec peeked into the window.

A woman was pounding on the walls inside, tears running down her face.

His first impulse was to mind his own business. But the woman seemed so miserable, he thought he should see if she needed help. He knocked on her door.

When she opened it, Erec gasped. The woman looked like she was thousands of years old. She was bent and stooped, with huge puffy circles around her eyes. Every bone of her skeleton showed through her skin, which was so loose and translucent that her wrinkles had wrinkles. She sniffed and blotted her face. "What do you want?"

"I'd like some help, actually. I have to clean a stable. . . ." Erec realized how desperate he was, asking this ancient woman to do hard labor for him.

"Help? Did you say help? I'd love some help myself. I can't stand the idea of being here a single day longer. Please, come inside."

Erec lingered in the doorway, afraid that he might get trapped. A long table inside was filled with steaming vials of liquids, piles of powders, scales, burners, and a microscope. Mirrors lined the walls. "What are you doing?"

"I've been working so hard. My job is to find a cure for aging. I have so many tools at my disposal, almost any chemical you can imagine. I have to try all of my cures on myself. Most have backfired." She gestured to her face sheepishly. "It would be so nice to have somebody else to try my medicines. Maybe they would work better on you." She leaned near Erec, reaching bony fingers toward him.

Erec jumped back, hands up. "No, thanks. I have a lot to do at the stables. Good luck with your cure."

A crowd jeered in the distance. Erec wandered toward the noise. Maybe somebody there would help him.

The girl in the sparkling white dress sat on a small white chair on a plot of grass. Erec had almost forgotten about her. She looked just as clean and beautiful as before. It seemed like forever since he had arrived and she had untied him from the target board. A group of people stood around her, shouting.

"You lazy, good-for-nothing girl! Look at you, spending your whole day doing nothing at all."

"Pig! You're a selfish pig, you are. Wasting all your time away."

"She thinks she's too good for us. Doesn't have to work, not her. Just like a little princess."

The girl rested her chin on her hand and watched some buzzards flying through the gray sky, looking totally bored.

"Hey, listen everyone," Erec shouted. "I really need some help. I've got to get out of here. My best friend is in terrible danger. If I can just get the stable clean, I can go. Will all of you give me a hand, just for a few days? I'd really appreciate it."

Everybody stopped short. Then they burst out laughing, slapping their sides and pointing at Erec as if he were a comedian.

"You got someone on the outside that needs you? That's the oldest line in the book. Good luck with that one, kid."

"Listen to him. Help him clean the stables. Yeah, I'll help you—after you do my job and get me out of here first."

"I'll help you." The girl in the chair stood up. Her voice rang like bells. "Let's go."

The people who had been jeering at her looked as amazed as Erec was.

"Good," someone said. "Let her find out what it's like to work all day. Then she'll come help me pick up all the garbage."

"Then you'll help me sweep the sand off of the beach, won'cha, girlie?"

The girl did not answer them but stepped lightly through the crowd and took Erec's hand. "Who are you?" she asked as they walked.

"My name is Erec Rex. I'm—"

"You're Erec Rex? I know exactly who you are. How did *you* get stuck in here?" Her voice was sweet and sympathetic. Erec almost cried with relief to have found a friend.

"I had to come here." He struggled to remember the reasons why. It was hard to think clearly in this place. "I have a friend who's in danger. I have to do my quest first, and then I can help her."

"I'm sorry. I don't understand. Who is in danger?" The girl's voice rang like bells.

"My best friend, Bethany. She's been captured by Baskania. I have to do twelve quests before I can become the king of Alypium. The Fates said I had to do my next quest before I can help Bethany escape."

"How awful. You must have taken a wrong turn and ended up here by accident, then. What was your quest supposed to be?"

"No, I didn't take a wrong turn. My quest was to meet King Augeas."

The girl stopped in her tracks, yanking Erec to a halt. A python slithered by, stopping in front of him. It waved its head back and forth as he slowly backed away. When Erec turned his attention to the girl, he was surprised to see tears filling her eyes. "*This* is what the Fates sent you to do?" She threw her arms around him and kissed his cheek.

His skin tingled where her lips were. He rubbed his face. "Why did you do that?"

"You've come to help me. I just know you have." She grinned at Erec.

"It looks more like you're the one helping me. I'll try my best to do what I can for you, but don't get your hopes up." He laughed. "I mean, look at me. I can't even clean a stable by myself." Erec looked over his shoulder and saw that the crowd had broken up. "Don't feel bad that they were picking on you. I think it's a compliment that you don't fit in to this place. Why is everyone so nasty here?"

"Most of them have been here a long time. It's not a nice place to live, even for a day, let alone thousands of years. I guess I'd be grumpy too. I think that they're mostly good people underneath, though."

Erec thought about the desperation of the old woman who was searching for a cure for aging, and the man who wanted the girl to help him sweep all the sand off the beach. "These jobs that the

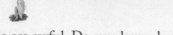

Nightmare King gave to people are awful. Do you know how many have made it out of here?"

She raised her eyebrows. "Do you actually think anyone can finish the jobs that they were given? I think that's part of his fun, seeing everyone slave away at ridiculous tasks with no chance of escaping." She shook her head.

"What was your job, then? Is that why you aren't bothering with it?" Erec was embarrassed and upset that he had spent so much time cleaning the disgusting stable if it really was impossible to do.

"I didn't get a job. That's why they're all so mean to me here. They're jealous." She shrugged her shoulders and her blond curls bounced up into the breeze. "Any of them could give up their jobs if they wanted to, but they're all afraid to stop trying. I think a part of them knows that what they're doing is futile, and it makes them angry to see me not wasting my time like they are."

"But why didn't King Augeas give you a job?"

"I think he was being extra safe, to make sure that I don't get out by some trick." She smiled. "I should introduce myself. My name is Wandabelle. I'm the Clown Fairy." She spun in a circle, and Erec saw golden gossamer wings waving on her back.

His eyes widened. "*You're* the Clown Fairy?" He considered that for a moment. "You must be the 'prize' that King Augeas was talking about." So that's why Balor was here, so that Baskania could make sure the Clown Fairy stayed prisoner. "How did you end up here? Did Baskania bring you?"

She nodded sadly. "He captured me by surprise—that's the only way I can be caught. I'm very fast, so if I know someone is coming I can always escape. Over the years people have caught me—it's good luck—but no one can keep me. I always find a way to escape." She sighed. "Looks like I'm finally trapped, though. I don't know why anyone would do this to me."

Erec remembered what Oscar had said in his letter. Baskania was going to give her to the Furies, and they would give him some big gift in return. She was just another soul for them to steal. A deluxe model to suit their vanity. Baskania could care less that she was the only thing holding the clown population together since their king and queen had died.

"We need to get you out of here. The clowns in Otherness need you."

Wandabelle hung her head. "I know. I'm afraid that I'm stuck, though." Another idea occurred to her, and she perked up. "Then again, with you here, anything can happen! You saved all the baby dragons when they were missing in Otherness."

"Well, yeah. But I had some help then—"

"And you rescued King Piter when he was hypnotized."

Erec grinned. "That was a while ago. I got lucky—"

"And you freed the bee hind that was messing up all of the Substance!"

"Whoa!" He smiled. "That was . . . well, that *was* pretty tough. You're right. I guess I am amazing." He laughed, which felt good, like his whole body was relaxing. "But the problem is, you're more amazing than I am. You're the only one who was keeping all of the clowns in the world alive. And you can escape from anywhere. So if you can't do anything to get out of here, I probably can't either."

"I don't believe that for a second. You specialize in fixing things. This is your area." She delicately waved an arm toward the crumbling buildings and filthy streets.

"Gee, thanks." He looked at the mess around him and chuckled. His situation didn't seem quite as bad when he had a smile on his face . . .

. . . which reminded him of something that someone once said to him. What was it? *The best way to walk into a nightmare is with a smile.* It really rang true. Someone wise had said it, he was sure. And he had a vague memory of eating cake.

The Hermit! Erec had forgotten all about him. Maybe the strange atmosphere here—or maybe it was the fact that he was asleep (Erec had to keep reminding himself that he was asleep) made it hard to think straight. The Hermit had taught Erec how to do finger magic, as he called it. And he had showed him something else. Something important that Erec needed to know.

If only he could remember what it was. He had the feeling that it was really the key. If only he could think straight . . .

Wandabelle surveyed the stable with a tight smile. "You'll never get this clean. You do know that, don't you?"

Erec looked at the piled mounds of stinking grunge and the slime oozing out of it and all over the floor. "It's doable. At least it's a finite mess, right? It will eventually come clean. Not like sweeping the sand off the beach, or something like that."

"I don't think so." Wandabelle pointed at the animals outside. "You know what's going to happen once you clear out enough room to bring them all in here, don't you? They'll make more of a mess faster than you can clean it up. He wouldn't have given you the job if you really could escape."

Erec began to feel desperate. "Maybe with help, then? I really have to get out of here fast."

"Let's try and see what we can do." She smiled.

Erec plowed his hands into the dung heaps and grimaced. "I'm really sorry. This is going to ruin your dress. I can't believe I'm asking the Clown Fairy to cover herself in animal poop."

Wandabelle's laugh tinkled through the stable. "I'm not above doing stable work. Anyway, my dress will be fine. I'm dirt-resistant. Goes along with my line of work, dealing with clowns. You can guess how often I get in the way of flying cream pies, even mud pies. It's important for me to keep looking nice, don't you think?"

Erec agreed that it couldn't hurt. Wandabelle grabbed an armful of sludge. Most of it melted, slipping onto the ground. Like she said, the dirt slid right off her dress and skin, leaving her sparkling clean.

"Wow! That's handy." Erec scooped up a huge pile of dung, which toppled back onto his head, leaving him covered. "Ugh!" He slid and fell into it and ended up rolling in the muck until he was completely covered.

Wandabelle laughed so hard that she almost fell over too.

"Really funny." Erec grabbed a handful of guck and threw it at her, but it bounced off and fell to the ground.

"Ahhh." Wandabelle fanned herself with her hand, teasing. "It's sooo nice to be clean. You really wouldn't imagine how great it feels!" She took a step and slipped, arms waving back in the air to catch herself, then tumbled next to Erec in the smelly goo. "Ugh!" She lifted a hand out of it, which of course remained perfectly clean.

Getting up, on the other hand, was not so easy. They both slipped and fell repeatedly until finally they found some dry ground to stand on, pulling themselves up with piles of dried dung. All in all, the effort was completely disgusting, but at the same time they were both laughing so hard that Erec almost didn't mind.

"The best way to walk into a nightmare is with a smile."

Wandabelle paused. "That's really wise. Did you just make that up?"

"No. An old friend said it to me. He *is* really wise."

Maybe Erec could show some wisdom too. The Hermit had brought him here. He believed, like Erec did, that the Fates knew what they were up to. That meant Erec had been sent here for a reason.

If he could just figure out what it might be.

CHAPTER SEVENTEEN
The Beauty of Dreams

I T WAS IMPOSSIBLE to tell how long Erec and Wandabelle moved small amounts of muck from the stable to the river. The work was going a little faster, which meant that Erec had to move more animals inside. Wandabelle had been right. The animals were amazingly quick to re-create the mess, to the point where they had to be moved outside again.

At least the job was more fun with a friend to work with.

"Do you notice that we never get hungry here?"

Wandabelle shrugged. "I don't eat much, anyway. Just a little dew now and then, when I'm in the mood."

"And we never have to sleep?"

"I don't ever sleep." She pursed her lips, correcting herself. "But I suppose I am sleeping now, though. I guess there is no choice here. That's probably why I can't escape."

"If only there was a way to wake you up." Erec gave that idea some thought. "Don't worry, Wandabelle. I'll do my best to get you out of here. Even if I end up leaving before you. I'll come back for you."

"Promise?"

"I promise." He looked around the stable. It was just as filled with gunk as when he first arrived. "That is, if I ever leave here at all."

Wandabelle fluttered through the air on her sparkling wings and landed in front of him. "We do need to escape, Erec. The clowns are in big trouble with me locked away. They won't last too long without a leader. I should have fixed things for them already, but I had no idea that I would be captured." She sighed. "You see, their old king and queen were—"

"I know. They were killed."

"In a sense." She touched a finger to Erec's nose. "Thank you for helping me."

His nose itched, and he rubbed where she tapped it. "No thanks yet." Erec crossed his arms and paced, careful not to slip in the guck. "I don't think this is doing any good. You're right. Let's not waste any more of our time here. We're going to find another way out."

They walked into the village, dodging tarantulas and running from a tribe of headhunters shooting arrows at them.

"Maybe we should both help someone else," Erec suggested. "It could get people into the right frame of mind. If we all shared the jobs, we might at least be able to get some people out of here."

Dark waves crashed onto the gray shore of a nearby beach. Erec saw a man sweeping the sand off the beach, not making a dent as the waves continuously pushed more right back around him. Crabs scuttled by, biting his ankles. That job looked like torture.

"Want some help down there?"

The man approached suspiciously, as if he didn't trust his ears. "What did you say, boy?"

"We'll sweep with you, if you like. Could help you get done faster."

His eyes bugged. "You would do that for me?"

"Sure." Erec and Wandabelle had no brooms, so they used their hands to push sand off the beach and into the water. Of course, all of the sand they moved rushed right back onto the beach with the next wave.

"Maybe we have to go faster," Erec suggested.

A few people gathered by the street above them, watching in amazement at the three of them working together.

"Come on down and join us," Erec called. "Maybe if we all pitch in, we can actually do this."

A few came down to the beach to watch or work, and others ran to spread the news. Soon the entire group of villagers was standing on the beach. Eyes bugged out of their heads, and hands clasped over their hearts.

"I haven't smiled in eons," a woman said. The deep lines in her face looked almost cracked in two from her grin.

"Well, don't just watch," Wandabelle shouted. "Push some sand into the water with us. It's fun!"

Oddly, it *was* fun. People ran forward, hands on the ground in front of them, splashing into the cold surf. Others scooted on their bottoms, pushing sand with their feet and giggling.

"I haven't done a wretched thing but clean toilets since I've been here—except for throwing me sabers at the lot of you." Erec recognized the man who was dressed like a pirate. "This is like paradise!"

"A vacation at the beach!"

The man who had spent thousands of years sweeping the sand was beside himself with joy. Tears streamed down his face. His broom fluttered faster than Erec could have imagined, spurred by renewed hope. "Thank you." He gripped Erec's shoulder. "Even if your idea doesn't work, I'll never forget this day. I feel so much better."

"Tomorrow," shouted the toilet scrubber, "we finish the beach. Then we all move on to hunting down the ants!"

A man with a bow and arrow clasped a hand over his chest. His chin trembled. "Thank you! And the day after that, we scrub the toilets! Then collect the garbage!"

Plans were made as people splashed and rolled in the water with glee.

"Oh, dear," Wandabelle whispered to Erec. "This isn't working at all. Have you noticed that there isn't any less sand now than before?"

Erec nodded. "They're a lot happier, though."

"True. But it would be nice to really get them out of here. We have to find some way to change things. . . ."

Change things. That phrase sounded familiar.

Change . . . That was what the Hermit had been teaching him. The thing he couldn't remember.

He could hear it now, his own voice, faint, in the back of his mind: *Change your dreams.*

That was it! The Hermit had showed him how to change his dreams. Well, this was a dream, wasn't it? Maybe he could change things here, too.

How had he done it before? He had placed objects near him while he slept. He could touch them, pull them into his dreams, make them become whatever he wanted them to be.

Erec tried to remember what he had with him now. His backpack had a lot of things. The Hermit had thrown shells and starfish into it. A nice round shell sounded perfect now. It would be much bigger here, inside his dream—their shared nightmares. But how would he find it and bring it here?

Control. He had to pay attention to his body. *Change your dreams.* Where was his body now, really? It took a certain awareness, he knew, to be able to tell while he slept. He had done it before.

Focus. Think.

You are asleep. *Change your dreams.* Realize that. Feel where your body is, what's around it.

A spark of awareness popped into his head. He grabbed onto it. His hands were empty, but something clung onto his back. It was his backpack, he was sure. Could he open it in his sleep? Was it possible?

With immense effort, Erec shoved himself forward and the backpack slid off his arms. The floor felt hard. The beach before him flickered, and then came back. He was lying on the sand, moaning. People were gathering around him.

"Are you okay?"

Forget this picture. Open the backpack. Erec felt torn between two worlds. The beach overwhelmed him with its sights and sounds. The other, the hard floor, only became solid if he really thought hard. He fought against the beach image, the dream.

Open the backpack. He felt a zipper, pulled. Was he really doing it? Or was this just another dream?

He felt things inside it. *Reach a hand in, Erec.*

He shuffled on the floor, still asleep but moving. He could sense things around him. People? He heard snores.

Or were those waves? No, they were waves crashing on the beach more ferociously than ever. People were gathered around him, talking about a seizure, wishing there was a doctor.

No! He had to keep focused. His hand roamed in his backpack. Feel for something round....

There it was. A sand dollar—in his grip.

No, it wasn't a sand dollar. It was an enormous fan. He pulled it right into the nightmare of the beach.

His hand became gigantic, like a skyscraper. It dragged something onto the road facing the beach. The thing was so big that it stretched into the clouds, reaching from one end of the beach to the other.

Everyone watched silently as his hand shrank to normal size. A solemn mood settled on the group. A miracle was happening.

"Um . . . we better move off of the beach." Erec jabbed a thumb toward the road. The villagers followed Erec silently, back behind the giant fan. "Grab onto the netting on the back of this thing and hold tight. I think it will create a lot of wind, even on this side."

People lined up, arms woven through the steel mesh behind the fan. Erec knew where the button was to turn it on, of course. It was his fan. And he knew that it would work.

With a swift kick, Erec flipped the switch. Fan blades began whirling. The pressure soon sucked him so tight against the steel that he could hardly breathe. The sand from the beach sailed far out over the ocean as easily as a giant would blow dust off a matchbox. Clumps of wet sand that lay beneath lifted away too, in huge chunks. Every time wet sand washed ashore it blew, too, followed by rocks that danced more like feathers. Soon the shore was a clean, bare slab of bedrock.

Erec kicked the fan off, and they all pried themselves away from the metal. In a blink, the fan vanished.

"I . . . I did it!" The man whose job was to clean the beach rejoiced, broom still in hand. "I can go home now! Thank you!" He hugged Erec and Wandabelle. "Thank you all! King Augeas? I can go!"

The king's face appeared in the sky. "Yes?" His voice was oily.

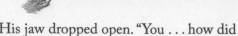

"You think you finished—" His jaw dropped open. "You . . . how did you do this? Did you get help? Because I don't know if that's fair."

The man waved his broom at the sky. "A deal is a deal, good king. Am I free to go?"

The king huffed and grumbled some. "Fine. But don't expect anyone you know to be alive anymore."

The sand sweeper vanished from the beach.

Villagers crowded around Erec and Wandabelle, crying and hugging them.

"You did it!"

"That is the first person ever to leave here!"

"How can we thank you?"

A shy voice asked, "Can you help me catch all the rats, you think?"

Erec winked. "I'll try my best, ma'am."

"How did you do that?" Wandabelle and Erec were sitting on a patch of grass. Villagers stood far enough away to give them space to talk, but close enough to shoo away the bigger cockroaches and fight off any wandering minotaurs that might bother them.

"It's a dream-control thing. I can bring objects from the real world into this nightmare we're all in."

She giggled. "I knew you could help us, Erec."

Neither said it, but both of them realized a sad fact: While Erec might be able to free the people that had a job, he still would not be able to help Wandabelle escape. The king had been smart not to make any deal with her.

"Are you going to get yourself out of here now?"

Erec shook his head. "I'm going to help everyone else escape first. I can't just leave them in this place." As he said it, he realized that if he succeeded, Wandabelle would be left in the nightmare alone. That sounded like a horrible idea.

She read what he was thinking from his face. "Don't worry about me," she said. "Being alone couldn't be worse than before, when everyone was awful to me."

Erec called out, "How many people live in this place?"

"Nineteen, before you two came," the toilet scrubber said, walking over. His voice was filled with awe. "So twenty-one. Guess it's twenty, now that Cadmus is free." He clapped Erec on the shoulder. "Puts me to shame, it does. We've done nothing for one another all this time, and your first day here you already set someone free."

"My first day? No, I've been here months."

The man laughed. "I remember back when I thought like that too. No, days are just very long here. Long and dreary. But the nights is worse. That's when all the nasties come out. They last forever, too, because we can't sleep."

This place was sheer torture, Erec thought. He felt like he had been here forever already. "Well, I guess I have my work cut out, trying to get everyone out before tonight." Erec smiled. "Don't tell the king how we're doing this, or he might figure out how to stop me."

"Aye, aye, cap'n. Griffin at yer service, here. Anything you need, you just tell me, ya hear?"

"Thanks, Griffin. Right now I'm just going to think a bit about blasting some blasted rats."

The beauty of dreams, Erec realized, is that anything can happen in them. Rats can be vanquished by starving serpents, inescapable traps, or even rodent-eating starfish if he chose. But the best way to catch them, he thought, was with starving cats. King Augeas wanted all the rats to be caught and eaten, and this covered all of the bases.

He struggled for that feeling of awareness, touching in his backpack for anything remotely catlike. Nothing seemed right.

Then Erec felt some very tiny bumps—sand that had fallen in

when the Hermit gave him the shells. Lots of grains of sand would make perfect little cats. His fingers slid along his backpack, scooping as much sand into his palm as he could.

"Look! He's out again, having another fit."

He was half in one place and half in another, split between universes. Ignore the voices, he told himself. Listen to the snores. Feel the sand. Pull it into your dream . . .

His hand came out big, but not as huge as before. Big enough to release about a hundred sandy-brown cats onto the grass. The sensation was amazing. His fingers felt like an opening between worlds. Erec grabbed one little cat by the tail as they scattered in search of food. "Come back and tell me when every last rat in this realm has been eaten. Then you all can go."

The cat mewed fiercely and ran off. People were staring at him in wonder. The cook's face was red and clenched into a knot. She tried to speak but was too choked-up, so she bowed low to Erec.

"Don't bow! Please. I'm just doing what anyone would do."

Wandabelle sent him a sideways glance. "Yeah, right. Anyone could figure out a way out of here, then? I told you, this is your specialty."

"I had some help, okay?" The Hermit had shown him how to change his dreams. All he had to do was remember how, and make it happen.

She laughed in delight.

"You're next, Griffin." Erec smiled at the pirate. "Your job is to clean toilets?"

"Not me, cap'n. I've only been here six hundred years, since me ship blew in. Let the older crew out first."

Erec addressed the crowd. "Were most of you brought here by King Augeas, then?"

"Most of us." A woman nodded. "But a few came later on expe-

ditions, voyages, or got lost at sea and ended up here." She hooked
a thumb at a woman in a long dress. "Mavis was sailing on a boat to
something called a 'new world' and ended up here. She was the only
one who survived. Everyone else with her was lost at sea, poor thing."

A haunted look distorted Mavis's gaunt and frayed face. She
looked as though she'd lived for seven hundred years in torture.
Bruises and scratches covered her arms and cheeks.

"What's your job here, Mavis?"

Her voice squeaked. "To climb the tallest tree here." She pointed
at a gigantic fir tree that towered over everything else in the realm.
"It's three hundred and seventy feet tall, a Douglas fir, King Augeas
told me. All I have to do is climb to the top. It should be simple,
right? But every time I get high enough, the wind whips me loose."
She frowned. "And the sharp leaves hurt." She frowned.

"I can help you with this one!" Wandabelle grabbed the woman
under her arms and flew her to the top of the tree. The top branches
were thin and the tip of the tree bent when Mavis clung onto it, but
her face lit with glee.

Soon King Augeas's face appeared in the sky. "What?" he cried,
enraged. "How could you have gotten up there? This is preposterous.
Have you cheated?"

Erec could not hear Mavis's reply, but King Augeas said, "Fine. I
guess I can't hold you here anymore. But if there's trickery going on
down there, I'll find out, you all hear me?"

When Mavis disappeared, the remaining townspeople hugged
one another and danced in the filthy streets.

"In a way, you've already set them free," Wandabelle whispered.
"From this day on they'll never go back to being mean and living so
horribly."

Griffin appeared with a sheepish look on his face. "I know you
could have let yourself out and left us here. So maybe you better

escape before King Augeas puts a stop to what you're doing. It wouldn't be fair if you ended up stuck in this place."

"Thanks, Griffin. But I can't leave you all here. I just wish I knew how to get Wandabelle out."

"What's her job, then?"

"The king never gave her one. He didn't want to risk her escaping at all."

Griffin fell to his knees before Wandabelle. "I'm so sorry, ma'am. When I think how awful we were to you . . . well, it makes me ashamed. We was just jealous, you know. You were too smart to do some dumb job, and we were too afraid to stop. But I didn't know that the king never made any deal with you at all. Now you're the one who could be jealous, and instead you're helping people."

Wandabelle's smile lit up her face. "Thank you, Griffin. I think this place was bringing out the worst of us all before Prince Erec showed up." She touched Griffin on the nose, and he scratched it right after.

"Prince?" Eyes darted toward Erec with new respect, and a few people bowed.

"No! Stop. I mean, I don't want to be called that, okay? Just . . . get up. Let's figure out how to get out of here."

One after the next, everyone's bargains with the king became settled. The woman Erec met on the road found a potion to stop aging in a pot shaped like a seashell. She smeared it all over her face and drank a few sips. A moment later she looked young and radiant. She threw her arms around Erec, crying.

After she was gone, the streets were completely cleaned by three snail shells that became enormous giants with strong water hoses. The last rat was eaten by the cats. People were vanishing and the king was getting angrier.

THE THREE FURIES

Soon only seven people were left, including Erec and Wandabelle. By this time King Augeas's face hung continuously in the sky, watching. "I don't know who is responsible for this—how that net appeared in the ocean to catch all the fish in the reef, or how that huge sponge scoured all the buildings. But I have an idea . . . Erec Rex. If you or that Clown Fairy found a way to trick me, don't think it's going to last. I'm watching you."

It was getting dark. Wild howls echoed through the air. They sounded more ferocious than regular wolf cries. Could werewolves lurk around here too? Erec didn't doubt it.

A huge full moon rose over the horizon, shedding ghostly light onto the village. Movement on the ground caught his eye. The white dirt road he stood on wiggled like it was alive.

"Get over here, man!" Griffin called to him. "Now is when the worms come out."

Erec bolted from the road, shaking some glowing white worms from his shoes and pants cuffs.

Griffin checked the sky. "At least there's a full moon tonight. You don't want to know how bad things are here when it's pitch-black."

"Don't any of the houses have lights in them?"

"You mean candles? Oil lamps? Never had anything here to make them with."

"I meant lightbulbs."

"Light balls? What are them things?" Griffin laughed. "Some newfangled torches, I guess?"

"When you get out of here, Griffin, you won't believe all the new inventions waiting for you."

"I'll stand guard if ye want to try and rest, cap'n. But ye won't be able to sleep. Nobody can here."

"That's okay. Let's keep working on freeing people."

"Seamus has to find a four-leaf clover, Ted has to capture all the werewolves (that answered Erec's question), Selene is supposed to weave a silk cloth out of dust, and Castor must build a ship that can travel into the skies. And of course, me with the toilets, and you with the stables." He scratched his head. "I hate to leave that little girl here alone, cap'n."

"I do too. I'll figure out a way to rescue her, even if I have to come back."

"Yer a good man."

"I'll be better once you're all free."

Erec closed his eyes. In the other world he felt his body on the cold floor, wiggled his fingers in his backpack. A bumpy shell, that could be a four-leaf clover. He pulled it into the nightmare world and handed it to Griffin. "Give this to Seamus. I'll see what else I can do."

"Aha!" King Augeas's face glowed on the huge full moon. "I see what you're doing! How are you bringing things into your dream like that?"

Erec could hear the king's voice both in the Nightmare Realm and where his body was lying, amid the snores. Ignoring Augeas, he focused on his sleeping body, reaching farther into his backpack.

"Are you moving? You can't be awake—"

What could clean toilets? A clam shell could be two parts of a spaceship, ready to be snapped together. A sand dollar was a magic spinning wheel. The round platter was a werewolf trap with a call that was irresistible to them.

"Arg! You're taking things from your backpack."

Erec's hand clenched on one more thing as the backpack was whipped away. Pull hard! In a flash the objects were yanked into the Nightmare Realm by his huge hands. "Castor, over here! Two parts of a working spaceship. If you have to build one, just snap these two halves together and send it into the air."

Castor rubbed his hands together, face filled with joy.

A giant oval of silver lay on the ground, making a hideous screeching noise. "Ted, do you hear that? This is a werewolf trap. Just stand near it, and soon they'll all be caught on top of it." Ted nodded, scared but determined.

"Selene, this is a magical spinning wheel. It will spin silk from dust. Get to work, quickly, before the king stops you."

"Thank you, Prince Erec!"

Griffin looked at him expectantly. Erec ran his fingers over what was in his hand. He had to make it clean toilets for Griffin.

"What have you got in your hand?" the king's voice screeched. "Give me that!"

It was his MagicLight.

A hose. A huge snake hose that would slither from one house to the next on its own, blasting water into each toilet until it sparkled.

Erec let go and the snake hose slid away just as he felt his hand yanked open. The other objects fell away.

His eyes opened into the moonlight. "I did it, Griffin! I got a huge water hose snake to clean every toilet perfectly!" He sighed, relieved. King Augeas cursed and screamed in the sky above. "I was just in time. He took everything else away from me."

Griffin looked pained. "What about you, cap'n? What about the stables?"

Erec stopped short. He had forgotten about himself. Maybe he could make the water hose snake clean the stables when they finished the toilets. They didn't seem built right for it, though. Plus, all of the other things he had brought into this place had vanished once they did their job.

He concentrated, reaching for his backpack, but it was gone. Something rough had grabbed his arms instead, and then they were stuck behind him. His arms were tied. Nothing else was in reach, nothing he could feel with his fingers.

Feeling helpless, he collapsed on the ground.

"Aye, cap'n. I won't be leaving you here."

"Go, Griffin. Your deal with King Augeas is done. You're the last, and I want to see you get out of here."

Griffin protested, but finally thanked Erec, promising to wait faithfully for him out in the real world.

Wandabelle sat down by Erec's side. At least the werewolves were gone, but howls of other creatures approached. Were they ghosts? Phantoms? Erec didn't want to know.

He had a feeling, though, that he was going to find out.

CHAPTER EIGHTEEN

The Best Present

EREC AND WANDABELLE sat back-to-back behind a bush and shut their eyes so they wouldn't see what horrible beasts were creeping around them. Erec remembered that Griffin's sabers had not hurt him when he first arrived. Nobody could die in the Nightmare Realm. So he really didn't have to worry. He preferred covering his ears, burying his head in his knees, and trying to block everything out to spending the night running away from his unknown fears. Every now and then he felt something furry or sharp running over him, and batted it away.

The night was passing so slowly. Erec missed sleeping . . . and then realized that he was, in fact, sleeping. Was he really stuck here permanently? Every time he tried feeling around for things to bring into his dream, his hands came up empty.

Poor Bethany. He gripped his arms tighter, wondering if she was okay. No matter how bad his situation looked, he knew it must be worse for her, chained to a desk, her mind rifled through like a book. What did she have to face? Death for certain. And if she wasn't lucky, she might give Baskania what he needed in order to destroy the world.

If only he could get away from this place. Tomorrow he would take another look at the stable. Maybe if he worked extra hard he could shovel it out with his hands faster than the animals could mess it up again.

At least he had a friend here. That was his only consolation. But he knew that he wasn't doing the Clown Fairy any good by staying here. If he got out, he could tell everyone where she was trapped. He would figure out some way to overcome King Augeas.

The night passed as slowly as the day had. It seemed an eternity before the sun rose. But even with the moonlight, cleaning the stable was too horrendous to do in the dark, so they waited.

When the morning finally came, King Augeas's face arrived with it, hanging in the sky. "You've ruined my realm, boy," he growled. "Now the only toys left to play with are you and that fairy girl. And don't think you did anyone any favors, either. I let them out, like I said I would. But how long do you think they'll last on Henrietta Island in the Arctic Ocean? They're all nicely frozen out there, I'm sure. Well, at least you two are stuck with me forever. Unless you finish cleaning all the muck out of that stable. So get to work. And no more tricks."

Erec's heart dropped. All of the people that he saved were dead? He thought about poor Mavis, so excited about climbing that tree. Little did she know she'd get cast into subzero temperatures and frozen to death.

If possible, the stable looked even worse than it had the day before. He had been stupid to let everyone out before he escaped. Now they were all dead, and Bethany was still locked away. There had been no way that he could turn his back on them, though. . . .

Wandabelle looked as desolate as Erec felt. "How could he have done that to those people? Is he truly heartless?"

The stench of the stable was overwhelming. Erec closed his eyes and tried to feel his body in the other world. Maybe if he stretched he could feel something that he could use here. Anything. But nothing was in his reach. Could he bring something into his dream just from imagining it? He tried to picture a giant backhoe tractor and mops. But even when he formed a clear picture of them in his head, he could not make them appear.

It was useless. He gave up and sank to his knees in the muck. Had he really blown his last chance of escape?

What must his mother be going through now? And his siblings? His father? He winced, thinking about how they would feel with him missing. Why hadn't he listened to his mother when she told him not to leave? He had really gone and done it now.

He could not believe that the Hermit had led him here to be trapped forever. Yes, he had taught Erec enough to escape, but not enough to get everyone out of there safely. Did the Fates really expect him to leave the others to suffer? The Fates were supposed to be right all of the time. But then again, King Piter had told him that they only knew what *could* happen—what people were capable of—not what *would* happen—what they would choose to do. So Erec had made the wrong choice. The Hermit's help had not been enough.

At least he had finally learned finger magic.

Erec froze, eyes wide.

Could the Hermit have taught him how to do that for a reason?

Wandabelle gave him a slight kick. "Get up, lazybones. We might as well—"

"Wait!" Erec put a hand up. "Let me think a minute. I have an idea." He could not bring any objects into the Nightmare Realm. He could not reach his remote control. But he could make things move with his finger at home. Could he do that here? He recalled how he had used the remote control on level three. It was such a peculiar sensation. Like a well of power sprang right out of his imagination.

As soon as he remembered the feeling, he knew he could reproduce it again. Erec stood and pointed to a mound of hardened animal droppings near his feet. In a small wave, part of the pile shot into the air. Some pieces flew to the roof, others wavered near the floor. Then the muck all dropped back to the stable floor.

"Hey, not bad!" Wandabelle grinned. "Look at this." She lifted a shiny pendant that dangled from a black ribbon around her neck and waved it in the air. A sudden wind blew by Erec's neck, and loud swishing noises zipped through the air. Then a bright streak shot like a lightning bolt into her pendant. The light reflected back in double into the stable. One of the beams shot to a small stack of dung near him, and the other shone on a similar one farther away.

The two mounds flew into the air, just like the pile Erec had lifted with finger magic. Seconds later, hers fell to the floor as well.

"You can do magic too?" Erec rubbed his hands together. "We can get this place clean together."

"Well, not really. But this can help." She held up the pendant, which looked like a small, round mirror. "This is a Doubler charm. It can pick up any magic that has been performed recently and repeat it twice. I mostly use it just for fun. It's not easy to direct." Her eyes met his. "But I'll do what I can with it."

A well of hope surged through Erec. "I think we'll be able to clean this place now. Stand away from the doors. I'll see if I can get one of these big piles out."

Droppings flew everywhere when he tried to levitate an enormous column of mud and dung. It was much harder to control than a small, solid object. The center of the stack liquefied when it moved, sloshing all over the floor, and harder bits struck the walls and ceiling. Only a small amount trickled out of the stable door.

Erec shrugged. "Well, it's better than using my hands ... I guess. If I keep practicing, it should get easier."

Wandabelle waved her Doubler charm in the air, repeating what Erec did, only doubling it with two more huge stacks. Two small amounts flew out of the door, but the inside of the stable was a mess. Foul dirt dripped from the ceiling in clumps.

Unfortunately, while practicing did make Erec more coordinated, the droppings would not stay together. Small bits refused to move along with the large ones, and the liquid moved separately. At one point he was able to raise all of the wet muck off the floor and sent it sailing through the door, but the next time he moved one of the piles, more slipped back down again.

Wandabelle gave up doubling what he did, at least until he figured out a better method. Instead she scooped up handfuls and carried them out to the river. Even though the process was faster, it still wasn't nearly enough. Erec would have to bring more animals in at some point, and then the mess would become just as bad again.

If only he were better at doing magic! He wished that he had practiced more. Erec thought about the other things he had done with the Hermit. Maybe he should use his dragon eyes again and see into his future. Things would probably be different now than they were before, since he was stuck in this place. Sure, he thought. He would probably see himself levitating mounds of mud ten, twenty, thirty years from now. No more drowning in water, or getting hit by a tidal wave.

He looked around and laughed. Too bad, he thought. A tidal wave was just what he needed here.

His eyes widened. "No way!" he shouted. "I got it! I think I have the answer." He paced back and forth. "A vision I saw in my future—it was the right thing for me to see, I guess. It's exactly what I need to do here. And I think it will work, too. C'mon!"

They went to the back of the stable and yanked some of the old boards off the wall. He concentrated hard, crooking a finger in the air, and pulled the wood planks out one at a time. Prying them loose was hard, as they were nailed in, but if he really focused his thoughts he could make them fly all the way back to the riverbed. Finally, most of the wall had been removed.

"What are you up to?" Wandabelle crossed her arms, amused.

"You'll see. I need to make sure the front doors are clear." Erec propped them open with rocks. "Wandabelle, I think you better stay away for this part. If you can fly into a tree, that would be the safest." A sour note nagged at him and he frowned. "Are you sure you'll be okay if I'm gone? Because if this works I'll be able to get out of here."

She nodded. "Of course. You need to rescue your friend, then you'll come back for me. Right?"

"You got it," he promised.

"Here, take this." She took off the Doubler charm and hung the black ribbon around Erec's neck. "I won't be needing it here. Maybe it will help you on your quest."

"Thanks, Wandabelle." Her Doubler charm hung next to his Amulet of Virtues and the Trwyth boar vial.

She fluttered up to a treetop while he walked to the riverbed.

Erec closed his eyes and took a deep breath. *Concentrate.* He had to get this right. A small stream of water would not wash out the stable. He had to steer the entire river to run through it. The opening he had made where the water would come inside was bigger than the doors where it would leave, so the water should swirl around and scour the place clean as it rushed through.

So, the whole river had to change its course. This task would take every ounce of energy he had. He lifted both his hands and, like a conductor, swept them high into the air. He struggled to keep his hands lifted. Energy raced through his mind and out of his hands . . . pulling . . . lifting.

Unlike the smaller objects he had moved, Erec could feel the weight of the water resisting him. He fought it, tugged harder. Mind over matter. This had to happen.

Without warning, splashes drifted onto his face. It was coming closer . . . the balance was tipping . . . just needed more power, more force . . .

A loud roar nearly deafened him. Before his eyes, a wall of water raced toward him, towering over him like a tsunami. He was immersed, whipped around in eddies until he didn't know which way was up.

It was impossible to tell which way the surface of the water was, but it was so far away he might never reach it before he ran out of breath. He shot forward like a bullet along with the rushing waves.

Erec crashed into the ground at the bottom of the flood, then bounced up again. Big clumps of green and brown goo swirled around him, picked up by the rushing river. He could not hold his breath any longer. His head spun, and he was choking.

Yet at the same time he was so relieved, so excited. Who cared if he inhaled the water and all the disgusting things in it? He sputtered and coughed, limbs flailing wildly in an attempt to reach air.

Things were turning gray. He needed oxygen. Instagills weren't working—maybe because he was in the Nightmare Realm. Just as he was about to pass out, something hit him hard on the head. Did he crash into a wall? It looked like a door. He burst through an opening and was thrown to the side of the onrushing flood. Water sloshed past him, spreading out across the fields.

Right before everything turned black, he gasped air.

Erec awoke with a hand on his cheek. Wandabelle was looking at him in concern. "You're okay! Thank goodness. I think you would have died, except that nobody can die here." She tilted her head toward the stable. "Well, you did it. That place is clean as a . . . as I am! Congratulations, Erec."

He searched her eyes for fear of being left alone, but could only see her joy. "I'll be back for you. I promise."

"I know. Remember, I've been around a long time. Spending a little while in this place means nothing to me."

"Thanks for helping me, Wandabelle."

"No, Erec. I didn't do anything. Thank *you*."

"King Augeas!" he shouted. "I cleaned out the stable. You have to let me go now."

The king's face appeared in the clouds. He looked stunned. "How did you . . . Ugh! Obnoxious brat. Fine, I don't want you around here anyway. You've caused nothing but problems since I took you in. Get out—now!"

Erec sat up on a cold floor, shivering. His hands were tied behind his back. King Augeas stood before him, glowering.

"C-could you p-please untie me?"

The king shrugged. "If you wish. You won't last one bit longer out there, though." When he yanked the rope from Erec's arms, their hands touched for a moment. The king's skin was smooth and icy.

Erec grabbed his backpack, which was lying across the room from where he had been asleep. "Were the others in here with me?"

"Yes, you fool. You've sent them all to their graves." A door opened into pure whiteness. Frozen wind rushed into the room. "Get out."

"Where is Wandabelle's body?"

"None of your business! Out of here. Now!"

Erec stumbled into the blizzard outside and the door slammed after him. The cold swooped into his bones. A vague noise echoed through his head, a drumbeat in the wind. After a moment he realized that it was the pounding chatter of his own teeth.

He spotted something red in the snow, a drop of blood, or a rose. He stooped for it, so stiff from the cold he almost toppled over.

It was, of all things, a snail shell. Erec scooped it up. The snail trembled in his hand—or maybe it was his hand that was shaking. He rubbed it to warm it up.

A sheet fluttered in front of him, like a white flag in the snow. With a dark flash, a hand beckoned him. He stumbled forward, falling. Something hard under him moved along the snow. Was it a sled? Where were the others? Their bodies must be frozen under the ice.

He was dragged around a cliff and down a hill. Hands pulled him through a door and it slammed shut. Then another door opened onto a bright scene of sun and sand.

Heat seared his skin like fire. People were laughing, chattering. Someone threw warm water on him and it burned.

"He's coming to! Cap'n, can you hear me?"

Erec's eyes flew open. It was Griffin! Was Erec dreaming? Was he alive?

"How did you get yer scrawny bones out of there?" Griffin laughed. "Your funny little friend here said that ye'd be out before long. Guy has faith in ye, he does."

Erec turned to see the Hermit with a smile twisted across his face. "Welcome back, Erec Rex. Have you had a nice birthday?"

"No." Erec pulled himself up, blinking the wetness out of his eye. "I'd say it was the worst one ever. But *this* is the best present."

"That's right, Erec Rex. Happy birthday."

The villagers told Erec how the Hermit had pulled each of them to safety into the Port-O-Door when they left the Nightmare Realm.

"—and he yanked me right off of the ice into this wonderful place like I've never seen."

"The food was amazing. I forgot how good it is to eat."

"I was the only one who ate in all those years. And it was all rat. Only rat. With a little blood, of course."

The thought made Erec shudder. It was so strange seeing the people who had populated his nightmare standing next to him in reality. They looked the same, but far more oddly out of place in the twenty-first century, on a sunny beach.

They were certainly happier than any lot Erec had ever seen. They swam in their clothing, dried out in the sun, and ate everything that they could find. The Serving Tray was working nonstop.

"Ice cream, you call this? I've never seen anything like this before. I shall never eat anything else again."

"Oh, you will once you taste this fancy concoction. It's called 'am-burn-ger.'"

"Where will all these people go?" Erec whispered to the Hermit. "They can't stay on this beach forever, can they?"

"I have just the place for them." He cleared his throat and stood. "I will take you all to wonderful lands to live. You will see new inventions that are so magical, like little boxes that let you talk to people who are far away; big boxes that show moving pictures inside." Eyes widened in awe as people gathered around to listen. "You will be paid money just to have fun and travel. From now on, you will call yourselves actors. You will go to places known as medieval festivals and fairs. They will love you. Follow me to your new lives!"

"Not me, matey." Griffin swiped his hand in a long line. "It's nae an actor's life fer me. I'm an adventurer, and I'll live and die by my wits." He bowed to Erec. "Cap'n, if ye'll have me, I'd be honored to travel with you awhile. I might be a little rusty in me navigational skills, but I've kept up me practice in throwing a mean saber."

Erec laughed. "I remember." He thought about how that would work. "I'm going to rescue a friend from an evil sorcerer who wants power over the whole world—and almost has it. This quest is going to be really dangerous."

Griffin set his hand on his saber. "I'm in, cap'n. Sounds perfect."

He settled in the sand next to Erec as the Hermit led the others to the Port-O-Door. Erec suddenly realized he was still gripping the red snail shell. He pulled a letter out of it.

Dear Erec,

I have to tell you, the Shadow Prince isn't as bad as we thought he was. I mean, I don't agree with him about what he's doing. Trying to get superpowers from the three Furies trapped in Tartarus is okay, I guess, but he shouldn't give them live people as a trade-off. And if the Furies do escape, I think it will be bad news. Baskania wants to control them, but I don't know if it will be that easy.

But, like I said, he's not so bad. He totally gets why I hate Rosco. Said I'm a smart kid, and he'd help me get even if I told him everything about Rosco that I knew. So, of course, I did. It's like he thinks there's some mystery about Rosco and me, and he wants to know what it is. He knows Rosco can read my mind, but he said it doesn't make sense. Rosco can't have that kind of power over me from far away. Even Baskania can't read minds from that far. Something is up, and he knows it just like I do.

I asked Baskania about Bethany, and he said that she's not trapped at all! She just agreed to stay with him awhile. He's paying her to do some research for him. So you don't have to worry about her. It turns out that story I overheard about her being a prisoner in Jakarta wasn't true—they knew that I was listening and were just trying to scare me. Baskania visits with her most of the time, anyway.

But anyway, he kind of understands me. It's just nice to have someone on my side after all this time.

He's decided to give the Clown Fairy to the Furies as soon as they agree to triple his powers. They'll probably do it too, because they're just drooling to get her. It's like a death sentence for her, so I feel bad. But, like Baskania says, better a fairy than another human, right?

Hope you're doing well.

Your friend,

Oscar

Erec was stunned. How could Oscar let Baskania trick him like that? He was vulnerable, of course, after being alone for so long and angry, his father dead. But switching over to Baskania's side was crazy. He would have to write back to Oscar as soon as he returned to King Piter's house.

Poor Wandabelle. He hoped she would be okay until he could help her. As soon as Bethany was safe.

Then thinking of the cheering villagers who escaped from their nightmares made him smile. They were okay. And he *would* rescue Bethany. Then he'd go back for Wandabelle. He was free, finally, and on his way.

The Hermit returned alone, dusting his hands together with a contented smile, like he had just dropped a box of donuts off at a police station. "They scooped the villagers right up. All of them got jobs on the spot."

Erec said, "It's strange. I realized how I could escape the Nightmare World from looking into my future. I wonder, if I hadn't seen into my future, would I have thought to have done the same thing? Did it just speed things up for me?"

The Hermit laughed. "That is what is so beautiful about the universe, Erec Rex. It's full of puzzles and poetry. Maybe it was a little loop. You told yourself what would happen, so it happened in your future, so you knew what to do when you were there. The whole event might have shaped the minute you looked through your dragon eyes." His eyes twinkled. "These things happen. Look at the Fates. Everything they tell you, all of your quests are like this. Just currents in the ocean. But sometimes currents can shift the whole tide of things to come."

"I thought tides shifted from the gravity of the moon."

"That makes you the Moon Prince, then." The Hermit lifted an eyebrow conspiratorially. "Reflecting the light of the Sun King, and held by the gravity of the Fates." He giggled to himself.

"Tha's it!" Griffin clapped Erec on the back. "You're the Prince of Light, you are. Going against the Shadow Prince. Tha's the feller that trapped Wandabelle, right?"

Erec liked the sound of that. The Prince of Light. "You know what this means, don't you? Now that I'm free?"

"Of course," the Hermit said. Which was a totally unsatisfactory answer for Erec, who wanted to tell him what he had been thinking.

"It means that I can get Bethany now. Will you come with me?"

"I'll be there in spirit." The Hermit laughed. "Bring some of your friends with you. Just remember, nobody owns a cat."

"What does that mean?" Erec blinked. He was sure the Hermit had been sitting on the sand by him a minute ago, but now all that was left was a warm breeze.

BOOK TWO

Tisiphone the Vengeful

HUMANS ARE FUNNY *creatures, in a pathetic sort of way. You'll say almost anything when you know you are in trouble. Lies, excuses, promises, apologies . . . I've heard it all.*

As if anything you could possibly say would make me spare your lives. Ha.

I think about that a lot, now that I am locked away in Tartarus. Let me tell you, it is not easy for me here, being the only level-headed one. I'm stuck with one sister who is furious at life, and another who is so jealous of my intellect she can barely communicate with me. I sorely miss taking care of you human beings. Making sure you do what you are supposed to. Destroying those who don't obey.

My lovely Harpies—who in some countries now are respected enough to be made into police officers—keep me informed of the goings-on of humankind. A pathetic state of affairs it has become in my absence. From my calculations, your misdeeds are adding up much faster than new humans are being born.

You know what that means, don't you? Yes, I believe you do.

You are all slated to die.

CHAPTER NINETEEN

Doubts

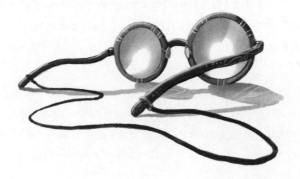

Dear Oscar,

If Baskania is listening to you, you have to try to talk
him out of giving the Clown Fairy to the Furies. It's the
worst thing he could do. Even giving one regular person
to them is terrible. It's like killing people, you know that.
But she is the only one keeping all of the clowns alive!
Giving her to the Furies is like murdering ten thousand!

Please, don't trust Baskania. I know he can act nice, but he is not. He might seem like he's your friend, but that's only because he wants something from you. He lied about Bethany. King Piter found out she's trapped there, chained to a desk. So don't believe what Baskania said. You were right about her being a prisoner in Jakarta.

You've been away from people who you care about for too long. You've been through so much, and you have nobody with you. I'm sure that's why you're even listening to him at all. I'd get away from him before he does something awful.

Your friend,

Erec

Erec took the snail into the Port-O-Door and picked a spot in Munich, Germany, to toss it out, so it could not be traced back to King Piter's house. He had snuck in with Griffin, keeping away from the windows so nobody would see them. Within moments, Griffin fell fast asleep on the couch.

He tried to think of what he would need on this trip to Jakarta. Too bad he didn't have a tribe of ninja warriors to take along with him, just waiting in his basement. One of these days he would explore the catacombs under the house, the huge winding hallways and rooms that used to be under the Castle Alypium. Who knew what might be hidden in there? King Piter built his new house right over them to protect his most prized possession, the Novikov Time

Bender. Erec had used it to travel back into his early childhood.

Wolfboy came up and nuzzled his hand, happy to see him. That set Erec to thinking. Wolfboy might be perfect to bring along. He wasn't exactly a guard dog, but he was a loyal friend. A dog that turned into a ferocious wenwolf during the full moon might come in handy.

If Erec took Wolfboy along, he would have to bring some wolfsbane to protect himself. Luckily, he knew where to find some. One other spot in the house led underground to Hecate Jekyll's old storerooms, which used to be below the Castle Alypium. She had kept not only wolfsbane down there but also more strange things than Erec had known existed.

A large iron plaque, round like a manhole cover, with a large closed eye carved into it, was set into the wood floor near a parlor that Erec rarely went into. The Castle Alypium kitchens used to be in this very spot, in what had been the east wing of the castle. Erec crouched by the cover and said, "One eye sees all."

The carved eye flicked wide open and looked around until it spotted Erec. It stared at him and winked. Then the thick metal circle rose and slid across the floor, revealing a hole with a ladder below. A light turned on in the storeroom below.

A shiver of excitement ran through Erec as he went down. This small room contained so much magic and mystery. It made him a little nervous to go in alone. If the plaque slammed shut above him, nobody would know where he was.

The room reminded him of Bethany, and one ingredient they had found there together. Maybe it could help him get out again if he got stuck inside: Nitrowisherine—a powerful explosive that granted a wish when it was set off. If even one drop fell to the floor it would cause a huge blast. He smiled. That would be the perfect potion to bring along.

In fact . . . could it be that there was an easier way to bring

Bethany back home after all? What if he set off the Nitrowisherine now and wished her to be here? He had not even considered it before, as the Fates had said there was only one way to save Bethany. But could trying hurt?

The potions and powders lined the shelves in alphabetical order, and Erec found the small glass Nitrowisherine jar in the *N* section. He had learned to be careful of what exactly he said when the Nitrowisherine detonated. If he only wished for them to be together, no doubt he would end up a prisoner at her side. "Here goes nothing." Erec opened it and squeezed the dropper until a single drop tumbled to the floor.

The room rocked with an earsplitting bang, and Erec was thrown against the shelves. None of the ingredients in the room seemed disturbed—likely they had a magical protection. But his back was sore. He pried himself off the bottles and jars behind him, wondering if the noise had woken Griffin. Then he remembered that the storeroom locked in sound, so no noise would carry above. "I wish Bethany was right here with me now, safe in my father's house, and would never be a prisoner of Baskania again."

He bit his lip, waiting. Nitrowisherine had never failed him yet. Maybe he would see her right now. He would tell her how sorry he was, and they could go on together, best friends, and never look back to this horrible time.

A glow, and then shimmering movement, filled the air. There was a subtle noise, and Bethany appeared—at least it reminded him of Bethany. Something like her shape wavered in the air. Shadows of her eyes caught his, trying to hold on. Then, with a look of sadness and longing, she faded away.

Erec stared at the empty space where Bethany had almost been. He slumped over in disappointment, even though he hadn't really expected the rescue to be that easy. It made sense, anyway. The Fates had said there was only one way. And she would never escape

Baskania's Draw unless Erec found her in his fortress and gave her the dragon blood to drink.

He decided to bring along the rest of the jar of Nitrowisherine. Even though it hadn't been able to break the Draw, it still was pretty powerful stuff. He found the wolfsbane on the *W* shelf and grabbed a handful to put in a bag.

Other shelves held some fascinating items such as eye jelly, worm tears, ground mummy bones, and flea ointment—guaranteed to keep dogs off any flea. He dropped a small vial labeled LAUGHTER in his pocket. Given how horrid the place was that he was headed, he thought laughter might be a good idea.

When he climbed out, the plaque slid back into place and its eye shut. Erec found a bag for the yellow-flowered wolfsbane and put it into his backpack along with the vial of laughter and the Nitrowisherine. Then he noticed a note on the kitchen table.

EREC,

WE ARE ALL WORRIED ABOUT YOU. I HOPE THIS NOTE FINDS YOU—QUICKLY—AND THAT YOU RETURN TO YOUR FAMILY. YOU KNOW WHERE WE ARE. PLEASE LET US KNOW THAT EVERYTHING IS OKAY.

YOURS,

JAM

He sighed. He would have to go back to Jam's Aunt Salsa's apartment in Americorth North before he left for Jakarta. They must be worried sick.

A strange noise came from one of the bedrooms. It sounded like a bulldozer scraping over a steel wool carpet. The sound grew louder as Erec tiptoed down the hall—and then he realized it was coming from his own bedroom. He peeked inside, then jumped back in shock when he saw a large figure like an enormous round ball on his bed.

Who could it be? The noise, now deafening, and apparently a snore, reverberated through his room.

Careful not to wake the sleeper, he slowly crept around his bed, until he could see the face of . . .

Dumpling Smith. Drool poured down her cheek, removing a trail of white makeup powder along with it and making an ashen puddle on his pillow.

Eeww! He bit his lip to hold in his reaction. He couldn't make a sound.

Because in front of her lay something that he wanted very badly.

His mother's Seeing Eyeglasses.

He measured the distance from the bed to the door. Could he grab them and run out without waking her? What was she doing here, anyway? Probably camping out, hoping that Danny and Sammy would come back here. Her friends were probably still in their apartment in New Jersey, trying to cover all their bases.

Erec put another foot in front of him and shifted his weight onto it.

Mrs. Smith groaned and turned onto her back, throwing an arm out near the eyeglasses and the other over her face. "I've got 'em," she muttered in her sleep. "Got 'em by their collars. They won't go away now. . . . Daaanny . . . Saaammy . . ."

He took another step and lifted the glasses off the bed. Moving faster, he exited the room on his toes.

"Hmph . . . ? What's that?" There was a loud creak. "Where are my glasses?"

Erec bounced away on his toes. "Wake up," he whispered, shaking Griffin. "We have to go."

Griffin sat up, yawning loudly. "Ready and set, matey?" He stood up, smacking his stomach. "Aye, it feels mighty good to sleep again in peace again, after all these years. Mighty good." Footsteps echoed down the hallway. "Who would that be?"

"Hurry. She's after us. Come on!" Erec grabbed Griffin's sleeve and pulled him toward the Port-O-Door.

"What?" Griffin asked, looking around. "We're not running from a girl, are we?"

"She's really big and strong."

Griffin laughed heartily and swung around. Two of the long sabers that swung from his belt were in his hands. "I'd like to see her bother us, cap'n. I'll dice her like a rotten tomato."

Dumpling Smith appeared in the doorway, eyes wide. She looked at Erec's hands. "My glasses!" Her voice was deep and rough. "Give those back, you hoodlum!" She dove toward them, arms in front of her.

Griffin stepped forward, swords whirling in the air. "Stand back, wench! And take yer last breath."

"Eek!" Mrs. Smith screamed and dove away as a saber shot over her shoulder. Wolfboy began to bark in response to the noise, not disturbed at all by the flying sabers.

"No! Stop, Griffin! Don't hurt her."

Griffin paused with an arm raised, saber waiting to fly from his grasp. "Aye, aye, cap'n. Are ye sure you want to spare this odd bird? It would feel good to fling a blade that actually made a cut, after all these years."

Mrs. Smith huddled against a wall, blubbering. "Spare me, please. I'm just trying to help everyone." She looked appealingly at Erec. "G-give me back my glasses?"

"They are *not* your glasses. They are my mother's. You stole them, and I'm bringing them back."

She stepped forward, hesitating. "Well, will you take me with you, then?"

"No! Absolutely not. You are to go away now, and leave my family alone. Understand me? And tell your boss—Baskania—that you're going to leave us alone now."

A look of fear washed over her face. "My boss? No . . . he's not my boss. I'm just trying to help. Really . . ."

Griffin whirled a saber in the air and she plastered herself against the wall. Her voice was faint and slick. "Okay. I'll go now." She smiled and nodded, then walked to the door. Instead of leaving, Dumpling hesitated. "Are you sure you don't want me to come with you? I'd love to see where your brother and sister were staying, make sure it was a nice place for them—"

"Get out!" Erec pointed at the door. She nodded and hurried out. Being fourteen was nice, he thought. Almost like being an adult. He didn't have to be afraid of people like Mrs. Smith anymore.

Of course, having a huge adult pirate under his command, with sabers drawn at his side, also helped. He was beginning to appreciate Griffin much more now.

Too bad Griffin hadn't been in New Jersey with him during his break. Danny and Sammy would have thought twice about teasing him then.

"Hurry. Let's go to the Port-O-Door before she can follow us. I don't want her to know where we went."

Erec grabbed a few bags of dog food and called Wolfboy into the Port-O-Door along with Griffin. He found 8 Anodyne Road on the Americorth North map. He hoped she didn't mind that he put the door right into her living room, like Jam had done last time. At least they wouldn't have to walk through the insane heat without UnderWear that way.

"Erec!" Sammy shouted. Everyone froze at the sight of Griffin walking in after him. Erec started to laugh, thinking how shocking a sight he must be. Griffin still carried a sharp saber in each hand, and he was dressed like a real pirate yanked off a ship in the 1500s, with his loose lacy shirt and vest shredded over his rippling muscles, a filthy torn rag tied like a bandana over his wild hair, and billowing knee breeches.

June put her hand over her heart. "Erec!" she called out in warning.

"It's okay, Mom. Griffin is my friend."

Griffin's eyes widened and he hugged his sabers to his chest. "Really, cap'n? A friend? I am honored." He fell onto one knee.

"Yes. Griffin is a *good* friend," Erec added. "He helped me with my fifth quest. And this is Wolfboy, for those who haven't met him. Sorry I snuck out," he said to June. "I just had to, for Bethany." He motioned to Jam. "You have to send this Port-O-Door back without us. Dumpling Smith was waiting in my father's house, and she might come back and try to see where we went."

As Jam quickly sent the Port-O-Door away, June gave him a hug. "We were so worried about you. I thought you had gone off to find King Augeas. After hearing that story from Jam I was terrified we'd never see you again. I'm just glad you're back safely. So, was there a different King Augeas that you met, then? A nice king somewhere?"

"No. I met the Nightmare King. I was there for what seemed like forever—but it ended up being just one day and night. It was awful." He shuddered. "But at least I helped a few other people get out of there."

"You missed your birthday, Erec." Zoey hugged his leg. "Mommy cried."

"We'll have cake today instead." He took out the Serving Tray, feeling bad.

"Young sir, are you sure that you finished your fifth quest?" Jam was looking at Erec's Amulet of Virtues. "Did you really meet King Augeas?"

Erec picked up the amulet. Only four of the twelve segments were lit up with colors. He wasn't surprised. "Well, the quest is not completely done. Someone is still trapped in the Nightmare Realm who I have to save. I understand now what the Fates meant about me saving Bethany before finishing the quest—they must have known it would happen like this."

"Who has to be saved?" Trevor asked. It was unusual for him to speak, so everyone was silent a moment.

"The Clown Fairy. Her name is Wandabelle."

"You found the Clown Fairy!" June became very alarmed. "She's trapped in the Nightmare Realm? Oh, how awful. At least you know where she is, though." She looked so hopeful that Erec could not bring himself to tell her that Wandabelle was in great danger.

Then he remembered what he was holding in his hand. He raised the Seeing Eyeglasses. "Look what I found!"

"Yeah!" Sammy jumped up and down, cheering.

Danny smacked Erec on the back. "All right, kid. Good job."

"Hey, you can't call me kid anymore. You know we're the same age, right?" Erec said, feeling a little reckless pointing that out.

"I'll call you kid, kid. We don't even know when your exact birthday is. Anyway, I'm sure I'm older than you." He winked. "Thanks for getting those glasses back. I guess we don't have to hide anymore."

"Yeah, except that Dumpling Smith and her pals are camped out both in New Jersey and Alypium looking for you. Life isn't back to usual yet."

"Usual?" Danny laughed. "When has life ever been usual for us? As far back as I can remember, we've always been moving around, living in tiny apartments. Then all this crazy stuff that's happened in this last year. No offense, guys, but this family is an odd bunch. Except for me and Sammy, of course."

Something Danny said caught Erec's attention. "As far as you can remember? How far back can you remember? Either of you?"

"I dunno." Danny shrugged. "I remember pretty soon after Mom adopted us. That first apartment, the blue one with the ugly black drapes." He shuddered.

"Yeah, me too." Sammy agreed. "I can't remember anything about our birth parents, though. Probably blocked them out since they abandoned us."

"Me too." Danny nodded.

A chill ran through Erec. Of course they couldn't remember. They had had their memories of those early days removed, just like he had, so they didn't know they were King Piter's children, destined to rule the Kingdoms of the Keepers. He was so tempted to tell them, but he bit his tongue.

"Erec's right," June said. "We should stay far away from King Piter's house, to be safe. But we don't have to burden your Aunt Salsa anymore, Jam."

"Burden?" Salsa exclaimed. "This has been the biggest treat for me! Young people to talk to—" She looked Griffin up and down. "Exciting things happening. I'd just die of boredom if you all left now. Please, consider this home until you need to move on."

"Thank you so much, Salsa." June gave her a hug.

"That's *Aunt* Salsa, honey. Now, let's get some nice snacks for our new guest." Aunt Salsa fawned over Griffin, who was more than pleased with her attention.

Erec suddenly remembered what else he could do with the

Seeing Eyeglasses. His eyes began to ache at the thought, he could feel them well up, and his heart pounded.

"Would you all excuse me?"

June could read his face, and she knew just what he was thinking. "Of course. Why don't you go find a quiet room." But she grabbed his shoulder as he walked by. "Are you sure you're okay using the glasses? You might not want to see—"

Erec pulled away. "I don't want to see, Mom. I have to see."

Erec sat on Aunt Salsa's bed, staring at the Seeing Eyeglasses, terrified. What if it was too late?

He struggled with himself, forcing his hands to bring them to his face. He slipped them over his eyes, and suddenly he was in a huge, darkly lit space. Bethany sat at a wooden desk, her arms chained tightly to her chair, eyes red and wide. Small metal cones were implanted in a circle around her scalp. An old picture of herself working in a notebook was frozen on the screen in front of her.

Someone was yelling. Baskania was furious, screaming, "Simpler! Can't you speak English? Tell me so I understand."

Erec gasped in reaction, without thinking.

"What was that?" Baskania spun around. "Who is here?" He paced, looking through the air.

Erec whipped the glasses off. How stupid he had been to make a sound. He waited before putting them back on, in case Baskania had some way he could detect that he was watching.

When he looked through them again, Bethany was talking, hoarse and exhausted. "I'm trying. It's just hard to put it in other words." Her voice droned on, patient. "Let's say you had a set of infinities. And the set of all sets included the set of infinities. But each of the infinities also included the set of all sets. It's biconditional, but I was sure one had to be lower bound. So, if you just think of the sets as half-closed intervals—I know that's not it at all, but it's just the easiest way to explain—that led me to the idea that the derivative I talked about being the counterexample which—"

A loud crack cut her off, and her head jerked to the side as if she had been slapped hard.

"If you continue to speak gobbledygook, then you will be punished again."

"No! Really . . . like I said, I was only nine when I wrote this out. I disproved all of it later. It can't be important, because it was wrong!"

Erec ground his teeth, furious. How dare Baskania treat her like this! It must have irked Baskania that Bethany had to talk down to him to explain all the math she knew. Fists clenched, he watched as Baskania grudgingly started the movie again. It played in fast forward through her entire life, but Baskania slowed it down whenever something interested him. "What was this thing you were so intently looking at? Did you notice something written on that candy wrapper?"

Bethany was reliving her past enough to recollect everything. She coughed, her voice thin. "I was reading the ingredients. Earlier that day Mrs. Shapiro had told us that some candies were made with an ingredient just like shellac. But that wasn't as bad for you as some of the coloring chemicals in them."

Baskania continued to sift through her mind. "Soon we'll stop and do another test of your reactions. Then you'll spend a while telling me anything that comes to your mind about magic, especially your unique understanding of it. Then later, another brain scan." He rubbed his chin. "Maybe I've been letting you off too easy. If you were less comfortable, maybe you would have more reason to help me, and we could end this all sooner."

Bethany stared ahead, defeated. Erec was amazed that she didn't answer. Her lips chattered as though she was freezing, and she was thin as a rail. Baskania probably was starving her slowly.

He threw off the glasses and flung himself onto the bed, not able to bear any more. He would put them on later, keep trying until Baskania was gone and he could talk to Bethany. A hot tear ran into his ear.

At least she was still alive, he told himself. He wasn't too late. Danen had used his magnet on her, and Erec had done most of his fifth quest. He just had to go back and rescue Wandabelle to finish it, he was sure. Why did it matter if he had completed part of that quest before saving Bethany? He wondered if he would ever know.

Now everything was in place. He even had the vial of dragon blood for her to drink. So, no matter how she was feeling now, he would make it all better soon.

After saying that to himself over and over, he fell into a deep sleep.

It was dark when he woke. Erec fingered the glasses. Out of habit, he had slipped their chain around his neck. They would be safe for sure that way.

Baskania had to be gone by now. There must be a time difference, he thought, between Americorth North and Jakarta in Upper Earth, but he wasn't sure what it was. In fact, Americorth North could be in any time zone at all, as there was no real sunrise or sunset. The lighting was artificial.

When he put the Seeing Eyeglasses on, light filled the huge room. Math books were strewn around the floor. Pads of paper were piled on the desk in front of her with notes and jottings. Bethany slept sitting at the desk, upright. Her cheek drifted toward her shoulder, but when it drooped too far she jolted upright again.

She looked so pathetic that Erec didn't want to wake her. On the other hand, if he waited too long, Baskania might come back.

"Bethany!" he whispered.

She made a humming sound and her shoulders jumped, but she did not open her eyes.

"Bethany!" Louder. "Wake up! It's me."

"Mmnh." She fought to turn over and lay down, but her arms were fastened tight at her sides. It looked awful.

Erec wished he could touch her hair, lift her face to wake her. He got close to her ear and shouted, "Bethany!"

She startled. "Wha—?" Then she looked around. A deep frown etched on her face and then she closed her eyes as if to shut the world out.

"Wake up! Bethany—it's me."

Her eyes jerked open and she looked around. "Erec?" Then her lids filled with tears and she choked down a sob.

"Bethany, can you hear me?"

"Stop!" She looked around at the empty room. "I'm going crazy."

"No. I've got my mom's Seeing Eyeglasses. I'm right next to you, you just can't see me."

"Erec?" She sat up straight. "Is it really you?" Fat tears streamed down her face. "Or am I hearing things? I think I've gone over the edge."

"No, it's really me. I promise. This is the first time I've had the glasses since you disappeared, or I would have used them sooner. Bethany . . . I'm so sorry. This is all my fault. I should have come back sooner and been with you in Alypium. Then this never would have happened. Can you ever forgive me?"

She smiled, but she looked so weak and worn out that Erec's heart crumpled. "Now I know it is you. Only you would make this all out to be your fault." A faint laugh escaped her lips. "This is Baskania's fault, Erec. Or that stupid prophecy's fault. I have no clue what information he needs." She sighed. "It's so good to hear your voice. I really miss you."

"I miss you, too. But don't worry. I'm coming to get you. It won't be too much longer. I found out you're in Jakarta—"

"No!" Her face got hard. "Don't come here, Erec. Don't even think about it."

"Bethany, do you think I'm going to let you stay a prisoner there? Of course I'll come get you out."

"You can't, Erec," she pleaded. Her eyes flashed around the room, not sure where he was. "This is Baskania's most highly guarded fortress. I'm sure you can find your way in—he'd want you to. But you'd never come out again." Her voice shook. "The only thing that is getting me through this is knowing that you are out there somewhere, doing okay. You're going to be a king someday. And I'm happy knowing that. Just promise you'll always remember me. That's all I want now."

"But the Fates said—"

"Forget the Fates, Erec. Forget me. Okay? Move on. I'm done here. The best part of my life was my time with you. I wouldn't change a thing that we did together." She cocked her head toward the movie screen. "In fact, I'm looking forward to reliving that part again, when we get there. That will be the grand finale before my life is over." She paused. "I just hope there isn't anything you've told me that we don't want Baskania to know about, or he'll see it on the screen."

Erec wanted to scream, throw things. But he understood how she felt. He would have said the same to her if he had been captured.

Not that it would stop him from coming to Jakarta, of course. "Bethany, I went to the Oracle and asked just what I had to do to get you out of there alive. They gave me a list of instructions, and all of them are done. I'm not just going to wander in there, clueless," he said, trying to laugh, despite the fact that he would, indeed, be completely clueless.

Her voice became very soft. "Erec, answer one thing for me."

"Yes?"

"The Fates told you what you could do to let me escape alive?"

"Yes, Bethany. They did."

"Did they say that you would also escape alive?"

Erec was silent. No. Of course, she was right. They had not mentioned that at all. It made sense to him now. The fortress was impenetrable. How could they both escape? For the first time, he had doubts.

So maybe it would be a trade-off, then. Her for him.

He would take it.

"Don't worry, Bethany. It will all work out all right. I'll make it."

He wished he believed it himself as much as he had before.

CHAPTER TWENTY

One Impossible Thing
Before Breakfast

WHEN EREC WOKE again, it was midday. Griffin continued to sleep, after having slept most of the previous day. Erec was sure sleep felt wonderful after centuries of being awake in a living nightmare. Finally Griffin rose, dusted himself off, and bowed to Aunt Salsa. "Aye, me lady. I'm at yer service for yer hospitality." He lifted her hand to his lips. "Yer but a beautiful rose, my sweet. Anything you need, just ask old Griffin, here."

"Oh, my." Aunt Salsa's fingers fluttered over her lips. "You're so sweet to an old lady." She plumped her black, spiky hair.

"Old? Ye must be kidding. Yer but a child in the dew, Salsa." Griffin winked at Erec.

Erec lowered his eyebrows at Griffin, hoping Griffin wasn't becoming attracted to all the jewelry hanging around Aunt Salsa's neck and dripping from her clothing. As much as Erec liked Griffin, he was a rough sort. Wolfboy liked him too. Erec noticed that Griffin snuck the dog some food from the Serving Tray every chance he got.

Four magical items now swung around Erec's neck: the Doubler charm that Wandabelle had given him, the Trwyth boar vial with four tiny colored spheres attached to it, his Amulet of Virtues that kept track of what quests he had finished, and now the Seeing Eyeglasses. As much as Erec wanted to keep watching Bethany with the glasses, it wasn't helping her escape. Being with her when Baskania was there was just too painful and didn't do either of them any good—but he would try to talk to her every night when she was alone.

How would he get Bethany out of Baskania's fortress? He wished the Hermit was going with him. What did he mean when he said he'd be there in spirit? And that strange remark about the cat? The Hermit suggested that Erec take friends with him. Help sounded like a great idea, but he didn't want to put anyone else in danger. Stealing a prisoner from the world's most powerful sorcerer's fortress would not be a walk in the park.

He wished he could ask Danny and Sammy to go with him. But he knew that would be wrong. They were destined to be the other two rulers of the Kingdoms of the Keepers. If he didn't survive, at least they could still be king and queen.

He didn't want to risk anyone's lives. Griffin insisted on coming with him, which was great. Maybe that was all the help he needed. Still, Erec remembered going on adventures with Jack, Jam, and other friends. He would like to have more company. Should he listen to the Hermit? Or keep his friends away from danger?

Then Erec almost laughed, remembering talking about this very issue with his friends on his last quest. They were on the Path of Wonder collecting the five Awen—the magical crystals that he attached to the Trwyth boar vial. He had wanted to protect all of his friends and climb across a crumbling ravine by himself to get one of the Awen. Jack had told him that he wasn't the only responsible one, and they all wanted to help. He had pointed out that they had a better chance if they all worked together.

Which probably was the case now. Erec decided he would let Jack know what he was doing and leave the decision up to him.

He was sure Jack was in Alypium somewhere. The cell phone that had been implanted in Jack's finger had stopped working, so he couldn't call him. But Jack usually spent afternoons in Paisley Park with his magic tutor. Erec might be able to find him there.

"Hey, Mom. Are you going to stay here with Jam's aunt?"

"I suppose we might for a while. She is so sweet, and we can't go back home until things are safe there. Now that that Dumpling Smith woman can't track Danny and Sammy down, we can go out and explore Americorth North. It will be like a vacation." She sighed. "As much as I've been working the last few years, I could use a break with you kids."

"You deserve it," Erec said. "It looks like I'll be here a while longer. Danny and Sammy can use a break too; once they find out they're going to be king and queen, things will be a little harder for them."

June's eyes flew open wide. "*Shhh!* Come here," she whispered, dragging him into an empty bedroom. "How do you know about that? *I* don't even know all the details. And at this rate, it might not happen."

"I saw it through my dragon eyes."

"Well, don't breathe a word to them, understand me? Like you, they're in hiding here, to be safe. It's bad enough that people are already starting to come after them. I've made a promise to your father to keep things under wraps."

"I know. I'm sorry to say anything here about it. And I won't tell them. But does it really make sense now for all of us to go back to New Jersey? The other kids would like living in Alypium too." He thought about the hordes of people after him there and realized that might not be the best choice of places to stay. "Or at least here in Aorth you could do magic, and you wouldn't have to work so hard."

"Let me talk to King Piter, and think about it. For now we'll just take a little break."

Erec cleared his throat, nervous about breaking the news to her. "I have to go for a while, Mom. I need to help Bethany." He hoped saying it in the least threatening way might keep her calm.

But it didn't work. "No, Erec," she cried. "You of all people can't waltz into one of Baskania's headquarters and expect to get out unharmed. It's too dangerous. I'm sure your father would agree with me."

"Mom, the Fates said that I could. I've found Danen, the man with that strong people magnet, and he's turned it on Bethany. I've finished most of my fifth quest. I even have a vial of dragon blood ready to give her. Everything is set. Now I just need to go there."

June shook her head firmly. "I can't let you do it. And this time, don't try to sneak away. I'll be watching you."

"But it's the only way, Mom. I can't just let Bethany die. You understand that, don't you? The Fates said it would work—"

"What did they say, exactly? That she would escape alive?"

"Yes."

"Did they say that *you* would escape alive?"

This was exactly what Bethany had asked him. But that wasn't going to stop him. "They don't go into that kind of detail. It doesn't matter—"

"*Doesn't matter?* No way, mister. It matters to me, I'll tell you that. Just forget about it."

"No, I meant it doesn't matter that they didn't explain that. They kind of . . . implied that I'd live, I think."

"You *think*." She started to pace back and forth. "Will you do me a favor? Please? Before you run off and get yourself killed, let's just talk to your father and Queen Posey. See what they say. Okay?"

"Can we talk to them today? Like now? Because this can't wait."

"Okay. Come with me." June found Jam in the kitchen with his aunt. "What is the best way to speak to King Piter and Queen Posey, Jam? Cell phone or e-mail?"

"Modom, I will speak to Queen Posey's staff and find out what they prefer. Just a moment, please." He held up his forefinger, shook it, and put it to his mouth. "Yes. I am calling from the Rex family. June O'Hara and Erec Rex wish to speak to the queen and to King Piter. Which way would they prefer to speak? Yes, I'll hold. . . ." He waited. ". . . Yes, hullo. We do have e-mail here. Very well." He pulled a paper pad from his vest and wrote on it. "Thank you. They will contact the king and queen shortly."

Jam bowed his head to June. "Modom, Queen Posey requests that you and Erec e-mail her. She is not listed, but you can find her servant here, and she will put them on." He handed June the paper. "Please use my aunt's e-mail in her room."

"Thank you so much, Jam," June gushed. "Erec, Jam is the most polite gentleman I have ever met. You would do well to learn from him."

Jam's face turned red and he exited the room quickly. June typed the name on the paper into the touch screen. "C-a-s-s-y D-e-r-b-y-s-h-i-n-s. There it is."

In a moment, a woman's picture lit up the screen. She wore a shiny cap of little scales on her head and a huge smile. June tapped on her image and the woman with the large smile and small cap appeared live on the screen. "Cassy Derbyshins, Castle Ashona. May I help you?"

"Yes. This is June O'Hara and Erec Rex. We would like to speak to King Piter and Queen Posey, please? Somebody just placed a call—"

"Oh, *yes*. Of course." Her smile widened to the point of cracking. "They're expecting you. One moment, please."

She disappeared, leaving a white screen. Soon Erec's father and aunt appeared. Erec was amazed at how healthy King Piter looked. He was tall and square-shouldered, and his face glowed. Being near Queen Posey's scepter had put more life in him than his own scepter had recently. The queen looked beautiful and radiant, long dark curls waving under her silver crown. The three thin, dark lines below each of her eyes made her look tired, but Erec knew they were from Instagills, like he had in his wrists, which let her breathe underwater.

"Erec!" King Piter cried. "And June. I've heard from my plants that you're doing well in Americorth North. Erec—you seem to have disappeared for a while, but I'm glad to see that you're back. Is everything okay?"

Queen Posey blew a kiss and waved.

Erec nodded. "I got my fifth quest and did some of it."

"Where did you go?"

"I had to meet King Augeas and introduce myself. Those were the quest instructions, at least. But I found out my real job was to save all the people in his Nightmare Realm. A certain one in particular."

"A certain one?" Queen Posey leaned forward, interested.

"The Clown Fairy. Her name is Wandabelle. Baskania took her there because it's the only place that can trap her. He's going to give her to the three Furies in exchange for some special powers."

"You *found* her?" King Piter's jaw dropped. "Thank goodness. So, she's in the Nightmare Realm? We have to figure out a way to save her right away. The clown societies are desperate for a leader. Many are sick and dying, others are wandering aimlessly in the wilderness. They won't survive without someone to rule them, and only the Clown Fairy can help." He pursed his lips in thought. "How were you able to escape King Augeas's realm? I can't believe you were there . . . and left. That is supposed to be impossible."

"The Hermit prepared me. I had to learn how to change my dreams and perform some magic. But I have no idea how to rescue Wandabelle. King Augeas was extra careful to give her no way out."

The king frowned. "I should go myself."

Queen Posey objected. "You can't do that, Piter. Look what happened when you were just a few days away from your scepter. And I can't risk leaving all of Ashona without a queen, and become trapped forever in a nightmare. We'll find the Hermit and ask him to go."

"Good luck with that," Erec said. "He seems to follow his own orders." He looked at his father. "Is Queen Posey—I mean Aunt Posey's scepter helping you more than . . . ours was? You look a million times better." Erec wasn't sure whether to refer to the scepter as his or his father's.

The king smiled. "It's far stronger, and I have completely recovered. So much that I forget my limitations."

June was confused. "I thought your scepter was the strongest, your highness."

"It was—when my castle was intact. That gave me strength to handle my scepter, as Posey has, and also let my scepter work at its highest power." He turned to his onscreen companion. "But you are right, dear sister. I would be a fool to leave your side. I will talk to the Hermit. He may know of a way."

A new voice behind Erec made him jump. "We all know a way, but some of our ways are wayward. Or just ways with words."

Erec spun around and found the Hermit perched on one foot like a flamingo in the middle of Aunt Salsa's bed. Her pink sheets were wrapped around him like a toga, and one of her pillowcases dangled from his bald head like an oversized cap.

"Hermit!" Erec was so happy to see him that he would have given him a hug—were he not so odd. "What a relief that you're here. We *all* need you now." He wondered if the Hermit would understand that Erec wanted him to help rescue Bethany, too, though the king was focused on Wandabelle.

"We all need you? No." The Hermit shook his head with a grin. "You need all *we*. Remember that." He nodded sagely as if he had settled everyone's problem, then sat on the bed with a look of contentment. Erec hoped Aunt Salsa didn't stroll in now and see the state of her bedsheets.

The king's voice took on a pleading tone. "Erec has found that the Clown Fairy is being held in King Augeas's Nightmare Realm. You, of course, know the significance of this information. Is there any way that you can release her? Do you think you are capable of doing that?"

"You are talking to the wrong person!" The Hermit laughed, then pointed at Erec. "Ask that guy over there. He's the only one who can save her."

Erec's eyes widened. "Me?"

The king and queen both protested. "I don't know," Queen Posey said. "It seems too dangerous for a boy, and a future king. He could get trapped there."

The Hermit rubbed his chin in thought. "I see. Did that explanation stop you when you were fulfilling your quests to become queen?"

She cleared her throat, taken by surprise. Everyone, including

Erec, had forgotten what the Hermit had subtly pointed out—that rescuing Wandabelle was part of Erec's fifth quest.

The king shook his head. "I don't know. These quests that Erec has done have been so dangerous. Visiting the Nightmare King? Joining the five Awen to the Twrch Trwyth? He could have easily died doing any of these things."

"Yet here he is!" The Hermit threw a hand toward Erec.

Erec nodded. "I guess the Fates know what they are doing."

The king nodded, solemn. "I know," he said quietly. "It's just hard for me, that's all. But you are right. If the Fates sent Erec there on a quest, likely he would be the only one able to help her." He put a hand over his eyes and sighed. "I suppose you'll watch over him again, Hermit. Are you going to leave now, Erec?"

"No, not yet. I have to do something else first." Erec gulped. "That's why we needed to talk to you."

June looked horrified. Erec was sure she was already upset that he would be returning to the Nightmare Realm. But after Piter had approved of it, both as king and as Erec's father, she could not argue.

"I have to rescue Bethany. You saw her; you know what's going on."

"Erec, leave that to me," King Piter said. "I've been working on it since I got here. Did you think I'd just leave Bethany trapped with Baskania? That girl is like a daughter to me. Her parents were so dear to your mother and me. If I had only kept a better eye on her, not been so obsessed with my scepter . . ." He shook his head. "I guess it's *your* scepter now. Anyway, with the help of my plants, I've found out where she is. It's not good news, I'm afraid. Baskania is keeping her at his most highly guarded fortress, in Jakarta, Indonesia."

"I know. Oscar told me in a letter. Baskania took Oscar in, and he's sending me all of the information he finds out."

King Piter sighed. "Poor Oscar. I hope he gets away before it's too late."

THE THREE FURIES

Erec nodded. "I also saw Bethany for myself, now that I have the Seeing Eyeglasses back. She's not doing well."

The king expected as much. "So we know where she is. I have been gathering information and talking to Posey. We have sent him a formal request to return Bethany. In response, we received a letter from Bethany saying she was fine, and to leave her alone. Baskania attached a note that she was doing important work, and we should be proud of her.

"We are preparing the Ashona army to invade and rescue her. The Alypium army is no longer at my disposal—Baskania has taken over there. President Inkle looks to him for instruction. But Ashona has outstanding fighters. They will break in and rescue her, no doubt."

"What if it doesn't work, though? I went to the Oracle and asked the Fates about Bethany. They said there was only one way to rescue her, and they gave me instructions. Nothing else will work." Everyone stared at him in silence, so he continued. "I had to find the man with the magnet, and get him to use it on Bethany. Then I had to do most of my fifth quest, which I did. Now I'm supposed to find Bethany, get her to drink dragon blood—which I have ready. That will break the Draw that Baskania put on her. It's the only way for her to make it out alive."

King Piter was speechless. In the silence, the Hermit sang, incongruously, "These are the sweetest, the funnest moments. The funniest time of your life. Woo-hoo!" He slapped his side and giggled.

"I don't know about this." King Piter looked stunned. "It's one thing to let you go back into the Nightmare Realm—at least you already escaped from there once, and it's part of a quest. How can I let you walk straight into Baskania's high-security fortress? What are the odds of you escaping?"

"That's what I told him." June's voice was hoarse. "This is ridiculous. He's a kid, remember that. Not some superhero. I don't know what he's thinking, even talking to the Fates about this at all. He should leave it to you. Your armies are much better equipped to march into that place than he is."

King Piter wasn't so sure. "The Fates said it was the only way she would escape alive?"

"Wait!" June threw her hands up in the air like stop signs. "There is a big problem here. The Fates said that Bethany would escape alive. *Could* escape alive is more like it. But they never said that *Erec* would escape alive. That would be impossible."

"The White Queen sometimes believes as many as six impossible things before breakfast." The Hermit giggled. "It just takes some practice. Here we only have one impossible thing before breakfast— no problem at all."

"Hermit." The king rubbed his eyes. "What do you advise here?"

"It's not for me to sell advice when three Fates have already given it for free."

"So you think Erec should go to Jakarta? That he would survive?"

The Hermit tipped his head in thought. "That depends on what you mean by 'survive.'"

"No!" June shouted. "Try another way."

King Piter was thoroughly unhappy. "I understand, June. Believe me. But look at all of the outcomes. What if Queen Posey's army attacked but could not get through to save Bethany? What if they did get through to her and she was killed in the rescue? And what would that do to Erec? Would he ever be the same again? If Queen Posey's army could help the girl, then the Fates would have said so at the Oracle. Now I see that sending the army would be a mistake. I'm afraid we'll have to leave it up to Erec."

"Leave it up to . . ." June's eyes were filling with tears. "I can't let that happen. I'm sorry."

King Piter's voice was soft. "How will you stop him, June? He knows everything. If he does not go, that will be because he chooses not to. He knows how you feel, but he also knows that his best friend will die if he doesn't save her."

June sniffed, tears running down her face. "Would you really run away and go . . . there?"

Erec hugged his mother, seeing how upset she was. "I would never hurt you on purpose. But I don't know how I can leave Bethany there to die. And what if Baskania pulls the information he wants out of her? If he learns the Final Magic? I think we're all forgetting about that problem. That could be the end of life as we know it."

June said, in a stiff voice, "I guess that there's no choice, then, is there?"

"If you go, Erec, you must be prepared," King Piter put in. "I will tell you a few things that will help you when you get to Jakarta."

"If you don't mind, I'm not going to be a part of this." June sniffed. "Erec, come talk to me when you're done." She left the room.

The king drew his mouth down sternly. "You better come back, you hear me, Erec?"

"I will." He shrugged. "Just tell me what I need to do and I'll do it."

"Okay. First of all, I have plants all over, but not in any of Baskania's compounds, fortresses, or corporate buildings. So I won't know what's going on while you're inside there. Keep the Seeing Eyeglasses with you—it's the only way you'll be able to communicate with anyone. The Jakarta fortress is going to be hard to break into. They say the entrance is hidden. It's located in an eye care shop, I've heard, but I don't know the details. In fact, it may be impossible for you to get inside at all."

The Hermit waggled his eyebrows. "Erec has his ways."

"One thing I do know," the king said. "All types of ferocious creatures guard that place. So you'll need to have someone with you that can tell you what to do to defeat them. I suppose the Hermit would be perfect for that."

"Oh, no. You are too kind." The Hermit was bouncing on the bed. "But I cannot come along with Erec. I have an appointment—for a haircut." He smoothed a hand over his bald scalp. "I do know someone, or should I say some*thing*, who would be perfect for that job."

The king caught on instantly. "You are right. I hadn't thought of that. But that's a good idea for a lot of reasons."

The Hermit nodded.

"Who? What?" Erec asked.

"There are creatures known as mynaraptors," King Piter said. "They are humongous birds. But they are also incredibly smart. A mynaraptor could advise you the best way to handle almost any creature that you come up against. Plus, they can help with transportation. One of these birds could fly a whole group of people around. They can talk your ear off, though."

Now Erec remembered. "I've seen one of those before—at least a baby mynaraptor. Bethany had to ride one in the Tribaffleon contest last summer in Alypium. Where would I find one now?"

"Same person, different place," the Hermit said.

"That's right," added the king. "Only one person I know runs a mynaraptor ranch. He's an expert in baby animals, and they're his favorite. Turns out they were going extinct before he started helping them out." The king laughed. "I'm glad he's found something that he's good at, finally."

"Who is it? Someone I've heard of?"

"Oh, I think so." King Piter nodded. "His name is Spartacus Kilroy."

THE THREE FURIES

CHAPTER TWENTY-ONE
Kilroy's Cuddles

"SPARTACUS KILROY? YOUR old AdviSeer? I haven't seen him for ages. Didn't he get in trouble for helping Hecate Jekyll hypnotize you all those years?"

"He didn't know that he was doing it," the king explained. "There was no reason to punish him when he just thought that he was helping me. Spartacus is happier with animals, I think. He is a nice person, but far too trusting. When he was surrounded by the wrong people, they walked all over him."

"So I need to bring a mynaraptor with me to Jakarta. That's in Upper Earth. I can't imagine what people there will think when they see it."

The Hermit said, "People see what they want to see, and hear what they want to hear. Unfortunately, smell is a different matter all together. And most of them have no taste at all."

Erec ignored this comment. "Where does Kilroy live now?"

The king said, "His farm is placed in the one spot where Alypium borders Otherness, in the flatlands. Jam knows where it is."

"Thanks. Is there anything else I need to know?"

The king nodded. "Take as many things with you as you think might help. I don't know what you might come up against. I would say to bring the scepter . . . but that would likely backfire. Neither of us is ready for that yet. The Fates would have told you if you needed it, I think."

For a second Erec craved the scepter as deeply as he ever had, but then he was glad he had sent it away. He counted himself lucky that the king hadn't said he was ready for it, or it would have appeared in his hands right now. "Okay. Thanks for the advice, Dad. I'll let you know how it went as soon as I get back."

"Best of luck to you, son."

June straightened his shirt and mussed his hair. "If you go, do it quick before I change my mind. Contact me with the Seeing Eyeglasses whenever you can, okay? I don't like this one bit . . . but I do understand. And I trust you. If anyone can do this, you can." She placed her fingers on his cheek. "Now, you better hurry, okay?"

"Yeah. Thanks, Mom. I love you."

"Love you, too." She gave him a hug.

Jam's Aunt Salsa packed a sack of snacks for them, even though Erec took the Serving Tray.

June was glad that Jam offered to go along with Erec and Griffin. Griffin bowed low to her. "Me lovely lady, I swear on me mother's grave that I will guard your son with me life. He has saved us from an eternal nightmare, and I can never repay him for that."

"Thank you, Griffin." With a grown man offering help, June perked up a little. "Don't let him do anything dangerous, all right?"

"Of course, me dear." He kissed her hand. "I'll be takin' care of all that part meself."

June looked less pale, if not satisfied, when she hugged Erec good-bye.

Against Jam's advice, Erec insisted on finding his good friend, Jack Hare, in Paisley Park before going to Spartacus Kilroy's ranch.

"Young sir, are you sure bringing friends is a good idea? You would risk his life on this trip?" He cleared his throat, uncomfortable disagreeing with Erec about anything.

"No, it's *not* a good idea, and I don't want to risk his life. Or yours or Griffin's, for that matter. But the Hermit told me to bring friends. His crazy advice is better than most people's. It's like he's clued in to what is going on more than anyone else." Erec's lips crept up into a half smile. "Maybe that's why he seems so odd. He just knows too much. Anyway, I'm leaving the decision up to Jack. He cares about Bethany too, and he would want the choice."

"Aye." Griffin nodded in agreement. "If Jack is any kind of man at all, he'll want to grab his sword and fight to the death. I know he'll be in with us."

Erec and Jam exchanged a look. They'd have to hold Griffin back from killing everyone in the fortress.

Erec pulled his sweatshirt hood over his head before they exited

Aunt Salsa's Port-O-Door into Paisley Park. Jam programmed the door to stay in the tree and wait for their return.

Entering the huge park full of paisley-shaped bushes brought him back to the afternoons he had spent here with his old tutor, Pimster Peebles. He frowned as he thought how quickly he had learned finger magic with the Hermit compared to how slowly Peebles had taught him.

Stone benches lined the lawn, nearly connecting the paisley shrubs like a maze. Wolfboy had fun jumping over the hedges and barking at squirrels. Kids with remote controls filled the spaces between them, instructed by their tutors. Many of them wore the traditional blue apprentice cloaks. Everywhere benches were clumsily lifted by spells, then tumbled back onto the ground, kids and pets were turned upside down, fires sprouted from fingers and then turned into icicles. Erec stumbled over a thin boy with snowy white hair who was so deep in meditation he had nearly become invisible.

"Ow!" The boy dusted himself off and stood, black eyes blazing. "Can't a kid get a break around here? Bad enough nobody talks to me, now I have to get kicked in the side?"

"Sorry." Erec thought the kid looked familiar. Where had he seen him before? "I'm just looking for a friend, and I wasn't watching where I was going."

"At least you have a friend." The boy shook Erec's hand. "My name is Erec Rex. But everyone calls me Connor Flannigan. Glad to meet you."

Erec sent a sideways glance to Jam, who looked amused. This kid was obviously nuts. No wonder people avoided him. "Well, nice to meet you, Erec Rex. Best of luck with your . . . meditation. Or sleep practice. Whatever it was you were doing down there." He waved, then remembered something before walking on. "Hey, do you work at a pet shop in the agora? I think I've seen you there."

"Yeah. I pick up a little cash there when I'm not practicing magic. Did you buy a pet?"

"I got a cat there once for my friend Oscar." A wave of regret washed over Erec when he thought about Oscar. What was he doing now? He hoped Oscar would come to his senses about Baskania soon.

As if he had summoned it with Nitrowisherine, a red snail shell with his name on it appeared on the ground like a smudge of paint in the dirt. Connor made a grab for it, but Erec snatched it first.

"Hey, that's for me!" Connor held his hand out, frustrated. "I've never had a snail come to me with my real name on it yet. It could be important."

Erec looked at him like he was crazy. "This is mine, Connor." He started to pull the letter out.

"But your name is Rick Ross!"

Erec laughed, remembering that Connor knew him by the name he used in the contests last summer. "Look." He flashed the letter to Connor. "It's from my friend Oscar."

"Who?" Connor looked confused, then disappointed. "Stupid mail service."

Erec walked away and read the letter.

Dear Erec,

I have huge news! Rosco just brought a proclamation to Baskania announcing that King Piter is officially resigning his throne! He's actually passing it on to Balor Stain. I wouldn't have believed it, but it has King Piter's real signature on it! The letters sparkle and they kind of split apart on the page when it's really signed by him. Nobody can forge it—and the Bureau of Bureaucrats has already stamped it as authentic.

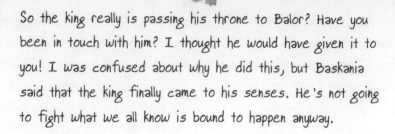

So the king really is passing his throne to Balor? Have you been in touch with him? I thought he would have given it to you! I was confused about why he did this, but Baskania said that the king finally came to his senses. He's not going to fight what we all know is bound to happen anyway.

Weird. But you were right about me not trusting Baskania. I still think he's not as bad as we used to think. But he didn't help me get back at Rosco like he said he would. After I told him everything I knew about Rosco, and all of the things we had done together when he was my tutor, he acted like it wasn't enough. And now that Rosco brought him this proclamation from King Piter, he's acting like Rosco is his favorite assistant ever.

Which makes me laugh, because he's calling me his "assistant" too. I guess that's his name for anyone who works for hm.

Oh, well.

I talked to him about Bethany again, and he said she is completely fine and happy. He even showed me a few letters that she wrote talking about how well things were going there.

Your friend,

Oscar

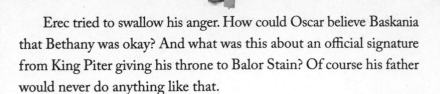

Erec tried to swallow his anger. How could Oscar believe Baskania that Bethany was okay? And what was this about an official signature from King Piter giving his throne to Balor Stain? Of course his father would never do anything like that.

So, Rosco was able to forge the king's unforgeable signature? What else could this guy do? He was as powerful as he was nasty. Erec remembered when he had believed in Rosco, and when Oscar had too. What a con man.

He asked Jam for a pen and paper, which of course he had ready, along with a board to write on.

Dear Oscar,

You have to believe me. Baskania is completely lying to you. Bethany is not happy, and she is not there by choice. I don't want to go into how I know this, because Rosco will read this letter when you get it. But you have to trust me.

And the king—my father—did not leave his throne to Balor Stain! I have no idea how Rosco got his signature, but he did not sign any proclamations.

I really think you should get away from there, fast. If Baskania wants you to help him so much, wouldn't it be better not to? It's like helping your worst enemy destroy the world. I really wish you could join me. This whole thing stinks.

Just met a crazy kid who said he was me. What a laugh.

Erec

He put the note in the shell and tossed it. Before Oscar got it and Rosco took it and traced it back to here, Erec would be long gone.

Just about when he was ready to give up looking, a tall kid with yellow-blond hair bounded into view. He was taking turns keeping a rock alight, passing it back and forth with a slim girl. Her straight black hair bounced against her shoulders as she ran.

"Hey, Jack!" Erec shouted. "It's me." He threw his hood back.

Jack and the girl turned around. Jack's face lit up with a grin at the same time as the girl's lips curled into a snarl. She dropped the rock and it fell, hitting Jack in the head.

"Ouch." He rubbed where the stone had bounced off, a smile still covering his face. "Erec! Jam! Wolfboy! I've been wondering what's going on with you. Man, I can't believe you're here. I visited Bethany a few times when you were in Upper Earth. But the last time I tried to go to your father's house, I was stopped by a water wall around it." He bent down to rub Wolfboy's ears. "Are you okay? I heard that your father passed his crown on to Balor Stain. I couldn't believe it. So I wondered if something happened to you."

"Nothing happened to me. And don't believe that King Piter would ever hand his kingdom over to Balor. Not in a million years. But Bethany is in trouble. Baskania captured her."

Jack's eyes widened and he grew paler than usual. "Bethany? No . . . No way. Are you sure? Can't your father get her back?"

Erec noticed that the girl was listening to them intently. Just then he recognized her: She was Bette Noir, an old friend of the Stain triplets. "Bette?" His mouth fell open in disbelief. "What are you doing here? Did your rotten friends send you to spy on Jack now? Isn't Oscar Felix enough for you?"

Bette's snarl deepened into a full-fledged sneer. "Erec Rex. Pretty brave of you to show your face around here. One little shout to one of the Alypium police birds up there and you'll be arrested on the spot." She jerked her thumb toward a Harpy flying overhead.

"Hey, guys. Cut it out." Jack put a hand on each of their shoulders. "I know it's hard to believe, Erec, but Bette is on our side. She was friends with the Stains, and Ward Gamin, and Rock Rayson. But she hates them all now. You know Balor. He thinks he's ten cuts above everyone else. Now that he has more power than ever, he's even worse. Bette's come to her senses about him."

Erec thought about Balor stuck with King Augeas and felt sorry for him. "He doesn't have as much power as he makes out."

Bette stuck her chin out. "I still like Ward. He's cute. But Rock won't even talk to me anymore."

Jack said to Erec, pleading, "C'mon. Give her a chance, okay?"

"After everything we've been through? Can I talk to you in private?"

Bette retreated, in a huff, to a bench not far away.

Jack crossed his arms and waited, with a look on his face like Erec had kicked a kitten. Patient and considerate as ever, Erec thought. Jack didn't have a suspicious bone in his body.

Erec, on the other hand, had more than enough suspicious bones to make up for ten of him. "Jack, this is confidential information. Please don't tell Bette anything, in case she still has connections with the Stains. We're going to Baskania's fortress in Jakarta to try to break Bethany out of there. I just wanted you to know, in case . . ." He didn't want to suggest that Jack come, or put any pressure on him at all. It had to be his idea entirely.

"Cuz we know you'd want to come and fight for her," Griffin said. "Yer a man, not a meece, right?"

Jack pulled back from Griffin in shock.

"Sorry," Erec said. "This is my friend, Griffin. We met in . . . somewhere far away from here. But he's helping me in Jakarta. Listen, don't feel like you have to come. I mean, don't come with us, okay? It's going to be really dangerous. The only reason we're going is the Fates said it was the only way to get Bethany out alive."

"The Fates said that?" Jack bit his lip. "Well . . . of course I'm going to go with you. This couldn't be any worse than the Path of Wonder, could it?" He laughed, remembering their past quest.

"*Yes.* It will be much worse. Picture every horrifying monster you know. We may not come back alive."

"I know. Look, it's Baskania's fortress. But Bethany is trapped in there. What am I going to do, just sit here when I know something we do could help her? I'll go nuts if I don't go. Just like you would."

"You would risk your life to save her?"

"If it comes to that. But I may not have to. You might need a lookout, or there are other things I could do to help. I'll come along and play it all by ear. Okay?"

Erec was filled with relief. He had not realized until now how much Jack's company made him feel better.

"We should ask Bette to come with us. She's pretty smart, and she might be able to help."

Erec's eyes narrowed at Jack. "How long have you been hanging out with her?"

"I dunno." Jack shrugged. "A few weeks?"

"You don't know anything about her. What if she was lying to you? Listen, Oscar is working for Baskania now. He thinks Baskania is his friend. Baskania has been feeding him stories, and using him to get information. That's probably what Bette is doing with you."

Jack looked over his shoulder at Bette sadly. "You really think so? I hate to just leave and not tell her where I'm going. We've been hanging out, and she'll think we're ditching her like the Stains did."

"So? Look, Bethany's life is on the line. There is no room for mistakes. If you would rather stay here with Bette, I understand—I think. But don't tell her a thing."

"Okay," Jack agreed. "I won't. But you have to let me tell two other people. They've been worried sick about you, and would really want to help too."

"Who, Rock Rayson and Ward Gamin?" Erec tried to calm down.

Jack held up a finger. "Be right back." He ran off and returned shortly with two girls. Erec immediately recognized them as Melody Avery, Bethany's good friend and old roommate, and Darla Will, a pal who had helped him out in the past.

Melody plunged past Jack and scooped Erec up in a hug. "Where have you been? I can't believe you let all this time go by. Hey, Jam!" She embraced the blushing butler. "Good to see you not steaming mad anymore."

Jam turned a darker shade of pink. It was hard to imagine polite Jam as spitting angry. But that was what the Awen of Harmony had done to him when he had held it on their last adventure.

"You were pretty funny then too, Melody." Erec laughed, although it had not been funny at the time.

A grin spread across Melody's dark-complexioned face and she pulled on one of her tight black curls. "All pretty fun to look back on. I'm glad you let me go with you guys."

Erec smiled remembering Melody's magical gift of producing beautiful music with her body. Each limb made the sound of a beautiful instrument, from flutes to violins. When he finally rescued Bethany he would have to ask Melody for an encore—he knew how much Bethany would love that.

Darla blinked behind her glasses, pulling on her stringy brown hair. "Hi, Erec. Glad to see you're okay."

"You too, Darla. Have you been out for a while?" Darla's unfortunate "gift" from birth was that she would get the same sickness or injury as anyone she knew or was around, only twenty-four hours ahead of them. She usually was recovering from one illness or another. This was the first time that Erec had seen her out of the royal hospital.

She nodded. "Luckily, everyone here has been okay. I mean, I've had a lot of colds and flus. But nothing too bad. Guess that means you'll all be in good shape tomorrow."

"Now that the castle is gone, where can you go when you're sick?"

"There's another hospital in Alypium." She shuddered. "It's more crowded, though. So when I was there, I kept getting one thing after the next, every time someone came in. It wasn't easy to convince them to let me out with pneumonia before I got whatever else was coming in next."

Jack sent Erec a meaningful look. "Tell them?"

Erec studied Darla and Melody, then nodded. Of course they deserved to know. "Don't tell a soul, okay? Only Jack and you two can know. Bethany is a prisoner in Baskania's fortress. He thinks she can tell him the secret to the Final Magic, because of that dumb prophesy. She has no clue what the secret is. I guess that's good, but he's not letting her out either way. I'm going to try and rescue her, and Jack—?"

"I'm going too."

"Count me in," Melody responded immediately. "She would go for me if I was a prisoner. I know that."

Darla sighed. "I'd love to go, really. But you know what would happen to me there."

Of course. Any fighting that happened would injure Darla a day in advance. She was pretty much guaranteed to be hurt or even die if anyone else did. Erec smiled at her. "Bethany would not want you to chance that." He added, "She doesn't want any of us to risk our lives. I talked to her with the Seeing Eyeglasses, and she was beside herself when I told her that I was coming."

"You saw her?" Melody jumped up and down, excited. "So she's okay?"

"For now. Not great, but okay . . . You guys are really amazing to come with me. Thanks."

"Oh, shut up." Jack rolled his eyes. "Let me tell my tutor I have to go on a quest with you. This is kind of a quest, isn't it? That should cover us."

"Me too!" Melody squeaked.

They ran off and were back in minutes. "Did you say we're going to see Spartacus Kilroy?" Jack said. "I thought he was in prison."

Melody laughed. "No, he was let off. Well, we better go now, right? I guess a suitcase wouldn't work if we're sneaking into a fortress, would it?"

Spartacus Kilroy lived in what looked like the opposite of a prison. His ranch spread over a hundred acres at the border of Alypium and Otherness. Sunlit cliffs towered over green fields. Raptors soared through the trees above, and a waterfall tumbled into mist just within sight. The ranch itself was in Alypium proper, which meant that the huge golden dome kept it at a warm, perfect temperature year-round.

Jam didn't set Aunt Salsa's Port-O-Door to stay and wait for them, as he figured that Spartacus Kilroy would have his own. Still, Erec felt stranded seeing it disappear.

A tall wooden fence with metal railings surrounded the property. Erec and his friends gathered in front of a huge gate with a sign reading KILROY'S CUDDLES: PRECIOUS PETKINS, FURRY FRIENDS, STINKY SWEETHEARTS, AND CUTE COMPANIONS. The grass in the fields appeared to be swirling around like paint in a mixer, with bits flying up into the air. Erec squinted, trying to get a better look.

"Wow!" Melody pointed. "Look at all of those leaping lizards! I've never seen so many in one place!"

The entire farm was swarming with the same leaping lizards that Erec had seen in the gardens of the Castle Alypium. They flew up into the air, often bashing into each other head on, and dropped onto the backs of others. Wolfboy watched, stock still, with a low growl.

"Man," Jack mumbled. "It's hard to hear them with all the commotion, but a few of them are talking about . . . what is it . . . 'fly worm stew'?" Jack's inborn gift was to understand animals. "Look, they're clearing a path down the middle."

Like a huge green zipper coming open, the hoards of leaping lizards parted down the middle, leaving a path of empty grass that widened until the lizards had nearly all run away. Straight down the path whirled huge blurs of green, like miniature emerald cyclones. Occasionally one of the blurs of motion stopped, revealing what looked like huge grinning toads.

"Dervish Toads!" Jack pointed with a grin. "I rode one of those during the baby animal race last summer, in the Tribaffleon contest. Almost makes me sick to my stomach remembering it. I think I was greener than it was at the end." He laughed. "I guess Kilroy was the one who supplied the animals."

They cautiously opened the gate, trying to avoid being knocked flat by spinning Dervish Toads as they walked toward a big white ranch house in the distance. Wolfboy, for all his bravado, stuck tight to Erec's side as they walked.

"Look at those." Erec nodded at an approaching herd of glittering white unicorns with golden horns. Several dozen pranced straight past them, gracefully dancing above the Dervish Toads without a problem. Erec did not blame Spartacus Kilroy for wanting to stay in such a wonderful place.

Other animals appeared as they approached a big red barn near the ranch house. Some of them looked almost normal, like turtles, rabbits, and mice, except that they were twenty times their normal sizes. Others Erec had never seen before. He recognized a triclops like the one he had ridden for the Tribaffleon contest. It looked like three horses connected together by a fur-covered bar through the center of their bodies. The three parts moved in tandem around the bar, one side going up when the other went down, just like carousel horses.

Erec immediately recognized Spartacus Kilroy, with his sandy blond hair and friendly green eyes. He looked more relaxed and happier than Erec had ever seen him. He no longer wore the starred blue cloak that used to be his trademark. Spartacus was tending to a shed full of sharp-beaked ducks in nests, deeply engaged in conversation with a few of them as he gathered their eggs in a basket and replaced their water buckets.

When he heard the group approaching, he looked up and waved. "Hi, folks! Spartacus Kilroy here. Best deals on all creatures you can—" He left off and stared in shock. "Erec Rex? I can't believe you're here. And . . . you're the head butler from the Castle Alypium, aren't you?" Spartacus looked at the others as if he might recognize them, then gave up. "Are you here to buy a pet? I see you already have a dog."

"No. Well, yes, I guess. I heard that you sell mynaraptors?"

"Yeah, I do." Spartacus gestured with his arm. "Come on in, guys. You want a snack? I've got some cookies. Not the best I've ever tasted, though. The flying cows like them better than I do."

As Spartacus turned to lead them inside, Erec wondered how much he could trust him. The way to saving Bethany was so fragile and narrow, he feared any wrong move could send them all tumbling into disaster.

CHAPTER TWENTY-TWO

An Even Trade

E REC PULLED HIS silver Serving Tray out of his backpack in Spartacus Kilroy's kitchen. "Don't worry about the snack. We can take care of it. Tray, some platters of warm cookies and brownies, please. And a pitcher of milk." He bit into a chocolate chip cookie that tasted fresh from the oven.

"Pretty nifty." Spartacus picked up the tray. "Can I have a lemon meringue pie square with chocolate melba toast topping?" The odd but tempting treat appeared on the tray and he took a bite. "Unbelievable. This is just like my mom used to make." He sat down and leaned back in his chair. "What brings you guys here? I've heard you've been up to some strange things, Erec, but I never know what to believe. After being lied to for ten years when I was King Piter's AdviSeer, I've lost my patience with people. I guess that's why I'm spending my time with animals now. They don't play games."

"I don't blame you." Jack laughed. "This place is amazing. If I wasn't a magic apprentice now, I'd love to work here."

Griffin stared in horror at the pie square until Spartacus asked the Serving Tray for another and slid it over to him. Griffin held it to his mouth, wavering between disgust and an effort to be polite. When he finally tasted a bite, his eyes lit up and he shoved the rest into his mouth.

"My door's open to you." Spartacus nodded at Griffin, stuffed the rest of his own pie square in his mouth and dusted his hands off. "I sure could use a hand. Seems like one creature or another is always in trouble. In fact, I got a call the other day. Two guys are going to stop by tomorrow for a job interview. First time anyone's been interested in working here. Anyway, even if they don't work out, I'm glad to be doing this. Some of these animals have been dying out in the wild, and now they're getting a new start here."

"Were you the one who brought the baby animals to the Tribaffleon contest?" Melody said.

He nodded. "This was my first job, way back when. It's really too bad I got sucked into that whole AdviSeer thing. I guess I let my vanity overcome me when I accepted that post. I should have known I couldn't do any of that stuff. They just wanted a dupe to follow orders. Someone who wasn't bright enough to catch on that there were problems."

Nobody knew what to say to that. Erec felt bad—Spartacus was such a nice guy. He shouldn't feel responsible for things he had done by mistake.

Spartacus broke the silence. "Have you all heard about the clown problem? Too bad I can't do anything for them. I tried to take some in, but as soon as they stopped wandering they got sick, and a few died. I made them go—I thought they would last longer on the move. Poor things roam around Otherness and get into trouble, searching for someone to guide them. Some get too weak to go on, though. They're not going to last long." He sighed. "It's such a shame what happened to their rulers ten years ago. And now with the Clown Fairy gone, it's a mess." They sat a while thinking about it. "So, why do you want a mynaraptor?"

Erec was not sure how much he could safely tell Spartacus. "Well . . . my father suggested that they know a lot about other creatures, and they're really smart. He said they make good companions."

"That's for sure." Spartacus laughed. "As long as you can stand the chatter. You have to know how to be firm with them, or they'll talk your ear off. Some people tape their beaks shut." He immediately became concerned. "You have to promise me you'll never do that. They're not the most popular pets, because people don't know how to handle them. I guess if you really want one, I can show you some." He asked the Serving Tray for a steak for Wolfboy, who was getting more and more spoiled.

"Okay." Erec remembered the baby mynaraptor that Bethany had rode upon during the Tribaffleon race. It was true—the thing babbled nonstop. Was that really what they needed?

Outside, Erec noticed a gazebo filled with beautiful women laughing and chatting. On a second glance he saw that they were not wearing bright plumed clothing, as he thought—instead, the lower half of their bodies was feathered and shaped like human-sized bird legs.

Spartacus caught Erec and Jack staring. "Those are Kinari. They weren't doing so well in Otherness. Kinari like to live close to humans, so they end up drifting across the border into Upper Earth sometimes. They need more Substance around them, though, to live, and there isn't enough there. So when they wander too far into Upper Earth, they don't make it back."

Jack frowned. "Kinari? They look like regular girls to me. I mean their clothes are—" His eyes widened when he noticed that the feathers were not just an outfit. "Ooh. Never mind."

Spartacus told them that the ducks with sharp, pointed beaks and long claws that he had been talking to were mynaraptors.

"That couldn't be right," Erec said. "My father said that they were enormous, and we all could ride on one of them."

"You could." Spartacus nodded eagerly. "They are huge."

Erec looked at the ducks skeptically. Even the baby mynaraptor that Bethany had ridden was much larger than these.

"Oh, excuse me." Spartacus laughed, then explained. "Right now they're small. The birds can hide their size. Look." He petted one of the birds on the back. The creature started babbling to him about water and noise levels on the farm. "*No*. Stop talking," he commanded. Then in a nicer tone, "Would you please show my guests your larger size?"

The thing gave a quick nod, then grew before their eyes until it loomed over all of them. Its legs stretched so that it resembled an enormous ostrich, and its elongated duck body widened. Soon it was twenty feet tall, with a broad back and immense wingspan.

"Whoa." Griffin looked up at it in awe.

The bird preened, enjoying the attention, then shrank back to duck size and hopped into its nest. "You know," it informed them, "I had an aunt once who met a little girl when she was small. I don't

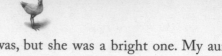

remember what her name was, but she was a bright one. My aunt loved her. They talked about many things—I think they even spoke of fish at one point. Fish are one of my favorite snacks, you know. If I had my way, then all the time I would just—"

"*Stop.*" Spartacus held a hand out and the thing shut its beak. He motioned for Erec and his friend to follow him back into the house. "It's getting dark. Why don't you all stay here tonight? Make yourself at home. I don't know what your plans are, but you can't do much right now. I'd love the company, anyway." He smiled. "Tomorrow morning I'm interviewing two guys for jobs. Other than that I'm just hanging around here, as usual."

The idea suited Erec fine. They might as well rest up. Who knew what tomorrow would hold?

Erec warned Jack and Jam before he put on the Seeing Eyeglasses in the small guest room they shared that night. Jam had insisted on taking the couch, leaving two cots for Erec and Jack.

"I'm going to talk to Bethany, so . . . if I sound like an idiot or get choked up, just try to ignore it, okay?"

He put the glasses on. Bethany sat in the same spot as before. The room was dark, but he could see her silhouette nodding to sleep and jerking upright again. He guessed the time difference was less than when he had been in Americorth North.

"Hey, Bethany!" he hissed, trying to keep his voice quiet. "Wake up. It's me."

After a long while her eyes opened and searched the room fearfully. "Erec? Is that you?"

Bethany looked even more exhausted than before. Dark circles sagged under her eyes and she wore a look of defeat. Erec felt bad to have woken her. From now on he would just watch her sleep, and only wake her if he had to.

"How are you holding up? It makes me sick to see you so sad."

"Not great." She shrugged as much as she could with her arms chained down. "I don't know how much longer I have. We're already up to age eleven of my life. That's only three more years until we hit my age now. Then I bet he'll take another route to seeing what's in my head." She sighed deeply. "I'm really afraid, Erec. I heard Baskania threatened the Memory Mogul within an inch of his life to find out where my earliest memories went. Turns out the guy keeps no records at all of who gets what memory. In a way I'm glad—that's less for Baskania to find out about me. But at the same time, it would at least give me longer to live."

Erec's skin prickled with hot anger. "Bethany, I'm coming to get you. And I'm not alone. A group of us are going. All you have to do is drink the dragon blood from the vial I give you. That will break the Draw that Baskania has on you. I know this is going to work, so try and hang in there."

"No," she begged him. Tears poured down her cheeks. "Please. You don't understand. You don't want to be anywhere near this place. You coming here would be the perfect gift for Baskania. Do you get that? He would love it. And it would kill me, to see you going through what I am—or worse. Knowing you are safe is the only thing holding me together. Baskania would probably take your eyes and destroy you right away. Think what would happen to the rest of the world if he gets your dragon eyes. You can't risk that."

Erec paused. He had not thought about his eyes. Of course Bethany wouldn't miss a point like that.

Well, he'd just have to be careful, and make sure Baskania didn't capture him.

He gulped. "It's going to be okay, Bethany. I promise you. Just remember to drink the dragon blood, okay?"

"Don't come, Erec." Her voice shook. "Promise me that you won't come."

Erec was torn between telling her what she wanted to hear, to comfort her, and telling her the truth. So he thought of something else he could promise. "Bethany, I promise it will all be okay."

He hoped he was telling the truth.

Erec woke with a vague memory of dreams that involved Bethany and Wandabelle escaping a prison on the backs of huge mynaraptors while he waved good-bye from inside a barred cell. He was relieved that he was okay after he woke up, but then he realized that he would rather have things the way they were in the dream, with Bethany and Wandabelle safe, as compared to now.

At least he had not had that awful dream with Earl Evirly starring as his father. Then he remembered—that dream had been removed by the Nightmare King. He smirked. What a great gift the king had given him. Erec hoped the king enjoyed keeping that horrible nightmare on his little glass collectors shelf. Good riddance.

It was hard to get out of bed, knowing that this might be the last morning of comfort he had in a long time—maybe forever. While he was dying to run straight to Jakarta, he was also terrified. His mother's words—and Bethany's—echoed in his mind. The Fates never said that *he* would get out safely. Was it possible?

By the time he walked into Spartacus Kilroy's kitchen, everyone else was feasting on a table full of foods from the Serving Tray. Omelets were passed around, along with chocolate blackberry pancakes, peanut butter-chocolate chip Belgian waffles, fried egg-sausage-cheese-honeybread stacks, and hearty gruel—ordered up by Griffin.

"This tray makes having guests easy." Spartacus laughed. "I have to find one of these things." A doorbell rang and Spartacus glanced at the clock on the wall. "Ooh—it's ten. Almost forgot about the fellas coming to interview for jobs. Do you mind if I talk to them first, and then get you your mynaraptor? I'd appreciate if you told me what you think about these guys too. Have to say, I don't trust my own judgment about people anymore."

Spartacus disappeared for a while. When he walked back into the room, two men followed him. One was short and squat, wearing an eye patch and a dirty brown sackcloth tied at his waist with a rope. Sparse gray hair drooped around his face, circling a mostly bald scalp. The other was very tall and dressed like a hunter, with broad shoulders thrown back and his head held high. Soft blue eyes gazed out under tousled dark hair.

Erec's jaw dropped.

"Let's keep this casual. May I introduce you to some friends of mine who are here? Then we can all chat about what the jobs will entail. This is Erec, Jack, Jam, Melody, and Griffin. And your names were Arthur and . . . Karen?"

"Kyron," the larger, younger man said, staring at Erec. "And my father here is Artie." His shocked face morphed into a huge grin. "Erec? You're *here*? I thought we'd never see you again."

"It's Erec Rex," Artie said slowly. "Youse saved us from that bad manticore beast that was after us." He lumbered toward Erec and gave him a hug.

Erec endured it a while, then pushed Artie gently away and stepped back. "Great to see you both. Are you doing okay?" His third quest had involved putting both Kyron and Artie in danger. Risking their lives was one of the hardest things he had ever done.

Kyron gave him a high five. "We can't thank you enough, man. It's so great to be free. We've been wandering all over the world, exploring and having fun. But Dad needs a place to settle down now. He's getting older, you know. I'm not too fond of Alypium—we've heard about all the crazy politics going on here. But this part seems more isolated." He shrugged. "Almost like farm life. And we're big animal fans." He laughed. "I haven't hunted a single dragon since we last saw you."

Erec shuddered, remembering Kyron's past profession. "Glad to hear that. I bet you'll like it here. This setup seems perfect for you guys."

"Yeah." Kyron nodded. "It's beautiful. As long as Baskania doesn't catch wind that we're here." He looked sharply at Spartacus, as if he had slipped. "That's something we need to discuss. My father and I are happy to work for food and a place to stay. A little money would be good, but we don't need a lot. But I have to find out where your allegiances lie. The fact that Erec is here is a good sign. You see, my father used to work for Baskania. 'Used to' being the key words. Baskania even took away his eye. Dad was the only one to ever quit service to Baskania and get away alive. He managed to get his eye back. One of these days I'm going to take him to Vulcan and see if he can reattach it."

Kilroy shrugged. "Allegiance? My allegiance is solely to my animals. I've learned my lesson and I stay away from the crazy power struggles that are going on. But I don't want you bringing any of that in here. This is a peaceful place—"

Kyron held a hand up. "We're as peaceful as they come. As long as you don't spread the word that we're here, we'd be grateful. I asked around about you before we called. I heard what had happened to you, and thought you might understand."

Kilroy considered this. "Baskania took advantage of you. Same happened to me. I'd be glad to help you out. You know anything about the type of creatures I keep here?"

"That's our specialty." Kyron glanced around the room. "Hey, Erec. Where's Bethany?"

At the mention of her name, Erec felt his stomach drop. Telling new people what had happened was like reliving it.

Jack saw Erec's expression and said, "She's been captured by Baskania. We're going off to save her."

Spartacus's eyes widened and he jumped to his feet. "What? That can't be. I remember that girl. Poor thing had such a nasty uncle taking care of her. Now this? What's wrong with that Shadow Prince? Can't he just leave people alone?"

Erec had forgotten that he wasn't going to tell Spartacus where they were going. "Don't say anything . . . okay? If they know we're coming—"

"Don't worry." Spartacus paced the room. "I won't breathe a word. I'm sick about this news. Really."

Kyron's face was clenched into a red knot. He informed Erec harshly, "I'm coming with you guys."

"You shouldn't, Kyron. But thanks." Erec looked around the room. "*None* of you should. It's walking into a pit of danger with no guarantee of getting out again, ever. You've fought enough awful things in your life, Kyron. You don't need to do this. Just settle down with your father, okay?"

Jam nodded. "Young sir is right. The two of you should let us handle this."

"Not possible." Kyron grasped the handle of a silver knife that hung from his leather belt. "Baskania has taken one thing from me after the next. Bethany is my friend, too. And after all you've done for us—well, I can't sit this one out."

Erec understood. "Thanks, Kyron. Thanks to all of you. Bethany would be so happy to know that this many people have volunteered to free her." He choked a laugh. "Actually she'd hate it. She doesn't even want me to face that danger. Oh, well. I'd feel the same way, I guess."

Artie had been staring at Erec as he talked, and he lifted up a shiny object dangling from a black ribbon around Erec's neck. "This here thing is pretty. Bethany was pretty too. Not like youse. Youse is nice, but not as pretty."

Erec was tempted to give the Doubler Charm pendant to Artie. He would probably appreciate it more than Erec did. Then again, Wandabelle had said that it might come in handy. Once he freed her—if he came back alive—it would be his gift to Artie.

Spartacus led them outside to the mynaraptor coop. A loud chatter slammed to a halt the minute they walked inside. Erec thought that they looked very intelligent, for ducklike creatures.

"Good job, guys!" Spartacus sounded like the coach of a kindergarten soccer team. "Right on the money! It's nice and quiet in here. Some of you have been listening really well. I can see there will be extra fish snacks tonight."

That promise was met by a chorus of suppressed cheers and squawks.

"Hey, you've all been great, and I'm so glad that you're staying here with me. Remember the day I told you that sometime someone may want to take one of you guys, for a pet?"

Several sharp beaks dropped in horror, and others put wings over their faces.

"No, it's not like that, guys. Nobody is taking you away forever. Okay? But one of you will get to go on a little adventure with my friends here. They need a smart bird who can teach them what to do with all of the strange creatures they're going to come across. And maybe fly them places if they need it. Is one of you up for an adventure?"

One of the birds raised a wing. "And where would we be going?"

Erec suddenly felt nervous. It had not occurred to him that the mynaraptor just might not want to go along with them. What creature in its right mind would *want* to go? But his father had said it was important to bring a mynaraptor. Erec held his breath, shuddering as he heard Spartacus's answer.

"Into Baskania's most highly guarded fortress in Jakarta, to rescue Erec's friend Bethany, who's a prisoner there."

Erec was sure that each of their heads would disappear completely under their wings, or even their nests. But, to his surprise, the birds began to jump in their nests, wings up with glee.

"Pick me! Pick me!"

"I want to go! I need a good story to tell!"

"No, me! Please! I'm the best there is at spilling all the details. Let me go!"

All of the birds wanted to go, not for the adventure itself, but for the vast amounts of storytelling they would get to do when they returned. It would give them a good reason for the others to listen to them talk.

The room grew noisy with chatter until Spartacus held up a hand. "Stop! I'm glad to see you are all willing to go. So I will choose the one of you that I think has earned it the most. Lalalalal, you were the first mynaraptor here, and you helped me train the rest to hold their tongues. You've been an exemplary model for the others. Would you like to take the trip with my friends?"

One of the birds fluttered from its nest onto the floor near Spartacus. "I would be honored." It bowed. "In fact, I was just saying the other day that this place has taught me some things that I had never even known existed before. Sheshesh here had been cut on a rock down by the stream, just a little cut, mind you, no blood, but enough to bother her. I hate any cuts, or any kind of pain, for that matter, but this time I noticed that—"

"Stop!" Spartacus held a hand up. The bird fell silent, but strutted proudly before the others. The others ignored him, either gazing up at the roof or completely turned so they were facing the wall.

Griffin cleared his throat. "Um, excuse me, cap'n?"

"Yes, Griffin?"

"May I please have the honor of carrying the bird on me shoulder?" He sounded both embarrassed and hopeful. "I once had a parrot. . . ."

Lalalalal sprung onto Griffin's shoulder and gripped it with long, ostrichlike claws.

Griffin petted its head as they walked out. "Good little birdie. I'll be takin' care of ye now."

Erec excused himself before they left for Jakarta. He had one more thing to do. It had been a while since he had used his dragon eyes to see into his future.

Before, he had asked to see something happy in his future, and he saw Danny and Sammy being crowned king and queen. He did have some control over his visions. This time he wanted to ask a darker question. One that, in fact, might change everything.

Tell me, he thought, *what will happen in Jakarta? Show me who will leave there, who gets out and who won't make it. Please, let me see us as we're escaping.*

Erec closed his eyes. He pictured the small, dark room in his head. After a few breaths he relaxed, shedding the stress he was feeling. The utter peacefulness in the room took him over. It was all good.

He knew where the next door was inside of the larger room he rested in. When he opened it, harmony and happiness filled him completely. This room was nearly pitch-black, and cozy. Two big windows in the front let in the slightest hint of light. These were his dragon eyes, he knew, his vision into his future. *Show me who lives, who escapes from Baskania's fortress in Jakarta.*

The box on the table held all of the answers. The warmth emanating from it gave him the strength he needed to see what he most

　　　　THE THREE FURIES

dreaded. Would Bethany be with him? Or would she be alone, with some of his friends, and Erec left behind or dead? He would save her, either way. But if a single one of his friends was not going to escape safely, he would not let them come.

When he touched the box, it pulsed with a reassuring beat that matched the beat of his own heart. He was ready now for whatever might lie ahead. The warm cord between the windows felt soft yet firm in his grasp as he pulled. The shades flew open.

Terror washed through him. Run! Escape! They had to get out of there. Fast.

It was hard to tell what was going on. So many people were running around him.

Chaos. Baskania was there.

Chaos. People running, shouting.

Erec pulled the cord and closed the shades as the vision faded to black. This would not do. His dragon eyes were showing him only what he wanted to see. He needed to slow down and really concentrate.

He put both hands on the warm box, willing it to give him the calmness inside to see what would really happen. Like a vacuum cleaner, it sucked his horror and fear out through his fingertips.

It was okay. He would escape from Baskania, then, wouldn't he? Or he would not have had the vision of running away with all of those people around him. Now he just had to see who else was there with him.

Slow, he thought. *Focus. Watch everything around you.*
He took a breath and pulled the cord again.

He was in an eyeglass shop. People were pouring out of the secret door in the back of the shop and running out the front door into the streets of Jakarta. The Port-O-Door was not far away. All they had to do was get safely around the corner and they would probably make it alive.

Bethany was a few feet in front of him. No, she was behind him. It was confusing. He was seeing her in different places, which didn't make sense. But the important thing was that she was escaping. Jam was there, and Griffin, Melody, Jack, and Kyron. They were all okay! He even spotted the mynaraptor clinging to Griffin's shoulder as he ran.

But where was Wolfboy? Heartache filled him. He knew that Wolfboy had been left behind.

Baskania was running, right behind Bethany! He was behind Erec, too. All over, somehow. How was he doing that? More people were everywhere, but it was hard to focus on those he wasn't looking for.

He had to get away, get out the door.

"There he is! There's Erec Rex. Get him!" A snakelike police officer wearing a tall stovepipe hat dove from behind the counter.

Erec's breath caught. There was no doubt what he saw, plain as day, before his eyes.

The officer sprang, flying through the air until he hit Erec's stomach. He slithered, wrapping himself around Erec's legs until they both tumbled, rolling, onto the floor.

Erec could see clearly, as if he was standing outside himself and watching the horrific events unfold. The officer opened his mouth wider than imaginable, long fangs poised over Erec's leg. In a flash, the snakelike thing bit, its jaws sinking deep into Erec's flesh.

Erec saw himself gasp and pass out. A few more police officers appeared, pulling Erec back through the hidden door.

"We've got him now, no worries," one of them said. "He's helpless. This one'll never escape again."

Erec had seen all that he needed. He pulled the cord and the shades closed over the windows. In a few moments he departed from the safety of the dark rooms and into what seemed like a harsh future.

Wolfboy, obviously, was not going to come with them. Erec would not have his faithful friend left behind in Baskania's fortress. He tried not to think about his own fate. At least Bethany would escape. And so would all of his friends. Unless something unforeseen happened, they would all get out unscathed.

As much as that relieved him, he was filled with fear. Going to Jakarta was like knowingly walking to the executioner's block. Bethany and his mother were right. How could he have expected to go that far into Baskania's territory and live? That had been ridiculous. No, he would be making an even trade. Him for her.

He could feel his shoulders shivering, and he tried to block out the terror he felt. Was there another way? Maybe if he didn't go along—if he let his friends go without him. He hesitated, hand on the doorknob, not ready to walk back into the room where everyone waited. Would they be able to read on his face that there would be big problems ahead?

No. He had to go back, one more time, and look through the dragon eyes. Could he see what would happen if he didn't go along with everyone else to Jakarta? Aoquesth, his dear dragon friend who gave Erec both of his own eyes and saved his life, had been able to picture alternate futures in his head. Erec had to try. . . .

I won't go along. I'll stay here with Spartacus. Jam, Jack, Melody, Kyron, and Griffin will go without me. Show me what will happen now. Show me their escape to freedom.

He closed his eyes and entered the familiar dark room. He would stay back, be safe. The door inside led into the darker room with the windows. They waited to show the new future, he could tell.

The box on the table was nearly buzzing with excitement. He rested a hand on it and felt a deep inner peace. Erec pulled the cord, and the shades flew up.

It was dark, quiet, and damp inside the cellar. A strange smell was in the air.

A bad feeling. Very bad.

They were too late. Bethany was dead.

Bodies piled near the wall. Jam, Griffin, Jack . . .

THE THREE FURIES

Erec pulled the cord and shut the shades. He didn't want to see more. He already knew.

If he did not go along, and trade his life for Bethany's, nobody else would return alive.

CHAPTER TWENTY-THREE
Windows to the Soul

"**Y**OUNG SIR. Is something wrong?"

Leave it to Jam to be the most perceptive . . . at least without Bethany there. She could read Erec like a book.

"No. I mean, I'm just worried. But I looked into the future with my dragon eyes. We all will get out safely except Wolfboy. Spartacus, could he possibly stay here with you until we get back? I think he'd really love it here."

"Of course!" Spartacus clapped and called Wolfboy over. "This guy will fit right in, won't you? And I know what you like to eat, don't I?"

Wolfboy jumped all over the friendly man, so much that he didn't notice when Jam took the dog food out of his backpack.

Erec was embarrassed that he was asking so much from Spartacus. "Can I give you some money to feed him while we're gone?"

Spartacus crossed his arms. "No way. He's my dog until you're back. I'll take care of him. No problem."

"Thank you." Erec bit his lip. "And if anything . . . were to happen to me, could he stay on here with you?"

"Of course! But you said you saw in the future that you'd all get back here okay." He raised an eyebrow.

"I did! But . . . just in case, I mean."

Jam looked sideways at Erec, but he didn't say anything. Luckily, nobody else seemed to notice Erec's black mood. So he forced a smile and said, "Let's go, guys! On to Jakarta. Hope Baskania's place isn't too hard to find!"

Spartacus Kilroy led the group through his house, patting Lalalalal on its head. "Remember, don't speak unless you're spoken to." He held a hand out, inviting them into his Port-O-Door. "I was pretty lucky to get this door—they're really expensive. But I guess that's one good thing about being an ex-AdviSeer. I still have a few connections. I don't know much about Upper Earth, but I've heard of Jakarta. It's supposed to be beautiful. A bustling city, and lots to do there."

Melody sighed. "Too bad we're not going for sightseeing."

Griffin pulled one of his sabers out and waved it in the air. The mynaraptor on his shoulder edged away from the blade flying by. "Speak for yerself, ye wench. I'm going to see the best sights of all. Me enemies' heads rolling at me feets."

"Watch out!" Melody lowered her eyebrows at Griffin. "You

nearly beheaded *me*. And don't call me wench, okay?"

Humbled, Griffin bowed. "Yes, ma'am. Mighty sorry, I am. I won't be nearly beheading you anymore, or any of you others. Pardon my witless—"

"That's enough!" Melody said, to shut him up. "Can we just find Jakarta and go?"

Jam scanned the map of Upper Earth in the Port-O-Door and tapped Indonesia, in Southeast Asia, about halfway between India and Australia. When the map of Indonesia popped up, Jack pointed at Jakarta on the northwest coast of Java, one of the country's many islands. Erec was glad that Jack and Jam were focused enough to find the cities. He was too nervous to concentrate at all.

This would have to change. He would need to focus if he was going to succeed. It was time to forget what his dragon eyes had shown him and move on. Who knew? Maybe they had been wrong.

Everyone eagerly scanned the map of Jakarta.

"Do we know where Baskania's fortress is?" Kyron asked.

Erec tried to remember what his father had told him. "I think you have to go through an eye care shop to get into the secret passage. . . ."

Everyone turned to stare at Erec.

Melody raised her eyebrows. "So, we're supposed to just walk the streets of this huge city and look for eye care shops? How many do you think there are in Jakarta? Are we supposed to just ask in each one, 'Hey, is this the passageway into the Shadow Prince's top secret fortress?' I'm sure we'll be guided right there."

Griffin sighed and filed a fingernail on his saber.

"That is one way you could get there," a voice rang from behind them.

The Hermit stood with an arm around Kilroy, as if he had been there all along. Kilroy turned to him in shock.

"But I would not recommend it. Asking around would be a one-way ticket into the worst part of Baskania's lair. I suppose your best shot is just to ask someone here who knows where it is." He paused dramatically. "Where would that person be? I don't know. Silly, silly me. None of you have been there. Who should we try?" He scanned the ceiling, then down along the floor as if a person who knew the answer might pop up at any minute.

"Do *you* know where it is?" Erec had a feeling that he did.

"Me? Little old me?" The Hermit giggled. "Let me ask. 'Hermit? Do you know where Baskania's hidden fortress is in Jakarta?' 'Why, yes! I do, Hermit!' 'Oh, really! That is wonderful. It's so good to have a wise, practical man like yourself among us, no?' 'Oh, you are too, too kind, Hermit. Truly a gentleman, you are.' 'No, it is *you* who are too kind. And smart, as well.' 'Why, thank you. Thank you for your sharp perception and unfailing wit.'" He wagged his eyebrows at the incredulous crowd gaping at him. "You all need to lighten up! Think of all the fun in store for you. What is challenge without appreciation? What is risk without daring? It's like eating meatloaf without chocolate sauce on top!"

Griffin responded with a loud "Yeah!" but the rest of the group was unmoved.

"All right, all right. You want answers, so answers I'll give. Look in south Jakarta on the map. You'll see an area called Kemang. Nice spot. Ritzy enough for the Prince of the Shadows. You may enjoy it so much there you won't want to come back." He giggled. "Okay, you've zoomed the map in to Kemang. Now find Jalan Kemang Raya. Jalan means street. You see it? Look where it crosses Jalan Bangka. Lots of nice stores and cafés there. Pretty art galleries. Near there, on Jalan Bangka, is a little store called Windows to the Soul—One Stop Eye Care Shop."

The name gave Erec a chill. Baskania was running an eye care shop in a nice section of Jakarta? How many people were going in to buy glasses and coming out with a glass eye?

"Ugh," Melody said, thinking the same thing.

"Oh, my." Jam worried his thumbs together nervously. "It doesn't sound like a safe place to shop."

The Hermit nodded. "Good thing you won't be buying. But be careful. You'll find an Identdetector around the front door. The clerk is supposed to check how important the store visitors are. Baskania would only want to take eyes from his most famous, wealthy, and powerful customers."

"An Identdetector?" Jack's eyes were wide. "That will show our true identity—and true appearance if we changed our looks. They'll know exactly who we are the minute we walk in. How will we sneak through into the fortress?"

The Hermit clicked his tongue. "That is a problem, isn't it? I do hope you work something out. It would be a shame for you to get caught and thrown in a prison cell before you even find the glasses."

"What glasses?" Kyron asked, confused. "It's an eye shop. Won't there be a lot of glasses there?"

"That's the point, isn't it?" The Hermit nodded at him as if Kyron had discovered something. "Many, many glasses. That makes it easy to hide the special pair, the ones that will let you find the secret door hidden in the shop."

"Hold on." Erec put his hands up. "One of the pairs of glasses will let us find the secret door? That sounds easy enough. If all of us try on glasses at the same time we can look through all of the ones in the store. One of us will find that pair and see the door soon enough, right?"

"Wrong." The Hermit beamed at Erec as if he had heartily agreed.

"Wrong? Why?"

"Ahh, do you think that Baskania would let people find his secret door so easily? That door is by invitation only." He wagged a finger at them. "You may only try on eyeglass frames one at a time. They are all behind the counter. The magic in the glasses that lets you see the door jumps from one pair to another. If you ask to see the frames that hold the power in them, it will move into another pair. Three times. So you have to pick the right four pairs of glasses in a row to get in. The clerk won't let you fish around—customers may try only four pairs on in this boutique. Of course, Baskania's special guests are told before they come which four pairs of glasses to ask for. The pattern changes every day. Not even the clerk knows which they are. Or where the door is—that changes too."

Griffin gnashed his teeth. "What if I just slash the place to smithereens? That invisible door will turn up soon enough then."

The Hermit crossed his arms and closed his eyes. "What will turn up then will be your head on a platter at Baskania's table. You would never find the door, but they would surely find you that way."

Melody grimaced at the thought. "But the clerk would have to know which pair the right glasses were, at least after someone else used them to find the passageway."

"No, no, no. Silly Melody Avery. Silly, silly girl. Silly head, full of fluff and music. After the right glasses are on, a customer can walk into the passage. But once the door shuts, the magic moves into a different pair of glasses, somewhere else, hidden again. So if the clerk doesn't follow you into the passageway, he won't be able to find it later."

"What if the clerk looks at the Identdetector after we go and sees that Erec Rex went through?" Kyron said.

The Hermit shrugged. "Maybe he will think you were asked to come. Bothering Baskania is not a mission he will do lightly, if he likes staying alive. But there are laws about reporting Erec Rex, too.

I suppose he would have to do that. It will be a hard choice for him—afraid to bother Baskania and afraid to not report Erec Rex."

Great, Erec thought. He'd be walking from a frying pan into an inferno—if he was lucky enough to figure out how to do it. "This seems impossible. I'm sure the store has tons of glasses. How am I supposed to ask for the right four pairs in a row? Baskania knew what he was doing—it's foolproof."

"Foolproof, yes," the Hermit agreed. "So do not attempt to go if you are a fool." One of his eyebrows shot high up on his bald head. "But, the real question is, is it dragon-proof?"

"Dragons!" Jack exclaimed. "We need to bring a dragon with us, right?"

Erec shook his head. Dragons were not allowed in Upper Earth. But that didn't bother him. He knew exactly what the Hermit was saying.

Jam set the Port-O-Door to wait for their return and wrote down Spartacus's code. It was hard finding a spot to put the door in the busy city. When they had zoomed the map in to Jalan Kemang Raya and Jalan Bangka, they discovered restaurants, nightclubs, art shops, and a few hotels, but everything was in clear view of people walking by. They finally agreed to put the Port-O-Door into the side of a luxury high-rise apartment condo farther down Jalan Kemang Raya, hoping it would look like a locked side entrance.

The time in Jakarta was only a few hours later than Alypium, so it was just after lunchtime, and the city was bustling. People walked into shops, and street vendors hawked their wares. The smell of their food carts was delicious. Erec, Jack, and Griffin eyed the bowls of meatball soup that one of the vendors was dishing up, and Melody was drawn to a dish called gado gado, which looked like peanut sauce on a salad with potatoes, eggs, and onions. Jam motioned them away, warning them about catching germs from street food.

"I know!" Melody spun around to face Erec. "Get your Serving Tray out. We'll stand around and block it so nobody sees, and you can ask it to give us the same things we see here, without the risk."

Erec produced lunches for everyone from the tray. Griffin approached eight different vendors to learn the names of what they sold, and he proceeded to put away more food than Erec had ever seen anyone eat, feeding some of it to Lalalalal, who liked most of the same things that Griffin did.

After they all agreed Indonesian food was delicious, they bubbled with excitement about their journey, but Erec's heart sunk. His only real hope was to keep his Serving Tray in whatever dungeon he ended up in. But what were the odds of that? Chances were he wouldn't end up in a dungeon at all after he was captured, like he saw in his vision. He'd be long gone. No, he should give the tray to someone else so it wouldn't go to waste.

Erec held out the Serving Tray. "Here, Jam. Why don't you hang onto this? I'm tired of carrying it. Okay?"

Jam put it into his own backpack, but eyed Erec suspiciously. "Young sir, are you sure you're feeling all right?"

Erec nodded. He tried to concentrate on the sights and sounds of Jakarta to distract himself from his awful fate. People stared at them as they walked by. Erec supposed three adults—dressed like a butler, a pirate with a bizarre duck on his shoulder, and a leather-clad wilderness hunter—might attract attention anywhere.

"This place is great." Melody looked around admiringly.

Griffin sighed and rubbed his stomach. "Aye, me lady. 'Tis a fine sight for sore eyes used to the Nightmare Realm."

Nightmare Realm! Erec stopped in his tracks. What would happen to Wandabelle when he was gone? Once he was caught by the snakelike officer and delivered to his enemy, who would save the Clown Fairy? He sighed and started walking again.

"You okay?" Jack asked, concerned.

"Yeah." Erec forced a smile. "Just thought I forgot something, but I didn't."

Jack shrugged and walked on, but Jam tapped his shoulder and whispered, "Young sir, I think I know what is going on. You spotted a problem when you looked into the future, didn't you? You've been acting funny ever since. I think you should stay out here and wait for us to bring Bethany back. Would you do that? *Please*, sir."

"No, Jam. Thanks . . . but that won't help anyway." Jam's face dropped. "Hey, Jam. It'll be okay. Really. I'm just a little nervous, that's all."

The butler let the point go. "Yes, sir. Or, I should say, sire. One of these days you'll be a great king, you know."

"Thanks, Jam." Erec did not have the heart to tell Jam that one of these days, very soon, he would be gone forever.

When they turned the corner on Jalan Bangka, Erec spotted a small sign in a neatly manicured lawn that read WINDOWS TO THE SOUL— ONE STOP EYE CARE SHOP. The small building was so quaint and pleasant he couldn't believe it was a portal to a terrifying fortress.

Kyron felt the same way. "Could this be it? It looks too . . ."

"Nice?" Melody said. "This shop is so sweet. Look at the flowers on the windowsills and the painted shutters."

"What I don't understand," Jack said, "is that there is no room for a fortress on this street at all. Do you think it all could be under-ground?"

"Hey, guys." Erec kept his voice hushed. "Don't forget there's an Identdetector on the door. We need to keep the clerk from seeing who I am, okay? Say my name is . . ."

"Rick Ross." Jack nodded. "The name worked well before. Might as well use it again."

"Good idea. And also, should we say we're with a traveling circus? I mean, if someone asks. The way we look might make people wonder."

Jam approved. "Good thinking, young sir."

They slowly filed into the shop. Erec checked the door frame as he walked in. A tube ran along the wall surrounding the door, glowing like a faint blue neon light. A small line extended from its side toward what looked like a fax machine. Paper spat onto the back counter each time someone walked through.

Without question, Erec's name was in the stack of papers. If the clerk saw it now, he would never have a chance to try on the glasses and find the hidden door. It would all be a matter of timing.

Which made him think. He could change the future, couldn't he? Maybe he could distract the clerk so that he would never find out who he was. If the clerk didn't know, then he wouldn't call for that awful police-snake thing, and on the way out Erec would never get bitten.

He stood straighter. What a great idea! He just had to be clever. This clerk wasn't expecting him to show up here. If he played his cards right, then he just might save his own life.

Looking around the shop was like déjà vu. The place was exactly as Erec had seen in his vision—except without people running all over. This was it. This was where he would either live or die.

Rows of eyeglasses lined the shelves behind the counter. The shop was decorated with framed needlepoint sayings. "Seeing is believing" and "Sleep with one eye open" were strange enough, but "See yourself through someone else's eyes" and "Go ahead, cry your eyes out" gave Erec the chills.

"May I help you?" The clerk—a man of average height, medium

brown hair, middling body size, and standard features—could have blended into any crowd. Even alone behind the counter he seemed to fade behind his own glasses into the rows of eyeglass frames behind him. The man glanced toward the stack of papers near the door.

In a quick move to distract him, Erec blurted, "*Hey!* We're all here, visiting in Jakarta. You having a good day here? Seems awful nice outside."

The clerk looked at him quizzically, and his friends stared as if he'd gone crazy. Erec didn't care. If only he could grab those papers away, he just might survive. If Jam had a match, maybe he could burn them.

The clerk smiled patiently. "Are you in need of a checkup? We highly recommend it here. You never know what eye disease you might be carrying."

Kyron pointed in shock at a display case full of eyes, made of glass, all peering out at him. "What are these for?"

"Those are top of the line. Nowadays so many people come down with eye problems that can only be solved by replacements. You would be surprised. Take a look around while I catch up on my paperwork." He moved down the counter toward the stack.

"*No!* I mean, please. I'm ready to try on frames now. Can you show me some?"

"Well." The clerk frowned as if he were deciding. "I usually like to do the exam first. It's quite important, you see. That will help me decide which frames would work best for you." He jiggled the glasses on his face and squinted at Erec. "You look familiar, young man. Have I seen you in here before?"

"N-no. I just have one of those faces." Erec forced a laugh. "People say that to me *all* the time. *Look!*" he shouted as the clerk took another step toward the stack of papers. "I really just came in here to try frames on. My eyes are perfect. I just had them checked."

"Yes, but where?" The clerk held a finger aloft. "Other eye centers don't have our expertise, our equipment. You wouldn't want to be walking around with harmful glasses, would you?" He took another step toward the papers.

"Okay—okay! Wait! I'll tell you what. If you let me try on frames first, then we'll all get eye exams. We won't let you do it any other way. That's it."

The clerk was very surprised. "You'll all get exams? They are free, of course."

Erec's friends didn't know what he was doing, but they all nodded.

"I better not lose an eye in this deal," Melody murmured in Erec's ear.

The clerk walked back and crossed his arms. "Well, son? Which would you like to see first?"

"Hmm. Jam? What do you think?" He waved for Jam to come closer, then whispered to him, "See if you can steal those papers. Light fire to them. Anything. Just get rid of them." He nodded at the stack by the door.

Jam strolled toward that part of the room while Erec looked at the frames. "Let me see . . ." He closed his eyes and brought his dragon eyes forward. The Hermit had suggested that finding the hidden passage was foolproof, but not dragon-proof. He better be right, Erec thought.

He squinted to hide his glowing green dragon eyes and put a hand over them like a visor, then he surveyed all of the frames again. The whole room appeared green. Lacy white netting, the Substance that carried all the world's magic, hung in the air. The eyeglass frames all looked dull and uniform. Nothing stood out.

Erec began to panic. What if this method didn't work? They would never get into the fortress. But then he saw a glimmer in the last pair of glasses in the bottom row on the right. It wasn't really a full sparkle, more like a hint of a thought of a sparkle.

"That one." He bent down. "The last pair on the right." He closed his eyes and let his normal blue eyes return.

"This?" The clerk laughed, picking up a pair of bright red, elongated women's cat eye frames. "You really want to see these?"

Erec shrugged, tried them on—to the great amusement of his friends—and handed them back.

The clerk was annoyed. "If you're all in here for a joke, you can just go now. I have serious work to do."

"No, I'm sorry. It's just—I'm looking for *special* frames, if you know what I mean."

The clerk raised an eyebrow. "Special frames, then? Well . . . all right." He frowned, searching Erec's face. "What is your name? You look very familiar."

"It's Rick. Rick Ross."

Erec closed his eyes, brought his dragon eyes forward again, and squinted to hide them. "Those. Up on top now. Top row, third from the left."

The clerk handed him a pair of nondescript metal frames. Erec put them on, then took them off without even looking at himself in the mirror. "No. You can put these back."

Jam came as close as he could to the papers, but they were lying on the back counter, out of his reach. Something long and gray stretched out of his sleeve, slowly making its way to the counter where the papers sat. *Please*, Erec thought, *please get the papers. Save my life, Jam!*

The clerk began to look where Erec was staring, so Erec jumped and shouted to catch his attention. "Look at me! I'm going to get glasses, everyone! Yeah!"

Now everyone was sure Erec had gone off the deep end.

"Wait." The clerk snapped his fingers. "I know where I've seen you. It was on a notice, somewhere. I'm sure. Did you win an award through The Corporation?"

"No, that was probably one of my look-alikes."

Erec shut his eyes and twisted them back until his dragon eyes were forward again. A pair of thin wire-rim granny glasses had the sparkle now. "Those, please. Right in the middle. Next to that pair. The tiny ones."

The clerk handed the glasses to Erec with growing interest. "Are you here for a *reason*, boy? I guess I'll know soon enough. Hmm. You do look very familiar."

Jam was stamping on something by the door. With a glance Erec saw a flash of light snuffed out under his feet, and a pile of ash. The papers were gone.

Jam had done it! Now the clerk would not know who he was, and he would not call for that terrible snake thing to come bite him when he left, capturing him forever!

He was free!

Erec shot a huge grin at Jam, who nodded back. A huge weight melted off Erec's shoulders. He felt like he could stand straight for the first time since he had seen into his future.

He swiveled his eyes again and found the final sparkling pair of glasses. "That one." He could hear the confidence in his own voice. "The brown-and-black plastic ones near the end."

"Horn-rimmed tortoise shell? I wouldn't have picked it for you." The clerk handed the frames to him, stroking his chin in thought. "Where have I seen you?" He looked at the back counter and became alarmed. "Where did my papers go?" Confused, the clerk strode to the back desk. "They were right here. I saw them. Did you take them?" He asked Jam accusingly.

Erec slipped the glasses on. He felt a funny tingle on his face. The room grew dark before his eyes, as if a rain cloud had drifted into the shop and plopped down to stay. He could not even see his friends through the gray mist.

He could not see, but he could hear quite well. The clerk was shouting, "Who took my papers? You're all going to have to walk in and out of here again. What are you, a bunch of crooks?"

Something bright, almost blinding, glowed when Erec turned around. A door. That was it, he was sure.

"That's *it*!" the clerk shouted. "You *are* crooks! *That's* where I've seen you. I knew it! You're Erec Rex, aren't you? Look, I have a notice right under the counter here, with your picture on it. This is you, all right. I'm calling the police right now, you hear me? That's the law around here. You're highly wanted, you . . . villain!"

Erec stumbled toward the glowing doorway, tripping over unknown objects on his way.

"Don't think you can get away from me. I'll have the cops here in no time. You won't get far."

Erec's hand grasped an icy knob and he twisted, yanked.

A freezing black wind blew through the doorway and into the shop, throwing him back. He perched the glasses up on his head, and the room came back into view. A door, made out of a thin part of the back wall, led into a dark hallway.

"Let's go!" He waved for everyone to go inside.

"Wait! Um . . . uh . . . were you invited here?" the clerk asked, confused. Erec's friends poured through the doorway, ignoring him. "Well, you must have been told to come, or you would never have known which glasses to pick. But I'll be watching for you. This is the only way back out, unless Baskania sends you somewhere himself. I'll have police ready, you hear me! I'm not going to let Erec Rex past me, you hear?"

The door slammed shut behind Erec, who was the last to go through, drowning out the clerk's threats.

CHAPTER TWENTY-FOUR
Lalalalal's Flight

EREC WAS GLAD that the hallway was long and dark, so nobody could see his face. He was sure it was twisted in fear, and he could feel his chin trembling.

So, that was it, then. He would die, after all. He had been so sure that Jam had fixed things, that he had been clever enough to change his fate. But the clerk was calling the snakelike police officer this very moment, probably. He would be there, waiting, just as Erec had seen in his vision. Erec couldn't escape his fate now.

The image of what he had seen popped into his head again. Everyone was running around in chaos. He couldn't avoid one particular spot, or try to be somewhere different to stay away from that snake thing. It seemed to fly through the air right toward him.

"Young sir?" Jam was walking next to him. "You seem upset again."

Erec shrugged, keeping his face turned away.

"That was the problem, wasn't it?" Jam asked. "A police officer will be waiting for you on the way out, won't he?"

Erec gurgled, "Mmm-hmm." A huge lump filled his throat, making it hard to speak.

Jam's hand patted his back. "Young sir, I will stand between you and any police officer in that room."

"No!" Erec found his voice. "It—he will get me either way. You need to stay away. Because . . . Jam?"

"Yes, sire?" Jam whispered.

"I need you and Griffin to go back to the Nightmare Realm and rescue Wandabelle for me. Would you do that?"

"Aye, aye, cap'n! At yer service." Griffin's voice boomed in the narrow hallway. Erec suddenly realized that the whole group had been listening to everything he had said.

"I don't understand," Jack said. "You're going to get caught on the way back? You saw that—and you're still coming with us?"

"I have to," he said simply. "It's the only way to save her. It wouldn't work if you went without me. I checked."

They walked a ways in silence, thinking about the sacrifice Erec was making.

"What if you waited here?" Melody asked. "Maybe that would work."

"No." Kyron patted Erec on the back. "It's too late, Melody. He might as well help us for this part. That's not the problem. It's when he goes back out again. But I'll fight for you, Erec. I battled a manticore every night for most of my life. Nobody else could do that and survive. I can fight a police officer. No problem."

That seemed to make everyone else feel better, so Erec didn't say anything more to upset them. Unfortunately, he had seen what would happen with his own eyes. The room would be far too crowded and confused for Kyron to stop the snake thing before it bit him. Then it would all be too late.

Light appeared at the end of the long hallway. They filed ahead, then came upon a narrow beach. Somehow they were outside now. They had entered a different world, far from the little shop in Jakarta. The sun was setting over the water, its light dancing on the ripples of the waves.

"Look!" Melody pointed over the water. A gigantic castle stretched across an entire island. Sharp black spires raked the sky like angry spikes, and lonely turrets spun into the air—perfect places for lost princesses and bearded prisoners.

"It looks like it's moving," Jack said.

In fact, it did. Tall gates encircled the castle, and they were swarming, it seemed. As Erec's eyes adjusted, he could see that it wasn't the gates themselves that were moving, but huge creatures in front of them.

"It's the guards," Jam whispered. "Ferocious beasts. All the worst types."

Kyron pulled his sword out and Griffin swung several sabers around.

"How do we even get there?" Jack asked, his voice filled with dread.

"Swim, I guess?" Kyron tested the water with his foot. Earsplitting screams filled the air and the ground shook. The water filled with small ball-like waves that raced toward them, all aimed at Kyron's foot. He yanked it out of the water just before a slew of skeleton fish with long, sharp teeth jumped into the air, snapping their jaws with frightening clicks. The fish fell back in the water, springing up again and again, but were unable to climb onto land.

Kyron panted, backing away from the shore. "What *were* those things?"

"Phantom barracudas," Griffin growled. "I haven't seen 'em since the old, old days, before I was a prisoner of the Nightmare King. They're only found in the dead of night, in the deepest parts of the blue sea. They rise over the graves of the pirate ships of old, which have sunk into the deep for all eternity. Nasty varmin, they are. Eat yer flesh right off yer bones, and chew through yer skeleton fer dessert."

"I guess swimming is out," Kyron said. "Any other . . . uh, ideas? We must be able to cross, if Baskania invites people in this way."

"Unless he picks them up personally," Erec said. "Maybe it's another way to keep people out."

"Hard to think he'd spend his precious time transporting people around," Kyron answered. "I don't think of him as a gracious host."

"Look at that thing over there." Melody pointed at a tall stand that jutted high into the air on the other shore. "Is that a . . ."

"It's a bridge!" Kyron said. "They must lower it when they're expecting someone. I bet it grows longer to stretch out this far. Little good it's going to do us from over here."

The mynaraptor on Griffin's shoulder was making a funny, muted squeal. Erec realized that it badly wanted to speak and was holding its tongue by their orders.

"Yes, Lalalalal? You want to say something?"

"Aaaaah." Lalalalal sighed in relief. "This reminds me of the time when I was in my nest at home, and I was talking to Huhuhuhuhuhu about the terrible weather we'd been having. She was so caught up in the details of the last storm that I couldn't get a word in edgewise! Can you imagine! It was dreadful having to sit there, waiting and waiting. Of course I had to say a few things when she was going on or I would have gone insane. I'll never forget that storm, by the way. It was a bit unusual, and I notice this type of thing about the weather, believe me. There was a certain pink-and-orange haze to the clouds as they darkened, and it made me wonder how—"

"Enough! Stop it!" Erec patted the bird's head. "Please, Lala—just tell us what you need to about this place."

Lalalalal looked annoyed. "You did bring me along for a reason, right?"

"Of course. To tell us about the creatures we run into. Quickly and quietly, right?"

"And . . . ?"

Erec was stumped. But Melody shouted, "To fly us places! Lala can grow big and fly us over the water, right?"

The bird nodded.

"Perfect," Erec said. "Now we just need to come up with a plan."

Devising a plan to avoid the hordes of nasty creatures awaiting them was much harder than they thought. They did not know who and what guarded the fortress. They decided to cross the water when it was dark, to avoid attention. Jack suggested going first, as it was his gift to understand animals. "I'll spy on them a while and let you know what they're up to."

Lalalalal was making loud choking noises, and the bird's eyes looked about to pop out of its head.

"Um, cap'n?" Griffin said. "Methinks the bird may have something to say."

"Yes, Lala?" Erec said. "Do you have an idea?"

The bird sighed with relief, stretching one claw, then another into the air from Griffin's shoulder. "Yes." It spoke slowly, with concentration, to keep on track. "Why don't I fly over first? With my small size nobody should notice me. I'll dip down to scout out the creatures, then find a good place to land when I bring all of you. Best we travel as quickly as possible."

Everyone agreed that was a good idea. Lalalalal sprang from Griffin's shoulder. The bird's broad wings became a blur as it rose into the evening sky. Soon it had flown out of sight.

After several rounds of passing the Serving Tray, after which Griffin took a short nap, Lalalalal returned. The mynaraptor settled onto Griffin's shoulder contentedly, looking at each of the travelers in anticipation.

The bird conspicuously waited to be asked what it saw, cocking its head to point out how its orders to stay quiet were ridiculous. Then it settled into a comfortable squat, leaned against Griffin's head, and fluffed its feathers.

"Aaaah, let's see," it said. "So much to tell. So much to talk about." It was very pleased, finally having the audience it had always dreamed of. "You know, I always say that creatures, birds especially, are only as good as the stories they have to tell, the things they have seen. My life has been interesting, mind you. I have had many experiences that would likely blow the wind out of your sail. Now, maybe my friend Griffin, here, could rival me a bit. But let me tell you something. Life is an adventure. Lived right, it will be a source of endless delights—"

Lalalalal paused, gazing in delight at the rapt attention that was paid to it. "I was born a very small bird, and penniless. My parents were quite wealthy, but frankly I was too small to hold even a farthing of it in my own claws. I spent quite a while that way, you see, which makes me rather understanding to the situation of the poorer birds I come across. Which reminds me of the time I met a beggar in a pumpkin field in Otherness. It was a human beggar, not a bird, which made the situation even worse I thought—"

"*Stop!*" Erec held a hand up. Lalalalal's beak snapped shut, and it lifted its jaw in protest. "Lala, can you please just tell us what you saw across the water?"

The bird sulked a minute, then said, "Am I allowed more than three words to answer?"

"Yes, of course. If you could just talk about what's waiting for us at the fortress, we'd appreciate it."

Lalalalal picked a loose feather out of its wing with its beak, then assumed an important air. "Well, all right. I'll skip ahead then, past the years of my childhood, on through my encounters with all types of sorcerers and fools, and even gloss over the great wisdom imparted upon my during my teachings by the great—"

"*Lala!*" Melody exclaimed. "Get to the point!"

Lalalalal must have decided that Melody was not to be messed with. It sighed. "Okay. First I flew around the castle. Nasty-looking creation, it is. The water goes completely around it, like a huge moat surrounding the island. Would be impossible to reach without flying. I'm sure those phantom piranhas would chew through a boat in seconds.

"After circling a few times, I perched in different spots to get a good look. The only entrance that I could find is right in front, facing us here. I guess that's not surprising, given Baskania would want to keep it hard to get inside or out again. The entire perimeter of the castle is surrounded by a horrid assortment of creatures, both living and dead. Really there were no deserted spots at all, although most of the nasty things were toward the front, around the door."

Melody's voice trembled. "What do you mean—living and *dead*?"

"Now, now," the mynaraptor said crossly. "Make up your mind.

Do you want me to tell you what I saw, in a logical order? Or do you want me to relate things my way, and make a good story of it? Because that would be a lot better, you know. It reminds me of what my old Uncle Jamesjamesjames once said. It takes more patience to whittle a flute from a stick than to use it as a bat. Which is rather a funny saying for mynaraptors, as we can't quite whittle sticks, now, can we? Or play flutes. But the idea is—"

"*Stop!*" Erec was trying to be patient. "Okay, if you could please continue, as you were before, and tell us everything you saw. I think you just started to talk about the island full of awful creatures over there. Was there any place that seemed safe for us to land?"

"*Ahem!*" The bird took a deep breath. "The largest part of the sickening crowd of evil beings on the island were in front, guarding the only entrance. But a good number wandered around the castle, some singly but mostly in groups. There were no windows on the lower floors either, likely to keep anyone from breaking inside, or moreso, escaping. The walls were made of a thick stone. From the windows higher up I could see that the stone was more than a foot deep. The sloped roofs were also made of stone. It was hard to place the type. The look was similar to slate, but it was colder and slippery.

"As far as the guards and creatures on the lookout there . . ." Lalalalal paused, enjoying everyone's baited breath. "Not a happy story, I'm afraid."

Erec noticed that the mynaraptor seemed quite happy. Was it really fearless, or were the creatures they would face be worth all the stories it could then tell about them later? It probably wouldn't face the kind of danger they would, anyway, as it could simply fly away at any time.

Lalalalal fluffed itself and shuffled a bit, flexing its horned legs. "Ah, yes. The creatures. An ugly lot, they are. Many different types, too. Looks like Baskania is a big fan of the undead when it comes to guarding his place. Not a dumb move, actually. Can't quite kill 'em. Lots of Vetalas down there. Don't want to get mixed up with that sort. I spotted zombies, too, but it looks like the Vetalas are in charge of 'em. There are specters flying all over the place. I didn't see those at first, you know, they're kind of see-through, like white winds. And there were some spirit warriors, too. Saw one shadow demon—probably more down there, though. You know what they say, when you got one shadow demon you've got a hundred.

"On top of that, hoards of minotaurs were running around wild, and some manticores, werewolves, and wenwolves." He chuckled. "I even spied a few lions and tigers roaming through, but they looked more creeped-out by the other things than truly ferocious, if you ask me. They kind of kept to themselves."

Erec's spirits plummeted, and the rest of the group looked as defeated as he did. The only creatures that didn't worry him were the shadow demons. He had faced one before and learned a big lesson from it. They got into peoples' minds and twisted their thinking, and if you started to believe them they would devour you. Walking through them would make them disappear. And maybe Kyron could defend them from a manticore, or a lion. But a tribe of lions? And what about all of those other undead things?

Lalalalal yawned, holding a feather over his sharp beak. "Oh, let's see, what else . . . ? The plant life wasn't too spectacular. There were some scrawny trees, not much else. Not that I saw any plant-eaters. No, those were all vicious meat-eaters. At least the ones that ate at all—"

"That's enough!" Melody shouted. "I think we get the idea. Erec, are you sure the Fates said we could rescue Bethany? Cuz it's not sounding too good."

He nodded, overwhelmed.

"What are minotaurs and manticores?" she asked, voice shaky.

Kyron whispered, "My father and I had a manticore chasing

us every night of our lives. They are relatives of the sphinx. Look like lions, only a lot bigger. They have huge mouths with long, sharp teeth, and their face looks kinda human. Their tails are spiny and spiked, and they use them like a club. But I can handle them . . . don't worry." Kyron's voice didn't sound as sure as his boast.

Plus, Erec wondered how many manticores Kyron could handle at once. He took a breath, tried to get a grip. "Do you remember the MONSTER race? There was a fake minotaur in it, and a real one showed up later in the party. They have the head and body of a bull, and their lower half is like a human giant. Minotaurs are nasty, but I took that one out—luckily I got a cloudy thought that told me to stab it in the eye with a glass shard. Sounds awful, but it was the only way. . . ." He shuddered at the memory. Was Baskania's fortress really filled with evil spirits like this? They would be crazy to walk into this place. "I know what. Maybe we could break a window up high to get inside."

Lalalalal shook his head. "Nope. I flew into a few to check that out for you—you can thank me for that one. Not pleasant, I'll let you know—and did that 'dumb bird flying into a window' bit. You'd be surprised how many times that's not a mistake. Birds like to see if they can get in and nip a few valuables. But those windows are extra strong. Magic strong. You'll never break in or out that way."

There went their only chance, Erec thought. Should they just land and see what would happen for Bethany's sake? "Hey, guys. This is way too risky. I'm going to go alone. You can all wait here for me. Sound okay?"

"Not a chance, cap'n," Griffin growled. "I'm at yer side the whole way. Made a promise to yer mother, I did. So don't ask again."

Backing him up, Kyron held out his sword. "We're in this together. I'm not afraid of the creatures there—at least not the ones I've heard of."

Jam's voice was more faint. "As always, I'm sticking with you, young sir. But I think we should look at this logically. There are certain . . . enemies that may not be a problem for you, Erec. The ghosts, for example. Ghosts cannot harm you, isn't that correct? And your Amulet of Virtues should shield you as well."

"True." Erec had found out that ghosts could not hurt him. They could not even touch him. This had something to do with his lineage, his mother had said. "But how many of those undead things are ghosts?"

"The specters and spirit warriors are ghosts," Jam said. "Spirit warriors are more of the plain variety, they come from humans who have passed on. They would probably be people that Baskania had killed in the past, and now he's keeping them on as part of his army. Specters are a nastier sort. Pure evil, and vicious, I'm afraid. Like a spirit gone wrong. But the shadow demons are not ghosts. I don't know about the Vetalas and zombies. . . ."

Lalalalal was clearing its throat loudly.

"Yes, Lala?"

It sighed. "They're not ghosts, either of 'em. A zombie is a dead body that has been activated back into life. Those things have no soul, and they're not the brightest either. That's why the Vetalas tell them what to do. Vetalas occupy the bodies of the dead, but they're something else altogether."

"Wait a minute!" Erec rooted through his backpack and found the clump of wolfsbane he had brought with him. "This will protect us from the wenwolves. My dog, Wolfboy, is a wenwolf—he turns into a huge wolf when there is a full moon. And it should keep the werewolves away too." Seeing the others look more hopeful, he went on. "The shadow demons can't hurt us if we walk right through them. Believe me, it's not as easy as it sounds. But I know I can do that. Once you all see me, you'll be past its control. Kyron and Griffin could probably handle the manticores, lions, tigers, and minotaurs. And the specters and spirit warriors can't bother me—but might hurt you all. What does that leave?"

"The Vetalas and the zombies." Jack sounded excited. "That's it."

"Doesn't sound quite as bad now," Melody agreed.

"Lalalalal?" Jam said. "Do you know any way to get past Vetalas or zombies?"

"Of course I do. But I'm afraid it won't be easy. You see, laughter will stop the Vetalas in their tracks. If you're truly fearless, and laugh at them, they will shy away from you. But it has to be true laughter, not forced. If you're not really laughing from the heart, the thing will close in for the kill."

"That's it?" Jack grinned. "No problem at all! Now that I know I only have to laugh, it'll be easy for me."

"No, it won't," Erec said. "Lala's right. I thought it would be a cinch to walk right through the shadow demon, because I knew in advance about it. Those things control your mind. If you have to be completely fearless to laugh, then none of us will be able to. They'll scare us to death, and our laughs won't be real enough, and we'll die."

Kyron shrugged. "At least we can try, right? I guess if even one of us can do it, that might throw them off."

"What about the zombies?" Erec asked. "What will stop them?"

"Oh, nothing," Lalalalal said. "Once they get going they just follow directions until they've done what they're told. They'll never quit trying."

"So," Jack said thoughtfully, "if one of us was able to laugh before the Vetalas told the zombies to kill us, we might survive? That is, if the specters and spirit warriors don't get us?"

The thought sounded so ridiculous that Erec almost laughed right then.

"Good thing you brought that wolfsbane," Jack said. "What other things did you take with you?"

Erec dug through his backpack. "Here's the wolfsbane." He pulled it out. "And this"—he grabbed a vial—"is the most important thing. Dragon's blood, to free Bethany from the Draw spell she's under."

Everyone stared at the vial in shock. Erec knew it sounded disgusting, but after all they had just heard he was surprised at their reaction to the vial.

Until he looked at his hand. It was empty.

He gasped. Now what would they do? This was the only way to rescue her! Where did the blood go? The outside of the vial looked clean enough.

Then he saw a label on the side of the vial. It read LAUGHTER.

"What?" His jaw dropped. He had completely forgotten. This was the vial of laughter he grabbed from Hecate Jekyll's storeroom. He dropped it into his lap and rooted through his backpack. "Here it is!" The vial of dragon blood was still full.

"You scared me, Erec," Melody said.

"Tell me about it. That's about all I brought, except this MagicLight, a little money, and this . . ." He took out a glass jar. "Nitrowisherine! This is an explosive, but when you set it off it grants you a wish. Well, it works most of the time, anyway. I already tried wishing to rescue Bethany and it didn't work. So this may help or not."

Jam pulled more items out of his backpack than Erec could believe fit into it, including snacks, remedies, tools, and things he couldn't identify. "I'm not sure if any of this will be of use. But if anyone needs a bandage or towel please let me know."

Erec held the laughter vial a while as he put his things away. "Do you suppose . . . Wait a minute. This could be just what we need."

Jack stared at it. "An empty vial?"

"It's laughter. A vial of pure laughter."

There was a silence, then everyone started talking at once.

"Perfect, Erec!" Melody gave him a hug. "We'll use it on the Vetalas! If they hear the laughter before they give orders to the zombies, we're home free!"

Erec thought they would be far from home free. But at least it was a place to start.

CHAPTER TWENTY-FIVE
Mind Reader Extraordinaire

THE MOON WAS high when Lalalal grew to full size on the beach. With a little struggling and a hand from Griffin, all six of them climbed onto the mynaraptor's back. Erec held the vial of laughter in one hand, and each of them carried some of the wolfsbane.

The mynaraptor made a strange noise that sounded like an engine starting and stopping, again and again.

"What's that?" Erec asked. "It sounds like it's out of gas."

"Methinks the thing is clearing its throat, cap'n. Maybe it has something it wants to say."

"Lala? You want to talk? Get straight to the point, okay?"

Lalalalal's voice was louder and fuller now that it was bigger. "I have a suggestion for you all. Unless you're all counting on landing in the middle of those beasts, you might want me to alight directly on a low roof I saw. It's dark enough that if we come around from the back, maybe none of them will notice us. Too bad you don't have any music with you. That would help calm some of the animals down, help a little."

"I can make music," Melody volunteered. "It's my gift from birth." She slid two fingers together and a light, lovely melody drifted into the air.

"Perfect," Erec said, then rushed to add, "but we can live without it if you decide to get off here and wait. It's your last chance, everyone."

"I'm coming, Erec. I have a good feeling about this. The Fates said we can do it, so let's go!"

They lifted into the air, bouncing higher with each beat of Lalalalal's huge wings until they blurred in a whir of motion. Erec, sitting in front, grabbed a handful of huge feathers to hang on to. Someone screamed behind him as they soared toward the moon— he was pretty sure it was Griffin. Riding so high was terrifying, with much less to hold on to than riding a dragon, but also amazingly beautiful, to watch the stars disappear and reappear as they rose through the clouds. Ripples of light danced on the black water beneath them. Erec tried not to think what would happen if one of them slipped and fell in.

Baskania's fortress really did look like a rogue castle gone bad, complete with black iron spikes on the turrets, carved images of terrifying creatures, and crooked Gothic peaks. Even the towers had towers jutting out of them, all of them pointed and foreboding.

As they closed in, masses of beings became visible outside. They looked terrifying even from a distance.

Lalalalal swerved in from the back, dropping straight down out of a low cloud onto a flat section of roof close to the ground. The bird skidded a bit, then stopped so fast that all of them tumbled, hanging on by handfuls of feathers.

As soon as they dropped onto the roof, Lalalalal shifted back to its small size and perched on Griffin's shoulder. From their vantage point, they could see the creatures below, some drifting aimlessly and others walking in groups. Sickly gray human-shaped beasts marched in rows around the huge building in an endless parade.

"Those must be the zombies," Jack whispered.

"Maybe we should stay up here awhile and get our bearings," Jam said.

"I don't think so," Erec said. "Even if the other things can't see us, the shadow demons will know we're here soon."

"But you said you could walk through them," Kyron said. "Then they can't hurt us."

"Yes. The shadow demons might not hurt us, but they will warn everyone else that we're here. I think we better catch them unprepared."

They all lay side by side, peeking over the edge of the roof. The sight was truly horrifying. Up close, the zombie troops were the worst sight Erec had ever laid eyes on. Flesh hung off of their half-exposed skeletons, and sharp fangs jutted from their bloodred mouths. But worst of all were their eyes, which glowed bone-white, with no iris or pupils at all. They made a loud hiss as they marched by, but did not speak.

Even the manticores and minotaurs, both of which would attack anything that moved, stayed clear of the zombies. When one of them did drift too close, however, a buzz of activity erupted. The victim disappeared fast as the zombies clustered around it, ravenously ripping it apart with their fangs and claws.

Nobody made a sound, but Erec was pretty sure they all were wondering where the Vetalas were. The spirit warriors were easy to identify as the translucent human-shaped beings roaming around with real rifles in their grasp. And the glowing white things whipping through the air like see-through sheets in the wind were likely the specters.

Suddenly, Erec heard voices from below.

"Something is wrong, Master Vetu." The voice echoed deep and clear. "I can sense it, but I don't know yet what it is. Maybe the Shadow Prince needs us."

The voice that responded sounded exactly the same, although slightly sarcastic. "Thank you, shadow demon. I appreciate your mental acuity, but I must remind you again that you are not allowed to form yourself in *my* appearance or use my voice while you are here. I wouldn't want to confuse the zombies as to who their master was. Anyhow, be sure to tell me when you figure out what the problem is."

"Of course, Master Vetu," a voice squeaked back, now sounding more like a squirrel that breathed in helium. "Anytime, anytime."

Out of the shadows a figure appeared in a long black cloak. Erec jumped when he saw what was inside its hood and heard Melody and Jack gasp at his sides. Three rotting heads were stacked atop one another. The eye sockets of each were deeply sunken, and the eyes themselves glowed bright red. It raised its hand, and two more cloaked creatures emerged and bowed.

Master Vetu spoke, the mouth in his middle head moving. "The shadow demon spoke of problems. I don't want to wait until it's too late to find out what's wrong. Let's stand guard by the front entrance,

THE THREE FURIES

put the zombies on high alert. Perhaps it is just a visitor coming, of course. But maybe someone on the inside has gotten loose. If that girl escapes, the Shadow Prince will have our heads."

Ghoulish laughter came from one of the other cloaks, and a skull-like head popped out and rolled down the slight hill where they stood. "Speaking of heads, it's time for a new one," it said.

"Get yourself a new right arm, while you're at it," Master Vetu said. "That one's about to drop off."

Master Vetu and the other cloaked creature drifted toward the front of the castle. The remaining Vetala raised an arm and uttered a high-pitched groan that sounded like a huge rusty hinge opening. Three zombies approached him, and in a minute he had shredded them into pieces. "Now . . . let's see which arm is the best. I think I'll take yours, thank you. And this head looks all right." He inserted the head and arm into his cloak and marched off.

"Wow," Griffin whispered. "Those things make manticores look like house pets."

"Ow!" Melody's arm was twisted into the air above her, elbow up and palm out, like she was a rag doll. "Make it stop!"

A wisp of white wavered in the air above her, and she lifted from the rooftop into it. "Help! Ow!"

Griffin slashed his sabers through the thing to no avail. The white wind drifted right around his blade and yanked Melody a foot into the air.

Erec jumped and grabbed her around the shoulders, but his weight didn't pull her down. Instead they both lifted higher. He stretched an arm up and waved it into the specter, trying to grab her arm back.

Everywhere Erec touched, the specter let go as if he had repelled it. In a moment the spirit drifted off and Erec and Melody plunked onto the roof.

"Ugh. That thing was so cold!" Melody hugged herself. "Thanks, Erec."

Kyron eyed the sky warily. "We better hurry, before we get swarmed by those things."

"Okay, plan," Jack said. "We dodge the zombies, try to hide from everything, make our way to the front door, open the laughter vial, and sneak inside while the Vetalas are still confused."

The plan sounded awful, but everyone nodded their heads. Staying where they were wasn't any better. They took turns jumping down into a bush and then hid behind it while a parade of zombies walked by.

"Look," Jack whispered. "They're all walking in the same direction on this side. The ones farther out are walking the other way. I bet that's so they don't bump into each other all of the time. They'd probably shred one another."

"Let's find a gap between the zombie groups and stay behind them."

A loud snorting pant with a gurgling growl came closer to their bush. A hairy wolflike creature shuffled toward them, clicking its claws together.

Jack tumbled back away from it, knocking Jam down, and Kyron whipped out his sword.

"Wolfsbane," Erec hissed. "See if it works."

Everyone whipped out a handful of leaves and waved them toward the werewolf. The thing whimpered, backing away, and then ran off.

"Good thinking, Erec," Kyron said. "How did you know to bring this stuff?"

"I actually took it because I brought my dog with me. Wolfboy turns into a wenwolf when there is a full moon." He gulped. "Oops. I forgot to tell Spartacus Kilroy about that. I hope we get back before the next full moon."

Nobody answered, maybe because they were feeling as doubtful as Erec. They waited for a gap between some zombie groups streaming by, then popped out of hiding, following their path.

"The zombies behind us can see us," Jack whispered. "They're only about thirty feet back."

But it seemed that the zombies could not tell Erec's group apart from the other zombies. Kyron and Griffin held sword and sabers out, close to their sides. "Not that bright, cap'n, are they?"

A gunshot rang out, and a bullet whizzed past right in front of Erec. He jumped backward, shaking, but Jam tugged him along. "Sir! The zombies are behind us. Keep moving."

Another shot blasted, this time almost hitting Melody. It cracked against the stone wall behind them.

"What *is* that?" Jack's voice shook.

"Look!" Kyron pointed at two spirit warriors squatting nearby, aiming their rifles at them. Jam jumped and darted forward at the sound of another gunshot.

Erec stood between his friends and the spirit warriors, arms out, shielding them.

"What are you doing?" Kyron sounded furious. "Making yourself a target?" He tried to pull Erec back.

"No. Ghosts can't hurt me."

"Maybe ghosts can't, but those are real bullets, kid. Now get down."

Two more shots whizzed by. Erec was glad that they spirit warriors weren't better marksmen. Maybe they had been bankers when they were alive. Eventually, though, one of these shots would hit a target.

"Be right back." Erec left the group and hurried across the field, just a few feet in front of an incoming group of zombies. He could smell their stale breath as he ran by. A minotaur watched him, snorting, and some lions licked their lips from a distance. Before the spirit warriors could take another shot, he dove on both of them, tackling them.

His body clunked straight to the ground as he passed through them. But because they were unable to touch him, the ghosts split apart into pieces around him. Their parts fizzled into the air, leaving the guns behind on the dirt.

Erec picked up the guns, not sure if they would help or not. He had never touched one in his life. But as the minotaur started closing in on him, followed by two hungry looking manticores, he held it up and considered it. The minotaur didn't seem to care one bit about the rifle, however. It pawed the ground, then charged at Erec, horns down.

Erec froze. He had no idea how to shoot the gun. Something silver sailed past his ear, knocking the minotaur flat.

One of Griffin's sabers stuck up from the minotaur's neck. Erec darted back, slamming to a stop to avoid running into a group of zombies, then raced ahead to join his friends.

They had managed to step back into a niche behind another bush to wait for him. Melody threw her arms around him and Jam patted his head.

"Young sir. Do be careful, please."

Jam's warning sounded so tame compared to their dreadful surroundings that all of them laughed for a moment.

"If only we can laugh like that around the Vetalas," Jack said.

Looking out, they slipped back into a gap between the roaming zombies, but by now they had attracted the attention of more minotaurs, and some lions and manticores. They crowded together, approaching steadily.

"Oh, dear," Lalalalal said. "Here we go."

A tiger sprang out of nowhere, but was too close to an incoming group of zombies. With amazing speed they closed in, reminding Erec of the phantom piranhas in the water, and the tiger was devoured.

The lions paced back and forth outside the zombie group. As soon as a gap opened, one of the lions sprang at them—but it was knocked to the side by a humongous manticore with huge, ravenous jaws.

Melody began rubbing her arms and fingers together, creating a haunting melody that seemed to slow the manticore down. Kyron was waving his sword out in front of everyone. He stabbed the manticore again and again, pushing it away. Of course, being a manticore it was impossible to destroy, and its wounds healed almost as fast as they were made. Kyron glanced back and forth between the manticore and a group of zombies that was coming closer. With a final stab he pushed the beast right into them.

As the zombies closed in, slashing away, Erec's group dashed toward the front of the castle. Erec looked back and saw the manticore tear itself away from the zombies, unharmed. "C'mon, guys. More zombies are getting closer behind us."

Kyron and Griffin shouldered the rifles. "Not too much farther, cap'n," Griffin growled. "If we can just make it around yon corner ahead, the doors may be within sight."

"Oh, no!" Melody shouted. "Look!"

The group of zombies in front of them finally noticed they were being followed. A half dozen of them had turned around and stood waiting, arms stretching toward them. The zombies behind them were closing in as well, and others walked by along the path beside them.

Gunfire resounded as Kyron shot into the zombie group. Griffin followed suit, shooting the ones behind them. A few of them staggered away, but then returned, coming toward them even with missing limbs.

"Go for their heads!" Kyron shouted. "It's the only way to stop them."

Griffin blasted the head off a zombie, and it staggered off to find it. They were close now on both sides, and there were no shrubs by the wall of the fortress to hide behind.

Erec felt dizzy. His knees buckled. This was it, he thought. He was about to pass out, and they'd never survive now. *Poor Bethany*, he thought. But instead of dropping to the ground a strange feeling came over him. His clothing was getting tight. He slipped off his backpack as something sharp pricked his back.

Even though it was dark out, everything turned a vivid green. His dragon eyes were out—they could see as well at night as in the day. Scales coated his skin. He felt wings flap. He had grown bigger than Griffin.

It was a cloudy thought. No vision appeared this time, just commands.

Jump.

Kick.

Breathe fire.

He knocked down a group of zombies with his breath and set fire to another horde. Several minotaurs closed in.

Spin, then pounce.

He knocked the minotaurs over with his tail, then dove on the approaching lions, sending them scrambling away.

More fire.

He breathed streams of fire into approaching zombies, burning them into smoke, and into manticores, making them run. Kyron and Griffin battled beasts behind him, with Jack, Melody, and Jam hiding between them. Melody continued to play a sweet refrain that slowed the beasts down a little.

Roll.

Erec rolled over a group of spirit warriors, disintegrating them. He discovered that specters were pulling Jam and Kyron into the air. They were clinging onto Griffin, who was lifting too.

Fly.

With a flap he spun in the air right where the specters drifted, and they whipped away, dropping Jam, Griffin, and Kyron to the ground.

Fly.

Swarms of specters zoomed in now, looking like the northern lights. Erec soared into them and they flew into all directions like fireworks.

Fly.

With a final sweep around Erec knocked out an approaching group of spirit warriors and scared away another minotaur. He hurried back to the group, stumbling as he returned to his normal size. In grave silence, Jam gave him his backpack. Melody had stopped playing music as the living beasts backed off, now afraid of them. Jack wiped sweat off his brow and handed the vial of laughter to Erec. "You dropped this."

Griffin was stunned. "Do you do this . . . often, cap'n? I didn't know you were part-dragon."

Kyron's jaw hung open. "You were so . . . even more . . . than the last time I saw you. Does it hurt?"

"Nah. I think we're okay, actually. No more spirit warriors have seen us, and I'd guess they're the only ones who might talk and tell the Vetalas that we're here."

"Good guess, but not exactly correct." Erec heard his own voice. In front of them stood an exact replica of himself.

He gulped, stunned. Everyone else looked back and forth between him and his look-alike.

"You're a . . ."

"You are right," his mirror image answered. "I am a shadow demon." It smiled warmly. "I can see you've had quite an evening. Very interesting, mind you. We don't get this kind of entertainment very often."

Erec took a breath. "Okay, guys. All you have to do is walk right through this thing."

Griffin stepped forward and the shadow demon morphed into a giant sea monster with three heads swaying from long necks. "I wouldn't do that." Its teeth snapped at them. "You'll die a horrible death." It shrank back into a boy that looked like Erec, except with two sea monster heads waving from his shoulders. "You see, I'm a lot more reasonable than that. I can help you all, you know. Just hear me out—I'm on your side. You just have to trust me. I'll get you right in to save your friend. Bethany, isn't it? I've been wanting to help her escape. Now that you're here, I can do it with you."

Kyron was nodding. Even Erec was starting to feel convinced, but an old memory struck him. Shadow demons manipulated people's thoughts. He had believed one once and almost died. Never again.

"Follow me, guys. Just walk right through him." Erec took a step closer, and the shadow demon changed into a huge Vetala with a stack of drooling heads with long fangs.

Erec shuddered and stepped back. "Careful, Erec!" Melody grabbed his shoulder. "Just listen to what he has to say. Maybe he can help us."

"No!" Erec was fighting his own thoughts as much as hers. He wanted to believe, to trust . . . but then he remembered how he had put his and his own mother's life in danger because he fell into this trap before. *"Never again!"*

Erec grabbed Griffin's and Jam's arms—the two people who were most likely to follow him anywhere, even to a sure death. "Hold on to the others. We're all going through. *Now!"*

The shadow demon hissed and swayed. It held its arms out to them, and in its deep Vetala voice it said, "That's right. Come right here. I'm hungry for a snack now. Unless you want to make a bargain and save your friend. Otherwise I'll enjoy this meal."

Erec pulled Jam and Griffin toward the demon, going against every instinct in his body. He started to doubt his own memory of the shadow demon he had met in the past, but he kept moving forward.

"That's right," the Vetala shadow demon hissed. "You're confused, aren't you, Erec? The shadow demon you met before was your friend, wasn't he? Just like I am. I only want to help, and now you're leading all of your friends to die. Tsk, tsk."

"Don't listen to it!" He yanked Jam and Griffin, and they pulled Jack, Kyron, and Melody behind, protesting all the way. "Come on!"

It started winning over his mind, confusing him. But he fought hard. As long as he thought about his mother and what had almost happened to her in the past when he made this mistake before . . .

The thing radiated heat and fear, and stepping close to it was almost more than Erec could handle. He fought against his entire being and stepped forward, face-to-face with the three sets of sharp jaws, tongues licking their chops, red blazing eyes burning down on him with fury.

He almost jumped back when it let out a screeching roar, but he held his ground. The others tugged behind him, but he would not let go. It was hard to remember even what he was doing this for, but he knew he had to keep going. He could not listen to it, or even to himself now.

Erec clenched his eyes shut, and with bravery that he never knew he had, he stepped straight into the beast.

The image of the Vetala dissolved around him as he passed through, turning into a clear, shimmering vapor that hung in the air. Griffin and Jam could still feel his hand, but seemed not to see him. They still gazed where the Vetala image had been, their faces masks of fear.

Its voice said, "There. Your friend is gone now. A tasty snack. Which of you would like to be the next course? Or would you rather reason with me?"

Erec tugged on their hands. "I'm here, guys! I'm okay! Trust me and walk through this thing."

He tugged, hearing the shadow demon saying that his voice was a fake. But Jam and Griffin must have believed him. Erec was amazed they would follow him into the jaws of death, but in a moment both of them were at his side.

Jack, Melody, and Kyron still stared at the image that had disappeared to the rest of them. "Yum," it said. "Are you going to be fools as well, or will you save yourselves and your friend Bethany?"

Erec, Jam, and Griffin all shouted at once that they were fine, which was all the others needed to hear. Jack took the longest to come through, but soon stood next to them.

They all hugged one another, most of them with tears in their eyes. Erec knew that even the last group to pass through the shadow demon needed tremendous courage and belief. The vision had disappeared, and a thin voice rang in the air. "Interesting. Well, I do say I'm disappointed. I would rather have enjoyed devouring you. But at least I'll have the pleasure of seeing you torn apart by the zombies, if the Vetalas don't want to do it themselves. I suppose you'll all make some nice new body parts for them."

"Do you . . . get a lot of company here?" Erec's friends looked at him strangely when he struck up a conversation with the shadow demon. "I mean, does it get boring for you?"

The thing sighed. "I suppose so. Always interesting starting fights between the Vetalas, spying in the fortress." It chuckled. "Just because you managed to walk through me doesn't mean that I don't know what you're thinking anymore, Erec Rex. That's me—mind reader extraordinaire. I know exactly why you are talking to me right now. You want to wheedle information out of me. Find out how to get inside the front door of the fortress. Like I would tell you that."

"Well," Erec said, deciding to push his luck, "why wouldn't you? Are you a slave of Baskania's? Do you have to follow his every command?"

"Pathetic attempt at manipulating me, boy. Even if I couldn't read your mind, I would not fall for that line. But to answer your question, I do what serves me best. Right now, since I can't consume you, you will serve for entertainment. Why would I help you? That wouldn't be interesting. Much more amusing to see you shredded."

"Wouldn't it be more fun if we had a chance to succeed? Then it would be more exciting—you wouldn't know how it would turn out."

"But there is only one way this can turn out," it said. "And that is with you shredded. There's no hope for you. . . . Ahh, I see . . . You have something else up your sleeve. You brought some bottled laughter with you. Even more exciting."

Erec wanted to kick himself. He should have gotten away from this thing sooner. Now it knew about the only chance they had of surviving. And if it told the Vetala about it—

"That's right. I know your secret now. But I doubt it will work. You don't even know how to use it. Maybe you'll get lucky. I can read minds, but unfortunately I can't read the future."

"How about a bet, then?" Kyron said. "If we get past the Vetala and the zombies, then you let us get inside the fortress."

"That's not for me to do," the shadow demon said. "But I will tell you this—for my amusement and benefit only. The one key to the doorway hangs on a chain around Master Vetu's neck. If you can get your hands on that, which I highly doubt, I will not stop you from entering the fortress."

"Aye," Griffin huffed. "You couldn't stop us anyway now. Even if ye wanted to."

"That is true, of course. But I did tell you where the key is. Remember, this is only for my personal gain, I assure you."

Somehow, chillingly, Erec knew that he was telling the truth.

CHAPTER TWENTY-SIX

Blind Followers

THEY STEPPED OVER piles of zombie parts as they wound their way toward the front of the fortress. The ground looked like a war had been fought there. Most of the zombies on this side of the building were gone, but more were coming, marching over the bodies of their comrades without noticing.

A brief peek around the corner to the front side of the fortress showed more zombies marching closer. A pack of wenwolves closed in, snarling around them.

"Wolfsbane!" Erec had dropped his, but everyone else made up for that, waving fronds toward the drooling beasts. The wenwolves backed away, whining, and trotted off.

A manticore watched them, pawing the ground. It looked like it was trying to decide whether to attack again. Erec bared his teeth at the thing and growled, holding his hands out like claws, and the manticore stepped back.

"Even that thing is afraid a ya." Griffin looked at Erec like he was scared of him too.

"We better hurry." Jack gulped. "No use waiting around here."

They headed toward the building entrance on a path that had been worn by zombies. The fortress was huge, so it was a while before the front doorway came into view. Erec felt a little better than before. At least they had survived this long. And if danger struck, maybe he'd get another cloudy thought. Without Griffin and Kyron warding off attacks and Melody making music, he might not have made it.

Lalalalal stepped onto Griffin's other shoulder to get farther from Erec, throwing him a wary glance.

"Hey, Lala. At least I'm on your side. Leave me alone."

A pointed gothic stone archway formed the entrance to the huge turreted castle. The three black cloaked Vetalas stood on the steps in front of it, talking. Their voices carried in low, hushed murmurs, and the red glow from their eyes blazed into the night.

Erec gripped the vial of laughter. "Listen, guys. I don't know if this will be enough. I know it sounds crazy, but try to see the funny side of this. Okay? I mean, if we can laugh, too, *really* laugh, that might help."

Everyone nodded, but not one of them was able to so much as crack a smile. Nothing seemed remotely funny about where they were now. Kyron and Griffin held weapons at the ready as they advanced, until finally all three Vetalas swung to face them.

"Well." Master Vetu stepped forward. His deep voice was slick and cold, and only his middle head spoke. "Looks like that shadow imp was right. Or maybe not. The thing said something was wrong. But I would have to disagree. This is something quite *right*." The bloodred mouths of all three of his hideous faces grinned, revealing dripping fangs. "Fresh flesh. How delightful. And a nice supply of parts, too."

"I get the girl's face," another one gargled.

Erec almost threw up picturing Melody's face in one of their cloaks, with those eyes and fangs. He tried to block the image from his mind. Before they could say more he twisted the cap and opened the vial.

There was silence. The vial vibrated in his hand but no sound came out. *No!* That was it? Was it was really empty? This was their only hope.

A blue mist curled in the vial and started to waft away. That was his laughter, then? Disappearing before his eyes? In a desperate attempt to stop it, not knowing if it would help, he raised the vial to his face and breathed in the mist.

"Hmp-he. B-ha!" His body shook like he had sneezed. Then he burst out in a fit of laughter so hard his sides hurt. He passed the vial to Kyron, at his side, who looked at him like he was insane. Erec doubled over, wanting Kyron to breathe in the mist but he was laughing too hard to speak. Finally he shoved it to Kyron's face.

Kyron's face lit with amusement and he laughed too, until he was pounding his fist into his legs. The others saw what was happening and passed the vial around until the thick blue mist was finally gone.

Not only was Erec laughing, but everything around him seemed hysterically funny. Melody's high fluttery laughter and Griffin's snorting were hilarious. Even the grotesque Vetalas ogling them with their rotting body parts and stacked heads were amusing. It seemed like someone had put them together for a Halloween costume show, but had completely overdone it. He looked at them, pointing, tears rolling down his face.

The others looked where he was pointing and joined in, doubling over at the sight of the Vetalas. Erec wiped the tears that were streaming down his face. His head and sides ached from laughing so hard, but this was the most fun he'd had in a long time. They would have to come back to this place. It was great.

It seemed comical that they had to take the key from Master Vetu's neck. Erec staggered forward, hooting with glee. Master Vetu glowered at him, drooling and baring his teeth. But this only made Erec laugh harder. He sniffed a few times and, chuckling, reached over to grab the key dangling from a chain around the Vetala's neck.

It was hard to control his movements, as he kept bending over in hysterics, so the first time he reached, his hand went too far into the Vetala's black hood. The back of his wrist banged into something slimy. A moment later, one of Master Vetu's heads was rolling on the ground near his feet.

"Oops!" Erec chortled. It seemed that nothing more amusing had ever happened in his life. "Look at that!" he screeched, pointing at the head. "It came off!" He doubled over, crying in laughter. Everyone behind him was guffawing just as loudly.

"Ohh-ahh." He grasped his side and stood again, in pain from his hysterics and barely able to breathe. Shaking in laughter, he reached one more time for the key on the chain. Master Vetu stood immobile watching them, stunned by their behavior. Erec pushed his hand into Vetu's hood again, but failing to look carefully, he again overshot and banged into something hard. A second head shook loose and fell out, rolling away.

"Aaaaah! Oh!" Erec felt like he was going to die of laughter. This could not have been staged better, he thought. One of the Vetala's heads was at his feet, glaring up at him angrily. He almost stepped on it by accident as he rocked in hysterics.

"Do it again," Griffin gasped, tears rolling down his red face. "Do the . . . third . . . one!" His snorts of delight filled the air.

Erec could not resist. He stuck an arm into the Vetala's hood and smacked the remaining head, which fell to the ground. "Eek!" He kicked it toward Griffin, whose face was contorted, snorting nonstop.

The key dangled in front of him, so he whisked it off the headless neck, which also was very amusing, and staggered back to his friends.

All of them looked to be in pain, gasping and rubbing their jaws and sides as they chuckled. Erec felt himself start to calm down. He waved his friends up the steps, thinking they should go inside while they were still laughing. But there didn't seem to be any urgency. The Vetalas were like some kind of a joke.

A voice came from the headless Master Vetu. "You think this is funny, do you? Let's see how funny you think this is." He raised a finger and pointed, to a chorus of appreciative chuckles, but nothing happened. This inspired more mirth.

But Erec realized that the Vetala was regaining his strength. They were laughing much less now. He fumbled the key into the lock, twisting.

A horrifying roar filled the air, coming from Master Vetu. Erec froze for a moment, then turned the key more, waiting for a latch to click. Nobody was laughing now. Kyron grabbed the key from Erec and jiggled it in the lock.

"*After them!*" Master Vetu screamed.

Zombies poured out of the woodwork in response to Master Vetu's command. They streamed toward the doorway, then up the steps. Vetu fastened one of his old heads back in place, and Erec failed to see any humor in it at all. In fact, the situation was horrifying.

"Got it!" Kyron shouted, pushing the door open. "Get in."

Erec's knees were weak and he felt faint, sick. Everything turned gray . . . and then it was green. He slipped off his backpack as he started to grow, and saw Griffin grab it from him. Spines burst from his back, scales coated his skin.

Zombies surrounded them in seconds, reaching around Erec for Jack and Kyron. His scales seemed to resist their claws.

Spin around, breathe fire.

He blasted some approaching zombies right before one grabbed for Melody, and knocked others away with his tail. Yet they poured onto the steps faster than Erec could destroy them.

Dive. Crush.

Kyron pushed Jack and Melody through the massive steel door and turned just in time to whip the head off one incoming zombie and then another with his sword. Griffin battled valiantly beside him, while Erec breathed a stream of fire onto another group lumbering toward them.

More fire. Claw.

Zombies all around had burst into flames, falling off the marble steps, but more kept coming.

"Get in there, Jam!" Kyron grabbed Jam, who was huddled on the ground, and pulled him inside to safety.

Erec was filled with relief that Melody, Jack, and Jam were okay. The Vetalas sprung forward with blazing red lightning streaking toward them from their fingers. Most of it swerved in midair and was sucked into the Amulet of Virtues, which hung on Erec's chest, protecting him from magic. But a small ray hit Kyron in the leg.

"Ow!" He winced in pain. "It burns!"

Zombies had crowded between them and the doorway, and Griffin fought to clear them away. "Go, Kyron! There's a space." He yanked Kyron through and pushed him toward the doorway.

The zombies seemed unable to enter the castle—Erec didn't blame Baskania for arranging that. Griffin's sabers flew as he and Erec cleared a path to the door, walking back-to-back toward it.

"*No!*" Master Vetu screamed. All three of the Vetalas held up craggy, clawed hands and sent bolts of red lightning streaming toward them. Erec heard Griffin try to laugh weakly, as if that might help. He threw Griffin behind him and let the red bolts swerve into his amulet.

Backing up, step after step, Erec breathing fire and Griffin swinging his blades, they finally reached the door again. One foot upon the door jamb, then another. Lalalalal, who had been hovering in the air just out of reach, flew away, calling, "I'll find you when you leave the fortress. Best I keep a lookout for you out here."

Erec wasn't sure if Lalalalal would be much help as a lookout, or if he was afraid to come inside. But either way, Lalalalal's job had been to help them get across and deal with the creatures outside of the fortress. There probably wasn't much he could do inside to help.

They fell back, closing the door behind them, and collapsed on the stone floor of a small anteroom. The door leading into the fortress was cracked open.

Griffin struggled to his feet and was about to swing the door open when Erec grabbed him. "Wait! We have to hide when we go through. Careful."

He peeked through the door and stopped in shock.

Jam, Melody, Jack, and Kyron stood together in a vast stone entryway, each with a thin black rope around their waists and wrists. A friendly-looking man with a black eye patch and dark hair spoke in an accent that sounded part British and part American. "I don't know," he said. "The shadow demon is never wrong, it seems. If he says there are two more of you, I'll tend to believe that. They'll turn up soon enough, no worries."

The shadow demon, who still appeared like a clear gleam in the air to Erec, hovered nearby. "I could help you right now, point out the other two, if you give me my reward."

"Wish I could, chum," the man said. "And I sure am glad for your help. But that's all up to the Shadow Prince, you know that. I'm sure he'll put your kind in charge out there when he knows what a big help you've been."

"And when he sees what kind of a mess the Vetalas have made of things," the shadow demon added. "They're inept. These kids were laughing at them. *Laughing.* I saw it for myself. One of them walked right up and swiped the key from around Vetu's neck. Pathetic."

"Yes, quite." The man looked pensive. "Can you give us a hint—will we see these two missing intruders soon?"

"I guess you'll have to wait until Baskania is back for any more of my help, if he's the only one who can repay me for all of my work. But don't worry. As soon as he's ready to put the Vetalas in their place, I'll give him everyone he wants."

The shadow demon dissolved into the air. Erec noticed as they had been talking that Kyron was working his silver sword against the thin black rope around him. He held his breath, watching as the rope began to fray. Silver, he remembered, was one of the only things that could cut through the magic rope Baskania had used on him in the past.

Kyron tugged against his sword a last time and the rope fell loose. He held up the rope to hide that he was free and slowly backed away from the others.

"Well, let's see," the man with the eye patch said. "It looks like you're going to be our guests for a while. We'll have a full search for your two other friends by morning, and they'll be joining you shortly. Until the Shadow Prince returns, you'll be staying in one of our comfortable, full-service prison cells. Then, if you are lucky, he may let you stay alive, for the small favor of one of your eyes and lifelong service. But there are no guarantees, unfortunately. My name is Ajax Hunter, by the way, if you need anything. Of course it may be hard to get a hold of me. Let me show you to your . . . quarters."

"Hya!" Kyron sprang forward, sword out, and sliced it through the ropes that twined from Ajax Hunter's hand around Jam, Melody, and Jack. He spun around and dashed into a hallway. "Come on!"

Ajax spun more black ropes out of his remote control, and they instantly wrapped around Jam, Jack, and Melody before they could follow. "No worries. As soon as the Shadow Prince returns he'll find all of your friends. In fact, he'll be so pleased that you stopped by! There's nothing as enjoyable as an unexpected visit, I always say." He pulled the three behind him and down another hallway, speaking into a cell phone in his finger. "Right. One intruder has escaped. He ran toward army headquarters. Two more are on the loose—try to find them all. It would look better."

Griffin and Erec stared at each other, stunned. For some reason they had assumed that once were inside the fortress they would be safe. But their problems were only just beginning.

Erec and Griffin stole quietly into the huge entryway, which was made entirely of gray stone from the domed ceiling to the floor. Several passageways led outward, and they picked one that pointed in a different direction than either Kyron or Ajax Hunter had gone.

Hallways branched and led to rooms that seemed to be living quarters for the servants. Erec was glad that it was the middle of the night, so nobody was wandering about.

Without warning, a man wearing a dark smock turned the corner and came toward them, carrying a tray with tea and crackers. Griffin grabbed for his saber, but Erec held up his hand like a stop sign and put a finger to his lips. The man approached casually, not looking at them, humming to himself. As he grew closer, they could see that neither of his eyes were real, and he was blind.

Erec and Griffin pressed back against the wall as the man ambled by, unaware. When he was out of sight Erec whispered, "Blind followers. Baskania keeps them as his servants—their reward for helping him is to give him both of their eyes."

"He wouldn't do that to . . ." Griffin didn't finish the sentence, but they both were worried about their friends who were captured.

"We'll just have to rescue them, won't we? Come on." A room off the hallway had a kitchenette and some dining tables, and beyond that were some bedrooms. They heard snoring coming from a few. Most of the doors were closed, but one was open. Inside, the room was empty. "Perfect."

They went in and shut the door. "I don't know how hard they'll search for us, but maybe they'll wait until people are up. We can hide under the bed, I guess."

Griffin rifled through a closet. "Or we could wear these." He threw some dark smocks on the bed. "Disguise ourselves as those blind guys. These have hoods on them too."

Erec picked one up. "That's a great idea! Then we can fit in, find our way around this place." He slid one on, and it fit perfectly, except for dragging on the floor a bit. Griffin's smock hung tighter, but was still long enough to reach his feet. Erec did not realize until silence surrounded him how tired he actually was.

But before even considering sleep he sat down and dug the Seeing Eyeglasses out from the tangle of things hanging off his neck. This time he thought about Jack, Melody, and Jam, and about how much he missed them. When he put the glasses on, he was looking at a small stone cell. Jack, Melody, and Jam were sleeping on stone benches that hung from the walls. There were no windows, and the door looked thick and heavy.

"Psst. Jam!"

Jam sat bolt upright and looked around. "I'm sorry. I thought I heard . . ." He started to lie back down.

"Jam! It's me, Erec. Are you okay?"

"Erec?" Jam was confused, then a look of realization crossed his face. "The eyeglasses?"

"Yeah. I can see you. Did anyone get hurt?"

"No, young sir," Jam whispered. "But I'm afraid we're stuck here." He sighed. "I wish you had kept the Serving Tray. Where are you?"

"I'm inside the fortress with Griffin. We're hiding out, but don't worry. We'll find you guys. Do you know which way they took you?"

"We went straight down the hallway to an elevator, up to the eleventh floor. Then it was hard to tell. We wound around a lot. But we're in a spot with concrete floors, rows of cells like this one."

"Does yours have a number on it?"

Jam thought. "It did. Can't see it from the inside, though. I'm pretty sure it was cell block ten. Almost positive."

"We'll get you out." Erec felt his eyes closing. "Don't worry, Jam."

He thought he heard Jam answer, but his words were drowned in a wave of sleep.

When Erec awoke, he jumped in shock at a large figure pacing the room in a dark smock.

"Eeeh?" the figure growled. "Yer finally awake, then?"

It took a second for Erec to process that this was Griffin, and to remember where he was. The events of yesterday seemed unreal. How could they have survived the Vetalas and all of those other insanely dangerous creatures out there? It gave him hope, though. Maybe things would only get easier from here.

For the first time he realized how close Bethany was now. Within walking distance. Even though his friends were imprisoned, everything seemed possible. Baskania wasn't even here. Erec would get them all out to safety. His vision of the future was true.

Then he remembered his vision of the future. It did show them all escaping—that *was* possible. But he knew what would happen then. Everyone else would run out of the eye care shop—Windows to the Soul—except for him. A police snake was waiting there, and would pounce and bite, then he would be carried back to this place alone and helpless. Nobody would be able to save him.

Erec gathered his courage and got up. "Jam, Melody, and Jack are in cell block ten on the eleventh floor. They took elevators up from that hallway that led down the middle. We should try to find them, and Bethany, too." Excitement raced through him. She was close now, and he would finally be able to see her again. If only they had more time together before he was captured in the shop by the snake.

He would make time, he decided. Before they left, he would have to find a place for them to go together, where he could tell her everything he'd been holding in all this time. They would have to fit a lifetime into a short talk.

Maybe he'd even give her another kiss.

Baskania's blind followers wandered the halls that they knew by heart, but people with sight walked past as well. Erec and Griffin played it safe, keeping their heads down and their hoods all the way forward. Erec decided to wear his backpack under his hooded smock. It made him look like a hunchback, but in this creepy place that was normal.

Griffin crashed into a blind servant by accident. The blind man tumbled to the floor, and Erec helped him up. "Sorry, sir."

"No worries, young man. You are young, aren't you? You sound it." The man was bald and wiry, with deep wrinkles in his face. He felt around the walls to orient himself again. "You still have a cane, then, I guess? A few more years and you won't need it anymore. I know this place like the back of my hand."

"How long have you been here?" Erec asked.

"Almost thirty years." He chuckled. "It's not as bad as you think. The first few years were hard, but you'll slowly realize that everything you're doing is for a great cause. World peace—remember! No matter how small your tasks are, from cooking breakfast for the servants to guarding the gemstones, it takes every cog in order to make a clock tick. So, welcome to cog life, boy. What's your name?"

"Uh . . . Rick. What's yours?"

"Heh-heh. They call me Maestro here. I used to conduct the London Philharmonic." He sighed. "Gives me a lot to think about. So many good memories. And the music is still all up here." He tapped his head.

Erec felt bad for Maestro. "Would you leave here if you could?"

"Well . . . I don't know about that. I do miss the real world, believe me. But I'm settled in my ways now. And content to be doing good work for a cause. It's best not to think about these things anyway—you'll see. Just get the lay of the land, and stay away from the bigwigs. That won't lead to anything but trouble." He frowned. "What's your job, Rick?"

"I . . . I'm just in training, still. They have me in the kitchens now, but they're trying to find a place for me."

"Do you want me to put a good word in for you? I've got it pretty cush, I admit. I'm in record keeping. I just file things in Braille. They like blind people to do that work, because we can't read the documents we're filing, only the Braille headings someone stamps on. It's a nice job—better than a hot kitchen, eh?"

Erec had an idea. "What are the records about?"

"Oh, everything, I guess. I can't quite read them, so I don't fully know. But the headings are about things like security, Eye of the World, Baskania's peace army, stored treasures, future development plans, all the minutes of what's taking place inside the fortress. The list goes on and on. It all ends up to be just useless paperwork, if you ask me."

Erec and Griffin's eyes met. "Wow. I'd really like to see—I mean, visit that place. It sounds interesting."

Maestro chuckled. "Don't worry. I still catch myself saying that I'll 'see' things sometimes. It's a hard habit to break. But you're in luck. Unless you're expected elsewhere, you might as well join me, because I'm headed straight to the archives now. Want to come along?"

"Sure!"

Griffin raised his hands in question, and Erec shrugged back to say he had no idea what Griffin should do. They walked behind Maestro in tandem a while, trying to match steps.

"Who's your friend?"

Erec and Griffin's eyes widened. Griffin pointed at himself questioningly.

Erec said, "Do you mean—"

"The fellow with you, who's following us? Sounds like a fellow, anyway. He's got heavy footsteps."

"Oh. That's my . . . uncle, Griffin. He's new too. We came here together."

Maestro nodded. "Well, that's nice for you, to know someone here. Unusual, though, to let you stay together."

"Yeah. They'll probably split us up once they decide where to put us . . . you know."

"Uh-huh. Turn right here now, and we're almost to the elevators." He pressed a button with Braille on it, and they filed in after him. "It's on six. Just keep a hand on a wall and follow my footsteps, you'll be fine."

Maestro punched a code into a box and the locked door clicked. "That's our sign. Follow me, then. There's good work to do in here. Let me introduce you to my friends."

"Hi, Maestro! Who you got with you today?"

"A few newbies. Boy named Rick and his uncle, Griffin. They might want to work here. I told him it beats the kitchens."

Erec noticed a video camera in the corner. He made sure his face was well covered, then picked up a paper and propped it in front, blocking its lens, in case it was recording them. While they made small talk with the archive workers, Erec and Griffin wandered the room looking at files.

The room was full of everything Erec wanted to know. If only he could bring this whole room back with him and give it to his father. But what he wanted the most were the records of what was going on inside the fortress. Maybe he could get a clue where Bethany was now.

She was so close! The thought gave him a chill.

He ran a finger along the cases of files. Some sat out, and others filled cabinets and locked cases. Griffin was stuffing paper into his pocket—Erec hoped whatever he found was useful.

As he scanned the room, he saw a file that made him stop cold. It was marked "Furies." He ripped it open and saw pages about each of the three Furies, their temperaments, and things they most wanted and enjoyed. In the front was a list of gifts that had been given to them, and were planned. Wandabelle's name was on the list.

Erec's hands tightened on the paper.

"Rick . . . did you hear that?" Maestro said. "Douglas asked if you were hungry."

"Um—yes." Erec realized he was quite hungry. "Do you have snacks in here?"

"No food's allowed in here, kid. But we're going to make a sandwich run. You sure you're not supposed to be somewhere?"

"Not right now. I'm starting a night shift tonight, so I have time off."

"You better rest, then! Let's go get some lunch now, okay?"

Erec scanned the page to see what it said about Wandabelle.

Clown Fairy: Wandabelle.

Stored in Nightmare Realm on April 1 for future trade.

Balor Stain to keep watch on situation with King Augeas.

Planned trade on May 1, for Tisiphone, in return for tripling Shadow Prince's power over the Substance. If Tisiphone and sisters refuse by this date to triple powers, the Clown Fairy is to be destroyed, and the Furies informed of such.

Clown Fairy to be released by Rosco Kroc using the alarm clock, which has been set. The Shadow Prince and King Augeas ensured that no other method of removal will succeed.

Clown society expected to fall into complete chaos. This will be advantageous, as surviving clowns can be reeducated to serve in Army of Peace.

Alarm clock is to be kept in the army security headquarters, Jakarta fortress, programmed, and at the ready.

"*Rick!* Are you with us? Hello, kid!"

"Um, I'm sorry. I just keep thinking about home. What did you say?"

"We're going to get some lunch. Want to join us?"

"I guess. Can we come back here after?"

Maestro looked doubtful. "A short visit is okay, but they frown on our taking things into our own hands. You're supposed to get your rest for night duty. Is it guard duty, then?"

"Yes." Erec thought that was a great idea for tonight. "It is."

Griffin held up a finger as he was reading more papers. Then he stuffed a folder under his smock.

"Oh, excuse me," Erec said. "Could we wait just another few minutes before going to lunch? I'm . . . not really that hungry yet." He looked through files as fast as he could.

"Sorry, kid. We're going now. Come on." Maestro smiled as he held the door open. Luckily he didn't expect Erec and Griffin to get to the door quickly. But even then, nothing else of interest jumped out before they left.

The click of the lock behind them sounded very final. Erec felt like breaking the door down and tearing the entire room apart to find out more information. But that was a straight ticket to the wrong side of cell block ten, he figured, so he quietly followed Maestro to the food hall.

CHAPTER TWENTY-SEVEN

Special Delivery

T HE ONLY THING that looked half-edible in the food hall was a ham sandwich. When Erec first took a bite, he choked so badly he wondered if it was poisoned—but then he realized it just tasted terrible. He really missed the Serving Tray. Griffin, though, didn't mind shoveling in the yellowish gruel that the others at the table ate. Then again, he had been stuck for hundreds of years with nightmarish rat stew, so anything tasted good to him.

They excused themselves quickly and found that the room they had stayed in was still empty. Griffin shut the door and pulled the folder he had taken from under his smock. "I found something about yer girlfriend, cap'n. Her name is Bethany, right?"

Erec's heart nearly stopped. "What? Let me see." He threw the stack of papers on the desk and sat down. Most of it was transcriptions of Bethany's memories that had been projected from her mind. "This whole packet is age seven. It starts in January. Dead of winter and Earl Evirly has her chained all day to his newsstand. When she cleans and does work, he gives her candy. Otherwise, she goes hungry." He threw the papers down. "Makes me sick. That guy was posing as her uncle, because Baskania ordered him to keep watch over her after he killed her real parents." He shuddered. "At least when I get her out of here, she'll have a good life to go back to. That's one thing I'll be happy to think about."

"You'll be with her, right? Yer makin' it sound like you're not coming back."

Erec didn't respond. He flipped through pages of Bethany's memories. Reading them didn't feel right—it was too much like spying, like reading her diary. And they wouldn't help him find her either. "Wait! Here's something different in the back." He spread stacks of tests that Bethany had taken across the desk, from math to free association to personality tests.

"They're keeping 'er busy, looks like." Griffin shook his head. "What do they want with 'er, anyway?"

"She's supposed to know something important. A prophecy said 'the secret of the Final Magic is hidden in the mind of the smallest child of the greatest seer of the first king of Alypium.' That's her. My father, King Piter, is the first king of Alypium. His greatest seer was Bethany's mother, before she was killed. Her name was Ruth Cleary. Bethany has one sibling, Pi, and he's older.

So somewhere in her mind is this secret that's supposed to show Baskania the way to rule the world. Which is pretty much what the Final Magic would let him do. My dad said that it would make him go mad and destroy everything, so let's hope he doesn't figure this out soon."

"And does Bethany know the secret, then?"

Erec shrugged. "She doesn't think so. But she's a math genius. No, that's not a strong enough word for it. She can speak math, if you know what I mean. So she probably does have it in her mind somewhere. . . ."

The pages didn't contain any more information. Erec pushed them aside and stood.

"Well, lookie here." Griffin placed a fat finger on one of the papers.

Erec grabbed the sheet. Right at the top of the page was written: "Bethany Cleary. Age 14. Prisoner #741-147. Contained unit, lab tower. High security."

"You did it!" Erec jumped for joy. "We found her. Now we just have to find the lab tower."

"It says 'high security,'" Griffin pointed out.

"I figured it would be. So we know where Bethany is, and where the others are. I'm going to put on the Seeing Eyeglasses and try to find Kyron."

Erec thought about his friend, Kyron, and how great it was to see him again. He hoped he was okay, and hadn't been captured yet. With Kyron on his mind, he put the Seeing Eyeglasses on.

He was marching in a corridor, moving alongside soldiers. Where was Kyron? Was he captured? But he could see no prisoner anywhere. Finally he noticed the face of the soldier marching next to him.

"Kyron?" he whispered.

Kyron jumped in shock and looked around, then fell back into step with the other soldiers.

Now wasn't the right time to talk to him, but Erec was glad that he was okay.

"Why don't ya use those things to talk to that girlfriend of yers and just ask 'er where they're keepin' 'er at?"

"I doubt she knows what it's called, or directions to get there. I haven't told her we're here yet. I want to, but Baskania is a mind reader. If she knows, then he'll probably know too, as soon as he's back."

"Looks like ee's going to hear it anyways, from both the shadow demon and that Ajax Hunter fella."

True enough, Erec thought, forming his plan. He had three places he needed to go, as soon as possible. Cell block ten, the lab tower contained unit, and army security headquarters—to find the alarm clock that was somehow set to free Wandabelle.

If they only had a map of the fortress, the rescues would be so much easier. Erec had an idea where cell block ten was, from Jam's description, but even that might be hard to find. A few of the blind followers seemed kind and trusting enough to ask questions, but he didn't want to raise anyone's suspicions.

At one point a group of soldiers hurried through, checking in rooms, but nobody noticed them. "I bet they're looking for us."

"Aye."

They wandered into an area filled with magical instruments, from all kinds of remote controls to magical weapons, vanishing caps, and MagicLights, as well as things Erec had never seen before.

A tall, thin man in a long black cloak swept before them. "What are *you* two doing here? No servants are allowed in these quarters. Don't you know anything?"

"Sorry, sir," Erec said. "We were just curious."

"Well, don't be." The man snickered. "Takes a brain to be curious. Now, off with you dunces, before I practice with one of these weapons on you." He wagged a finger at them, and dunce caps appeared on Erec and Griffin's heads, on top of their hoods.

He heard Griffin snarl, which worried him. If Griffin picked a fight, they'd be found out right away. Plus, they were supposed to be blind. "Shh." He winked at Griffin, getting a great idea. Under his smock Erec felt for the Doubler Charm that Wandabelle had given him. He waved it back and forth under the cloth, unsure if it would work.

A blast of wind puffed under Erec's smock, so he spun around to hide it. "Let's go," he said. "Sorry to bother you."

As he walked to the door a small bolt of lightning formed in the air and shot toward him. He couldn't see it enter the pendant, but was sure it did. Then two identical beams burst out again, zinging toward the people behind him.

Erec hoped he had blocked the light beams, and that nobody noticed. He glanced behind him to see the men talking together, paying no attention to the lowly servants who were leaving.

Suddenly four of them were wearing dunce caps on their heads. A fight arose among them, accusing one another of making them appear, as Erec and Griffin snuck out.

Erec almost giggled, but bit his tongue. He heard a small snort from Griffin.

"So tha's how that charm works?" Griffin said once they were in the hallway.

"Yeah. It's just for fun, really. You can't direct where it goes. But it's all I have from Wandabelle, so I'm holding onto it." He gave it a squeeze and hoped that someone would rescue her before it was too late.

***

Erec and Griffin walked down a hall with purpose, as if they knew just where they were headed. Actually, they had no clue. Somehow, something would give them a lead to where Bethany was. It had to—time was ticking. If only Erec knew what to do . . .

Wood-framed glass double doors appeared at the end of hallway, immediately attracting Erec's interest. He could tell that they led to someplace official. Could this be the Army Security Headquarters, maybe?

But as they approached, a sign near the doors became visible, reading LEYEBRARY.

"That's odd," Erec said. "Want to take a look?"

They pulled their hoods forward more, and Erec hunched over. With his backpack under his smock he was sure he looked ancient.

The leyebrary did not contain books. Instead, jars and jars of eyes floating in liquid filled the shelves of the massive space. Erec could hear Griffin gagging quietly under his hood. The eyes didn't bother him, but he could not believe how many were there. Somehow he thought that Baskania carried inside him all of the eyes he had taken from people—they emerged for him to see through whenever he needed to look through the other eye of its owner, and to read their thoughts. But he had thousands here, all categorized into sections such as "politicians," "athletes," and "recent additions."

A woman sat at a desk, thumbing through stacks of index cards. "What do you have, a new deposit?"

Erec tried to make his voice sound old, but probably just came across like he had a bad cold. "Just checking to see if you need help. We have some time free now."

The woman flipped through a file cabinet. "Well, you can run a delivery for me. We have a few new ones in that the boss wants now. They've just been processed and are ready for use. One of these is really important, they say—it has to go in right away." She stood up and gathered a few small jars of eyes and put them on a tray. "Ajax Hunter will be taking these personally. Now run along."

Erec made his voice scratchy. "Um . . . Where can we find Ajax Hunter now?"

She looked irritated. "How should I know? You delivery types are supposed to have all that information. You better hurry along."

Griffin carried the tray—apparently the woman thought he would be better at holding the precious cargo than his hoarse hump-backed companion. They stole back down the hallway, Griffin gagging all the way.

"Take these." He thrust the tray at Erec. "I can't look at 'em"

Erec took over the tray. Ten small jars held floating lumps, some of which were looking at him. Names were written on the lids. *Robert Jeho. Carly Stampers. Marty Allen. Red Friedman. Oscar Felix.*

Erec almost dropped the tray. His stomach rose into his throat. "I have to sit down. Quick."

"I knew them eyes would get to yas."

They found a room filled with computers and rows of people at desks. At an empty table by the front, Erec collapsed into a chair. "This." He tapped the jar with Oscar's name on it. "This is my good friend. Oscar Felix." He wanted to say more, but choked on the words, glad that his hood was hiding the tears rolling down his face.

"Cap'n." Griffin lowered his head. "We will avenge this, right?"

Erec shrugged. "I'd be happy just to leave this place safely with everyone. Revenge sounds like a luxury. I wish I knew if Baskania forced him to do this, or just talked him into it. I don't know if it even matters, either way." He shuddered with revulsion, then grabbed Oscar's eye jar. "Well, I'm not letting it happen. We're stealing it back so Oscar can put his eye back in." He paused. "Maybe *you* should find Oscar after we're done here and give it to him. I guess I won't make it that far."

"Don't think that way, cap'n. I'll fight to the death to get you back home alive."

"I know, Griffin. Thank you, by the way. You're a real friend."

"Aw, shucks, cap'n. Now yer making me get all soppy. Let's shut up about this before I have to sock ye one, okay?"

Erec agreed. Getting socked by Griffin was not what he needed at the moment, on top of everything else.

He stashed Oscar's eye in his backpack and stood up. "We're saving Oscar. And maybe we'll get Ajax Hunter in trouble, too. We're delivery guys now. I guess that's a good reason to learn where everything is in the fortress—like the Army Security Headquarters, the lab tower contained unit, and cell block ten, right?"

After asking around, they finally found the office known as delivery central. Smocked blind followers, with and without hoods, canes, and trays, bustled in and out. Erec and Griffin got in a line. Locators, sitting behind a counter, gave information about where people were at the moment for deliveries.

Griffin tapped Erec's shoulder. "Turn around, cap'n."

Before them on the wall—nonsensically, as the deliverers were blind—was painted a schematic map of each floor of the fortress. Some of the blind servants ran a hand across it as if they were looking for something, which was when he saw that the paint was raised, with Braille words as well as painted ones describing the rooms.

"Try not to look like we're staring at it," Erec whispered. "Remember, we're blind." He stayed in line and stood still, studying the maps. There was the front entrance. Here is where they turned and followed the hallways into the servants' quarters. The lunch room, the leyebrary . . . what floor were the archives on? Oh, on the sixth.

Jam, Melody, and Jack had been taken straight back from the front door. Jam said they took elevators to the eleventh floor and followed passages back. . . . There they were! Erec's breath caught. He saw rows of cell blocks on the eleventh floor. He stepped out of line and ran his finger over it as if he were blind. Cell block ten. Right there.

Kyron had run the opposite way. That led straight into the army wing. Floors and floors of training facilities, research and development, officer entertainment, sleeping quarters . . . and on the top, thirtieth floor, the Security Headquarters. There it was. The alarm clock that could save Wandabelle from the Nightmare Realm.

Now where was the lab tower? He felt himself shaking. If he could just see it, and know where Bethany was, how close they finally were. Not on the first floor. Not on the second. He couldn't find it anywhere. Then he noticed other maps off to the side that didn't fit in with the rest. They were small, round floor plans, broken into levels. . . . Towers! Here were maps of dozens of the towers that sprouted from the huge complex.

Where was it? He traced a finger along some of them, running it over the Braille to fit in with the others. Many weren't labeled, some were dungeon towers, which sounded ghastly. A sorcery tower—that was a big one—and a few empty ones . . .

Then he spotted it. The lab tower. It wasn't tall, just six stories. And the top level was labeled CONTAINED.

Erec rested a finger on it. Bethany was right there. So close now. Everything he wanted was within his reach.

They had kept the tray of eyes, which made roaming around the complex look more official, but took a few more of the jars off and left them under a desk in an empty room. When the tray finally was turned in—not that Erec planned on doing it himself—it might throw more suspicion on him if only Oscar's was missing. If it was just one of several misplaced eyes, nobody would make the connection right away.

The room they stayed in was still empty, so they went back inside to make plans. Erec decided to try looking for Kyron again. He thought about how good of a friend he was, and how much he missed having Kyron around. Then he slipped the Seeing Eyeglasses on.

Suddenly he was in a huge mess hall full of uniformed men chowing down on dinner. Kyron sat at a crowded table, speaking to nobody and eating some gray slop.

"Kyron," Erec whispered. But the noise level was so loud that Kyron didn't hear a thing.

Erec could talk louder without anyone noticing. Everyone around Kyron was wrapped up in conversations—they probably wouldn't notice another voice nearby. "Kyron. *Kyron!*"

Kyron glanced up in shock, then looked around.

"Kyron, it's me. I'm right here, but you can't see me."

Kyron continued to search around him and under the table.

"Go somewhere quiet. Can you get away? Just get up and go."

A few people around Kyron started to look at him funny as he was staring at the ceiling and then looking under his plate. An officer nearby tapped his head to hint that Kyron was crazy.

Erec sighed in frustration. "It's *me*, Erec. I'm wearing glasses that let me see you, and you can hear me. Leave that place, okay? Go!"

Though mystified, Kyron got up and walked toward the door.

"Do you have a room, or somewhere quiet to go?"

Kyron jumped when he heard Erec's voice, as if he was not expecting it again. "Erec? Can you hear me?"

"Yes, I can hear you. But so can everyone else, so stay quiet. Find someplace where you are alone so nobody hears me, either."

Kyron went into a narrow hallway that led to an empty room stacked with bunk beds. He sat down on one. "Are you still here?" He looked around the room.

"I am right next to you, but you can't see me. I can see you, though.

These glasses I have are magical. They let me see people I miss."

He nodded. "Did they catch you and Griffin?"

"No. We saw you escape, and we stayed hidden. What happened when you ran away?"

"I got lucky. The halls were pretty deserted, and I kept going until I got lost. This army officer came out in the hall and grabbed me—I thought it was going to come to a fight, but he had no clue who I was. He assumed I was one of the new recruits trying to escape. So he sat me down with a 'Look, Sonny' talk about how there was no way out, and it was my time to serve humanity, all that. Tossed me into this barracks filled with bunk beds, so I found an empty one and fell asleep. Everyone assumes I'm just another new guy. They even gave me fatigues."

"Good. We got lucky too. And we found out where Bethany is. Jam, Melody, and Jack are in cell block ten. We need to meet you somewhere and try to get them out."

"I'm ready anytime. I don't know my way around this place, though."

"Have you heard of the Army Security Headquarters? It's up on the thirtieth floor of the military wing."

Kyron shook his head. "Why?"

"We need to get something up there. It's really important. I think it will be hard to find, and I'm sure it's highly guarded."

"What is it?" Kyron leaned forward, interested.

"An alarm clock."

Kyron raised an eyebrow. "I don't think I heard you right. An alarm clock?"

"Yep."

"We're risking our lives to get a highly guarded alarm clock?"

"Yes. It's more than just a regular alarm clock, though. It's the only hope for Wandabelle—the Clown Fairy. Its alarm is set to let her leave Nightmare Realm, and we have to free her before Baskania comes for her."

"Okay, then. Let me check into it. No need for you guys to risk your necks going up there."

"I don't know, Kyron. Griffin would be pretty angry if you had a good sword fight without him, I think."

Griffin slammed his hand down on the table. "What did Kyron say? Planning to get that clock without us? Tell him I'll do him in meself if he doesn't take me along."

"Did you hear that, Kyron?" Erec said. "Why don't we meet you and we'll all go up? What floor are you on?"

They made arrangements to meet at a mess hall on the third floor of the army wing. After one more peek at the maps in delivery central, memorizing all that they could, they picked their way through the fortress more easily. Everyone stepped out of their way when they saw the eyeballs Erec was carrying, avoiding him as if he was diseased.

Erec laughed. He fit in so well here—with a hunchback, a hooded smock, and a tray of eyeballs—that nobody bothered them. Kyron looked right past them as they approached, then jumped when Erec's voice came from under his hood.

"Is that . . . ?"

"It's us."

"But what's that . . . You don't look right. . . ."

"Shh. It's my backpack."

"Oohhh."

They found the elevator and took it to the thirtieth floor. Griffin held his sabers under his smock. Kyron had fitted his sword inside his shirt back.

"Any ideas of what we're going to do?" Kyron asked.

Erec shook his head. "Just see if we can find out where the alarm clock is. We could always sneak back later and try to steal it."

Kyron nodded. "I have an idea."

The elevator opened into a small room. A secretary sat behind a tall counter and a burly guard stood at the end of it, before a closed door. Both of them looked up when Erec, Kyron, and Griffin filed out of the elevator. Erec figured they must not have many unexpected visitors.

Kyron smiled broadly. "I've been asked to get an updated list of everything stored up here, and where it is. Ajax Hunter wants it right away."

The secretary sighed, annoyed. She glanced through Erec and Griffin as though servants were invisible. "It's going to take me a while to update it. Do you want to come back in an hour?"

Erec cheered inside at Kyron's idea. How perfect—a list would show where things were. It made sense that she would be organized.

Kyron leaned on the counter. "Would you like to be the one to tell Mr. Hunter that he can't have his list now? Should I bring him here, so you can explain your limitations to him? Or can you think of another way to make this work?"

She was flustered. "Hhff. I'll try and do it quicker, then. But I can only work so fast. Will he settle for an older version—like last week's?"

Kyron conferred with Erec, who nodded slightly. "I suppose so. But . . . what would probably be better is to give me last week's list, and then I'll walk through and look at any new items. I can add them myself."

The secretary looked doubtful. "Do you have a top-security pass on you? That's the only way you can go in. Plus, it would take you as long as it takes me to find everything."

"That's no problem," Kyron said. "I don't need to find all of it. I know the specific things Ajax is looking for. So it will be quick." He held his hand out for a paper.

"What about your security pass? That's a requirement to get into the vaults. I haven't seen you up here before."

Kyron held out his hands. "Why would Ajax need to give me a pass? He assumed you would be up-to-date by now, and have the new list ready. If I go back empty-handed it'll be your head, not mine. I have these guys as my witnesses." He waved a hand toward Erec and Griffin. "I'm taking them with me to deliver fresh eyes to Ajax along with the papers. So let's go."

The secretary seemed unsure what to do. "I'm sorry," she said slowly, "but I have to follow the rules. Nobody can go back without a pass."

"Okay." Kyron shrugged. "It's your head on a post, not mine. Just give me last week's papers and I'll tell Ajax that was the best you could do."

She put her head into her hand. "It's not my fault." Her voice cracked. "I'm overworked. I don't have enough time in the day to do everything they expect. Now I'm going to get in trouble for it?"

Kyron sounded sympathetic. "Look, we're *all* overworked here. Why don't we figure out another way to handle this?" He pointed at the guard. "What if he goes back there with me? I'm sure he's got a pass. That'll keep my visit on the up-and-up, right?"

She shrugged. "I guess. It's not protocol, but . . ."

"Great. Get me the old list and let's go."

He grabbed the papers and a pen from the desk. The guard didn't look thrilled either about accompanying Kyron back into the storage rooms.

"Well, come along then." Kyron impatiently waved Erec and Griffin to come. "We don't have all day."

"Um, they're not allowed to go back there." The secretary stood up, concerned.

"I can't let them out of my sight. Well, not them, exactly. But the precious cargo they're holding. You can't expect me to leave those eyes unattended? Unless *you* have the authority to carry them, and then you can come back with me, and they'll wait out here."

"But . . ." She finally surrendered. "Just—just go quick and get it over with."

"Thanks, ma'am." Kyron nodded, and Erec and Griffin followed him and the guard into the storage rooms.

They looked around in wonder at the shelves piled with all kinds of rare treasures. It was too bad Oscar wasn't here, Erec thought. He had the inborn magical gift of being able to tell if things were valuable just by looking at them. Of course, everything here was probably valuable.

A chill ran through him when he realized that a part of Oscar was with him right now, in his backpack. He would have to remember to give his backpack to Jam when they left, so he could find Oscar and give him his eye back.

Odd crystals glowed in different colors on shelves, and some large boxes hummed and shook. One peculiar object caught Erec's eye. It was a small block of amber with something inside it. When he looked closer, he saw a bee trapped inside the block, petrified there. The poor thing, he thought. It reminded him of the missing bees in Upper Earth. What was Baskania planning to do with this thing?

Nobody was looking, so he ran a hand over the shelf and swiped it off, putting it in his pocket under the smock. Stealing from an evil sorcerer seemed like doing a good deed, somehow.

"Okay, where are the newer items?" Kyron asked the guard.

The guard shrugged. "There are some in every room. Here." He waved at an area, then walked into another room, annoyed.

"I see." Kyron picked an object off a table, examined it, and jotted on his paper. He frowned, making more notes, then looked up. "Where is the alarm clock? I know that is one issue of concern. It might have to be moved."

"Over in that room." The guard thumbed in another direction. "In the locked trunk."

"Hmm." Everyone followed Kyron into the room. "Locked, huh? And you have the key, right?"

The guard took a keychain from his pocket. "You need to see it?"

"I'd better." Kyron tried to sound official, but Erec could hear the excitement in his voice.

After jangling the keys a bit, the guard found the right one and fit it into the lock. He threw the lid open and stood back, as if this was his usual procedure.

The box shook a bit, then a pair of tiny hinged, metallic limbs appeared over its side. A moving alarm clock pulled itself out of the box, stretched, took a few steps, looked around, then plopped down as if disappointed she was still in the vaults.

And it was definitely a "she." Erec thought it looked identical to his lifelike alarm clock from home, except with feminine eyes and a bow on top of its face. His mother had bought his from a Vulcan store, but for some reason he had always thought his was the only one.

So, this was the alarm clock that was set to save Wandabelle? Interesting. He supposed it would be able to do more than a normal clock, anyway.

Griffin exclaimed, "Hmph!" Erec hoped he didn't attract attention, but the guard took no notice.

"I see." Kyron picked the thing up, its tiny metal legs kicking. "We'll just have to take this back with us. Ajax Hunter wants to get it ready for use now."

"Put it back." The guard pointed at the box. "Nothing goes out of here. *Nothing.*"

"Now, see here—"

"That means no." He walked closer to Kyron and pulled out a remote control.

Erec gasped. Kyron's sword was no match for magic.

Magic. The only thing Erec could think to do, fast, was waggle his finger at the remote control. *Pull. Move.*

Erec felt the familiar power well up inside, then shoot out of his fingertip toward the guard. Commanding magic was like riding a bicycle—it got easier every time he did it.

The remote shot from the guard's hand toward him. The guard drew back, stunned, then assumed Kyron had done it. "You! Hands up!" He pulled a wooden club out of his holster and raised it, looking for his remote.

Kyron put his hands up, reaching behind his back for his sword. Then he brought it down fast, knocking the guard's club clear across the room. Griffin started to react, but Erec grabbed him. "Let Kyron get him," he whispered. "No use alerting them about two blind servants as well as a military guy."

Griffin reluctantly stepped back as Kyron forced the guard against the wall, still holding the wiggling clock. Nobody wanted to hurt the guard, but they did not see anything to lock him in or tie him up with so they could escape. Kyron raised his sword again.

"No!" Erec gasped. There had to be another way. Maybe he could try using finger magic. The rope that Ajax Hunter had used on Jam, Jack, and Melody worked well. Erec doubted he could do it, but tried to imagine the rope spinning from his finger. *Concentrate.* The same power surged through him. Somewhere in his mind, he was able to take that and spin it into a black cord that spun straight from his finger toward the guard. It wrapped around him, tight, sealing itself off at its end.

Kyron blinked in surprise. "You did that?" He tossed the clock to Erec, who caught it carefully. He grabbed a sheet that was folded on one of the shelves, wrapped the clock inside it, and stuffed it into his backpack.

The secretary looked blasé as they left. "Done already?"

"Yep. The guard said he'll be out in a few minutes."

"All right. Over here, then." She pulled a black stick out from behind the counter and walked toward Kyron.

"What's this?"

"Just the usual check. I have to make sure you don't have any of the stored items on your person." She ran it up and down over Kyron, finding nothing.

Erec tensed. He could see Kyron scratching his shoulder, ready to grab for his sword when she ran her scan stick over Erec. But instead she walked back to the counter. "All right. See you later."

The lowly blind followers were so completely trusted they didn't even merit a check. What would one of them do with a valuable item, anyway?

The three had run far from the army wing before the guard could get loose. Erec found another long, hooded smock in their room and gave it to Kyron. "Time to change personas again."

"What about you?" Kyron asked. "A hunchbacked servant won't be too hard to find."

Erec slid his backpack to his front. "What about a potbellied one? That should throw them off our track." He laughed. So far the plan was going perfectly. Soon he would find Bethany. Wandabelle would be freed. And he . . .

Don't think about that, he told himself. Just think about Bethany. She was all that mattered.

CHAPTER TWENTY-EIGHT

An Interesting Crowd

THREE BLIND SERVANTS shuffled down the hallway toward the central elevators. One was tall and thin, another muscular and stout, and the third had a huge belly. They went up to the eleventh floor and wandered back toward the concrete cell blocks.

Guards swarmed in and out of the area. As soon as Erec, Griffin, and Kyron stepped foot onto the concrete floor, a guard's head snapped up.

"Back!" He waved a stick. "Step back."

Erec said, "But we're supposed to deliver—"

"Over here!" the guard shouted. "We've found them!"

Before Kyron or Griffin could grab their weapons or Erec could think of doing magic, a dozen remote controls pointed at them, freezing them to the spot. A guard walked over and flipped all three of their hoods back.

"This one's definitely Erec Rex. The boss'll be happy now."

"Just in the nick of time, too." Another one nodded. "The Shadow Prince will be here tomorrow. It's going to look better with them locked up."

"Phew." A third guard wiped his brow. "I didn't think we'd be able to do it. The place is so big." He laughed. "Until three 'blind servants' walked into the prison cell blocks. That was a bit of a giveaway."

"Should we throw 'em in the same cell as the other ones? Might look good to keep them together, like we caught 'em all at the same time—or close to it. This will be a great surprise for the Shadow Prince when he gets back." He chuckled.

The three were unfrozen and dragged straight to cell block ten. Erec wiggled his finger and tried to spin a rope out, but he couldn't concentrate. They were thrown inside, and the concrete door slammed shut after them.

After the initial excitement of being reunited, disappointment filled the room. Jam was relieved that Erec was all right, but upset that they all were trapped now. Griffin kicked the door with loud bangs until he was exhausted, then plopped on the floor.

Erec felt sick. How could they have failed? They were so close to freeing their friends. They *had* to get free. He'd seen it in his vision.

Then an awful thought occurred to him. He was able to change the future—that he knew. What if he had done something different than originally planned, and that had changed the outcome of everything? He thought hard, wondering if there were unusual decisions he had made.

Was it the magic? He had spun a rope from his finger. He had never done that before. Maybe that wasn't supposed to happen. Maybe that changed everything.

But what else could they have done to get away? If he hadn't used the rope, Kyron might have killed the guard with his sword. Or maybe the guard would have chased them somewhere and they would still be safe. They still had to rescue their friends, though.

Well, it was too late to worry about it now. Baskania would be here tomorrow. At least everyone was alive.

Even though the cell was crowded, Erec decided to put his Seeing Eyeglasses on. This might be the only time he would ever talk to Bethany again. Instantly, the room on the top floor of the lab tower appeared.

She was alone at her desk, eyes closed. "Bethany?"

Her eyes popped open. "Erec?" She looked terrible. Her eyes were sunken and her lips blue. "I'm glad you're here. I don't have a lot longer, you know."

"I'm really here, Bethany. I'm in the fortress, with you."

"Oh, Erec." Her voice was faint. "You came for me. I didn't want you to. But . . . but I'm glad you're close. I wish we could be together before . . . before this is all over."

More than anything, Erec wanted to say that he was about to save her, that she should just hold on and he'd be at her side. "I'm sorry, Bethany."

"No, Erec. Please. You rescued me already from my awful life. Nothing could be as bad as where I was when you found me. I've lived a lifetime of magic since then, all in less than a year. This was more than I ever dreamed of. Even if it ends this way."

"I . . . You're my best friend, Bethany."

"You're mine, too, Erec."

They sat a moment in silence, listening to each other breathe, until it became too painful. "Love you," he whispered, and pulled the glasses off his face.

Even though the cell was full, nobody said a word.

Erec sat upright on the hard stone bench. Everyone around him was asleep. Was it night still? His watch said four in the morning, but he had no idea if it magically changed to the right time zone or not.

He grabbed his backpack and rooted through it. Dragon blood vial, fake serving tray, MagicLight. Where was it? There was a glass jar—but he jumped when he saw Oscar's eye staring back at him. Erec put it back and dug some more. There. Another glass jar.

This one held Nitrowisherine.

He had to think hard. Wishing Bethany could escape the lab tower wouldn't work. He already had tried that. So the only thing left to do was to wish that all of them could be there with her. Then she could drink the dragon blood.

It was worth a try. The concrete cell was thick, and probably filled with magic. Breaking out wouldn't be easy. He decided to use all the Nitrowisherine left in the jar—which wasn't a lot—and hope for the best.

Jam was watching him. "Is young sir okay? Would you like a meal from the Serving Tray?"

"No thanks, Jam." He shook Griffin by the shoulder. "Help me wake everyone up, okay?"

Soon all six of them were sitting up, Melody yawning and Jack stretching.

"Listen, guys," Erec said quietly. "I have an explosive here called Nitrowisherine. After it detonates, it grants you a wish. So I'm going to wish for us all to join Bethany, so we can help her escape. Okay?"

Jack's jaw dropped open. "You can get us out of here? Oh, *man*. That's great."

Melody started jumping up and down.

"This might not work, guys. Once my mom was a prisoner in King Pluto's dungeon. Nitrowisherine was only *part* of what it took to blast her out."

Jam thought about that. "Well, dungeons are usually higher security than prison cells. The really bad prisoners get moved to the dungeons."

"Cross your fingers. We'll see soon enough." They all crowded into the corner of the cell, arms covering their faces. Erec held the vial of dragon blood to his chest. "I'll throw it at the far wall, but the whole room will shake. And *be careful* not to accidentally wish for something before I do, even in your head. I'll wish out loud. That should help."

They steadied themselves as Erec counted. "One . . . two . . . three!" He hurled the glass jar into the wall across from them. It shattered and then—

Ka-*boom!* The walls and floor shook, knocking them over in a heap. Concrete benches dropped from the walls, breaking into pieces. Cracks ran through the stone around them as the room continued to shudder.

"I wish we were all with Bethany in the lab tower!"

The world grew quiet and still. The room around them instantly expanded—but that wasn't right. They were in another room altogether. It was huge, with a high, domed ceiling and dust motes floating in the air. Tables nearby were piled with papers and odd equipment. Erec peered through the dim lighting. She had to be here somewhere. . . .

Bethany, chained to her desk, seemed so small and weak she almost faded into the background. Big red eyes stared back at him in disbelief. She was as pale as the piles of papers stacked on her desk.

THE THREE FURIES

Even the math books here were giving her no comfort.

He imagined what they must look like, six people appearing at once in a tangled heap on the floor, getting up and dusting themselves off. Erec's hood was half up, Griffin's was off, but he wasn't somebody Bethany would recognize. She probably thought she was imagining this whole thing.

Erec pulled his hood off and walked up to Bethany. She gazed up at him, arms chained tight at her sides to the chair. The metal cones dug into her scalp—Baskania probably used them to pull her memories out. She looked so pathetic. Hot tears ran down his cheeks as he smoothed her hair back.

"Here." He untwisted the vial of dragon blood and held it out. "You better drink this right away. I don't know when people will be coming."

Then he realized that her hands were chained down. "Oh, sorry. Let me do it for you."

Her voice sounded worn-down. "I'll try. I haven't eaten in a while."

Erec held the vial to her lips, sure that the idea of drinking purple dragon blood was disgusting. But she dutifully swallowed. He raised it higher until the last drops were gone.

"We did it, Bethany! That dragon blood broke the Draw Baskania put on you. Now we're free to go—once I can get you out of here. Look—Kyron's here! Can you believe it? He's got a silver sword. Maybe it can cut through these chains."

An odd transformation was happening to Bethany as he spoke. At first he was worried that the dragon blood was making her sick. She turned a purplish color, then a ruddy red. But after that she looked better than he had ever seen her. Her skin glowed, and her eyes sparkled. A huge smile spread over her face.

"You're *here*!" she cried. "That stuff was great. I mean, it didn't taste great. Kind of like spicy metal. But I've never felt this good—this strong! It's like I could break these chains myself." She tugged on one side and then the other, and the steel links on both sides snapped like breadsticks. When she jumped up, the metal cones in her head popped out, bouncing onto the floor. Her skin healed immediately where they had been. "It feels so *good* to *move*! I'm surprised I'm not sore and stiff from being tied there for so long, but I guess the dragon blood helps that, too."

Erec remembered one time that he had tasted dragon blood. After his first quest he had been badly injured. Patchouli had given him just one drop of her blood to heal him, and he felt stronger than a steam engine, all his pain gone. He couldn't imagine what Bethany must feel like, having drunk a whole vial of that blood. Maybe it was like how he felt when he turned part-dragon.

Bethany squealed and raced to Erec, throwing her arms around him and burying her face in his shoulder. "You did it. You're here, and you saved me. I can't believe it!"

"*Don't* believe it." A dark voice rang out. Baskania stepped out of the shadows with a flourish of his black cape. "As far as I can see, nobody has been saved or gone anywhere at all. In fact, it seems to be just the opposite. I return, expecting to extract the final memories from my captive. But look! To my great surprise, I have several gifts waiting for me. First, someone has finally located your earliest memories, Bethany. The ones that were removed from you after your parents were killed." He shoved a frightened boy in front of him. "This boy here apparently was given your oldest memories at an early age when he was adopted. And second, Erec Rex has delivered himself straight to me. What a treat! This could not be better." He cackled with glee.

Baskania had a third eye in the middle of his forehead today, and it was glancing around the room. This was not as many as he usually had adorning his face—and he wore an eye patch over the hole that still waited for Erec's dragon eye. His silver-gray hair led to a sharp widow's peak and his thin lips curled into a sneer. "Oh, I see you've vacated your seat for the moment, Bethany. Well, that's good timing, isn't it?" He pushed the boy behind the desk where Bethany had been held. "Come on, Ajax. Fasten the projectors on to him."

Ajax Hunter appeared from behind Baskania, metal cones in his hand. The boy squirmed and protested as Ajax pushed them into his scalp, but with a wave of Ajax's finger the boy froze.

Baskania smiled. "Always nice to have an audience for exciting events. I suppose I will enjoy Bethany seeing her early past, remembering what her parents were like before I ordered them to be killed. So sentimental." He yawned. "And after we've all enjoyed the nice movie, and the suspense of whether or not I have at last learned how to do the Final Magic, then I'll get rid of all of you. Erec, I'm delighted to have two dragon eyes now, to accompany my new, great powers."

Everyone's eyes were glued to the screen where the boy's memory replacement—Bethany's earliest memories—were projected. But they did not start with Bethany as a baby. She looked about three years old, tugging on her mother's skirt. "I'm tired," she complained. "Pick me up. I've walked three hundred and forty-two steps by myself." She put her arms in the air and jumped. "Up-ee! Up! Up!"

"Now, Bethany." Her mother, Ruth, sighed. "You know it's too hard for me to hold you now. It won't be much longer, maybe a few weeks, okay? Why don't you sit down and think about how many seconds there are in two weeks, okay?"

She bent and patted Bethany on the head. But something about Ruth's shape caught everybody's eye.

When she stood, her condition was obvious.

Bethany's mother was pregnant.

Baskania swung around to Bethany. "Is this true? Do you have a younger sibling?"

She shrugged, frightened. "I . . . I don't remember. I didn't know I had any siblings before. That memory was all taken from me."

Baskania growled. "Forward this a few weeks."

Ajax flicked his head at the projector, and the movie spun ahead in time. Bethany was on a couch holding a tiny, bald baby in her arms, kissing its forehead. Her older brother, Pi, raced by. "Don't drop him! Cuz he won't bounce, he'll just hit, right there, on the floor, and slide three point seven eight inches, and then he'll get hurt and cry, and you will be in trouble!"

Bethany watched her young self in the movie, eyes wide and glistening. "I have a baby brother," she whispered.

"He's not a baby anymore." Erec said. "We'll find him."

"No." Baskania's voice was controlled, furious. "*I'll* find him. You have a younger sibling. Do you know what this means? I've wasted all of my time with you. The prophecy wasn't about you. You weren't the youngest child of the greatest seer of the first king of Alypium. I need your little brother." He raised his fist. "You'll all pay for this! There's no need to keep any of you alive one second longer." Baskania pointed a finger at Bethany and a black mist shot out toward her.

Erec stepped in to shield her, and the mist was sucked straight into his Amulet of Virtues.

"I'd forgotten about that thing," Baskania said, sneering. "That will make my job a little trickier. But you're my captives now. I have all the time in the world to destroy you."

"We are not your captives." Erec took a step closer to him. "We're leaving, right now. You can't stop us."

Baskania pointed at Erec again and again, sending daggers, ropes, and lightning bolts at him, but all of them were sucked right into his amulet.

"You see?" Erec raised his hands. "You can't hurt me now."

Baskania's face was dark with anger. "So foolish. So very, very foolish. You'll find out before long just what I can do to you. But, in the meantime, I'd like you to try to find Bethany, to rescue her at all." With a flourish, the air in the room rippled. Bethany stepped apart into two identical Bethanys, who stepped apart to make four, then eight, and on and on until the room was full of identical girls.

Cackling, Baskania pointed at one Bethany after the next, sending black puffs of air that knocked them to the ground. "Isn't this fun? It's like a game. Will I kill the real Bethany before you can find her? Too bad there's no way for you to tell the difference!"

Shocked, Erec looked around wildly. What could he do? In a half-formed thought he grabbed the Doubler charm that Wandabelle had given him. Its power was unpredictable, but maybe he could use it to make even more Bethanys. That would protect the one real one until he could find her.

He waved the shiny charm in the air, hoping that it picked up the spell that had multiplied Bethany, and not the little deathly blasts Baskania was making. *Please,* he begged. It was a much larger spell, and it had made that gigantic ripple through the room.

A blast of wind raced through the room, and a ripple of lightning zipped through the air, straight at Erec. Baskania watched, confused, as the light entered Erec's pendant, and two identical bolts shot out into the air. They spun a moment as if deciding where to go. Then one turned back and hit Erec, and another headed straight for Baskania.

Erec had a strange feeling, like something was coming alive inside him. He wanted to pull away from it, and when he did, another version of himself stepped out and stood at his side, staring at him in awe. Then both of them felt it again, and soon there were four Erecs, then eight. The room was getting mobbed with Erecs, Bethanys . . . and Baskanias! The Doubler charm had hit him with the spell too, and the room filled in chaos with imitation people.

Soon the feeling ended, but the room was packed with individuals who looked just like him, Baskania, and Bethany. All of the Baskanias glared around the room, pointing at people, but Erec noticed that no smoke was coming from their fingers. They must have been doing the same thing that the original Baskania was, but without his powers.

Good. So they were just crowding the room, getting in the way. He called for Bethany, but after he did, all of the other Erecs started calling for her too. Not in a chorus, and not even in the exact same way. But they were all looking around, searching, just as Erec was.

The Bethanys were answering "Yes?" all over the room. It would be impossible to find Bethany in this mess and get her out of here.

Jack, Jam, and Griffin were stunned. Erec could not even see Melody or Kyron in the crowd. He had to figure out a way to determine which of these Bethanys was real. The other ones probably didn't have her math powers. He asked a Bethany by his side, "What's two thousand divided by two?"

She shrugged and went back to calling out for Erec, not even caring that she had just spoken to him. So, the imitations really only cared about imitating the originals, then. They had no agenda of their own.

Baskanias stalked through the crowds glowering and pointing at Erecs and Bethanys. But Erec noticed something strange. One of the figures walking by had Erec's head on Baskania's body. How did that happen?

Then he saw the cause. A Bethany and Baskania imitation crashed into each other by accident and combined on the spot into an odd-looking creature that looked like Bethany's legs and arms coming from Baskania's body and head. The clothing was strange in configuration, too, with his cloak tucked into her jeans. The resulting figure took turns acting like Bethany and Baskania as if that was totally normal.

He scanned the crowd for a Bethany that was doing things before the others, but it was too hard to tell which was leading. If only he could see the difference, and find her, maybe they could escape in all the chaos. . . .

Wait! A thought flashed into his head. *The eyeglass shop!* He was the only one who could see the magical frames, because of his dragon eyes. Maybe that would work here, too.

He spun his eyes in his head, and everything glowed bright green. The imitation people that filled the room looked almost see-through. Bethany was off to the side of the room, smashed in a crowd of imitations. The real Baskania was coming closer to him, zapping imitations as he walked.

Something bumped into him, hard . . . literally *into* him. One of the imitation people had collided with him. Erec looked down at himself, afraid to discover that he had become some odd combination of parts.

But instead he appeared completely like Baskania. Seeing himself look like his worst enemy, someone who terrified him, took his breath away for a moment. Had he *become* Baskania, then? Was *he* an imitation now?

But his mind was working just fine. He was in control of his body. He tried to use his dragon eyes again, but they wouldn't work at all. Somehow, having this imitation skin over him was messing with his powers.

The real Baskania came into view. Real magic shot from his finger, knocking people over. That gave Erec an idea. He wiggled a finger, trying to send Baskania up into the air. Power welled inside him, and he could feel it come all the way to his fingertip . . . but then it was blocked. He couldn't do any magic with this Baskania skin on.

That led him to another thought. If the fake Baskania covering him took away all of his powers, then maybe that would work the other way, too. He shoved his way through the crowd until he was at the side of the real Baskania—who took no notice of him, looking as he was. Erec grabbed an imitation Erec firmly and shoved it hard, straight into Baskania.

The Erec imitation combined with the real Baskania. What was left was someone who looked just like Erec.

Baskania, looking like Erec, scowled at himself angrily. "What's this about?" He growled, pointing at himself, but nothing happened. He shook his finger. "What's wrong with me?" He pointed at an Erec imitation and realized he could do no magic with the Erec skin on.

Erec grinned with relief. It was time to find Bethany. He called for her—and soon all of the Baskanias were calling for Bethany. *Great*, he thought. Just what he wanted, to be the new leader of a band of imitations of his arch enemy.

The Erecs were cursing and growling, in imitation of their new leader.

Erec shoved through the room to where he had seen Bethany. Right in the middle of the tangle was one who looked at him fearfully, and ducked behind some imitations. That had to be her, he thought. The others didn't pay attention to him.

"Bethany!" he called out. But he realized his voice was now Baskania's. How would she know it was really him? "It's me, Erec," he called to her. "We switched bodies. It's really me. We have to get out of here!"

She peeked at him, doubtful, and shuddered when she saw him. All around them Baskanias were calling out, "It's me, Erec!"

"Come on." He held out his hand. "Would Baskania know that I said I loved you last night?"

"He might." Bethany stepped forward. "But he also would have tried to kill me by now. This isn't quite his . . . style. I can tell it's you."

The Baskanias were not able to keep up with their exact conversation, but they were chattering animatedly with the Bethanys in the room. Erec threw his arms around her, but Bethany pushed him back. "Sorry. I'm not quite ready to hug Baskania yet."

Laughing, he grabbed Bethany's wrist and headed for their other friends. The Erecs were screaming, "You idiot. It's me!" and the Baskanias were dragging Bethanys behind them.

Kyron, Griffin, Jack, Jam, and Melody were gathered in a tight cluster, watching in amazement. The boy who had Bethany's memory was standing with them now. When Erec walked up to them, holding Bethany, they all cowered.

"Guys," he whispered. "It's me, Erec. Long story, but you have to believe me. We're getting out of here now."

Bethany nodded. "It's really him. You guys ready to go?'

Melody looked doubtful. "You don't look like Erec."

"I know. But Baskania doesn't look like himself either now. That's a good thing. He can't use his powers—for now, at least."

"He sounds like me cap'n. Kind of." Griffin scowled. "If yer me cap'n, tell me what my job was in the Nightmare Realm."

Erec laughed, wishing his laugh sounded less spooky. "You were the best toilet cleaner there was. Just needed a little help from a big water-hose-snake-thing."

"It's him," Griffin declared. "Let's go!"

They all grabbed hands and headed through the crowds toward the door. All of the Erecs were facing a bewildered Ajax Hunter, screaming at him. "If I only had my powers I'd skin you alive, Ajax."

Erec walked up to Ajax, trying to speak in arrogant, low tones. "Pathetic, aren't they? Lock them all up. I've got Bethany and the others. I'm going to take care of them personally. Don't let me be disturbed."

Ajax nodded. "Of course, my prince." He bowed. "I'm sorry. If there was anything I could have done—"

"I'll deal with you later," Erec sneered, as did all of the Baskanias behind him.

"Don't *listen* to that thing! It's not me!" one of the Erecs screamed, followed by the others.

Erec did not stay to see what happened. He and his friends found a hallway with elevators and waited for one to take them to the first floor. Baskanias and Bethanys followed them out, crowding in the elevator with them until it was full. Others had to wait for more elevators to come.

"Looks like we're not getting rid of them," Bethany said.

Erec shrugged. "I don't know how long these phony guys will last. I'm looking forward to seeing the reaction we get downstairs."

The reaction on the main floor was profound. From army generals to secretaries, people fell back in horror when they saw masses of their leader, a hundred Shadow Princes, storming down the hallways. Most of the witnesses probably assumed that this was part of some new plan, but that didn't make the sight less terrifying. Elevators full of Baskanias and Bethanys poured more hordes into the halls. The only people who did not react at all were the blind followers, who scurried around immune to the goings-on.

"How do we get out of here?" Bethany asked.

Erec paused. Out the front door were the Vetalas, and the shadow demon who would doubtless know exactly who he was. That was a problem, because he had no powers at all now with this Baskania skin on. If he couldn't even use his dragon eyes, he probably couldn't get cloudy thoughts if he needed them. The laughter vial was used up.

He grabbed the collar of an army officer who was pressed up against the wall, trying to stay out of the way.

"Yes, my prince." The officer tried to bow. "Can I help you, sir?"

"Lower the bridge to the Jakarta entrance. Can you do that?"

He bowed again. "Y-yes, sir! I'll go to the bridge corps now, sir. Anything else, sir?"

Erec thought. "Yes. I want a path cleared outside, so none of . . .

us is bothered by the beasts out there on the way to the bridge. Is that understood?"

The officer looked confused. "You're taking the bridge across to the Jakarta entrance?"

Erec raised his voice to cover any slip he might have made. "Yes, are you deaf?" he roared. "Are *you* questioning my decisions?"

"N-no! Sorry sir. W-would you like the usual exit opened up, I mean? So no path will have to be ... cleared ... out there?" His voice had raised to a tiny peep.

"Of course," Erec cried. "Just making sure you knew what you were doing, officer."

"Oh! Thank you." The officer bowed repeatedly, then ran to obey.

Erec grimaced at Bethany. "Do you think I pulled that one off?"

She nodded. "Only thing is, now we have to find the way to the 'usual exit.'"

"No problem." Erec led the crowds down a hall toward the army wing. He grabbed the next officer he saw. "You! Lead the way to the *usual exit*. The bridge better be down by now."

The officer looked bewildered. "The usual *guest* exit to the bridge to Jakarta, sir?" he squeaked. "You want me to take you there?"

"Yes." Erec released him. "I want you to clear the way for us. This place is a zoo today."

"Of course, sir. With pleasure." The officer walked before the growing crowd of Baskanias and Bethanys, and the few odd people walking with them. Up a flight of stairs and down more hallways, people and imitations marched in a never-ending parade, until finally reaching a steel wall.

"Open!" the officer yelled, and men at a control desk in the room, eyes wide at the sight before them, pulled levers and made the steel slide apart in two pieces.

A bridge led right out of the room and across the water. Surrounding it, the entire way, was a clear glistening bubble that looked like plastic. They all filed onto the bridge. Under them, zombies marched and manticores leaped up at them, and specters swept by, but none was able to get through the barrier around them. Lalalalal appeared, spiraling down from the air and landing on Griffin's shoulder.

"Looks like we made it." Erec grinned at Bethany.

He face wrinkled into a frown. "Sorry. It's still hard to get over your . . . looks. I hope you can get this mask removed when we're home."

Erec melted inside when she said "home." Were they really going to be okay? Then his stomach tightened, thinking about what awaited him in Windows to the Soul eye care shop. This was it for him. He only had a few minutes left with Bethany. And he could not kiss her now, looking like this. If only they had more time to talk . . .

That's when the truth hit him. He looked like Baskania now. No police snake was going to bite him looking like this. He would get out, with everyone else! He was going to make it!

"Yeah!" Erec shouted, throwing a fist in the air. He grabbed Bethany and gave her a huge hug, even though she shoved him away. "We're going to make it! Let's go!"

The bridge was a quarter of a mile long, and they ran the whole way to the small beach on the other side. Erec, Bethany, Jam, Jack, Melody, Kyron, the boy with Bethany's memories, and Griffin, with Lalalalal on his shoulder, crowded into the passageway that led back into the shop.

"Act calm, everyone. There's a police snake waiting for us, so we have to be careful." Erec held his breath as he opened the door to the shop.

This time the door opened behind the counter, carrying shelves of eyeglasses. The clerk swung around expectantly. "Here they come, officer . . . oh! Excuse me. I didn't know . . ." He looked terrified as Baskania strode into the room, followed by Erec's friends.

Erec looked down on the clerk in disgust. "You are to keep this door open until everyone has gotten through. Is that understood?"

By this time more Baskanias had filed out into the shop. The clerk held his hand over his heart, mouth open. "Yes, master. I-I saw Erec Rex before. If he comes back—"

"Have him arrested, immediately."

Erec turned to run out the door. He had to get out fast, before anything went wrong.

But then he heard his old voice, screaming in rage. "You idiots! Do you think you can get rid of me that easily? I might not have my powers now, but I know ways around this place. And when I get back to normal, you will all pay!"

Baskania, looking exactly like Erec, burst through the door behind them. He ran toward Erec with a ferocious expression. Yet, exactly as Erec had seen in his future, the clerk shouted, "There he is! There's Erec Rex. Get him!"

A snakelike police officer wearing a tall stovepipe hat dove from behind the counter.

Erec's breath caught. His vision was unfolding, plain as day, before his eyes.

The officer sprang, flying through the air until he hit Baskania in the stomach. He slithered, wrapping himself around what he thought were Erec's legs until they both tumbled, rolling, onto the floor. Then he opened his mouth wider than imaginable, long fangs poised over Baskania's leg. In a flash, the snakelike thing bit, its jaws sinking deep into flesh.

Erec saw what looked like himself gasping and passing out. A few more police officers appeared, pulling "Erec" back with them through the hidden door.

"We've got him now, no worries," one of them said. "He's help-less. This one'll never escape again."

CHAPTER TWENTY-NINE

Your Sworn Enemy

EREC FELT STRANGE being in a normal city in Upper Earth after seeing zombies and specters just one minute earlier. But not as strange as it was for the citizens of Kemang, in South Jakarta, to see mobs of identical people jogging down their streets. People pointed, stared, and ran away in fear.

Erec realized that Baskania's appearance made the problem even worse. Half the people walking by wore long black cloaks and had a third eye in the middle of their foreheads. He wondered if the people living in Kemang would chalk it up to some kind of mass nightmare. Erec would have to make sure that none of the Baskania replicas were left behind to roam around, terrifying people.

"Look!" Kyron pointed. Behind them, legions of Erecs poured out of the eye care shop, far more than the police officers could capture on their own. They looked aimless, with nobody to follow. So Kyron ushered them along after the Bethanys and Baskanias, and soon they all fell into step.

"How many of us do you think there are?" Erec asked Bethany.

"I counted a few times when we were in the fortress. There were one hundred of each of us in the beginning, so three hundred. But a few of them combined into other things, and some got killed by Baskania. I'd guess there're about two hundred and fifty left."

Jam led the way to the Port-O-Door and pulled out the stored password. Moments later, the door to Spartacus Kilroy's house was open, and they all trotted through.

Safe! It felt so good to be back in Alypium again. He had done it! Bethany was rescued, and the Draw spell was broken. More than that, Baskania wouldn't bother trying to capture her again. The prophecy hadn't been about her all along.

Spartacus Kilroy heard the commotion and ran into the room, then stepped back in shock when he saw Erec.

"Spartacus!" Erec ran up and gave him a hug. "You wouldn't believe what happened."

Spartacus looked like he would faint. Jam raced over and sat him down. "I know it looks odd, sir. But that man is not Baskania. It's Erec Rex, sir. He just . . . looks like Baskania right now."

Before Spartacus could adjust to that idea, hordes of Baskanias, Bethanys, and Erecs poured into his home. His lips moved silently for a moment, then his eyes crossed, and he passed out.

"Oops!" Erec wasn't sure how he should have handled the introductions, but there probably was a better way. Griffin ushered the look-alikes outside, which seemed like a good idea. Once out in the open, the Bethanys, Erecs, and Baskanias huddled in separate groups. The Bethanys and Baskanias peered inside the windows and tried to emulate their doubles inside.

They waited for all of the imitations to get through, and then Kyron and Griffin went back into Jakarta through the Port-O-Door to look for any stragglers. Lalalalal raced through an open window and straight to his coop, excited to relay all of his adventures to his friends. Jam took the boy who had Bethany's early memories back through the Port-O-Door to his home and then returned.

Erec was floating inside. Everything was perfect. Everything except . . .

He felt like he was being picky, but he didn't want to look like his archenemy anymore.

"Picky, picky boy." Erec spun around to see the Hermit, shaking his head and tut-tutting. "It's always something, isn't it? Never satisfied." He handed Erec a cup of steaming brown liquid that smelled rancid. "Why don't you have a drink?"

Erec looked at it in disgust, then gulped it down. He nearly choked—it tasted worse than it looked. "What was that?"

"Just a little health drink. Bathwater from the muglumps in Salsaban. Like it?"

Erec looked down at himself. He still looked just like Baskania. "It's not working."

"Oh, I think it is. Your complexion is a little brighter, I think." He giggled.

"You mean, that wasn't supposed to turn me back into my normal self?" He pointed at the Hermit and said in his most threatening Baskania voice, "I'll get you someday."

The Hermit laughed joyously. "It would be fun to keep you like this forever. But if you really want to look like yourself again, swallow this." He handed Erec a vial of purple liquid.

Erec eyed it suspiciously. "Is this going to give me green polka-dots?"

But the Hermit had disappeared. Erec opened the vial. It resembled the dragon blood that Bethany had drunk to remove the Draw spell. He took one sip and felt something inside dissolve. A figure resembling Baskania stepped out of him, looked at himself with relief, and darted away. Erec looked in the mirror, afraid to see. . . .

His normal face looked back at him, then grinned. "Bethany!" He ran out to find her. At first he couldn't tell which one she was, as a host of Bethanys were wandering around inside. But once he swiveled his dragon eyes around, there was no question.

The Erecs inside and out rejoiced, imitating him with vigor. The Baskanias, however, grew confused with their leader gone.

Erec grabbed Bethany's hand. "Let's get out of here. Jam, do you think Aunt Salsa would mind if we all came to her house? I mean, not all the imitations. Just us."

"Not at all, young sir."

"Um, Spartacus? Would it be okay if these fake look-alike things stayed on your farm for a little while, just until we find a place for them? I hate to ask, but . . ."

Spartacus nodded weakly. "It's just going to take me a little while to get used to seeing the Shadow Prince all over my house."

"I'd keep them outside. Maybe they can help out here." The offer was lame, Erec knew, but Spartacus agreed with a strained smile.

Jam led Erec and Bethany to the Port-O-Door. Erec could not help but notice the wistful look on the faces of the Bethanys and Erecs as they watched them disappear.

***

June would not stop hugging Erec and Bethany, until finally it got embarrassing. She sniffed, whispering to Erec, "I'm so ashamed. I told you not to go, and when I think what would have happened to her . . ."

"You didn't know. Of course you said that. You're my mom."

After telling the story about twenty times from different perspectives, they started to feel like they had really had a great adventure.

"Remember how funny Master Vetu looked when his rotting heads rolled to the ground?"

Those who had not been there shuddered, but everyone else burst into laughter, remembering how funny it had seemed at the time.

Erec had not eaten anything good for a long while, and the cookies that Aunt Salsa kept bringing from the kitchen were amazing. Bethany took one bite and swooned. "I never thought I'd eat real food again."

After Aunt Salsa heard that, she produced snack after snack for Bethany until finally she was holding her stomach and groaning.

"Can we go somewhere and talk, Bethany?" Erec said.

Looking up brightly, she nodded.

"We'll be right back, guys." Bethany followed him into Aunt Salsa's Port-O-Door. "Let's see. Otherness. Here's Nemea. Remember the first time we went there, and found the entrance to the Nevervarld?"

She laughed. They left the door in a tree and sat on a log in the woods, enjoying the quiet.

Nemea was as beautiful as he remembered it. The sun hung golden, streaming rays like spotlights through the thick branches overhead. Birds called out in the sky.

"Look!" Bethany pointed at a dragon flying high overhead.

They were finally alone together. She was back home again. With him.

This was the best day of his life.

Bethany grinned. "Now I've been saved twice by a prince."

"Hey, you've saved me, too. Remember pulling me out of the Nevervarld? I'd still be in there if not for you."

She didn't answer. Instead she looked out into the distance. "You know, I really thought my life was over. It was horrible there. Miserable, lonely, painful, scary. But the whole time I kept thinking it wasn't really that bad. You were still safe, and that made it all okay. I don't know if you realize how much you've given me. After my parents died, everything was gone. My life really started again when I met you." She shrugged. "So I kept on thinking that even if I died, every moment of this last year made up for it a million times over."

"And I kept hating myself for letting you get caught. I should have come back sooner, and been there for you."

"You didn't know that this would happen. King Piter was there— we all thought I'd be safe with him around."

Erec nodded. "When I came back, I couldn't believe what had happened to him. He was a mess. Completely obsessed by his scepter. He's with Queen Posey now, luckily, and doing a lot better."

Bethany slid down and leaned back on the log so she could look up at the sky, and Erec joined her. Huge birds soared overhead, and they spotted occasional dragons.

"I have a little brother," Bethany said, as if just realizing for the first time. "He would be eleven now. Pi never said anything about him, and King Piter didn't either. I wonder where he is."

Whoever he was, the kid was in a lot of danger now, Erec thought. But he didn't want to remind Bethany of that after all she'd been through.

"I hope he's okay. I really want to meet him. This means I have a real family!" She turned partly toward him. "I mean, it was fine with just me and Pi. But to have more than just us two . . . Do you know there are entire cultures in places like the Amazon that have only three numbers? One, two, and more-than-two. My family is now of the highest order." She laughed. "Sorry. After being alone so long, I'm letting my inner math geek slip out. I try to keep it under control."

"It's okay, Bethany. I like you, inner math geek and all."

She giggled. "And I like you too, inner Prince Charming hero and all."

"Shut up." He threw a handful of leaves at her.

She glanced around her. ". . . six . . . you threw approximately seventeen leaves at me, which should be only about one hundredth of your ability. Which makes you either incredibly weak, or lazy—I'm not sure which." She laughed and tossed a few back at him.

"Oh, yeah?" Erec tried to hide his grin, and wagged his finger, looking at all the leaves around them on the forest floor. He focused on the feeling the Hermit had taught him, and felt his strength well up inside, then shoot out his finger. *Lift.* Leaves all around them lifted. *Whirl.* They spun through the air like a little cyclone. He brought them straight over Bethany and released, and for a few minutes it rained leaves down on both of them.

Bethany laughed, kicking her feet in the air and scattering them. Soon they were both covered in a leaf pile. Bethany kicked around inside and threw some into the air. Then she looked at Erec with a smirk. "Is that all you can do, Prince Charming? I thought by now you could make the whole forest come down."

"That's it. I'm returning you to Baskania." He called out, pointing, "Hey! She's right here! Come and get her!"

She laughed. "You're stuck with me now." She pulled herself up to a full sitting position. "By the way, how did you learn finger magic? That's amazing."

"The Hermit." Erec wondered where he was now. He guessed he'd see him again when he did his next quest. Which reminded him—

"My fifth quest isn't done," he announced. He lifted the Amulet of Virtues on his chest. Only four of its twelve segments glowed with color for the four quests he had completed. "Wandabelle, the Clown Fairy, is still trapped in the Nightmare Realm. But guess what I found in Baskania's fortress? The only way to free her is a special alarm clock, and we broke into the Army Security Headquarters and got it!" He rose to his feet. "I need to save her as soon as I can. That place is awful. Plus, the clowns need her. They're starting to die off because they need a leader to survive. Their rulers were killed ten years ago, and the Clown Fairy was all that was holding them together."

"Why was she stuck in there?" Bethany frowned. "That's awful!"

"Guess who did it? Baskania. He's holding her there, since it's the only place she can't escape from, and on May first he's going to give her to one of the three Furies—Tisiphone—in exchange for tripling his powers. Then he wants to use the remaining clowns that don't die out and train them for his armies."

Bethany looked pale. "We better get her out fast, Erec. As soon as Baskania gets wind that the alarm clock is stolen, I bet he'll move her somewhere else. Do you think he already knows?"

Erec thought about the guard that they had left tied up in the Army Security Headquarters. The secretary had probably found him soon after, and they both would have reported what happened. "Yeah. Good point. Baskania may be trapped in his own prison cell right now, looking like me, but that can't last forever. We're going to have to be really careful. . . . What am I saying 'we' for? The last thing *you* need is to go somewhere and risk your life right now. How about a nice vacation in Americorth North with my mom and Jam, and his nice Aunt Salsa? You can see all the sights down there with them and stay far away from Baskania. Sound good?"

She glared at him, then lay against the log and closed her eyes. "I don't know, Erec. I can completely understand how you feel. Believe me. After all of this, both of us just want to know that everyone is safe. And believe me, taking a break with your family sounds better than you can imagine right now. But I don't want to let you out of my sight. It sounds weird, but we've been apart for so long, the idea of you going to some Nightmare Realm without me freaks me out." She shrugged. "Imagine if you were sitting home and I was going by myself."

Erec didn't want to imagine that. "It would be awful." He laughed. "I don't want to let you out of my sight either. But it's easier for me knowing that you're somewhere safe."

They sat in silence a while, before Bethany said, "I'm going to do the smart thing, not what I want to do, just this once. I'll stay with your mom. But I don't ever want to hear you trying to protect me again, okay?"

He looked at her in surprise. "What made you decide that?"

She shrugged. "The dragon's blood you gave me really perked me up. But I can feel it starting to wear off. I haven't really slept in months. I think I'm going to be so wiped out, I won't be able to go with you." She scratched her head, puzzled. "I know this sounds weird, but a really unusual thing helped me get out of the fortress. I could feel the dragon blood break the Draw that Baskania put on me. But something else was holding me too. It was like Baskania had willed me to stay, and I wouldn't have been able to override it. It's hard to describe.

"But after the Draw was gone, I felt this powerful urge to get going. I know this sounds crazy, but I really needed to go to this place called Cinnalim, in Otherness. Can you believe it? Like some odd urge to take a vacation possessed me . . . and that's what let me escape with you. I don't even *know* anything about Cinnalim, except that they have that amazing chocolate rain there. But I really want to go now and see what that place is all about. I get the feeling it's incredible. So, when you finish your quest I'll get a day or two of sleep, then I'll go to Cinnalim. Do you want to meet me there?"

Erec laughed, knowing what happened. "I know why you want to go there, Bethany. A man there called Danen has a people-magnet, and he's pulling you to him. That was the first thing that the Fates said I had to do to get you out alive—to go to Cinnalim and get Danen to use his magnet on you." He was amazed that things had worked out as well as they had. What if he had done all of this without the magnet on? Would Bethany have remained stuck?

"Ooh, you've been to Cinnalim?" Bethany leaned forward, excited. "Tell me all about it. Was it beautiful?"

"Yes," Erec admitted. "And the rain was pretty good too—if you're careful not to eat the bugs that fall in with it."

She bounced up and down in excitement. "I can't wait to see it!"

"Danen's going to have to turn his magnet off you. And if you go, you'll have to be really careful there—Baskania might pop in unannounced, or have people watching. But maybe you and Jam can go down there together and ask Danen to switch the magnet off."

Her eyes lit up. "Maybe we should just go *now*. I can always sleep *there*, right?"

"No," Erec said firmly. "You're going to be exhausted soon. And going is not completely safe. So plan it out right, okay?"

She nodded, biting her lip.

"Let's go back and talk to Jam about it," he suggested. "Oh, guess what? You're not going to believe this. But I know for sure now that Danny and Sammy are King Piter's other triplets—my lost brother and sister!"

"What?" She clapped her hands together. "How did you find that out?"

"I had a few different hints. Dumpling Smith and her gang kept trying to steal them away. She was our old babysitter—she's got to be working for Baskania. But what told me for sure was using my dragon eyes to see into the future. I asked to see something good that would happen, and I saw Danny and Sammy being crowned king and queen! I remember it was the best feeling. I'm guessing Sammy will replace Queen Posey, and Danny will rule Aorth instead of King Pluto. My mom said something about it too. But Danny and Sammy *can't* find out yet. Remember what happened when I learned who I was too early? So keep it a secret, okay?"

"Of course," she agreed. "Maybe they can go with you to finish your fifth quest."

He nodded. "That's just what I was hoping."

A few minutes after they returned, the dragon blood wore off. Bethany's eyes were closing. Zoey and Trevor were at her sides, arms around her, and she seemed to be melting into them. Erec was glad that she was no longer talking about going to Cinnalim immediately.

Aunt Salsa tucked Bethany away in a quiet room with trays of snacks and water surrounding her bed, in case she woke hungry. Erec peeked in to say good-bye, but she was sound asleep.

He took Jam and his Aunt Salsa aside. "Could you make sure she stays away from the Port-O-Door until she's had enough sleep? Danen's magnet in Cinnalim is pulling her to go back there. Jam, would you mind going there with her when she's ready, and getting Danen to turn his magnet off now? Unless you can do it by phone."

"They didn't give us their number, young sir, but I can see if they're listed." Jam spoke into his finger briefly. "Alas, as I was afraid. I'll go with her when she's ready, then, young sir."

"Thanks." Erec took the alarm clock out of his backpack and unwrapped it from the sheet. Relieved to be let out, it stretched and took a little walk around the carpet. "How are you set to work, little thing? What do I do to free Wandabelle from the Nightmare Realm?"

The thing toddled around a while, happy to explore the room.

"Look at that," Sammy said, delighted. "It's so cute. I never knew there were girl versions of our clock."

Danny laughed. "Did you bring this back as a souvenir? I'd have thought that you'd be the last person to get another alarm clock, seeing how annoyed you always are with the one at home."

"Well, this one's going to do something a lot more important than just wake me up. It's set to rescue the Clown Fairy from the Nightmare Realm. Getting her out will finish my fifth quest."

"Wow." Sammy was impressed. "The clowns are in danger, right? You think this will work?"

"I hope so. You guys feel like coming with me?"

Danny jumped to his feet. "Thought you'd never ask! I'm ready for a little excitement. Let's do it!"

Sammy shrugged. "Now that Mrs. Smith doesn't have Mom's glasses anymore, we can go anywhere. Why was she trying so hard to find us, anyway?"

Erec bit his tongue. "I'm so glad you're coming with me. It's going to be great to have my . . . brother and sister with me this time."

"They're comin' with us, cap'n?" Griffin frowned, sizing Danny and Sammy up. "I dunno. Ye think they can handle it there?"

"Yup." Erec nodded. "They're pretty tough. But only three people are supposed to do the quests together. Griffin, do you mind waiting this one out?"

Griffin's mouth fell open. "Yer mean . . . you don't want me with you—yer loyal matey, sworn to yer service? You think these two'll do better in the Nightmare Realm than me, who's lived there for years?"

Griffin was truly insulted. It did seem silly not to let him come along. Who cared about the three-only rule, anyway? Erec wasn't even sure who had made that up. During his fourth quest he brought a lot more people with him, but during the most important part he ended up alone. "You're right, Griffin." He smiled. "I wouldn't dream of going without you. So, it's the four of us, then?"

"Check this thing out," Danny said. He held the sheet that Erec had wrapped around the alarm clock in front of his face, then flipped it the other way. From one side Erec could see Danny right through it, like it was clear plastic. From the other side it was an opaque white sheet. "Where did you get this?"

"It was on a shelf in the Army Security Headquarters. I thought it was just a regular sheet." He smiled. "Of course, why would they keep a regular sheet in that place?"

Danny tossed it over Erec's head, and everything went completely black and silent. "Hey. Get this off me." The words seemed to hit the cloth and echo back to him. Either nobody in the room was speaking, or it kept out sound, too. He struggled to pull it off, but was unable. "Help! I'm stuck!"

It seemed like forever before Danny lifted the sheet off him. "What, did you like it under there?"

"No way. That thing traps you completely. And you can't see or hear a thing with it on. We better get rid of it before Zoey puts it over herself." Thinking again, he wrapped the clock back into the sheet and put it in his backpack, to make sure it didn't escape. His alarm clock at home had a way of getting in and out of tight spots.

"That's funny," Sammy said. "We could see you perfectly through it, like it wasn't even there. I didn't hear you say a thing. It just looked like you were pushing out into the air around you for some reason."

"Look what's out here," Jack said, pointing. A red snail shell sat on Aunt Salsa's windowsill.

"How did it get all the way up here?" Erec asked.

"In Aorth snails drop out of the sky. Well, it's really just earth above us. But they're pretty good at aiming for windowsills. You

　　　　　　　　　　　　THE THREE FURIES

have to check who it's addressed to, though. Sometimes they're off."

"No, this one's for me." Erec opened the window and grabbed it before the heat blasted in. The letter in the snail was blotchy and crumpled.

Dear Erec,

I wasn't going to write to you at all, but I decided to send this one last letter. Not because I used to think we were friends, or anything soppy like that, but because I wanted the chance to tell you how much I hate your guts.

Turns out your little schemes and lies worked pretty well on me. Congratulations. You used me and my stupid trust in you. All of this time I was hiding, for your sake. I thought if I ran into you, then Baskania would know where you were. Imagine how I felt when I found out that you planned this whole trick on me because you thought it was funny. Well, ha, ha, ha.

Guess what? Baskania showed me all of your letters to him. I saw for myself how you wanted to work with him, like I am, and how you were begging to be one of the kings like the Stain brothers. And then I saw how you wanted him to set me up for crimes that I hadn't committed! I bet you're surprised I found out about all of this, but the Shadow Prince showed me your plans. I thought you were my friend! How stupid could I be? You were jealous because I had a father, and you didn't. Thanks a lot. If the Shadow Prince wasn't on my side, and things had gone your way, the police would have been

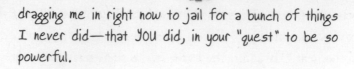

dragging me in right now to jail for a bunch of things I never did—that YOU did, in your "quest" to be so powerful.

I wish I could say it was nice to know you. Tell Jack, who I guess is still being conned by you, that there is a place for him here when he figures out what kind of a person you are. And Bethany—I heard about all the horrible things she did when she was supposed to be working for the Shadow Prince. She's no better than you are. Guess I'm not such a good judge of people.

I hope I never hear from you again. Just so you know, you've earned a spot almost as low as Rosco on my all-time hatred list.

Your sworn enemy,

Oscar Felix

Erec was stunned. Oscar's eye was in his backpack. He had probably given it to Baskania willingly. Baskania had completely turned him upside down. He was lost. What would Baskania make him do? Was there any way to make him know the truth?

Probably not. Erec gazed out the window, feeling empty.

"What did it say?" Jack asked. Erec handed him the letter.

Jack read the letter, becoming more and more alarmed. "We have to do something. We can't let that jerk ruin Oscar's life. Poor guy. This isn't fair."

"I know. Let's think about what to do. Maybe you could meet

him somewhere, give him his eye, and talk to him. If he sees me or Bethany, he'd happily turn us in."

Jack nodded. "I'll wait here until you're back from this quest, and we'll figure out the best way to approach him. Melody, do you want to go home or hang out here?"

"I think I'll head home, as long as you don't mind."

"No problem." Erec grinned at her. "Thanks again for coming along. If you hadn't sung and calmed the animals down, I don't know if everyone would have made it inside the fortress."

She shuddered at the ugly memory. "I'm just glad Bethany is okay." She gave Erec, Jack, and Jam hugs, then left through the Port-O-Door.

"Mom? I have to finish my fifth quest. Danny and Sammy are coming with me, okay?"

June was shocked. "I don't think that's a good idea. . . ."

"Why?" Sammy asked. "Mrs. Smith can't track us down now, without the Seeing Eyeglasses."

"Yeah." Danny laughed. "Don't tell me little Erec can do anything that I can't do."

That's true, Erec thought. They all were cut from the same cloth.

June wasn't convinced. "I wouldn't want anything to happen to you two."

"Thanks a lot," Erec said.

"No." June said, annoyed. "That's not what I mean. Erec, you're used to facing this kind of danger. The quests are meant for you."

Erec shot her a knowing look. "Not *only* me. You know what I mean."

"I don't know at all."

Someone behind Erec thought this conversation was funny, and started giggling. Erec turned around, surprised to find the Hermit perched on the kitchen table in the lotus position wearing a huge turban and loincloth made of silver UnderWear material. "Oh, June. Mother to the world. Set it down, June. These are not children. They have destinies to fulfill."

June's face reddened. "I . . . oh, okay. You three can go. But be careful, all right? This is not easy for me."

"Thanks, Mom." Erec gave her a hug.

The Hermit raised a finger. "Now, who is ready to get really cold?"

CHAPTER THIRTY

The One

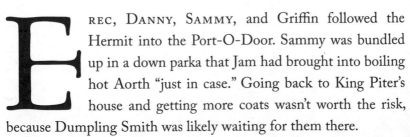

EREC, DANNY, SAMMY, and Griffin followed the Hermit into the Port-O-Door. Sammy was bundled up in a down parka that Jam had brought into boiling hot Aorth "just in case." Going back to King Piter's house and getting more coats wasn't worth the risk, because Dumpling Smith was likely waiting for them there.

"Can we put the Port-O-Door closer to King Augeas's realm this time?" Erec asked.

"I think I planned it perfectly when you went last," the Hermit said. "You collapsed and fell in at just the right time."

"Maybe now we can try just climbing in, instead of collapsing," Erec suggested.

The Hermit gave him a look of long suffering. "Always the renegade."

Griffin was trembling, and Erec knew why. "You don't have to go back, you know. You've spent more than enough time in that place. Why risk more problems, Griffin? I wouldn't blame you at all for staying here."

"Nay," Griffin cried. "This is one trip I'd rather die than miss, me hearty. If I have a chance to take revenge on King Augeas for all he's done, then good luck stoppin' me."

"Danny and Sammy, everything will seem like a horrible nightmare there. And I don't know exactly how we'll get out of his realm. I hope the alarm clock helps all of us."

"The harder part might be getting back into it," the Hermit suggested. "King Augeas is likely mad at you for ruining his little world. He'll figure that you're back to save the Clown Fairy, and probably kick you out to freeze in the Arctic snow."

Erec hadn't considered that possibility. "Oh, that's wonderful. So, our plan is to go die in a frozen wasteland? Good thing Mom's not in here. She'd be cheering that on, all right."

The Hermit nodded gravely. "That is your plan. To die in the snow. Unless you care to make another one."

Erec looked at the clock in his hand. "I wish I knew how this thing worked. That would help."

The Hermit raised an eyebrow. "You don't know how to work an alarm clock? A fourteen-year-old boy? Not too tech-savvy, are we?"

"I can use a regular alarm clock," Erec replied hotly. "This one is set to get Wandabelle out. But how is it set?" He looked at the buttons on the side. One of them, in the same place where he set his own clock, was pressed in. When he looked close, in very small print in a little display box next to it, was a date and time: MAY 1, 2 P.M. A small dial was set near the button. Erec turned it and the date changed. "April thirtieth now. What date is it today?"

"April twenty-ninth," Sammy said. "It's four p.m."

"The twenty-ninth!" Erec could not believe it. "My birthday seems like it was years ago. Wandabelle's been sitting in that awful place so long." He felt awful for her. Erec's watch said four o'clock, and he turned the clock hands so they were synchronized. "I'm going to set the alarm for today, then. April twenty-ninth, at five p.m. Does that sound okay? We have to be really careful. Baskania knows we have the alarm clock. He'll be on the lookout for us there."

"Do you think he's waiting there for us now?" Danny said.

"I don't know if he's gotten out of his own jail yet. He might still look like me." Erec laughed. "He's not the type to wait long, anyway, especially not someplace cold and nasty like that. He'd send someone else." Then he remembered. "Balor Stain! Poor kid's been stationed there to keep his eye on things—his one eye. Baskania has Balor's other one, so he can see what Balor is seeing whenever he feels like it."

"Cap'n, I'll take 'im out, first thing. Before 'e even sees yer there, I'll swipe that Balor Stain with me saber, and lights out fer 'im."

As tempting as that sounded, Erec couldn't do it. "We . . . can't kill him, Griffin."

"Speak fer yerself, cap'n. I surely can, and I can show ye—"

"No, please don't. Let's think of something else. We need a way that we could keep him from seeing us, or knowing we're there." The answer came to him. "I know. What about that sheet I found in Baskania's Army Security Headquarters? If Griffin throws it over Balor before he sees the rest of us, Balor won't be able to see. It's like blacking out the lens of a security camera." Erec felt bad for Balor. "Imagine your own father sticking you somewhere awful just to use you like a security camera."

He took the sheet out of his backpack, zipping the alarm clock carefully back inside, and opened it up. They tested it to make sure which was the right side to throw over Balor. If it was put on backward, the person under it could see and hear everything.

"So . . . I guess the plan is *not* to get thrown back into the Nightmare Realm, and not to be kicked out to freeze in the polar ice. We're going to let the alarm wake Wandabelle—I know! King Augeas kept our bodies in a room when we were living in his nightmare. I didn't see her in there, though. If I can find where she is sleeping, I'll put the clock wherever she is. When it goes off it will wake her up, and we can get her out of there."

"So, the rest of us just have to distract King Augeas, keep him talking?"

"I guess." Erec smirked. "You know, I have an idea of what I'd like to say to him. It would be fun to mess with him a little."

Danny had grown more unsure. "Um, how wrong can things go here?"

"Very, very wrong," Erec answered. "You sure you want to come?"

He nodded quickly. "Not to be outdone by my little bro."

Sammy grimaced, but she nodded too.

Griffin held the sheet at the ready. The Hermit pulled up the map of Upper Earth and found Henrietta Island in the De Long archipelago sitting in the East Siberian Sea. He enlarged it a few times, then put the Port-O-Door into a huge ice spike, like a giant clear stalagmite, projecting from a snow-covered crest.

They opened the door into blistering winds that knocked them back inside the vestibule a few times before they could stagger out. The only way to forge against the penetrating gale was to bend all the way forward and lean into it. Griffin and Sammy fell into the snow, and the others tugged them to their feet. The Hermit led the way, wrapped in a white toga.

The small island sloped up to form a steep crest on one side from which huge cliffs fell into the sea. Little penguins scurried out of their way as they walked toward the spot where the cliffs met an inlet of sea. Erec wasn't sure how his legs were able to move—they had no feeling left in them, and seemed more like dead logs. He wanted to ask his sister and brother if they were okay, but could form no words in such cold.

This time he did not collapse when they reached the icy cove. As the Hermit pointed down to the spot, Griffin bravely jumped in and was sucked away. Danny and Sammy looked at Erec in horror, as if to say they would not, in a million years, follow him. Erec waited, body shaking, hoping Griffin had time to throw the sheet over Balor. If that did not go right, they would have a lot more problems soon.

Sammy's face was blue, and she looked like she was about to pass out. Erec had to get her warm, fast. He took her hand and jumped into the cove and down the tunnel, knowing Danny would follow his sister anywhere.

Everything was white. Warmer now. But blinding white. Empty.

Erec staggered, but was standing on his feet in the tall white chambers. Griffin stood next to him with a smug look on his face. Erec felt much more comfortable here than he had the last time. After living here before, he did not need to adjust. Griffin was alert as well. But Danny and Sammy sat on the floor, gazing around them in a daze.

King Augeas laughed heartily from his huge throne of ice. His voice dripped with sarcasm. "Look who's come back here. Surprise, surprise. It's Prince Erec. And he's brought more royalty with him this time too. Oh, goody, goody. We can have ourselves a little royal tea. Three kings and a queen. How delightful."

Erec glanced at Danny and Sammy to see if they had picked that up, but they still were blinking in confusion. In the smaller throne, Balor Stain looked almost as dazed himself. He was bluish, still wrapped in black and red furs, and stared ahead, seeming unaware that Erec was there. Erec could not see the sheet over him, but he feebly pushed his arms out against something. Balor did not have much fight left in him anymore.

Erec was relieved that Griffin was able to have tossed the invisible sheet over Balor. He wondered how he had managed it. Maybe Griffin made it look like he was waving his arms in the air and bowing to King Augeas.

The king's skin sparkled like the ice around him. "I assume you've come back for the Clown Fairy. You're not going to take her, you know. Only one key can unlock her from here, and it's buried safely very far away." Seeing that Erec wasn't dismayed, he added, "I have to say, I don't trust you, boy. You tend to find strange ways out of things. Normally I'd love to have my guests back, but you were too much of a problem." He smiled. "Griffin, on the other hand, you are more than welcome to return." As he cackled, the sick laughter echoed from the ice-covered walls of the round cavern.

"Actually," Erec said, smiling at Griffin, "we came back for a different reason."

"And what might that be?" The king's eyes glittered.

"We actually liked it here. Griffin and I got to be friends, and we were talking. This place is a lot better than hanging out in Upper Earth, or the Kingdoms of the Keepers. You know why?"

The king frowned. "No," he said coldly. "Why do you think that?"

"Because you can't die here. Look at Griffin. He's hundreds and hundreds of years old. How much longer would he have where I come from? Fifty years? One small accident and he could be a goner."

Griffin nodded. "Much safer here, sire."

"But even more than that," Erec said, "we actually *missed* living here. It was far better. Like living a dream."

Amazement registered on the king's face. "A *dream*, you say? More like a nightmare, right?"

"No," Erec replied. "It was great here. You got rid of my worst nightmare, remember? And instead I was given all of the funny and cool things in your realm. I like to think of it as the 'Sweet Dream Realm.'"

"The 'Sweet Dream Realm'?" King Augeas asked, unsettled. "You enjoyed the monsters, then?" Erec spread his arms out wide. "What could be better than monsters that can't kill you? That's a complete ego boost. But my favorite part were the spiders. I love spiders. Always wanted some for pets. Just too hard to find so many of them back home. Yes, the spiders were great."

Griffin nodded. "Aye. Meself, I loved the food. Nobody serves a good rat stew like I could get here. Seasoned with blood, just like I likes it. That alone was enough to bring me back."

Griffin sounded so convincing, Erec wondered if he really did like rat stew. But he nodded and rubbed his stomach, playing along. "Umm, you're making me hungry, Griffin. But for me, I liked the work even more than the food, good as that was. Good, honest labor, hands to the earth. Just doesn't exist anywhere else. Where I'm from, everyone's too concerned about making money. Here, I learned to like getting my hands dirty just for the sake of hard work. That's what it's all about, right, Griffin?"

"You bet." He sniffed. "Got any of that stew around?"

"Don't tell me you liked the fleas and characters from people's nightmares walking around?" the king asked. His face looked whiter than usual.

"Nightmares?" Erec pretended to be confused. "I did notice some interesting folks around. They were all great, I thought. Really nice, too. And the fleas, well . . . what are a few fleas among friends? That's what my mom always says."

"I miss the fleas." Griffin sighed.

"Am I that out of touch?" King Augeas frowned. "What would be a bad thing, then? Something you wouldn't want to be around?"

"Cakes." Erec made a face. "Sugary things—rot your teeth out. And too many smiling, happy faces. Now, *that* is scary. Makes you wonder what people are up to."

"And parrots," Griffin added. "I hate parrots."

"Anyway, we decided it would be much more fun to live here, forever, instead of short, miserable lives out there. So I brought Danny and Sammy here. We'll bring back more people too, if you want. Build this place back up again."

Hope flashed across King Augeas's face, then he looked skeptical. "So you've come for a visit and plan to leave again? What is it you really want, Erec Rex?"

"Just to discuss this idea with you. We could stay if you like. Or we could bring a huge crowd back with us. It's up to you."

The king liked having a decision to make. "I suppose more people would be better. As you returned on your own, I suppose you will likely come back. But before I let you leave, these two owe me something. I do have a rule, you know. One nightmare each, for my collection."

Danny and Sammy were now more awake. Erec glanced at his watch. It was 4:50. He had ten minutes to find Wandabelle before the alarm went off.

"You." The king pointed at Danny. "Kneel before me."

Danny stumbled toward the king. Erec gave him a nod of encouragement. Danny kneeled at the throne and looked up into the king's eyes. A shimmering haze lifted from Danny, surrounding him.

"That's a good one," King Augeas said, excited. "I'll take it."

Danny lifted off the floor, screaming, then collapsed to the ground. Out of him stepped a humongous duck, twenty feet tall. A shadow version of Danny pulled himself out of his own chest and began to run from the duck.

Everyone in the room was transfixed by the dream characters, except for Balor, who sat unaware with the sheet over him. King Augeas watched, spellbound.

Now was the time. Erec scoured the room but could not see any exits. Where did King Augeas take the sleeping bodies from here? Erec had been in the other room, but didn't know how they connected. He had to find the way.

Griffin was motioning to him, pointing at Balor. Erec looked harder. Under his throne it was dark, like a hole. King Augeas had balanced Balor's throne over the opening to his Nightmare Realm, probably just as one more way to torture him.

Erec slowly drifted close to Balor. He sat on the floor and leaned against the smaller ice throne. King Augeas was rubbing his hands together, caught up in the giant duck chasing Danny down the street.

What a weird nightmare, Erec thought.

Griffin sat next to him. Then, in one swift motion, Erec slid under the throne and down the hole.

A short drop led to the room where Erec had woken from the Nightmare Realm. He could see the way outside into the arctic snow, but no other doors or openings. Nor did he see any sign of a sleeping Wandabelle. Could King Augeas have hidden her somewhere?

Erec searched, frustrated. Where could she be? His watch read 4:55. Danny's nightmare could be over at any minute.

There was nothing else to do. He set the clock down. "Be loud, okay, girl? You have to find the Clown Fairy and save her. It's really important."

He climbed as far up into the tunnel as he could and jumped to reach for the ledge. Griffin's hand was there, and he pulled Erec out easily. Erec slid on his stomach under Balor's throne.

The figures from Danny's nightmare were growing hazy and shrinking. Soon they were tiny statues, spinning through the room into the trophy case alongside the others. Danny looked exhausted, but the king was brimming with excitement. He beckoned Sammy forward. She resisted, but Erec waved her on.

She kneeled before the king and looked into his eyes, hers widening in fright with what she saw there.

Erec did not wait any longer. He had to act fast. He reached up and pulled Balor Stain off of the ice throne.

"What are ye doing, cap'n? We going to do 'im in after all?"

"I'm saving him." Balor felt like a block of ice. Erec pushed him down the hole under the throne and heard him thud at the bottom. "Look at that." He peeked down the hole. "He has no idea where he is. Everything is black with the sheet over him, and he's just fallen down a hole. And he's still barely moving. This isn't the Balor I know and hate."

Sammy had dropped flat on the cave floor, and the king was leaning forward eagerly. Out of her was climbing Rosco Kroc, Danny, herself, Erec, and June.

Erec looked at his watch. 5:01. Had the alarm clock gone off? He hadn't heard anything. He had to get back down there and check. He would reset it if he had to. What now?

He pulled Danny over. "We're getting out of here soon. I'm going to push you down a hole now. I'm coming too." Danny dropped down, landing on Balor, then Erec slid after, landing on top of them both.

The alarm clock walked around as if nothing had happened. Erec's heart dropped. He couldn't leave Wandabelle here. But they didn't have much time. He felt the walls for a trap door. "Wandabelle!" he called out. "Are you here?"

"I am!" she exclaimed. Her voice sounded faint but close. When he swung around, though, nobody was there. "Thank you for saving me. That alarm clock woke me right up!" He turned again but saw nobody but Balor lying still on the floor and Danny rubbing his head.

"I'm right here, silly!" He felt a tug on his earlobe, and his hand shot up to it. Something fluttered in the air near his face. Wandabelle, about one inch tall, was flying in front of him.

"Is that you? Are you okay? How did you get so . . . small?"

"I'm always small." She laughed. "But in the Nightmare Realm we were all the same size, for some reason. I knew you'd get me out of there, Erec Rex! You're my hero!" She gave him a tiny kiss on the tip of his nose, which then itched like he got a mosquito bite.

"Stay here. I have to get Griffin and Sammy. Then we're getting out of here." The alarm clock looked up at him fearfully, as if it didn't want to be left behind, so he tossed it into his backpack. He pulled the sheet off Balor, turning him so he was facing the wall and could not see anything. Then he climbed back up in the tunnel. Griffin pulled him through the hole again.

Sammy's nightmare was in full force. Erec told Griffin, "Wandabelle's free, and she's tiny, like a little butterfly! Go down there. You'll see the door—get Wandabelle, Danny, and Balor out to safety. Cover Balor's eyes so he can't see anything. The Hermit should meet us out there. I'll bring Sammy down as soon as I can."

He was afraid to take her in the middle of her nightmare, in case it hurt her in some way. Plus King Augeas would certainly realize what was going on. So he waited, poised next to the king with the sheet. As soon as her dream figures started to grow small, Erec dropped the sheet over the king's head.

King Augeas looked around in shock, pushing madly at the

sheet. His mouth was moving, but Erec could not hear what he said.

Erec grabbed Sammy, who was nearly unconscious, and slid down the hole with her. Running as fast as he could, they burst out the door in the swirling wintery winds.

The white seemed to go on forever, sucking the life and heat out of him as he staggered ahead. Snow blew into his face, freezing icy tears on his cheeks.

Sammy was heavy in his arms. Erec wasn't sure if she was awake, and hoped for her sake that she wasn't. Was Griffin able to carry Balor and Danny? he wondered. Had he found Wandabelle? And where were they? Where was the Hermit?

He wasn't so worried about Wandabelle. Now that she was freed from the Nightmare Realm, she would be fine. No place on Earth could hold her back. She was a fairy and had lived hundreds of years. Nonetheless, Erec would miss her. He wished Bethany had had a chance to meet her.

That made him smile, even in the wintery cold. Bethany was safe. Wandabelle was safe. And now the clowns would all be safe again. Too bad for Baskania. They would go on living normal lives, instead of dying out and being made to serve in his armies.

A flash of darkness appeared in the light, and then another. That was odd. Erec was quite sure that they were hands. He staggered ahead on legs like lead weights. Another dark hand appeared, this time in front of his face. It grabbed him by the collar and yanked—

—and he was inside the vestibule of the Port-O-Door, safe and sound. It shut behind him. Crowded in with him were the Hermit, Griffin, Balor, and Danny, now standing. Griffin had Balor in a head-lock so he couldn't see anything around him. Balor wasn't resisting one bit. Sammy was stirring a little, so Erec set her down.

She opened her eyes. "Wha—where are we? Was that real? I think I just fell asleep and had a nightmare."

"A real nightmare, I guess," Erec said. "We've done it. Thanks, guys."

Danny shot him a cutting look. "Thanks? We didn't do anything—except give you dead weight to carry. You're the one that saved Wandabelle."

Erec shook his head. "You did exactly what we needed. I couldn't have snuck away if you and Sammy didn't let him take your nightmares out. If Griffin and I were alone, how would we have distracted the king?"

Sammy was alert enough now to laugh. "So, does this mean we won't have those nightmares anymore?" She turned to Danny and laughed. "What was that about the giant duck?"

Danny's face reddened. "I haven't had that one for a long time. I was still little."

"I don't know." Sammy giggled. "You looked pretty old in the dream."

"Shut up, sis."

"What'er we going to do with this landlubber, cap'n?" Griffin dug his knuckles into Balor's head.

"Hermit?" Erec said. "Could you make the Port-O-Door open in Alypium? That's where you live, isn't it, Balor?"

His voice was muffled and defeated. "Umph. We live in Aorth and Alypium. Mom's in Alypium now, cuz they're building a . . ."

"A what?"

"Forget it."

Griffin twisted Balor's neck. "Answer 'im, ye filthy varmint, unless you want me to rearrange yer head so it permanently looks over yer backside."

Balor screeched in pain. "Stop! Ah—ah, I'll tell him!" He sneered.

"He'll find out soon enough, anyway. They're building a castle for me in Alypium. Damon, Dollick and I finished most of our quests, and we'll be ready to rule soon."

"Your quests?" Erec noticed the twelve-segmented Amulet that mimicked his Amulet of Virtues dangling from Balor's neck. Nine of its segments were filled in. "How did you get that fake Amulet? I know it's not real—I'm the only one that the Fates let draw quests from Al's Well. You guys didn't even get an amulet from the first quest, and we were all there together."

"Who cares about the Fates," Balor spat. "They only like you, for some dumb reason. So we're making up our own game."

"For some reason? Maybe it's because I'm King Piter's kid, the rightful heir to the throne. Ever think about that for a reason? What reason do you have to rule? Your father—or clone, I should say—was never a king. He only wanted to be."

"He was more than a king, you fool. My clone-father invented this whole place with his own two hands. He *made* the Kingdoms of the Keepers so that he could rule it—if your family hadn't stepped in the way all those years ago. The Shadow Prince is the most powerful person on the planet."

That brought a question to Erec's mind. "What is Baskania's inborn magical gift?"

"Unh," Balor groaned as Griffin pushed his face into the wall. "Don't you know? Where have you been living, in a hole? The Shadow Prince was born with a special connection with the Substance. He can communicate with it and make it do what he wants."

"And you and your brothers? Do you have that same gift?"

Balor didn't answer, so Griffin gave him a yank.

"Ow! Cut it out. I don't have to answer that dumb question."

Griffin jerked Balor's head hard.

"Aaawwww. Stop! Okay. I don't have a stupid magical gift, okay?

I guess clones don't get them. But that only makes me better, right? I do things myself, without relying on gifts to help me."

Erec was not sure if he felt more sorry for him or sickened by him. "So, do you want to be dropped off at your new palace, then?"

"No, take me home. My mom is at our house on Silver Street." The Hermit, who had been waiting patiently, brought up the Alypium map and found Balor's street. Balor seemed to droop into Griffin's arms, defeated. "Hey, Erec?"

"Yes?"

"Why did you save me?"

"Who knows? Maybe I'm a nice person. Just be glad and shut up."

That seemed to make Balor angry. "I'm not just your enemy, idiot. I'm a clone of your worst enemy. I tried to kill you, and . . . and don't think I won't again. What's wrong with you?"

"I don't know." Erec shrugged. "You're a kid. You can still change your mind and grow up to be half-decent, maybe."

The Hermit opened the door and Griffin shoved Balor onto the street. Erec's ear itched, but when he scratched it, a voice said, "Watch it! You almost knocked me over!"

"Wandabelle?"

She fluttered out in front of him. "Who did you think it was? The tooth fairy?" She flashed a tiny grin. "And what was that business about not trying to find me before you left?"

"I—I thought Griffin had you. Or that you went on your own. I'm sorry."

"I tried to take her," Griffin put in, apologetic. "But she wouldn't have it. Said you were saving her the whole way today."

Erec laughed. "I'm so glad you're free, Wandabelle. Do you want to come meet my family before going back to do . . . whatever it is that you do?"

Her laugh rang like a silver bell. "As a matter of fact, that was *exactly* my plan. I have an important task to do, you know, for the clowns. And I need all of your help to do it."

Erec remembered her talking about fixing things "once and for all" for the clowns. Something she should have done before, that only she could make happen. "Is this what you were talking about?"

She nodded. "It's high time. Do you mind helping me?"

He grinned. "There's nothing I'd rather do."

Danny and Sammy were delighted with Wandabelle, and they happily agreed to help too. Sammy let Wandabelle ride on the tip of her nose while the Hermit opened the door into Aunt Salsa's apartment.

Bethany flew over and threw her arms around Erec. "You're safe! I've never been so glad to see anybody in my life." Erec was feeling mighty glad himself until she said, "They wouldn't let me leave until you were back. You were tying up the Port-O-Door. Come on! Let's go! Cinnalim is waiting."

Aunt Salsa rolled her eyes. "You can't imagine how hard it was to keep her here," she whispered. "I caught her trying to jump out of the window at one point." She pointed at Bethany. "You would have shriveled from the heat before you spattered on the ground! Is she always this impatient?"

Erec laughed, thinking about Danen's person magnet. "I know what you're going through, Bethany. I feel that way when I get a cloudy thought. If anything stops me from doing it, I go nuts."

"Let's go, then!" She took his hand and pulled him toward the Port-O-Door.

"Wait a minute. We have to help Wandabelle."

The Clown Fairy fluttered by. Her voice tinkled. "Go on, Erec. I'm going right now to help the clowns and get things straightened out for them. I won't need you and your family's help right away. I've waited for years for this. Another few days won't matter. It actually gives me time to arrange everything." She sounded excited.

"You heard her!" Bethany was too excited to ask what Wandabelle was talking about, or even care that a fairy was floating around in the room. "Jam, you coming?"

"Yes, modom." He presented her with a backpack. "Ready, young sir?"

Erec could tell that Jam had been exasperated trying to keep Bethany from leaving. She jumped up and down, clapping her hands as Jam found Cinnalim on the map of Otherness.

"Now that I know where Danen's compound is, I'll put us closer. . . ."

"So, you finished your fifth quest, then?" Bethany picked up Erec's Amulet of Virtues. "I wonder why it's not lighting up yet."

Erec hadn't thought about it, but it was true. His fifth quest was done, wasn't it? He had saved the Clown Fairy. Nobody was left in the Nightmare Realm, not even Balor Stain. Maybe something was wrong with it. All of the death rays and black magic that it had absorbed when Baskania was trying to kill him must have damaged it. He let the thought go as Jam opened the door into the hot Cinnalim sunshine.

Bethany whirled out onto the beach. "It's *beautiful*! I knew this place would be this great. Look at the waves rolling in. The temperature is perfect." She ran to the water and trailed her hand through a wave. "It's warm. We should swim . . . but no. Up that cliff. Look at those gorgeous mansions up there! I want to go!"

She raced ahead to steep stone steps carved into the hillside and ran up two at a time. Erec and Jam chased after her.

"Careful, Bethany! Go slow. Just in case Baskania might be around."

"Eek! Look at this place." Bethany pointed out the gazebos, gardens, pools, and tennis courts. "Let's go in there." She ran toward

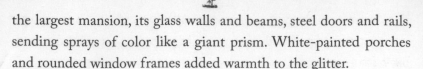

the largest mansion, its glass walls and beams, steel doors and rails, sending sprays of color like a giant prism. White-painted porches and rounded window frames added warmth to the glitter.

"Slow down!" Erec grabbed her arm, and Jam caught her other one. Inside the open door, surrounded by his never-ending party, sat Danen Nomad on his throne of money.

Bethany melted when she saw him, dropping to her knees. "Look at him! I can't believe it. He's the one—the man I want to spend the rest of my life with."

Erec was, against his better judgment, starting to feel jealous. "That old guy? Look at him, Bethany. His underwear is made of money."

"It is?" She swooned. "How dreamy!"

Erec spotted Ajax Hunter across the crowded room standing near Danen. He was looking at his watch, as if tired of standing around. He must have been stationed here by Baskania, just in case Erec showed up.

Bethany almost ran right toward him, but Erec pulled her down. "Ajax Hunter is right over there. You have to wait."

"*Wait!* I've waited my whole life for this moment. What did you say his name was?" Her voice sounded so dreamy it was making Erec sick.

"Can I help you?"

Erec looked up to see Mike, the big security guard who they had met before. "You have to get Danen to turn his magnet off Bethany. Quick!"

Mike frowned. "It's not been easy, what you've put us through," he said. "Baskania hasn't been back here, luckily. So he doesn't know about Mr. Danen using the magnet on Bethany. But he's had people stationed here since your visit, watching. They don't know why you came, it sounds like. In fact, Ajax Hunter said that after this week they won't be bothering us anymore—if we promise to turn you in if you ever show up. So this wasn't the best time to visit. Maybe come back next week?"

"No!" Bethany gasped. "It kills me to think of leaving!"

Erec shot Mike an annoyed look. "Can you just send a message to Danen that we say thank you and please let her go now? We're never going to get her out of here otherwise. I don't think you want Bethany hanging around and getting caught here either. That would lead to more questions."

Mike sighed and disappeared. Erec and Jam pulled Bethany out of the door, struggling, and sat out of sight.

"Just . . . let . . . me . . . go." Bethany twisted and fought against their grasp. "It's lovely in there. Great people to meet." Then, as if just realizing something, her jaw dropped. "We should live here! You can still do your quests. Go to Alypium when you have to draw one from Al's Well. But this can be our home base!"

Erec didn't bother answering.

All of a sudden, Bethany held still. She looked around, and then back at the house, frowning. "Was that Ajax Hunter in there?"

"Yup."

"Then what are we *doing* here? Let's go!"

Erec did not let go at first, wondering if she was trying to fake them out and get inside the house. "You don't want to meet Danen Nomad anymore?"

"Who, that guy inside? Not if he's standing next to Ajax Hunter. What's the big deal about him, anyway?"

He squinted at her, starting to smile. "Isn't he 'the one'? The perfect man that you want to spend your life with?"

Bethany turned pink, remembering. "Um, did I say that? I guess that magnet is turned off now. How embarrassing!"

Erec grinned with relief. "Okay, let's go home."

CHAPTER THIRTY-ONE

Schmaltzberry Pies

JUNE GAVE EREC a huge hug when they returned. "I haven't said congratulations yet for saving the Clown Fairy." She was very relieved. "You don't know how important that was. Wandabelle has been flying in and out of here—the little thing is all excited. Did she tell you what's going on?"

Erec answered. "She's doing something to secure the future of the clowns, I think. Something only she can do so they'll always be safe."

June looked at him closely. "She didn't give any details, though?"

"No. But she wants us all to help."

Surprising Erec, June sniffed and forced a smile on her face. "Okay."

"Are you all right, Mom?"

"Yeah." She ruffled his hair. "Just wanted to spend a little time at home with all of you. You know."

"We'll be able to do that soon, Mom. Don't worry."

Wandabelle fluttered up to Erec and kissed his nose, making him itch tremendously, then fluttered to Danny's ear. "It's time! Everything is ready. I have all of the special ingredients, whipped them all together." She giggled. "Come on! All of you!"

"All of us?" Erec asked confused. "You don't want everyone here to go, do you?"

"Of course!" Wandabelle's voice tinkled.

"I mean, my mom should probably stay here with Nell, Trevor, and Zoey, I think."

"Nonsense! They should come too. This trip is perfectly safe, I assure you. And I'd be very disappointed if Aunt Salsa didn't join us."

Aunt Salsa covered her mouth, giggling in delight. "Should I bring anything?"

"Not at all. Except we have to hurry!"

Everyone filed after the little fairy into the Port-O-Door, and she directed Jam to which part of Otherness to pull up on the map. "Over there. Enlarge the part that says 'Smoolie.' Now put the Port-O-Door into that big field there. Yes, the tree on that side is fine."

They stepped out into the most gorgeous place Erec had ever seen. The large field surrounded by groves of trees was absolutely spectacular. Each tree looked like a work of art, the leaves glistening green as if they had been painted with neon light. The sapphire sky seemed to melt around everything. Sunlight streaked from high above and made the air gleam and shimmer. The birds, the grass . . . everything seemed more like a painting than real.

Erec had visited many beautiful places, but never anywhere like Smoolie. It took a moment for him to adjust before he even noticed the crowds on the open lawn. Hundreds of clowns filled the clearing. Some of them juggled and did acrobatics, but most stood talking animatedly, facing straight ahead.

Wandabelle led Erec's group to the front of the clearing. Curiously enough, he spotted two large pies set atop thrones.

"Stand here—all of you." Wandabelle gestured to the front of the large crowd. She flew to the front of the crowd and sat on the grass. At first it was hard to see her. But she raised her arms and grew larger, shooting up to the sky, until she was thirty feet tall. Her voice boomed.

"Thank you all for coming here, to share with me a day that will go down in clown history! Many of you have been working hard for years to bring us to this point, that we can provide true safety for clowns. So let me say, long live the clowns!"

The crowd behind Erec screamed and cheered. "Long live the clowns!"

After they had settled down, Wandabelle continued. "We've been through a lot lately. Our numbers have dropped. We've almost suffered a disaster. For clowns without leaders cannot go on. And the Shadow Prince, who wanted to be your new leader, would have made you slaves.

"So, I'd like to thank our hero for today. Let's give a big cheer for Erec Rex! He freed me from my prison in the Nightmare Realm! And he has brought with him our new future—a future of hope for all!"

Wild cheering erupted behind Erec, and a few people slapped him on the back. He felt his face turn red. Why all this? He didn't need this attention. But at the same time he felt himself grinning.

"So, it's for Erec, as well as all of us, that I'm going to tell a little story. This is the story of the clowns. Our trials, our perils, and now—our victory!"

Amid the screams and cheers, Erec thought he heard circus music playing in the background.

"Many hundreds of years ago, a fairy princess had a dream. It was about a new nation of people whose mission was to spread joy and delight across all lands. And out of this dream sprang a wonderful reality. The princess made a wish. And the wish came true. The first clowns were born, and they prospered, following their Clown Fairy with love and devotion.

"As time went on, the clowns needed more than just their guardian protector to care for them, loyal as I was. They thrived with structure and deserved some of their own kind to lead them with wisdom and respect. So, one glorious day, I wished that kind of leadership for you. Two objects floated down from the sky, drifting on little parasols. They were quickly recognized as two of the most beautiful clowns ever seen.

"Queen Shalimar and King Derby stepped into their rightful places as the rulers of the clowns. I blessed them with the gift of ages—that as long as there was a clown on this earth, then they would live to rule. For many hundreds of years they lived happily and at peace with their subjects.

"When the Kingdoms of the Keepers formed five hundred years ago, the clowns happily accepted the invitation to live in settlements in Otherness and move completely out of Upper Earth. Baskania offered us safety and room to do as we wanted, without being disturbed by others. We trusted him and found no reason to doubt his good will.

"But ten years ago, Baskania's men went on a murderous spree, destroying most of King Piter's castle in Alypium, in an attempt to take over. Among his other plans, we found out that he also intended to take the lives of our precious rulers.

"Clown intelligence is the best there is. We have spy networks everywhere. So of course we learned the plot to take Queen Shalimar's and King Derby's lives. The king and queen brought their top advisors in to discuss the matter, and it was decided that they go into hiding. Their death would be staged. The deed was complicated, but with my help we were able to fool the killers.

"But to stay safe, Shalimar and Derby would have to stay out of sight. As soon as Baskania learned that they were alive, he would be back again. So we decided to take our own action. The rulers remained hidden while we came up with the most glorious and wonderful invention of all time. Something that would not only protect our rulers, but every clown alive as well.

"It was an Aeronautic Castle—a special structure that humans or clowns could never build alone. It took fairy work along with years of clown labor and assistance to create. But finally it has been finished. And so I reveal to you now: the Aeronautic Castle." She waved her arm, and the air before them rippled. A gigantic, shimmering clear castle appeared behind her, stretching into the sky. Its edges and beams shone, but most of it was completely transparent, which gave it the appearance of an immense, palace-shaped bubble. Amazingly, the entire thing was floating in the air, a few feet off the ground.

"This, my friends, provides safety. This gives us freedom. Once your rulers return here, nobody will ever be able to harm them, or you, again." She smiled. "Which brings me to the last part of my story." She gestured at the two thrones with pies sitting atop them. "Your rulers. They are here."

A frantic buzzing filled the air. Erec looked at the pies in shock. Their king and queen had disguised themselves as pies ten years ago? How dangerous was that? Anyone could have eaten them, he thought. And in clown country, it was amazing nobody had thrown them into someone's face by now.

"Yes." Wandabelle smiled. "As you've guessed, these are not ordinary pies. No, they are special shmaltzberry pies. And you know what that means."

Shmaltzberry pies? Erec had never heard of such a thing. They didn't look very appetizing, either. But that was probably a good thing if clown rulers were hiding in them. Erec turned to his side and found that June was moved by the story, tears rolling down her face.

"Our rulers are ready to return now. They have hidden themselves well, even from their own selves, as you can see. That was the safest way for everyone, so nobody would suspect anything. Right now"—she glanced at the pies—"they do not know that they are our rulers. But it is time to wake them up."

Erec froze in shock. Dumpling Smith and her tall companion, Kookles, ran up behind the thrones. How did Mrs. Smith find them? Had someone told her where they were? They searched the crowd and spotted Danny and Sammy.

Worse yet, they grabbed the pies on the thrones. It all happened so fast that Erec could barely react. Baskania must have found out where the clown rulers were hiding after all. He sent his assistants to destroy them.

Dumpling and Kookles stole the pies and ran straight toward Erec's family. His breath caught. He would not let them hurt anyone now. What were they doing?

Then, unexpectedly, Dumpling Smith and Kookles threw the two pies into the faces of Danny and Sammy.

Erec spun around in horror. Had that killed the clown king and queen? And what did it do to Danny and Sammy? Pie goop dripped down, covering them . . . melting into them.

The air surrounding both of the twins sparkled like diamonds. They rose in the air, turning slowly . . . and changing. . . .

Sammy's nose started to puff out, and Danny's hair turned a bright orange. What was in those pies? And why were they changing his brother and sister?

Dumpling and Kookles were stretched flat on the ground before them. Why was that? Were the twins about to explode or something? But instead they only began to look funnier. Sammy's nose was quite large now, and her cheeks puffed a bit too. Danny's eyebrows became high and arched, his nose turned red.

They looked like clowns.

The twins spun gently to the ground, big grins on their faces. They gave each other a big hug, hugged everyone in their family, then slowly walked toward the thrones.

Wandabelle looked down on them with delight. "After being gone for the last ten years, they have now returned to you—your illustrious Queen Shalimar and King Derby!"

Danny and Sammy blew kisses toward the crowd. Were they actually going to pretend that they were the clown queen and king? Erec thought. Why were the clowns going along with this?

Wandabelle said, "I think your king and queen would like to say something to you all." She pulled a branch off a tree and set it up like a microphone in front of them, and it worked like a microphone.

"Loyal subjects," Danny said, waving. "We have returned!" The crowd erupted in cheers. "It has been a long time since we've gone into hiding in Upper Earth. During that time, Shalimar and I did not know who we were. But June O'Hara, Erec Rex, Nell Rex, Trevor Rex, and Zoey Rex gave us protection, love, shelter, and even their name. We all owe a debt of gratitude to this family, who will always be a part of our family for all eternity."

That was Danny's voice, Erec thought. But Danny never talked like that. His mind still could not wrap around what was happening.

Then his vision returned to him. When he had looked into the future with his dragon eyes. Danny and Sammy were being crowned king and queen. That vision had shown only two thrones. Erec had been watching, not ruling with them.

Danny and Sammy really *were* the clown king and queen.

He had had no idea.

Sammy beamed like a true queen. "It is so good to be back with you. I didn't even know how much I missed you until now that my memory has returned. Thank you for building us this Aeronautic Castle." She held her hand over her heart. "You are the best, most loyal subjects a queen could ever have."

Erec looked at his mother. "Did you know this?"

Her mouth quirked in a smile. "When I took you to watch over, I agreed to take them as well." She sniffed. "It's still hard to say good-bye."

Erec gave her a hug. "It's not good-bye. We'll visit a lot, right?" His throat caught, but he didn't want his mother to know he felt the same way.

She nodded. "Yes. A lot."

"Come inside the new Aeronautic Castle," Wandabelle announced. "The coronation will begin!"

The castle lowered to the ground, and shimmering clear steps descended onto the field. Danny and Sammy, or Derby and Shalimar, were carried inside on their thrones, and the huge crowd of clowns followed in full celebration mode. Flutes were played, balls juggled, tubas blared, and gymnast clowns did flips over one another on the way inside. Erec had to be careful not to get trampled.

The floor inside was a garden of dirt, filled from wall to wall with huge white daisies. He and his family made their way to the front of the huge, sparkling throne room. From the inside, the palace was not clear at all, but it still gleamed with gold and warm colors everywhere. Dumpling Smith and Kookles approached King Derby and Queen Shalimar and bowed low before placing crowns on their heads.

Erec whispered to Nell and Trevor, "So . . . it looks like Mrs. Smith and Kookles didn't work for Baskania after all. They were clown spies."

Nell leaned forward on her walker. "So she really *was* trying to protect them."

Wild applause and cheers shook the walls, and the floor vibrated from all the dancing and celebration. On two tall thrones before him, his brother and sister, Danny and Sammy, sat glowing. They wore tall, pointed crowns of gold, diamonds, and emeralds capping each tip. Sammy giggled, waving at the masses celebrating behind Erec.

June, standing next to him, could not wipe the grin off her face. "Isn't this wonderful? I thought it would never happen. Now everybody knows!"

Erec crossed his arms and nodded. "Now we all know." And he knew everything would be better now.

The celebrations lasted into the night. Erec and Bethany wandered outside, tired and overwhelmed.

"Look." Bethany pointed at his chest. "Your Amulet of Virtues—another segment lit up now!"

Erec lifted it out. Another of the twelve slices glowed, this one a silvery white. A small black symbol was revealed in the segment. "I'm going to look at it with my dragon eyes, so I can read what it says. You can look away if it weirds you out."

"Nah, I'm used to it."

He turned his eyes around, and everything became green. The symbol was easy to read: It said "Love."

Erec let his eyes return to normal as he thought about his quest and what it had meant.

"Love?" Bethany asked, puzzled. "Does that mean you love Danny and Sammy . . . or Wandabelle?"

"I suppose that's part of it." He suppressed a smile. "But they're not the main thing that kept me going."

She looked at him shyly, then took his hand. They walked awhile in silence.

The next day featured a series of feasts, music, and more entertainment than Erec could imagine. He had a hard time adjusting to the fact that Danny and Sammy were a king and queen, especially of clowns. He had gotten used to the idea that they were his birth siblings, destined to rule the Kingdoms of the Keepers with him.

Sammy-Shalimar was getting fussed over by a group of clowns with makeup. "*Look* at you!" one of them was saying. "You look so serious! Let's fix you up a bit, okay? I've got some nice hair frizz; you'll be gorgeous in no time."

"Why, thank you, Trixie! What a warm welcome home this is."

"You're so pale! Here, let me put a little red on your cheeks."

Paint was applied, smudged, rinsed off, and reapplied until everyone, including Queen Shalimar, was satisfied. Although she did appear a bit clownish, Erec thought it was a nice in-between look.

"So," he asked Sammy-Shalimar, "is Danny your brother or your husband?"

She laughed. "He's my brother. We rule equally, but someday we may each choose to marry someone." She winked at Kookles, who stood by her, admiringly. "You know, I have to thank Dumpling Smith. There was a reason that I liked her so much, even though I should have been afraid of her."

Erec laughed. "I guess this is why you and Danny could read

those letters that she sent that were written in . . . she wrote them in pie, didn't she?"

Sammy cracked up with him, and for a moment he felt like things were as they always had been, just like they were sitting at their kitchen table in New Jersey.

But as Erec walked away, he felt a new sense of loss. He found Bethany watching an acrobatic show and pulled her aside. "I guess this means that my triplet brother and sister are really still missing. I was so glad to have found them—and now they're gone again."

She patted his arm. "They're somewhere out there. We'll figure it out. I have a little brother waiting for me to find him, too."

Erec sighed. It was time to go home.

Everything was perfect. There was no need to ever go anywhere else again. Erec and Bethany sat with Jack, Jam, Trevor, June, and Aunt Salsa in her living room, talking about the clown coronation and how great Sammy looked with the bright makeup on. Zoey ran around like a banshee, the only one who was not at all tired.

It was safe, quiet, and almost boring. Exactly the way Erec wanted it to stay forever. Some of the quests had been fun, some had been harrowing. But as far as he was concerned they were over. There was nothing that could get him to venture back out into the world when he had everything he always wanted right here.

Kyron had gone back to help Spartacus deal with the colonies of Erecs, Bethanys, and Baskanias that were still camping on his property, and with a little persuasion Erec got Griffin to join him. Griffin didn't like stepping down from his post of guarding Erec, but he finally agreed to go where he was more needed.

Erec took Oscar's eye out of his backpack and gave it to Jack. "Can you get this to him? He works in the Green House, but I doubt it's safe to go in there. Someone might steal the eye right back again."

"I'll see if I can find him on his way into the Green House and get him meet to meet with me in Paisley Park. Poor guy. Baskania's really turned his head around. I've known him for a long time, and I bet I can straighten him out."

"Let me know how it goes, okay? Thanks, Jack."

Jack held up the eye. "I'm glad you found this. What a close call." He went into Aunt Salsa's Port-O-Door and left for Alypium.

When everyone was hungry, they passed around the Serving Tray. Zoey sat in Bethany's lap and grabbed the silver tray. "I want chocolate rain from Cimm-lim." She laughed when a bag of it appeared in front of her. "Tell me about the bad fortress you were in. What was the scariest part?"

"Oohh, I don't know." Bethany thought. "I guess seeing Baskania was the scariest. I don't like him a lot." She rubbed Zoey's head, then said to Erec, "It was creepy. I ended up hearing bits and pieces of their plans and what was going on. I couldn't really piece it together, though. Ajax Hunter kept bragging to Baskania about all these people he was getting. Sometimes he named famous people, other times just big groups. But I've been thinking about it, and putting it together with Wandabelle. They mentioned her name too. And I have a really bad feeling about it."

Erec understood what she meant. "Those were all people that Baskania is giving to the Furies?"

She nodded, pale. "There were a lot of them. And I'm pretty sure that's what they were talking about."

"How many?" Erec began to feel worried.

"Ajax Hunter managed to get a group of nine hundred people together and took them . . . I guess to the Furies. That was the first big group. It was a fantasy convention in America. People showed up from all over expecting to meet authors, get signed books, and listen to panels. But someone got them all to march in some kind of costume parade, and the next thing they knew they were walking into the cave."

"The *first*? How many big groups did he get?"

"A few. They kept talking about that cave, and I didn't know why they would want people to be in a cave. But I'm remembering now something about taking the Clown Fairy there. It has to be the Furies' cave."

Erec tried to calm down. "Do you know how many people Baskania has taken there already?"

She nodded. "Ajax said they were up to two thousand four hundred. And they were bringing another five hundred in next—they're probably already there. Oh, this is awful. Those poor people! What are the Furies going to do with them, do you think?"

Erec could hardly speak. He had no idea that Baskania was working this fast. "We have to tell my father. Someone has to do something right away."

Bethany looked concerned. "I'm sorry. I should have told you sooner. I just—" She looked down. "I was so caught up in the Cinnalim thing. How stupid was that?"

"You couldn't help that."

"And then Danny and Sammy—I mean Derby and Shalimar's coronation. It's not right, though. Bad things might be happening to these people. You're right. We should ask your father why the Furies want so many people there."

He stared at her. "I never told you, did I? Bethany, things are a lot worse than you think they are. The Furies are trapped in a place called Tartarus. There is only one thing that will let them escape: three thousand human souls. Souls. Not living beings. So you can imagine what's happening to the people Baskania is sending there. Once they have three thousand, the Furies can use the souls to escape in. And if they get out of Tartarus it will be complete chaos. The

Furies hate their sisters, the Fates, so it will turn into some kind of cosmic war between them. You can imagine what that would be like for us.

"Oscar said in a letter that Baskania was planning on giving the Furies two thousand nine hundred and ninety-nine people, and holding on to that last one person until they meet all of his demands. I think he wants the Furies to take commands from him when they escape. They're desperate enough that they might agree to anything.

"I thought the process would take years, though. Three thousand people, gradually picked off one at a time. But if he's sending them in groups of almost a thousand, we're in huge trouble."

The room was silent as everybody absorbed this information. Just when they all had felt so safe and comfortable, an awful danger was looming over them. It threatened not just Erec's family, but all of humanity.

"Jam?" Erec said. "Can you get my father and Queen Posey on e-mail again?"

"Certainly, young sir." Jam's forehead creased with worry, and he hurried to find his notes on the contact person at Queen Posey's undersea palace. "I'll be right back."

The Hermit could solve this problem, Erec thought. Or his father could—with help from Queen Posey if he still was too weak to do it himself. Another person had to take care of this disaster. Maybe even his missing triplet brother and sister, whoever they were. *Some*one else besides him.

But a tiny voice told him that none of them would be able to. The Fates were watching him, he thought. And they were laughing.

BOOK THREE

Megaera the Jealous

W HEN TRIPLETS ARE born, there is always a youngest, even if it is only by a minute. I am that girl. No matter how strong my powers are, how many years of wisdom are under my belt, I will always be the one looked down upon, belittled.

To make it worse, we have three older sisters—Decima, Nona, and Morta—who think they are so much better than us, and trust us so little, that they locked us away forever. If only I could be one of them, and enjoy the kind of lives they lead—it pains me to no end. They are free of bitterness, and full of laughter.

It's not fair. I've spent millennia wishing, wanting what they have.

Knowing I'm never going to get it makes me want to shred them into tiny pieces and watch the wind blow them away. Only then might I finally be at peace.

It's not just the Fates, though, that drive me insane. Every single one of you creatures out there, free in the world, makes me sick. How sweet your lives must be! What I would give to have what you carelessly throw away every single day! You all deserve to die torturous deaths.

My life is a painful joke. Surrounded by one sister who is always furious at me, and another who makes me pay for every tiny thing I've done wrong, my long days are more of a prison than any you could imagine.

This knowledge of my existence has gnawed away at my heart until the once-beating thing has completely gone. And every time a bit of my heart threatens to grow back, it's eaten away again faster than it can form. All that is left is a wasteland of misery for me, and an insatiable desire to get even with my sisters, the Fates, and every last human soul on this planet. Even newborn babies make my stomach turn. They don't know how sweet their lives are, they take it all for granted. I want to see the world decimated. And maybe then I will finally have nothing to feel envious for. This is what I deserve.

CHAPTER THIRTY-TWO
A Productive Swim

KING PITER WAS stunned when Erec told him the news. "Are you sure you heard that right, Bethany? They may have twenty-nine hundred souls in Tartarus already? That would leave only a hundred more before the Furies could escape."

Bethany's face crumpled. "I heard that a while ago. The number could be higher by now easily."

"Hold on." King Piter had to go find a chair. Soon he was sitting, face in his hands. They watched him in silence, all of them feeling the same pressure. At last he sniffed sharply and lifted his head. "There's nothing we can do, then. It's over. I'd like you all to come here, to Ashona. First of all, it will be the most protected place. When the Furies get out they'll wreak havoc everywhere, and no doubt Ashona will be affected too. But it's more hidden, with all the sea life in the way. We might have more time here. Plus, I'd like for us to be together now. I don't know how much longer we'll have."

If Erec was frightened before, that was nothing compared to the hopelessness he felt now. "But we have to do something, right? We can't just let the world end!"

"I hope not, Erec. Nobody knows how much the Furies will wreck. The world could end, yes. So, until we know, let's stay together down here."

Posey appeared on the screen. "I agree. Would you like a few minutes to get your things together? I'll come bring you here. It's easier."

"Baskania is getting powers in exchange for giving people to the Furies," Erec pointed out. "You know the Draw he used on Bethany? That was in exchange for souls. He's planning to give them all the people they need to escape minus one, and when they're really desperate he's going to make them promise to serve him once he lets them go free."

King Piter couldn't believe it. "He's crazy. Baskania actually thinks the Furies will be his slaves? They're powerful beyond even his imagination. And wild and reckless, too."

"But they'll do anything to get out of Tartarus, won't they? Maybe even do favors for Baskania."

The king's mouth fell open. "Our problems are far worse than I imagined. I was worried about the world ending from the conflict between the Fates and the Furies. But if he's commanding the Furies, Baskania will destroy everything before that has a chance to happen."

"Isn't there *anything* you can do? Or the Hermit?"

King Piter dismissed that idea. "It's far too dangerous. The Furies are not to be trifled with. Stay far, far away, Erec. All we can hope for is a little time here together before the Furies are unleashed."

"I guess I can't do any more quests, then." Erec laughed bitterly. Oddly, he would miss doing them, even though a moment ago he had foresworn leaving Aunt Salsa's apartment ever again.

Piter's face darkened. "Erec—you have to promise me. This is really important."

"Okay. What is it?"

"The quests. Get them out of your mind. Stay far away from Al's Well, all right?"

Erec didn't see the connection. "Why are you thinking that?"

"The Fates have been using you to fix serious problems. And it's obvious from what they've asked you to do that your safety is not their main concern. So I wouldn't be surprised if the Fates plan on throwing you right into the middle of this mess. As much as I believe in them, I have to put my foot down this time. You are going nowhere near Tartarus, Erec. You are not getting involved with the three Furies. Sending you to see King Augeas was bad enough. I want you alive, you understand me?"

Erec remained silent. Would the Fates really involve him in this disaster? And if they did, would he stop the Furies? Or was his father right, and he would die? Then again, weren't they all going to die anyway if the Furies escaped Tartarus?

The king could read Erec's expression. "Son, don't even think about it. You don't mess with the Furies any more than you would mess with the Fates, if you'd like to stay alive."

"Okay." His father was probably right. Erec shouldn't even consider it. Let someone else take care of this one, he thought ... hoping there was somebody—like his father—who could.

The king saw his hopeful expression and shook his head sadly. "I'm afraid I can't. I couldn't even protect Bethany."

"You shouldn't be sorry," Bethany said. "That scepter was messing with you—Erec told me all about it. I didn't exactly come and tell you I was leaving. How would you have known that Baskania put a Draw on me?"

That made Erec feel worse. "Yeah, *I'm* the one she sent a letter to, saying she was leaving. I should have been able to stop her."

Bethany said, exasperated, "Would you two stop blaming yourselves for everything? You sent me a letter back right away, telling me not to go, didn't you? And you did come right away. It was just too late. Nothing could have stopped me, anyway."

The king was looking down, upset, mumbling to himself, and Erec decided to cheer him up. "Everything turned out all right, anyway. But you're not going to believe this. It turns out Bethany has a younger brother! The whole prophecy had nothing to do with her all along."

"I know it." The king's voice was deathly quiet. "Ruth Cleary had three children. Her youngest was just a baby when she died."

Erec stared at the screen, suddenly realizing a new twist to this tale. Of course his father would have been aware of that. Bethany's mother was his AdviSeer, and she lived in the Castle Alypium. "Why didn't you say something, Dad? Why didn't you tell Baskania he had the wrong person, so he would let Bethany go? Or, even ... way back when he first found out about the prophecy, before he even took Bethany. You could have gotten word out then, so we all knew. Then Bethany wouldn't have been captured."

King Piter's eyes were wet and heavy with grief. "You are right, Erec. I could have done that, and saved Bethany's misery. Maybe even saved her life, if you had not been able to. But I couldn't. If he actually knew . . ."

"*What?* You let Bethany get captured on purpose? You let her be a *decoy*?" Erec rubbed his ears as if he had heard wrong.

"No. I didn't want her to get captured at all! I thought I could keep her safe—"

"But you couldn't, could you?" A burst of rage seared through Erec. "Instead you spent all your time thinking about yourself and the precious little scepter. You kept such a horrible watch on Bethany, it was no wonder she was caught. And you didn't even do the simplest thing to protect her—let everyone know that she wasn't the one Baskania wanted to begin with."

"Erec." June reached out to stop him.

He flicked her hand off his shoulder and spun around. "Did you know too? Tell me, Mom. Were you in on this, setting up Bethany?"

Her face blanched. "It . . . wasn't my choice, Erec. I had to listen to your father, the king."

"Wasn't your choice?" He heard himself shouting, but didn't bother to control himself. "That's interesting. So you take no responsibility for what you do, then? If you think you can't defy your king, just take a good look at him. He can barely even hold himself together. His castle is gone, his scepter is gone. Look at him. You want to see somebody defy him? Well, just watch me. I'll show you how it's done. I think I'll start by drawing a quest from Al's Well. Didn't you forbid me to do that, *father*? Then it's exactly what I'll do."

King Piter was hunched over, shoulders shaking. Was he crying? No wonder he felt guilty. He had a real reason to.

Tears were streaming down June's face. She might not have made the decision, Erec thought, but she chose to follow it. He looked around the room. . . . Jam . . .

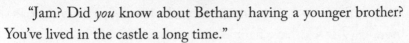

"Jam? Did *you* know about Bethany having a younger brother? You've lived in the castle a long time."

He shook his head solemnly. "No, young sir. I am sorry. I came to the Castle Alypium after this happened. So sorry. I had no idea that Bethany had a younger brother. Sorry, sir. So sorry."

Erec almost laughed, despite his misery. "Jam! Stop apologizing. You've done nothing wrong, and you didn't even know. So why are you the only one saying you're sorry?"

"Sorry, sir. I'm sorry about that. Sorry."

"Jam, cut it out!"

"Sorry. I will. Sorry." He was looking more flustered.

"Jam!"

"Sorry . . . yes." He bit his lip before another "sorry" escaped.

"I *am* sorry." June sounded hoarse. "Maybe I was wrong. I just did what I thought I had to. Which was keeping my mouth shut about certain things. I didn't tell you who you were all those years, and you hated me for a while because of that. But then you found out why, and I thought you understood." She sniffed. "I'll say this, Erec. In King Piter's defense, it's not as straightforward as it sounds. Saving Bethany would involve risking her brother's life."

"Oh, okay. So, her brother is more important than she is, then?"

"No." June shook her head. "It's not that. He's weaker, though."

Erec thought he was going to go through the roof. "Like that would have made a difference there! Griffin is the strongest person I know, and he wouldn't last there either. Why couldn't you find Bethany's brother and protect him, then? Keep Baskania away from him?"

"There was another risk, Erec." King Piter sounded choked up. "What if I couldn't protect him, and he was caught like Bethany? Baskania really would have found the secret to the Final Magic. That would have been the end of everything."

"It's the end of everything now, looks like," Erec said. "If it had been me, I would have figured out a way to keep her little brother really safe. Not whiling my time away playing with a scepter. Or you could have at least used the scepter to do something good, like keeping Bethany *and* her brother safe."

"Erec, June is right. It's complicated. When you come here we'll talk, and I'll see if I can help you understand—"

"I'm not coming." Erec crossed his arms.

The king looked distraught. "Of course you are. All of you. We'll spend our last days together. Bethany too. And I hope you'll forgive me, and try to understand what I was thinking."

"I will never forgive you. Let's start there. And I will not be spending my last days there. I'm going to get my quest. And, if these are our last days, I'll be spending my time actually trying to do something about that." He switched off the e-mail and walked out of the room.

After a while of sitting alone in bed, trying to calm himself, Bethany walked in and sat next to him. Erec expected her to defend his father, like she had so many times in the past, and he didn't want to hear it. But instead she sat silently, staring at her feet.

"I can't believe he did that to you."

When he raised his eyes, he was surprised to see tears rolling down her face. She nodded. "I know."

Erec dropped his head onto his knees. Of course, this news would be even harder on her than on him. She had thought of Piter as her own father. He was all she had, with both of her parents dead. And he had sold her down the river. Erec's fists clenched. How *dare* he do this to Bethany? What must she feel like now? She had lived with Earl Evirly for all of those years—him not loving her, just taking advantage of her. And now King Piter proved to be no better.

Erec put his arm around her shoulders, which made her cry

harder. He wished he knew the right thing to say. "I'm sorry, Bethany."

She laughed through her tears. "Stop it. You sound like Jam."

They both cracked up for a minute, then Bethany hugged her knees. Erec smiled at her. "You know what really matters, Bethany? You do have a real family. Pi loves you, and your new brother will too, once we find him. And we will find him, okay? I'll make sure of that. And you also have me. I mean, I know I'm not your family or anything. But I'll do anything for you. Who cares about what King Piter thinks? He's my real father—and I don't even want him. I'm officially giving him up. So neither of us have parents now. We're even."

Bethany looked at him out of the corner of her eye, a smile forming on her cheeks. "You have June, still."

"Yeah." Erec pondered that. "I guess the jury's still out on her. Not sure if I'm forgiving her for this one."

"I have. It wasn't her fault, really. Think of all the other things King Piter told her not to talk about, like who you really were, and Danny and Sammy. Those were all for good reasons. So she thought she had to listen." Bethany shrugged.

"I guess so. It'll take me a little time to get used to that, but you're probably right. I still have another mother to find too—my birth mother. She's around somewhere, I just know it."

"We'll find her, too. Your birth mother, my younger brother, and your missing triplet siblings. Guess we have our work cut out." She laughed.

It was good to see Bethany smile again. "Yeah. But you know the first thing I have to do, don't you?"

Bethany looked like she didn't want to hear the answer.

"I'm getting the next quest," Erec said firmly. "I have to find out what it is. Maybe there is an easy thing I can do that would make all of the difference with the Furies. I'm going to pull the quest out and see what it says, that's all. Then I'll decide what to do."

She was troubled, but she understood. "That sounds reasonable. Except it is so hard to get your quests now. Didn't you say you had to have a dragon fly you there last time?"

"Yup. Little Erec," Erec said, cracking a smile. "You've got to meet him. He's gotten so big since we saved him."

"Since *you* saved him. You always share all the credit with everyone."

"No, I don't."

She winked at him. "That's what I like about you."

"Okay, then. Maybe I do." A grin spread over his face.

"So, are you going to call Patchouli and Little Erec to help you get to Al's Well again?"

"I don't know. It was really dangerous last time. I don't want little Erec to get shot. There has to be another way."

He racked his brain. How else could he get into the Labor Society? Guards were posted everywhere, waiting for him. Even if he slipped through the front door, he couldn't get into Al's Well that way. Only the side door, where Janus was, gave him access to where he needed to go. And that door was crowded with armed guards.

Last time he had dropped from the sky on a dragon's back. Too bad he couldn't bring a cloudy thought on and sprout wings. Even if he did, how would he get back again? Turn on another cloudy thought and fly home?

"Wait a minute," Bethany said. "Remember that time you got flushed out of Al's Well into those water tunnels, and you ended up in the castle pool table?"

Erec sat up straight. That was the answer!

"Too bad that pool table is gone," Bethany said.

"But the water tunnel that led to it is still there. It's outside my father's house, in the gardens. He made it into a pool. That's perfect! I'll go in and try to find my way back to Al's Well." As he said that, he remembered how easy it was to get lost inside those tunnels.

"I'll go with you! That will be fun."

He was glad she volunteered to come. "All right. We're the only two who can do it, with our Instagills. Why not?"

"First thing in the morning, then?"

"We're on."

June didn't say much when they left, but her eyes were teary. Erec decided that he had forgiven her and gave her a hug. "We're just going to draw the sixth quest from the well and see what it is. It doesn't mean I'm going to do it."

"Be careful."

Erec was relieved to find nobody in his father's house. It occurred to him that Mrs. Smith would no longer be hounding them, now that her king and queen were restored to power. So, she really was a clown. That explained her strange looks a lot.

They weren't planning to go outside Alypium, so no coats were in order. Erec pointed out the window. "That's the pool. You ready?"

Bethany nodded. The two of them raced outside and jumped in. As soon as he submerged, Erec felt the Instagills open in his wrists. After a moment to adjust, he was breathing underwater like a fish. It felt great to be swimming. The water streamed around him, warm and comfortable.

"Here's the hole." He pointed at an opening at the bottom a few feet wide.

"Let's go!" Erec could hear Bethany almost as well as when they were on land. She was watching the little gills opening and closing in her palms with amazement. Then she dove toward the hole in the bottom. Erec followed her. It had been a while since he had been in these water passages, but it all came right back to him. Even though they were underground, an unseen light source filled the tunnels.

Openings branched off in several directions, leading to more tunnels and more openings. He remembered that a few led up into lakes, or even puddles or swamps. But no markings showed which way to go, so they just looked into a few as they passed by. Nothing looked like it led up into a well.

Regardless, it was fun swimming together. After a few kicks to send him in one direction a current took over, pushing him along that way, and then all he had to do was float while it carried him. For fun, Bethany kicked herself upward, down, then backward, just to make the current around her change and send her different ways.

"We can't go too far away," she said. "Al's Well is in Alypium. If we swim too long in any one direction, we should turn back again."

"That makes sense. The only problem is that this current is carrying us faster than you'd think. Remember how quickly we got out near an ocean last time?"

"Ooh—you're right." Bethany stopped going forward and swam in circles. "It is hard to judge how far we're going."

A few fish swam by, making Erec wonder if they were near a lake. They turned and plunged into a tunnel that led up and into a stream in the wilderness. He popped his head above water and gasped for breath as his body adjusted to the air.

"Look!" Overhead, two dragons soared through the air. One was a reddish purple, and the smaller one a deeper green.

Bethany choked slightly on the water. "Next time I'm staying under until I know where we are." She coughed until her breathing was clear. "We must be in Otherness somewhere. Oh, Erec. We're completely lost. I should have known this would happen in these tunnels."

"I wish there was a map." Erec shivered. "Let's go back down. It feels warmer and a lot better when my Instagills are out."

It was clear that they were well lost. Erec wished he had brought

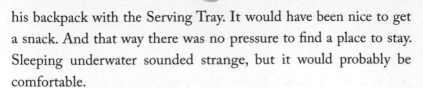

his backpack with the Serving Tray. It would have been nice to get a snack. And that way there was no pressure to find a place to stay. Sleeping underwater sounded strange, but it would probably be comfortable.

They meandered a while, starting to feel hopeless, and then Bethany pointed toward a flutter of activity. "Look! Something is going on over there." They swam close enough to see fish flurrying around something that looked like a treasure chest. Erec spied a flash of greenish hair and an arm. As they drifted closer, however, something huge rushed at them, teeth bared.

"Eek!" Bethany and Erec kicked hard and darted away from whatever it was. Luckily, the creature did not chase them. After they were far enough away, it went back to whatever dark corner it lived in.

"I'm about ready to call it a day," Erec said as they floated farther in an unknown direction. "What do you think?"

Bethany frowned. "I don't know. Look over there."

Erec turned to an odd sight. A very tall, thin man, with large gills waving from both sides of his neck, stood completely still in a wide alcove. Gray hair fluttered around his head in the water, and he watched them with a grave look on his face. His clothing, a blue camouflage one-piece suit, looked odd—not that Erec would expect to see any certain style of clothing on someone who lived underwater. Nonetheless, Erec was quite relieved to see someone who might help them find their way around.

They swam over to the man. "Hello," Erec said. "I'm afraid we're lost. Can you point us in the direction of Alypium, please?"

The man cleared his throat. His voice was goofy, and he extended all of his vowels a great deal and screeched sharply. "Excuse me? Are you just barging in here? Can't you see that we're having some important festivities right now? If you don't mind coming back in an hour or so, I think we'd be more inclined to help you then."

Erec and Bethany looked at each other. Nobody else was around that they could see.

"Sir," Bethany said gently. "We would love to come back later, but we're very tired and need to get home soon. Is there a way you could tell us now, if you know where Alypium is from here?"

"Oh, very well." He rolled his eyes. "I may deign to help you two gentlemen. But first I must confer with my fellow villagers. Do you mind waiting a moment?"

"Of course," she said.

The man turned so that he was facing away from them and continued to remain stock still. In a few moments he turned back. "We decided that you must pass a test, if you want help to find your way back. I know how to get all over the place. But I'm going to ask you each two very difficult questions. If you answer correctly, then I will take you wherever you want to go in the tunnels in Alypium. But if you *don't* . . ." He leaned forward, leering menacingly.

"Yes?" Erec said. "If we don't, then what?"

"*Then* . . . I will drown you in massive quantities of water!"

Erec looked at the water all around them, deciding that the guy was certifiably crazy. But they had nothing to lose. "Okay. Can we help each other with the answers?"

The man nodded. "You will have to. The questions are extremely difficult."

"Okay." Erec nodded. "Go ahead, then."

"You first." He pointed at Erec. "Your first question: What . . . is my favorite supper?"

Erec looked around, dumbfounded. "Um . . . fish?"

"Correct. You may live for question number two."

"Phew!" Erec shot Bethany a bewildered look. "Okay."

"Your second question is: If e to the i-x equals the cosine of x plus i times the sine of x, i being the imaginary unit, then how can you represent a point, z, in the complex plane?"

Erec froze, but Bethany chuckled as if the man had asked what two plus two was. Erec rolled his hand out toward her, hoping she would take over.

Which she happily did. "Euler's formula—so basic it's beautiful. Simple, really. i is the square root of negative one, of course. That used to be my favorite number! And it's kind of a trick question, so shame on you. Because if you want to express z in Cartesian coordinates it could be done simply, say as z equals x plus i-y, or z equals x minus i-y. But integrating Euler's formula you can express z in polar coordinates. Which then would be the absolute value of z times the sum of the cosine of theta plus i times the sine of theta, which equals the absolute value of z times e to the i-theta. And so on."

The man nodded at her, entirely unimpressed. "Correct." He rolled his rs for a long time. Erec wondered if the man actually knew the correct answer or not. Bethany's response was so enthusiastic that it was hard to doubt her.

"Now your turn, sir." The man turned to Bethany, who looked slightly annoyed at being called "sir." "Your first question is: What . . . is your name?"

Bethany laughed with relief. "Bethany Cleary."

"And second . . . how do you spell it?"

She started to say, "$B \ldots E \ldots T$—"

But Erec shouted over her, "No!" They both looked at him—Bethany's eyes wide with surprise—as he said, "$I \ldots T$!"

The man pointed at Erec. "Correct again! You have passed your test. So now I will guide you. Where did you say you wanted to go again? Directly under the famous geyser of Granitsia? Well, follow me, then." He took two paces to the left. "Here we are. Good day, now!"

"No," Erec said. "We need to go to Alypium. If you can take us to Al's Well we'd really appreciate it."

"Oh, all right, then." The man huffed a bit, then swam out before them.

Erec and Bethany followed him easily back in the direction they had come from. In fact, Erec recognized enough to see that they were indeed retracing their footsteps, which was a good sign.

"Thanks for helping me with the spelling test!" Bethany laughed. "How did you know that's what he meant?"

"Zoey used to do that to me all the time: 'Spell it.' Thanks for helping me with the math part."

"Easier for me than spelling 'it.' Kind of funny."

After a sharp bend, the water had a strange feeling, like it was both hot and cold at the same time. It was uncomfortable, like it was awakening all of the nerves in Erec's body. Soon, it was both burning and freezing.

He recognized the feeling immediately. These were the waters of the Fates. He must be very close to Al's Well.

The man swam a little farther and pointed up to a small hole where sunlight streamed in. "Now I will go back to my village," he said. "They are all awaiting my return anxiously." He held a hand out, as if waiting for a tip.

Erec had no money on him. "Um, thank you."

The man did not budge. Bethany shot Erec a look and shrugged.

The man cleared his throat and jabbed his hand toward Bethany.

"Um, we don't have any money," she said. "I'm sorry."

"Then you will have to give me a tip of another kind."

"Okay," she said. "Think positive thoughts. How's that?"

The man was very satisfied. "Thank you, kind sir. Now I must return."

"What an oddball," Erec said. "Well, at least he led us to the right place." He swam up to the hole, right under the inside of the toilet seat where Al's Well was. A bit of sunny sky with white fluffy clouds was visible. Erec searched all over, but did not see a paper with his quest on it.

A shadow appeared in the sunlight above him. He looked up to see Al's face peering down at him. "Oh, hey dere, Erec! Heard a little rumbling down here, and I thought something was up. Good ta see ya. I was wondering when you'd come back."

"Hi, Al! I'm just looking for my next quest down here." He wondered how odd he looked, inside a toilet.

Al cupped a hand behind his ear. "Are you talking? Cuz I can't hear ya in there."

Erec stuck his head into the air of the toilet bowl, coughing as he caught his breath. Well, he thought. This wasn't a view he had every day. "I'm here to get my sixth quest. Couldn't think of another safe way to get here."

Al was dressed, as usual, in overalls with a tool belt. He hesitated, looking pained. "Erec—could ya do something for me, pal? Go back down dere, seeing as you're a good swimmer an' all, and see if you can get over dat way." He jabbed a thumb over his shoulder toward the Labor Society. "Dere's a bathroom inside where Janus is, so maybe you can find a pipe leading inside. If you can get over dere and sign dat pad of his, dat would make it all official, you know? Seems like the girls like it dat way."

"I'll try." Erec groaned, but he knew Al was right. "See you soon, I hope."

"Good." Al nodded.

Erec plunged back into the water and his gills popped open again. "I guess I have to find Janus. Let's be careful to remember our way back here." The two of them swam slowly, paying attention to the details of the water tunnels. A few wide pipes led straight up into the Labor Society building. "You better wait here, okay, Bethany? I'll be back in a minute."

Erec felt nervous swimming into the building's water pipes. Most were too narrow to enter, but the main section was wide enough. He remembered the way he had come in, and looked all around for what might lead to sinks.

Straight above him was a row of openings where light shone in. He hoped he had swum far enough in. Maybe this was Janus's shop. Erec swam straight up into a circular hole and looked up.

A rim ran around the gap, like in Al's Well. And something was moving up there. Was it Janus?

A woman was bustling around, doing something with her clothing. She glanced down and saw Erec's face. She screamed, loud and long. After a few repeated screeches, she stumbled away. "Someone's spying in the toilets! A man is in here!"

Erec disappeared in a flash. Oops! Luckily he hadn't gotten there a few minutes later. That would have been awkward—and disgusting. That thought made him worry about the kind of water he was swimming around in.

He passed a few more rows of openings, this time staying far away, looking for a smaller bathroom. Janus's shop should be at the farthest end of the building. So he kept going until the pipes stopped.

Right above him, tiny bars of light shone through a drain. He hoped he was in the right place. "Janus!" he called out. "Can you hear me? Janus!"

Eventually he heard Janus's voice. "Is somebody here? Anybody? Old Janus is hearing things, I think. Too much time alone has finally caught up with me." Janus began sobbing so loud that Erec was afraid he wouldn't hear anything.

"Janus! Over here—I'm in the sink."

Janus scuffled closer, and Erec could see his shadow falling over the drain holes. "I'm hearing voices in the sink now. My, oh my. What's become of me?"

"You're not hearing things! I'm in the counter under the sink, looking through the drain. It's me, Erec Rex!"

Janus bent over and peered into the drain, then pulled out a screwdriver and yanked it off to reveal Erec's eye looking through. "It *is* you. Oh, how lovely to have company." Then he looked around suspiciously. "You're not supposed to be here," he whispered. "They want me to call and report you if I see you, you know."

"Please don't let anyone know! I just need to sign your pad, so I can get my quest. Okay?"

Janus's face cleared. "Of course I'll let you. The Shadow Prince says he's my new boss, but I've been here hundreds of years. My only bosses are the three girls, you know. That never changes. And I heard your next quest is ready. I'll be back with that pad." He shuffled away and returned with the paper pad and a quill pen. "How are we going to do this?"

Erec reached two fingers through the hole into the air. "Just put the pen in my hand, and hold the paper for me, okay?" Something was pushed between his fingers, and he grasped it tightly. "Is the paper there?"

Janus pushed the paper pad toward Erec's fingers, holding it steady. "There you go. Sign this."

Erec could feel a firm surface against the pen's tip, so he signed his name. He was sure it was the sloppiest signature he had ever made. "Did that work?"

Janus pulled the pad back, and Erec saw the paper splitting where the ink marked on it, light streaming through.

"You're fine," Janus whispered. "Best of luck, Erec Rex." He took back the pen.

"Thanks, Janus."

Erec swam back the way he'd come in, and shimmied down the pipe to find Bethany waiting under the building. They swam back, the water getting hotter and colder as they went.

Al was waiting by the well, peering inside when Erec returned. Erec searched around in the water. It had to be here somewhere. He closed his eyes and felt . . . something warm in his hand. Thick paper. This had to be his next quest.

He waved the paper at Al, who winked at him and pulled the toilet handle—

—and Erec and Bethany were flushed, spinning fast through the water tunnels, whirling as the water became normal again. Then, splash! They burst through a hole into the pool in King Piter's gardens.

Coughing and sputtering, the two ran inside and found towels to dry off. "We got it!" Erec waved the paper over his head.

"That was quite a swim." Bethany grinned, drying off her hair.

Erec collapsed onto a couch, not caring if he made it wet. Something was bothering him, but he could not put a finger on it. They were back, and okay. They had accomplished their goal. . . .

Oh, yes. The thing in his hand. He would have to look at it, he supposed. But he really didn't want to. His father had warned him to stay far away. What would it tell him to do? Something awful? Deadly?

He shouldn't think that way. The odds were just as good that it would have something simple on it. Maybe he just had to stop Rosco from finding something, or help Balor Stain get himself together again. Little things sometimes had a big effect, he told himself. One thing led to another. Maybe just the smallest action could save the world from what Baskania was doing.

"So, what does it say?" Bethany asked. "Have you read it yet?"

Erec looked at the paper and turned it around. He guessed now was as good a time as any.

He read the paper in his hand.

Give yourself to the three Furies.

CHAPTER THIRTY-THREE

Noble Revenge

"**S**O, WHAT DOES it say?" Bethany plopped beside Erec on the couch.

Hiding his shock, he held the paper to his chest. "Nothing. Don't worry about it."

Bethany put her hand out. "Come on. It says nothing at all? So this quest is a freebie, I guess? That's pretty lucky."

"Look, I don't want to talk about it." Erec did not want to even think about it. What this quest was telling him to do was crazy. His

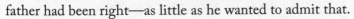

father had been right—as little as he wanted to admit that.

"Come *on!*" Bethany grabbed the paper and read it. "Give yourself to the three Furies. . . . Is this a joke? That's your quest—to basically kill yourself? Donate your soul so that the Furies can escape and destroy the world? Great." She dropped her head into her hand. "Why did the Fates bother giving you twelve quests if you won't be around to do the rest of them? Your amulet should just have six segments on it." She handed the paper back. "Well, I guess that's one to chuck off, huh?"

He was puzzled. "It doesn't even make sense, anyway. Why would the Fates want me to help the Furies escape?" A nagging thought crept into his mind. None of his quests had made sense right away. But, then again, none had asked him to do anything so insanely dangerous before.

Erec started to feel guilty. If he didn't give himself, how much worse would things get for the rest of the world? If only he could know in advance what all his options were . . . what would happen if he ignored his quest . . .

He couldn't think about it right now. "Tell you what. Let's have a Serving Tray special. I'm starving. What's your order, Bethany?"

"Mmm. I'll have to go with a veggie cheese omelet, a pancake on the side, French fries, and a chocolate milkshake."

"That covers all the food groups." He laughed, handing over her order. "I'll take a double cheeseburger with tomato and ketchup—those fries look good, I'll have more of those—an apple, cut up, and warm chocolate brownies." Food appeared, looking amazing. "Can you believe that crazy guy who was just standing there underwater? 'What . . . is my favorite food.' What a nut!"

She giggled. "At least he helped us out, though. We were so much farther away than I thought."

The food was delicious, as usual. Erec bit into a French fry, trying to forget the paper sticking out of his pocket. "What are we going to do? It doesn't seem safe to stay here. King Piter isn't going to be able to live here anymore. I guess until I'm king, Alypium won't have a ruler. Except for Balor, when he finishes his fake quests and takes over. Nobody will be here to oppose him, I guess."

That thought made him feel even more guilty. If he didn't do this quest, would he still become king? He didn't think so. That meant he really would be handing Alypium over to Balor Stain.

Bethany looked at him funny. "You know, it's not up to your father anymore."

"What's not?"

"This whole thing." She waved around the room. "Taking care of Alypium. Deciding what to do with the scepter, the quests. They're all your decisions now, Erec."

Although it was hard to grasp, he knew it was true. The scepter was undoubtedly his now, as were the quests. If he wanted to defend Alypium from a future of Balor Stain and Baskania, nobody was stopping him—but himself. "So, do you think I should hand myself over to the three Furies, then? Would that really help anything—me dying that way?"

She shrugged. "You're right. This is a crazy situation."

A thought occurred to Erec. If he did give himself up to the Furies and died, maybe his sacrifice would protect everyone else. He had two other lost triplet siblings out there. Maybe they would be found and they could finish the remaining six quests. They would become the next rulers. He slowly raised his eyes to Bethany's, wondering if she was thinking the same thing.

She must have been, because she said, "You can't just die. There has to be another way. The Fates aren't perfect, are they?"

If she really had wanted to protect him from the Furies, that was the worst thing she could have said. As far as he was concerned, the

Fates were perfect. They showed him how to save Bethany, didn't they? Up until now, they sent him only on quests he could handle, and they had always been right.

So . . . what if he didn't do the quest? They would all die then, anyway? But if he gave himself up to the Furies, maybe everyone else might survive.

"Erec, I don't like that look on your face. Stop thinking about it, okay? Let's . . . I know. Let's go to the library and look up information about the Furies. Maybe we'll find clues that will change—"

"Erec? Bethany?" A familiar voice called into the room.

Erec jumped to his feet. "Who is it?"

Jack wandered in from the hallway. "Hey, guys. I went to Jam's Aunt Salsa's to find you, and they said you went to get another quest. I'm glad I caught you here. Just used her Port-O-Door." He thumbed over his shoulder.

"Come in, Jack." Bethany patted the couch. "Did you talk to Oscar?"

"That's what I wanted to tell you about. He wouldn't see me. But I kept trying to get messages through. Every day I went to the Green House and caught him on his way in, but he just snubbed me. I was afraid to give him his eye back in front of people, or even before I talked to him. He might have just handed it back over to Baskania and turned me in as a thief. I don't know. Anyway, I wasn't giving up, so I kept going back every day.

"This morning one of the secretaries told me that he just quit. He said he had to do something, and he might return and work there again, or maybe not."

"Do you think I should try to find him?" Erec said. "Maybe we need to see each other face-to-face. Where do you think he went?" Erec had a bad feeling he knew.

"Oh, no!" Bethany exclaimed. "He's figured out how to take revenge on Rosco, hasn't he?"

"I don't know," Erec said, although he had a sinking feeling that she was right.

"Where else would he go? I don't think he's off searching for us. Getting revenge on Rosco has been all he's talked about since he went into hiding. Rosco killed his father; he ruined his life. I'm just afraid what he might do. He can't get too far if Rosco can read his mind. This might be the end of him, Erec."

"I should go find him, if I can."

"I don't know," Jack said. "Isn't that what we've been trying to avoid? If Oscar sees you somewhere, then Rosco will know where you are, and he'll tell Baskania. . . . Remember how every time we were with Oscar lately Baskania appeared a few minutes later? I think it's too dangerous."

"*Chickens,*" a familiar voice spat. "Too *dangerous*, isn't it? You all don't know one thing about dangerous." Oscar walked into the room, his face as red as his hair. A black patch was strapped across one eye. "Long time no see, *friends*. Good to know you're still sitting around in comfort together, while I've been out there learning about life the hard way."

"Oscar!" Bethany rushed over to him, but he pushed her away.

"Give it a rest, beauty. I'm onto your tricks. Don't think you can suck me into believing in you again. Little-miss-nice-girl is just a sham. Turns out you're only out for yourself, like your friends here. Not a kind bone in your body. You all make me sick." He stuck his chest out, hands on his hips.

"Oscar, what are you doing here?" Erec said. "Listen, you have to believe us. Baskania's been lying to you. He doesn't care about you." Erec looked around the room fearfully, wondering if Baskania was going to appear.

"That's right." Oscar smirked at him. "Be afraid. I hope the Shadow Prince does show up here. I'm not hiding out anymore for

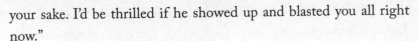

your sake. I'd be thrilled if he showed up and blasted you all right now."

"No, you wouldn't," Jack said.

"Oh, yes, I would. And as far as Baskania lying to me, I don't doubt that at all. Why wouldn't he lie to me? I like him. He's been the only one nice to me, the only person that understands me. Nobody else treats me right. First my own dad . . ." He wiped his eyes and stopped talking. When he went on, his voice was tight. "And then Rosco, who *really* took advantage of me, completely ruined my life. Then you, my best and only friends. So why not Baskania? Believe me, I don't trust anyone anymore."

"Then why can't you believe me? Those letters that Baskania showed you weren't real. He made those up! We've always been on your side."

Oscar laughed bitterly. "That's just what the Shadow Prince said you'd say. Of course. But he showed me more than your wonderful letters, great as those were. You didn't know, but he recorded you talking to him. And you too." He pointed at Bethany. "I know everything. And I know what kind of lies you're capable of, both of you. You two would say anything to get what you want. Or just to make me suffer for your sick amusement. And you." He pointed to Jack. "I used to think you were a good guy. I actually think you really *were* a good guy, until these two influenced you. That was one thing that Rosco was right about. The three of you never included me. Notice I'm the only one here who never was on a quest with Erec. Rosco was right about that, too, wasn't he?"

"Look." Erec put his hands up, showing he meant no harm. "Calm down. It's not like that, okay? We have something for you. I see you have an eye patch on. Well, I know why."

"It doesn't take a rocket scientist to figure that out. I'm in with the Shadow Prince now. And don't give me any of your holier-than-thou garbage about that, either. You all wish that he'd take you in too. But you know nothing about the man. It turns out, funny enough, that he's the one with the principles, not you all. I wanted to help out with his causes, because I understand what it's like to really care about things." He shook his head in disgust. "You all have no idea what I went through for you, living in hiding, just so I didn't accidentally see you, so Rosco and Baskania wouldn't come find you. Not one of you would have done that for me." He laughed. "Now I know why Baskania wanted to get rid of you so badly. It turns out he was right all along." He shoved his way past Jack farther into the room.

"Wait! Look, we can prove to you that we're on your side. We have your eye, in a jar. I stole it back for you from Baskania! Jack was trying to give it back to you. We're your friends, Oscar. Why would I lie to you?"

Oscar looked at Erec in disbelief. "You won't stop at anything, will you? Now I'm supposed to believe that you magically stole back the eye that I gave to Baskania? As if I even wanted it back? As if he wasn't ten million times more powerful than you? He would never let you take it from him. You *will* say anything." He shook his head with disgust.

"Look! I'll show you." Erec rooted around in his backpack, then he remembered that he gave the eye to Jack. "You have Oscar's eye, don't you, Jack?"

"Oh, yeah!" Jack searched his pockets, but he turned up nothing.

"What about you, Bethany?" Oscar faked a sweet smile. "Are you going to claim to have it now too? And maybe you have my father somewhere, safely tucked away for me? You saved him from Rosco? Go ahead. This is actually starting to get funny." He looked around. "Where is Baskania, anyway? I wonder what's taking him so long. It would be really nice to see him destroy all of you right now, before I finish my mission."

"What's your mission?" Bethany said. "It's not just to sic Baskania on us?"

"Get real, Bethany. As if I'd waste one more second of my precious time on you losers. And I mean that in every sense of the word. Baskania will be here soon enough, I bet. I'll leave you to him. Now, if you don't mind, I have something important to do." He shoved past them, kicking rugs and chairs out of the way. It looked like he was searching the floor. "I know it's around here somewhere."

"What are you looking for?" Jack said. "Can we help you?"

"*Can we help you?*" Oscar imitated him. "No, you can shut up and wait to be killed by the Shadow Prince."

Erec himself was wondering why Baskania had not appeared yet. "Why are you here, Oscar? What did you come for?"

"Revenge. What do you think?"

"I thought you said you weren't wasting any time on us," Bethany said. "Am I missing something?" She crossed her arms, annoyed.

"What?" Oscar's jaw dropped in mock horror. "The math brain is missing something? Impossible. Better recalculate, Bethany." He shoved a desk aside and stormed into another room, kicking rugs away as he went. "It's got to be here somewhere."

Erec, Jack, and Bethany followed him from a distance. Oscar continued to search the floors, room by room, until finally he said, "Aha!" He yanked a small rug from the side of the dining room, revealing a trapdoor in the floor. "This has to be it." Oscar yanked on a slit in the side of a plank, and the door lifted on hinges, revealing stone steps going down into lit tunnels.

Erec stepped back in shock. So here was the entrance to the catacombs that were under the Castle Alypium. His father had built this house to cover them after the castle disappeared. Something valuable was hidden in these catacombs, and all four of them knew what it was.

The Novikov Time Bender. King Piter's time machine.

That had to be what Oscar was heading for. Erec had caught him down there once before, studying the Time Bender. He remembered it like it was yesterday. Erec had asked him why, and Oscar had said, "I had to see it again. I just had to. Can't explain. I've been thinking about it, that's all. I had some ideas I needed to talk to Homer about." Had Oscar ever talked to Homer, the golden ghost who was guarding the Time Bender?

"What are you going to do?" Bethany squeaked. Erec could tell she was worried for Oscar's sake, although Oscar wouldn't see it that way.

"Something I've been planning for a long time." Oscar ran down the stairs, and the other three followed him. "It took me a while to get all the information I needed, but now I'm ready. And *nothing* is going to stop me. So don't get in my way."

Something struck Erec as familiar when Oscar said that. Nothing will stop him. Where had he heard that before?

Wait a minute. It was in writing. He had read it somewhere. *Nothing can stop Oscar.*

"If you think you're going to use the Novikov Time Bender, give it up," she said. "Homer will never let you."

"He let Erec use it to go back in time to when he was a kid. Of course he'll let me. He has only one rule, remember?"

Erec did remember. Homer would only let people use the Time Bender if their motivation was pure. Would that include Oscar? Pure hate and revenge shouldn't count, Erec thought. Anyway, he couldn't be up to any good. If Homer didn't stop Oscar, then he'd have to.

Nothing can stop Oscar. Then he remembered. Months ago, he had experienced the Awen of Knowledge, which let him know the truth of everything that existed. For a short time it gave him a complete understanding of his past, present, and future. Before all of that knowledge disappeared, he wrote a letter to himself, giving himself advice. The letter had read like a list, saying things like "forgive your father for his mistakes," "tell Jam how great he is," and "trust yourself." But one of the lines that he had not understood before jumped out at him.

Nothing can stop Oscar. It's written in the fabric of time. So just help him.

A vague memory of writing that hovered around him, although he had no idea why he would have said it. But everything had fit together then. So, he was supposed to help Oscar?

Oscar led them straight into the room. Homer, the golden ghost, hovered in the air like a cross between a man and a golden cloud.

The room was bare except for a tall, thin box made of solid gold, with windowed glass doors that opened on the front like a telephone booth. A small television screen extended from its side. The Novikov Time Bender. The last time Erec had seen it was when he had used it to travel back into his early childhood. When he had stepped back out of it, Oscar had been looking at it, planning something.

But how could Oscar use the Time Bender for revenge against Rosco?

"Welcome back, Erec, Oscar, Jack, and Bethany," Homer said. "So good to see you all here." Something in his voice made it sound like he knew perfectly well what was going on. He smiled contentedly.

"I need to use the Time Bender," Oscar announced. "I have to travel back in time. It's very important."

"I know." Homer smiled. "And your motivations are pure, Oscar. But, as you must imagine, the results will not be happy ones. Are you sure this is the choice that you want to make?"

"Positive." Oscar sounded resolute. "There is nothing for me here anymore."

"I don't get it," Jack said. "Are you staying there? How far back are you going?"

Oscar swung around, a wild look on his face. "How come you guys are still bothering me? What's wrong with the Shadow Prince—isn't Rosco telling him where you are today? All right, then. I'm going back to when Rosco was a young kid. And I'm going to fight him to the death. Don't bother thanking me, I wouldn't expect any of you to show any gratitude. But you'll all benefit too, you know. Once I do this, it will be like Rosco never existed. You won't be bothered by Baskania anymore—now or in the past, I guess. However it works out, I'm sure it will only help *you* all."

Erec was stunned. "Wait, don't do this for us. I don't want you killing anyone—"

Oscar laughed bitterly. "Don't worry, *King* Erec. I'm not doing anything for you. Believe me, this is revenge for my own sake, pure and simple."

Bethany turned to Homer. "You heard that! Are you letting him go back in time to get revenge on someone? That shouldn't be allowed."

Homer floated gently toward the Time Bender, not at all disturbed by the conversation. "The truth is more complicated." He sighed. "Oscar is quite upset with you, and the way he is wording things makes it sound like revenge is the main reason for his trip. But he is being quite noble, I assure you."

"Noble?" Jack said. "He's trying to go back in time and kill someone."

Oscar spun around in a fury. "*Yes*, Jack. Noble. Thank you, Homer. Obviously none of you have ever understood me one bit. You don't think it's ever noble to kill someone? What about the knights in the old days? Weren't they noble?"

"I don't know." Jack hesitated. "But killing someone is not right."

Oscar's fists clenched. His eyes were red and tearing up. "What if you're killing someone who would later go on and kill *hundreds* of people? Ever think of it that way? I'm squashing one rat when it's too defenseless to fight back, who would otherwise go on to kill and kill and kill. And I'm giving up my own life for it. Ever think of that? No. None of you would, would you? You're all *selfish*. Of course you wouldn't understand this. And of course you would call what I'm doing *bad*, when really it's the most noble thing of all." Tears were streaming down his face, and he was mopping them up with his sleeve, embarrassed.

"You're giving up your own life?" Jack looked bewildered.

Erec said, "He's going back to a time before he was born. If you do that with the Time Bender, you can never come back again. He'll be stranded there."

"Don't do it, Oscar." Bethany stepped closer and tried to put a hand on him, but he moved away. "We want you here. You're our friend. We can help you."

Oscar snarled. "I've seen your help, and your 'friendship.' All you want to do is use me, laugh at me, and step on me. That's been clarified. Oh, yeah, and lie to me. That 'stealing my eye back' one was really great. Now, time for me to go, guys. Wish I could say it was nice knowing you."

"Where's Rosco?" Erec looked around. "Don't you think he would turn up here and stop you if he could read your mind?"

"I planned this for a day when he was in important meetings with Baskania, all the way in Jakarta, in Upper Earth. So it should take him a while to get back here, I'd think."

"Wouldn't he know your plans in advance, though?" Bethany asked.

Oscar shrugged. "He's not here, is he? So I'm not going to worry about it. Looks like it's his loss this time. His *total* loss. And everyone

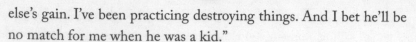

else's gain. I've been practicing destroying things. And I bet he'll be no match for me when he was a kid."

"What about your mom, Oscar?" Jack looked distraught. "She'll be all alone."

"No, she won't. Don't you see? My father will be alive again. Rosco would never have killed him. That will be the best part of all this for me. I'm saving my father's life." He closed his eyes. "There's no reason for me to hang around here, anyway. I don't have anyone here, except the Shadow Prince. I'm sure I can find him when I go back in time. He'll be around then, too. Maybe I could even find my parents back then . . . but my father doesn't like me around anyway. They won't miss me."

Erec spoke slowly, as if this wasn't real. "You're actually going to *kill* Rosco."

"You learn quick, king of nothing. It's kind of funny, too. Because Rosco used to tell me that someday I was going to save his life. Ha, ha. Guess the joke's on him. Now get out of my way, all of you." Oscar opened the doors of the Time Bender and stepped inside. "My only regret is that what I'm doing is actually helping you three. I wish Baskania had gotten here by now, so I could see you all be done away with, but I guess he was too busy in Jakarta. Too bad for that."

Jack ran up to stop him, but Erec held him back. "We have to let him go."

Jack looked frantic. "We *can't* let him go back there! He'll be stuck forever. He could get into real trouble."

Nothing can stop Oscar. It's written in the fabric of time. So just help him.

"It's too late." Erec let Jack go, and Jack rushed forward to pull Oscar out of the Time Bender, but Oscar easily pushed him away.

"I need to go back twenty years, to Ricochet Street in Alypium. The house of Donald and Liza Kroc, parents of Bobby Kroc. That's

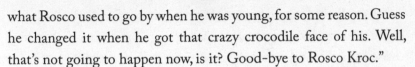

what Rosco used to go by when he was young, for some reason. Guess he changed it when he got that crazy crocodile face of his. Well, that's not going to happen now, is it? Good-bye to Rosco Kroc."

"*No!*" Bethany shouted. "Oscar, don't do it. We really have your eye, okay? We are your friends. Stay with us!"

Erec could tell that her words were painful to Oscar. He shut his eyes tight as if to block what he so wanted to believe. "Just leave me alone. My decision is made. Take me to see Bobby Kroc, Homer. I'm ready for him."

"You're going to go kill a baby?" Bethany's eyes were wide.

"No, for your information," Oscar spat. "I'm above that. Remember—Homer said I was noble. I decided to make it fair and even. I'm going back to when Rosco was about my age. It will be a fight to the death, but I plan on winning it."

"The Time Bender cannot take you to a different place," Homer said. "Only a different time. So you will be here, in this room, twenty years earlier. If you were going back—or forward—to a time when you were alive, then you would be in your body as it looked at that time, and appear either younger or older than you are now. Your current body would stay here, in the Time Bender, awaiting your return. But because you are choosing to go back to a time before you were born, which is not recommended, you will stay in your current body and disappear into that time. Instead of watching you on the screen the whole time you are gone, we will only be able to see you for a while, and the picture will fade away."

Oscar stuck his chin out, trying to be brave. "I'm ready, Homer. Twenty years back."

"You will see three dials on the side wall. They will set the year, month, and day of your visit."

As Oscar was turning the dials, Jack dove at his feet. "I'm not letting you do it!"

Oscar kicked him away and shut the glass doors. He finished dialing, and a wind raced through the room. In moments, a small cyclone swirled around the Time Bender, whirling dust and pebbles around so fast that they could no longer see Oscar through the window.

"He's gone," Erec whispered. They all felt his loss immediately. The wind storm quieted down as fast as it started. As afraid as Erec was to look, he still did. The Novikov Time Bender was empty.

CHAPTER THIRTY-FOUR
The Fate of Bobby Kroc

EREC, BETHANY, AND Jack sat, frozen, in front of the screen attached to the side of the golden Time Bender. Nobody had spoken. In fact, it seemed like nobody had taken a breath.

They watched Oscar walk through the castle and out its front door. It was before Erec was born. Bethany's parents were still alive then, Erec was thinking, and his own mother was still living there as well.

The only familiar person Oscar ran into in the castle was Balthazar Ugry, the second of King Piter's AdviSeers, along with Bethany's mother, Ruth Cleary. Ugry gave Oscar a funny look, but maybe that was because he had not seen him there before and kids were not usually found roaming in the castle. Oscar hurried by Ugry and passed quickly out the door and into the heart of Alypium.

It was odd watching on the television screen, as if what they were seeing was not really happening. In an odd way it wasn't, Erec thought. They were watching now something that had occurred a long time ago. Yet, at the same time, it felt immediate, and was—from Oscar's perspective. He was walking down the streets with a fierce determination, as if he was afraid of losing his focus.

What would he do? Erec thought. Would he really kill Rosco? He was sure Bethany and Jack were wondering the same thing. Maybe Oscar would just fight him awhile, convince him to be different. If Oscar went back in time and befriended Rosco, he could have taught him to be a different person.

No, that would never happen, he realized. Oscar would not befriend the person who killed his father, as well as all those other people.

As they watched the screen, it occurred to Erec that Baskania had never shown up. He hadn't shown up the last time Oscar saw him near the Time Bender either. Was Rosco keeping the Time Bender a secret from Baskania?

The sun was shining in Alypium twenty years ago as Oscar turned the corner onto Ricochet Street. A few houses down, a boy sat in front of a tree, holding a remote control and a blue toy airplane on his lap. Next to him was a dog . . . yes, Erec was pretty sure it was a dog . . . with a face like a crocodile. One dog ear waggled from its scale-covered head. Next to the boy was a hideous-looking doll that also had a head full of green scales and nasty spiked teeth jutting from its elongated mouth. The boy had a smug look on his face and was tossing his remote control into the air and catching it as Oscar approached him.

"What's your name?" Oscar asked the boy. Erec cringed, not wanting to hear the answer.

"Bobby Kroc." The boy shrugged. "What's it to you?"

"Only everything." Oscar strode up to him, bent down, and slugged Bobby in the face. "*That* is for my father."

Bobby Kroc jumped to his feet, remote control in his hand. "You're messing with the wrong guy, kid." He pointed his remote at Oscar. But before he could do anything with it, Oscar crooked all of his fingers toward him, like claws. Streams of white light flashed from Oscar's fingers. They struck Bobby, who jerked back into the air. He spun, flailing, and landed on the grass.

"Oh, no, you don't." Bobby sounded weak, but he was able to point his remote at Oscar. A green stream of light blasted toward Oscar, but Oscar darted out of the way. He bent his fingers again, shooting more light at Bobby.

"Ow! Ooohh." Bobby rolled around in pain. He managed to grab Oscar's ankles, pulling him to the ground. Then he dove on Oscar, punching. Oscar kicked him away, but Bobby sprang back, pinning his hands down.

"I've developed a specialty, kid. In honor of my last name. You mess with a Kroc, you become a croc." He pressed his remote control, murmured a word, and green light shot at Oscar, hitting him in the face.

"Ugh! Aaagh!" Oscar screamed in pain, hands over his face. The boy sat up, snickering and dusting himself off. Oscar rolled on the grass, rubbing his eyes and cheeks. Something green was growing on them. Scales.

Oscar sat up, panting, feeling his face changing. His nose began to stick out in a funny way, growing into a snout. *"No!"*

Then he stood, shrouded in fury. His head looked like the dog's did, like a crocodile. He screamed again with ferocious passion. "What have you done? *What have you done?*" He dove on Bobby, fists flying. In a minute, he had Bobby in a stranglehold. Oscar pointed his fingers at him. Crooked streaks of light crashed again and again into Bobby's face.

Bobby became weaker and soon his eyes closed. Oscar stood, shooting more and more rays into the boy, even after he lay completely still.

Oscar looked around fearfully. Nobody was on the street. He started dragging the boy's body away, but stopped, not sure what to do. He disappeared behind the tree—it looked like he might have thrown up. Then he pulled the boy's shirt and pants off and put them on himself. He pointed his fingers at the boy and said a word under his breath, and Bobby Kroc vanished.

Oscar collapsed under the tree, crying. The dog growled at him, but he took no notice. He kept touching his crocodile face, as if he could not believe what he felt.

Erec could not believe it either. What had happened?

"Oscar." Oscar said his own name softly into the ground. "Oscar. Oscar. Oscar. Oscar. OscarOscarOscarOscar . . ." He was shaking now, his voice weaker. "OscarOscaroscaroscaRoscaRoscaRoscaRosco. Rosco. Rosco. Rosco."

Bobby Kroc's parents walked outside and looked down in horror. "Bobby?" his mother said. "What have you done to your . . . face?"

"We'll fix it." His father sounded sickened. "I knew you weren't responsible enough to be an apprentice yet. Oh, no! Look at the dog! Get in there." He pointed toward the house, and Oscar slowly followed the dog inside.

The screen was fading as Oscar followed the Krocs into their house. It was hazy and hard to hear, but the Kroc parents were arguing and Oscar was staring at the dog. It was hard to read his expression through his crocodile guise.

And then the screen went black.

The room fell silent. Erec, Jack, and Bethany continued to stare at the blank screen, afraid to look away as if it might make everything they had seen real. Erec didn't even want to think . . . although ideas kept creeping into his head. Ones that he didn't want to face.

Finally Bethany started bawling. Tears streamed down her face. Erec put an arm around her and bit his lip. It was all he could do to keep from crying with her. What he had just seen could not be true. It couldn't be . . .

Jack said, "He killed Rosco. So now Rosco never existed."

"No." Erec shook his head, wiping his eyes. "It doesn't work like that. We still remember Rosco. He walked with us to the Labor Society when I drew my first quest. If Oscar killed Rosco, then he would be gone from our minds. Once I went back in time, and something changed for that really nice guy, Olwen Cullwich. It had to do with the way he died. But once the past changed for him, all of those old memories evaporated." He sniffed.

Bethany shot a glance at Jack. "You know what happened. Come on."

More silence followed as the three pondered what they had seen.

Jack got up and kicked a wall. "*No!* I refuse to believe it. Oscar was my best friend." He started to hyperventilate. "That's it. I'm going back to get him!" He dove toward the Time Bender. "I can use it, can't I, Homer? My motive is pure—to save my friend."

"It is," Homer agreed. "You want to give your life up to save your friend."

"No!" Bethany grabbed Jack and pulled him back. "You can't! I know you'd do anything for him. But think about your parents, your family. You'd never be able to see them again. You would be stuck back in time."

"Jack, if anyone should go back, it's me," Erec said. "Let me go find him."

"You can't—" Bethany gasped in horror. "Oh, *no*! I can't believe it. This is all my fault!"

"What?" Jack and Erec looked at her, confused.

Bethany pulled a small jar out of a bag she was carrying. "I totally forgot I had this. Jack was holding it when he first came in, and he set it on a table. I guess I stuck it in my bag so it wouldn't get lost. But with everything going on, I wasn't thinking. I totally forgot I had it!" Oscar's eye floated in the jar, surveying the room.

Bethany huddled over the jar. She gasped and then let loose with a flood of tears. "It's my fault. If I had only remembered I had the jar, Oscar would have believed us. He wouldn't have gone back and—"

"I don't know, Bethany. I'm not sure we could have changed anything. He had to go after Rosco. . . ." Erec choked up. Tears streamed down his face. He looked at Jack, who was crying, soundlessly, too.

A loud sniff came from the corner of the room. From the shadows, a small and wiry figure with piercing green eyes appeared in a black cape. Thick olive-colored scales covered most of his face and bald head, revealing occasional blotches of pink skin. His jaw and nose protruded like a reptile, and his mouth was long and wide.

Rosco Kroc. Erec's breath caught in his throat and he jumped to his feet. Was he going to kill them? Capture them or call Baskania?

But he was confused, too, after what he had just seen. Who was Rosco Kroc?

Then he noticed that Rosco had tears streaming down his face. Nobody spoke, but everyone's eyes were searching his, looking for Oscar. . . .

"Oscar?" Bethany said. "Is that really you?"

Rosco nodded, and she ran up and threw her arms around him. He bent his head into her shoulder, then pushed her away and sat on the floor, knees to his chest. "Don't . . . Stay away from me."

"But—what happened to you? I don't understand," Bethany said.

Rosco held a hand up and wiped his face. "I'll tell you everything. But then you have to go away and leave me alone. And . . . I'm sorry. I never deserved you as friends. I . . . didn't know. I really didn't know."

Jack sat next to him and spoke quietly. "What didn't you know?"

"That . . ." Rosco's voice choked up. "You really did care. Look," he pointed at the jar with his eye in it. "Bethany even really had my eye. You don't know how many years I looked back on this day and thought of you as liars. I was sure that the moment I disappeared, you all would be laughing and telling mean stories about me. You could care less that I was gone. All these years I believed what Baskania told me. I even . . ." His voice shut down on him as he contemplated the horrors of his life. "But I had to come back and watch today, see it all again for myself. Something made me. It was like . . . watching my own birth. I wanted to see you all as you really were, confirm how selfish you were, hear you with my own ears. But I never expected . . . never thought it was like this." He picked up the jar with his eye in it. "The Shadow Prince never told me that he didn't have my eye. I assumed he had it all along . . . but I never felt him using it like other people talked about."

"Rosco . . . Oscar?" Erec said. "What happened after you went back in time?"

"I remember it like it was five minutes ago. And, in a weird way, I guess it was five minutes ago. But twenty years have gone by since then, and here I am. I was so angry at all of you. So mad at Rosco for everything he had done." He took a breath, then laughed. "I still am, I guess. I became Rosco, and now I'm still angry at myself. But anyway, back then—I took the Time Bender back to go find Bobby

Kroc, sure that he was going to grow up and become the Rosco Kroc I hated so much. And I did what I swore to myself I would. I killed him. I know how that must sound." He shook his head.

"But Bobby was never going to grow up to be Rosco, was he?" Bethany said.

"No. That's the joke of it, I guess. I didn't see that until he was dead. There I was with the face of a crocodile, and he was lying on the ground. I realized I was going to be in big trouble. I didn't know anyone who might help me. It occurred to me that I might be spending the rest of my life in jail. But with my face gone I could disguise myself as Bobby, and make him vanish so nobody would know what happened. I put his clothes on, made him disappear.

"And that's when the irony hit me. I was posing as Bobby Kroc. I was going to be Rosco Kroc. And I had the crocodile face now to go with it. I had set out to kill Rosco Kroc, and instead I had given birth to him. And his first act was murder."

Erec sank to the floor next to Rosco. "It's okay, Oscar. You didn't know."

"No," Oscar said, shaking his head. "I knew. I'm not worthy of any of you. Maybe I once was, a long time ago. But I've done many horrible things since then."

"What happened next, Oscar?" Bethany asked. "Were the Krocs nice to you?"

"I guess." He nodded. "I avoided them as much as I could. It was hard to face them, knowing what I had done to their son, Bobby, even if they never knew. Sometimes they would look at me, and I'd be afraid they could tell. But it was just my guilty conscience, I think. They took me to see Vulcan himself to try to change my looks back. I was so afraid that they would find out who I was, that I wasn't their son, Bobby. But"—he gestured to his face—"as you can see, there was no danger of that. It's impossible to make people's looks return to the way they were. And compared to having a crocodile head, this wasn't bad.

"It didn't take long for me to find Baskania. He took me in right away as his assistant. It was interesting, though. This time with him, things were different. I was already a murderer, a villain, in my own mind. I didn't trust a soul, and was more bitter than you can imagine. So I looked at him more like an equal, a friend, than a boss. And he treated me that way too. He didn't know why this croc-faced boy found him, but he was impressed with my abilities and interest in him. I just wanted to be a part of something, to be accepted. That was always my downfall, I guess. My father never really accepted me, and I had wanted that so badly. So I was always looking for it in other people. And now, with my face so deformed, nobody wanted to be around me.

"But Baskania did. He liked me. At the time . . . I guess I thought he even loved me like a son. When I first found him, I waited for him to recognize me as Oscar Felix. But then I realized that he would not have heard of me back then. I was just some new kid with scales on his face. Years later, when he befriended Oscar—my old self—in Alypium, I wondered if he would make the connection between us then. But he couldn't. Baskania could read Oscar's mind, but Oscar didn't know he was connected to me either."

"Couldn't Baskania read your mind?" Erec asked.

"Oddly, no. I don't know why . . . if the scales blocked him, or my distrust in everyone—maybe I was too guarded. Or maybe going back in time closed some pathway off in me. I'll never know, I guess. Perhaps that is one of the reasons that the Shadow Prince took an interest in me—I was a bit intriguing to him. And angry. That attracted him too.

"But he never could see that I was Oscar, and I wasn't about to tell him. That would only give him more power over me, of course.

And one other thing I would never tell him about—" He pointed at the Novikov Time Bender. "This was my machine, not his. Baskania would have gone back in time to dominate the world if he knew about this."

"Is that why Baskania didn't appear the last time I saw Oscar down here?"

He nodded. "I wanted to turn you in and see you finally destroyed. I had hated all of you for so long. But not if it would risk the Shadow Prince finding the Time Bender."

"So . . . *that* was your connection with Oscar?" Jack said. "You weren't reading his mind—"

"No, I wasn't. I didn't have to read his mind. Anything that Oscar lived through was in my own memory of my past. When you invited Oscar to the castle that time with King Piter gone, as soon as you made the decision and I decided to come, once it all happened, then boom—it had happened in my past. I just simply remembered it. And, of course, I was happy to tell Baskania that you were at the castle.

"So, from the moment that Baskania decided that he wanted to capture you—sometime after he lost the dragon eye to you and before your quests started—I turned you in each time that I remembered where you would be. Each time Oscar had seen you. Until now.

"It was strange. Some of the things I remembered all along— things that didn't change. But other things, like when you decided to write a letter to Oscar, or invite him to meet you somewhere, those would only pop into my memory after you invited him, or wrote the letter. So the memories would appear in my head just before things happened. I guess I learned a lot about how time works through all of this."

Bethany looked both fascinated and horrified. "Why aren't you calling Baskania here now? You could have turned us all in."

Oscar shrugged, laughing under his breath. "Why would I? You don't get it, do you?"

Everyone watched him, waiting.

"I wanted to come here and see you all on this day for myself. See how terrible you were, revel in my pain and hurt. And then I was going to do something awful to you." He shuddered. "I am so sorry. I was wrong. All these years I lived a lie. Baskania had fed it to me a long time ago, when I was your age, as Oscar. He poisoned me against you. And as I changed into Rosco Kroc, that lie grew and grew until I had such a different view of you three. . . . You're just kids! And look at you. All wanting to go back in time to save me, at the expense of your own lives. Crying, missing me. Look, you even have my eye! Even that sick lie I thought you told me was true!

"Why would I ever hand you over to Baskania now? I've finally found my old friends from my distant past. The only real friends I ever had in my life." He laughed loudly. "And after all this time, you're still kids at that same age. How strange is that?"

Nobody was sure what to do. They sat a while in silence, and then Bethany pushed the jar with Oscar's eye toward him. "Here. Maybe you can get it reattached. It doesn't even look like your eye is gone."

"It's one of the new substitute eyes. They look pretty good, don't they?" He picked up the jar. "I don't know. It's probably too late to put this thing back in. It's been sitting in a jar for twenty years now."

"No, it hasn't," Bethany said. "Erec found it only a few weeks ago. He stole it back for you when he broke me out of Baskania's fortress in Jakarta."

"Only a few weeks? I guess so. How strange." He looked at his eye. "You really stole this for me?" Oscar-Rosco shook his head in disbelief. "And I was trying to get you killed." He pushed the eye away, sounding miserable. "I don't deserve this. I don't deserve any of you. But don't worry. I promise I will never harm you again."

"Oscar, you deserve everything you can get." Bethany patted his arm. "After what you've been through, you need a friend. And we're all still your friends. No matter what."

Oscar-Rosco's voice sounded bitter. "You don't know what you're talking about. I've done more terrible things than you know. With Baskania, one thing led to another. . . . I was a murderer when I met him, and I had lost myself. I would have done anything to be accepted, honored, a part of things. And he gave me all that . . . for a price. It's too late for me, kids. I'll do what I can for you. But I don't deserve your friendship."

"That's too bad." Jack's face was red, defiant. "It seems to me, though, that you don't have a choice. We're your friends, like it or not. Do what you want, Oscar, but we're here for you."

Oscar's voice rose, sounding pitiful. "You want to hang around with a murderer? A power-hungry criminal? What's wrong with you?"

"That's all in the past now," Erec said, trying to smile. "We just lost you, but now we have you back again, don't we? All of the bad stuff you did when you became Rosco, we all understand why that happened. You turned evil from hanging out with Baskania too much. That's what he does to people, right? But you don't have to stay that way. Do you? I think a brand-new part of your life could start now."

"Start brand-new," Oscar-Rosco mused. "I don't think I have a choice, really. Everything is different now. All of the lies I was living are exposed."

"That settles it." Bethany took his hand. "Time for Rosco to disappear, and Oscar to become our friend again."

Going to Rosco's apartment was strange, but he assured them that it was the safest place for them now. Erec could not help but wonder if Rosco was really setting them up. Maybe Baskania would barge in at any second. But he was acting like their old friend Oscar, and Erec decided to trust him.

The apartment was luxurious, filled with beautiful art and expensive furniture. Erec kept thinking how strange it was to be looking at his friend as an adult. He found himself staring at Rosco, searching for hints of Oscar. His eyes were the same as Oscar's. Erec noticed that one of Rosco's eyes looked slightly lighter—that was probably his fake eye. Even the way he tilted his head when he laughed and the sound of his chuckle were the same as they used to be.

"You have to stay away from King Piter's house," Rosco told them. "Baskania removed the water wall, and soon he is going to plant guards there, looking for you. They're building Balor Stain a huge castle right on the grounds where King Piter's castle used to be. Baskania could have put it anywhere, but he wanted to rub it in your father's face."

That reminded Erec. "Oscar wrote to me . . . I mean, you wrote to me in a letter that you—Rosco—somehow forged my father's signature on an official proclamation. It said that he was handing over his kingdom to Balor Stain. I don't believe that, obviously. But how did you do it? His real signature is not something you can fake. . . ."

Rosco looked away, ashamed. "I told you, I've done a lot of bad things. This one was nothing compared to . . . But I'm sorry. A long time ago I got King Piter's autograph, when I was a kid. I always carried it around with me in my pocket. Didn't think it would travel back in time with me, but it did. I kept it as the years went by, like a souvenir from the past—or future. But don't get me wrong. I was more than happy to use it against the king." He shrugged. "Still want to hang around with me?"

Erec nodded. "You were someone else then, Oscar. Anyway, I know what it's like to be angry at my father. I don't know if I'm ever going to forgive him for what he did to Bethany."

Rosco sat up straight. "What happened?"

"King Piter knew all along that Bethany has a younger brother somewhere. He could have told everyone and she would have never been captured."

Bethany's lip was trembling.

Erec put an arm around her. "I'm sorry for bringing it up. Bad thing to think about."

"No," she said. "It's not that. It's just . . . King Piter didn't think he was letting me get captured. He thought I was safe with him, and I guess I was until that scepter messed him all up. He probably thought it was all under control—and not telling anyone about my brother *was* his way of protecting him. I don't even know my little brother, but I'm glad he wasn't captured."

As they talked, it sunk in how good it felt to be finally sitting with Oscar again, not afraid that Baskania would appear because they were with him. "It's really good to have you back, Oscar."

Rosco grinned. "Yeah, I was thinking the same thing. You've really come a long way, Erec." Then his face dropped. "It's a shame, though. We reach this point again where we can finally hang out together, and it's all going to be over soon."

"Why?" As soon as he asked, though, he regretted it. He was sure he knew the answer.

"The Furies. Baskania is releasing them soon. Forget what he would have done to the world with the Final Magic. This is really going to be the end. I hate to be the one to bring you the bad news, but it's better that you hear it now. Take care of what you need to before it's all over. At least we can say that things got fixed between us before the world ended, right?"

"Do you really think the world is going to end when he lets the Furies out?" Erec asked.

"Probably. It's not going to be good, I'll tell you that. The three Furies have been enraged at their sisters for so many thousands of years they'll no doubt wreak havoc on the world. And, if that wasn't bad enough, if they want to escape they'll have to agree to be Baskania's slaves. Just wait to see what he does with that kind of power. Destroy kingdoms, bring down countries, kill everyone who disagrees with him . . . and it won't stop. He'll just get worse when he sees how invincible he is." Rosco sighed. "I'd have put a stop to this if I could. But he's far out of my league."

"Yeah," Erec murmured. "We knew about this." The quest paper weighed heavily in his pocket. *He* was supposed to stop them, right? Nobody else. The Fates knew what they were doing, he thought . . . at least they always had in the past. Bethany had said that it was all his decision now. King Piter wasn't in power anymore.

"How soon is Baskania letting the Furies loose?"

Rosco sighed. "He's already given them all the humans they need to escape—minus one person. And Baskania has the last guy ready to go. Grabbed him right off his ranch—it was one of King Piter's old AdviSeers. He's giving the Furies a few days to stew about it, and then he's going to bring that last man to them the day after tomorrow. By then they'll be ready to bargain, he thinks."

Erec's stomach knotted. "An old AdviSeer? Who is it?" It could only be one person—

"His name is Spartacus Kilroy." Rosco looked at the horror on their faces. "Oh, of course. You knew him. He was at the castle during the contests. I know. I was disgusted too. Poor Spartacus never hurt anyone. But he didn't trick King Piter enough for Baskania's taste, I guess. So now he's giving Spartacus 'a last chance to really help him.' Sick, huh?"

Erec broke out in a sweat. This wasn't really happening. The day after tomorrow Baskania was handing Spartacus Kilroy to the three Furies, killing him immediately and setting them free. Then everyone else would probably die as a result.

The answer seemed simple, all of a sudden. The Fates had given him a quest. He would just have to do it.

CHAPTER THIRTY-FIVE

Love, Chocolate, Conversation, and Massive Death

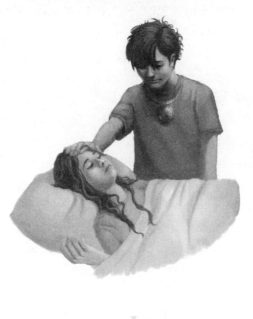

THE DAY AFTER tomorrow? Rosco's words kept bashing into Erec's mind like harsh waves against a rocky shore. *The day after tomorrow.* So Erec had one day left before handing himself over to the three Furies. One day left to live.

What would you do if you had one day left to live? Erec asked himself. All of those times he had played around with silly questions like that in the past . . . it always seemed like a dumb game, a joke.

But now that he really had only one day left, he realized that his answer would be nothing like he thought. Nothing at all. He would not go skydiving, or fly off to a foreign country. He would not try to meet his favorite sports heroes, or get together with the most beautiful girl he could find. In fact, none of those things appealed to him right now.

The only things that sounded nice—or even right at all—were spending quiet time alone with Bethany, and also his mother and siblings. He would have to say good-bye to Danny and Sammy, too. Or Derby and Shalimar . . . no, he decided. They would always just be Danny and Sammy to him.

This wasn't a quest anymore, really. Quests had a different feel. They were something risky, where he might be able to succeed, accomplish a goal. Sure, giving his soul to the three Furies so they could release themselves was accomplishing something, he assumed. The Fates wouldn't send him there for no reason. And a lot was at stake. But going to Tartarus was more of an ending than a quest. A grand finale, a good-bye.

Jack and Rosco were talking happily together, but their words drifted right over Erec's head. Bethany kept looking at him strangely. Telling her—and June—would be so hard. They would try to stop him, of course. In fact, that might just ruin their last day together. All of the arguing about it, crying . . .

Maybe he shouldn't say anything at all. What if they were able to stop him, lock him up or something? Then Baskania would give Spartacus to them, and the Furies would escape. If he was going to give himself to the Furies, he would have to do it soon.

His mind whirred through what he should do with his last minutes. He would not waste a moment on sleep. It would be better to watch Bethany sleep, think his last thoughts, write something down. If only he knew exactly how long he had. . . . "Rosco," he interrupted.

"What time is Baskania giving Spartacus Kilroy to the Fates, the day after tomorrow?"

Rosco's green eyes focused on Erec. "Mid-morning. Probably about ten, I'd think. The Shadow Prince has a few earlier commitments that morning."

Good. Erec's eyes closed. So he would go first thing that morning. That left the whole day tomorrow for himself.

When he opened his eyes again, Bethany was squinting at him, her mouth twisted.

He winked back, kissed one of his fingers, and blew the kiss at her. She blushed.

It was amazing what having only one day left to live gave him the courage to do.

Erec, Bethany, and Jack went back to Aunt Salsa's apartment to sleep. Rosco stayed in his own place, saying he should keep on pretending things were the same. He would try to find out the details about Baskania's plans with the Furies. He also said that he had an idea about how he might help, but would not tell them the details.

June threw her arms around Erec when he walked in. "You're okay! I was so worried about you. Did you get the quest?"

He nodded. That was the last thing he wanted to talk about. "Hey, Aunt Salsa. Do you have a library around here?"

"Of course." She walked up with a plate of finger sandwiches and cookies, looking happier than ever with all her company. "Just a few blocks away. It's closed for the evening, but you can put on some UnderWear and go in the morning."

"Thanks."

June had an arm around Bethany. "What was your quest?" she asked, interested.

"I don't know." Erec looked at his watch. "It's stupid. Anyway, with everything going on with the Furies, I won't be doing a quest now. Right? We should just have a great day together tomorrow and then go to stay with my dad and Queen Posey in Ashona the next day."

June nodded and gave him a loving kiss on the cheek. Bethany studied him, however, as if she didn't know who she was looking at.

When everyone finished their snacks and straggled off to bed, Erec walked back into the kitchen and found Jam. "Hey, thanks for everything you've done for me this last year. Really. You've been a great friend to me."

Jam turned his head and cocked an eyebrow. "Is everything okay, young sir?"

"Yeah, sure. I just wanted you to know."

Jam smiled. "Thank you, young sir."

Erec wandered back to the room he had shared with Danny and saw Trevor asleep in Danny's bed. Probably missing him, Erec thought. He felt a twinge of guilt, knowing that Trevor, Nell, Zoey, and his mother would be miserable when he was gone. Then again, that wasn't as bad as the alternative. Better that they were alive. They would get over it eventually.

Trevor snored lightly, a Cyclops action figure in his hand. Erec looked at the freckles on his face, watched him breathing. Why had he never noticed the little dimple on Trevor's chin before? Erec had probably never watched him sleep until now. Funny how having such a short time left on Earth made him pay attention.

He waited until he was sure everyone was sleeping, then walked into his mother's room. She looked so peaceful sleeping. So what if he never got to know his birth mother? Nobody could ever have been a better parent to him than June. He regretted all of the times recently that he blamed her for things that were really his father's fault. Why did he have to upset her so much? What he was about to do would hurt her for the rest of her life. If only he had been kinder before . . .

When watching her sleep became too much, he peeked into the room where Bethany slept in one bed, and Nell and Zoey shared the other. He could not look at Bethany—for some reason it frightened him. But he stood near his sisters awhile and thought about times that they had spent together. When he was gone, who would protect Nell if kids teased her about her walker? Then again, he had been gone so much lately, she must have been fending for herself. Danny and Sammy wouldn't even be around to help her anymore. A twinge of guilt stabbed him. She, and his whole family, would pay for this quest. It wasn't fair to any of them.

But that's the way life is, he thought. No guarantees. Nothing is fair. He had been pretty lucky up until now. If this was the way it had to end, then that was that. He smiled when Zoey stretched—for a moment her eyes opened and she said something that was a blur of words, then she turned over, asleep again. How long before she forgot about him? She was so young.

Bethany's presence seemed to loom behind him, like a wind whipping into a storm that might wipe him out if he did not turn around. But how hard would it be to see her face? How painful? Finally he forced himself to look.

Her head rested peacefully on her white pillow, with a serene look as if life were perfect. Instead of feeling sad, Erec was overcome with happiness and peace himself. She would be okay. Sure, she would be sad for a while when he was gone. But she would eventually recover and live a great life. What he was doing would let everyone live, he hoped. The Fates would not be sending him to his death unless it was going to foil Baskania's plans. And Bethany's expression sealed the deal for him.

He wished he could give himself to the three Furies right now.

He was ready. Staying around another day would make it harder. And there wasn't anything stopping him. . . .

But he owed his family one last day together. He would try to say everything he always wished he had. Also, part of him gripped on to his life like a vise. How could he give up his last moments?

His eyes were closing despite himself. Okay, he decided. He would sleep now so he could be at his best tomorrow. But he would stay up on his final night and enjoy each last breath.

"So," Bethany chirped in the morning. "Are we going to the library? Anyone else want to come?"

Jack volunteered, but Nell, Trevor, and Zoey wanted to go to the famous Americorth North volcano museum with June before they left the next day. "I don't live far from here," Jack said. "Look." He pulled a paper out of his pocket and showed it to Erec and Bethany. The detailed map had a path outlined on it leading from Aunt Salsa's apartment to Jack's house. "I got this from those crazy druids in Avalon. No matter where I am, this map always shows the way to my house in Aorth. I thought it was a gag gift, but it actually is pretty cool."

They all put on shiny silver UnderWear over their clothing to keep the intense heat at bay, and slipped out of the door. Boiling air blasted in Erec's face for a fraction of a second before his UnderWear took over and a cool wind blew from the suit and hood. They followed Jack down the street for a few blocks, then turned a corner to see a towering building shaped like a giant open book.

"Cool library!" Bethany squealed. "I hope it has some good math books. Good idea coming here, Erec."

"I don't know," Jack said. "You may have liked the volcano museum better."

A tall, thin woman with white hair and pursed lips sat behind

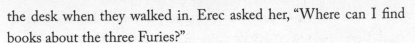

the desk when they walked in. Erec asked her, "Where can I find books about the three Furies?"

"On the third floor, in the mythology section, under *F*."

Mythology? Erec thought. Didn't people believe the Furies were real?

Bethany shot him a suspicious glance. "Was there a reason we came here today, Erec?"

"I wanted to find out about them, seeing that they're going to be released into our world tomorrow."

She shrugged. "I guess that makes sense. You're not thinking about doing anything stupid, are you?"

He hesitated, then said heartily, "Not at all." That was easy, he thought. Doing his quest might be the hardest—and last—thing he would ever do. But saving everyone he loved was definitely not stupid.

They climbed the stairs and found a row of books about the three Furies on a shelf. "Look at this one." Jack pulled out a book called *Alecto's Anger Management Workshop: A Completely New Approach to Your Problems.* He flipped it open. "Talks about throwing priceless vases, and . . . wow, smashing people with baseball bats. Man." He put it back on the shelf.

"This one is interesting." Bethany was holding *Anger, Vengeance, Jealousy, and Other Stunning Traits of the Three Beautiful Prisoners of Tartarus.* She laughed. "Big surprise. They wrote this one. I didn't know the Furies were authors."

"I guess they have a lot of time on their hands," Erec said. He noticed a book called *Dream Vacations in Tartarus* and pulled it off the shelf. "This shouldn't be allowed. It's trying to get people to go visit Tartarus, saying how great it is, and all these fun things you can do for free. Personal chefs, horseback rides, free babysitting . . . The minute people arrived they'd be killed, wouldn't they?"

"At least these are all in the mythology section," Bethany said. "I hope that would keep people from believing what they read."

"Here's a good one." Jack handed a thin cloth-covered book to Erec called *Writings of Megaera.* Erec flipped it open.

> When triplets are born, there is always a youngest, even if it is only by a minute. I am that girl. No matter how strong my powers are, how many years of wisdom are under my belt, I will always be the one looked down upon, belittled.
>
> To make it worse, we have three older sisters—Decima, Nona, and Morta—who think they are so much better than us, and trust us so little, that they locked us away forever. If only I could be one of them, enjoy the kind of lives they lead—it pains me to no end. They are free of bitterness, and full of laughter.
>
> It's not fair. I've spent millennia wishing, wanting what they have. Knowing I'm never to get it makes me want to shred them into tiny pieces and watch the wind blow them away. Only then might I finally be at peace.

He skimmed further in the book.

> For example, one of the things that I treasured the most when I was free was my amber collection. I had captured the finest of each type of living specimen, every species from humans to the simplest of viruses. My molten amber mixture was the purest, finest flowing liquid sunlight that

existed. I found a pure spring of it under what had been a forest for thousands of years, and I was able to keep it melted and ready to cover anything I found. The amber alone was exquisite—a fossil of the sap of oaks, maples, and pines perfectly blended so that not even a ripple or streak was to be seen. And the specimens themselves . . . how can I forget the bobcat caught mid-leap, its glorious paw waving at me through the amber like it was a fly caught in honey.

As expected, my sisters would find problems with anything I loved. The Fates always disapproved that I was ending the lives of my gems, although I assured them that their lives were simple and meaningless compared to my pleasure. Plus, this way I would glorify them always. They would never truly die. Alecto was so angry that she wouldn't speak to me because I was wasting my time on frivolity. And Tisiphone enjoyed destroying my creations whenever she could find them as a punishment for going against my sisters' wishes. But I was able to hide them from her, mostly. Amber was truly my one source of joy.

So, what happened on the day when my sisters, the Fates, imprisoned Alecto, Tisiphone, and myself in Tartarus? Did they bother to warn me, let me take my priceless collection along? Of course not. It floats around out there still, for unappreciative wastrels to find and use as they wish. Such is my life.

"She's miserable," Bethany said. "I almost feel sorry for her."

"Except for the killing and preserving animals from each species out there," Jack added. "And people. I wonder how often she updated her collection."

"Probably all the time," Erec said. He thought of his backpack at Aunt Salsa's house. In Baskania's fortress he had found a bee captured in amber. Could it possibly be Megaera's? Baskania must have kept it for a reason.

Bethany was flipping through *What do Furies Really Want?: Love, Chocolate, Conversation, and Massive Death.* "I don't want to look at these books anymore. There's nothing but bad news. We can't stop these three from escaping from Tartarus tomorrow, anyway. I'd rather have a last good day, not think about what's going to happen."

Erec pointed at the book. "Is it that awful?"

She nodded. "Basically. Alecto is ready to annihilate us all in a fit of rage, Tisiphone will happily punish us with death for all of our misdeeds, and Megaera wants to shred us out of jealousy. Not much happiness and light among the three of them."

Erec agreed. "Let's go do something fun. Thanks for coming here with me, guys. And, uh, just so you know, thanks to both of you for everything. You've been amazing friends. I'll never forget . . ." He realized that he wouldn't live long enough to forget a single moment of today.

Jack slapped him on the back. "You, too, guy. Guess tomorrow might be the end for us, huh? Let's not think about it, okay?"

Erec couldn't help but smile when he said that. No, he thought. Tomorrow will not be the end for you. That's the greatest part of this. Only he would be gone, he was sure. Everyone else would be just fine.

The day whizzed by too fast. They couldn't find any cloud cream shops in Aorth, but Jack took them to Molten Lava Sundaes. Erec ordered a molten amber parfait in honor of Megaera and his bee, although it tasted more like honey than hot liquid rock on the ice cream. Super A Fastaurants were all over, even more than in Upper Earth, it seemed.

The three paid a surprise visit to Jack's family. They had thought he was studying with his tutor in Alypium. Jack didn't have the heart to let his family know that they had one more day to live, but Erec could see the tears in his eyes when he hugged his parents. "Do you two mind if I stay here a few days?" he asked them. Then he turned to Erec and Bethany. "You can stay with us, guys, if you want."

"Or—does your family all want to come to Ashona with us?" Bethany said. "It would be a fun vacation."

"We better not, dear," Jack's mother said. "Too many things to do here. And Jack, I'm surprised you're taking a break like this. Your tutor won't like you getting behind in your studies."

He nodded, unable to explain. Erec wanted to tell him that it would be okay, but Jack would see soon enough.

Bethany and Erec found their way back to Aunt Salsa's. Danny and Sammy were talking to everyone on e-mail, decked out in royal robes with their hair standing on end, clown style. Everyone was saying their good-byes, just in case, not knowing what the next day would hold.

The day ended with more hugging, weeping, and storytelling. Erec felt lighter with each tear, however. He was the only one who knew, the only one who was strangely relieved. If everything went right, all of his family and friends would go on to share many more stories together—and think back to the times they had spent with Erec. He would live on in their memories.

The night sped by like lightning, even though Erec did not sleep a wink. He had no problem staying awake, actually. His mind raced with a mixture of fear, excitement, and desire to capture each last second of the feeling of being alive. Air felt cold as he sucked it in through his nose, and his warm breath caressed him on its way out. He could feel his blood flowing, the electricity running through his nerves. Life felt so good. Why hadn't he paid attention like this every day of his life? Why hadn't he noticed more?

He ran his fingers along the walls as he walked into the rooms of his loved ones. Every tiny bump under the paint was so beautiful he wanted to cry. Would he remember this world after he left it? Would he be able to look down and see everyone . . . or even stay on as a ghost?

It occurred to him that he could use his dragon eyes one last time to see into his future. But did he want to? Aoquesth had avoided it unless he had to. He had said that knowing when and how he would die would have ruined his life. Then again, Erec thought, he only had a few hours left to ruin. Why not take a look?

Unless . . . What if the way he would go was horrible? What if he saw himself in pain, dying slowly? Would he still have the guts to give himself to the Furies?

A small voice inside asked—*what if?* What if the Fates were wrong and him giving his life up wouldn't save anyone at all? They hadn't exactly come out and said that's what would happen, did they?

No. But at the same time, he was sure of it. All of his quests ended up helping people. And this was the big threat now.

In the end, Erec decided to take a glance into his future. He was too curious not to. Heck, there were only a few more hours left, he would find out soon enough. But he wasn't going to waste any more of his precious time sleeping tonight, and it gave him something to do. He hoped he didn't see something awful. That would make it so much harder to hand himself over to the Furies.

Then it occurred to him—he might not see anything at all.

Would there be nothing but darkness? Would he see his own funeral?

Pushing all thoughts from his head, he sat on his bed and crossed his legs. He tried to relax, which was hard with the tension clicking through him, and imagined entering a small, dark room inside his mind.

Once he stepped inside, everything became more peaceful. All of the burdens were lifted. Erec was tempted to stay there forever . . . but he knew that wouldn't help anybody. He found the doorway into the smaller, darker room and went inside. Here an even greater calm swept over him. All seemed right with the world. A living, beating thing, like a heart, was nearby on a table . . . the box that knew everything that existed, all the whys and hows in the universe. Wisdom he once had known himself, when he experienced the Awen of Knowledge. Too bad he had given that up, he thought.

He reached to touch the boar-shaped vial that still hung around his neck, with small glass balls attached to it. There it was, the yellow glass ball attached to the boar's snout. It was a part of the Awen of Knowledge. He would be able to use it one time, when he broke it. But he had no idea how it would work. The only glass ball he had broken so far was the blue one—the Awen of Sight—when he had saved Bethany and her brother Pi from Baskania a few months ago. It had filled the air with such a dense fog that nobody around him could see a thing—except for him. He had been able to see clearly when everyone around him was blinded.

What would happen if he used the yellow ball—the Awen of Knowledge? If he broke it when he was in before the Furies killed him . . . he would know if there was a way to get out alive and stop them from destroying the world.

Yes! It felt great to have a plan. He looked at the other Awen balls attached to the boar vial. The green and black ones on its feet were the Awen of Beauty and Creation, and the red one on its tail was the Awen of Harmony. The magic of the Awen crystals was one of the most powerful forces in the universe. He hoped the remnants that hung around his neck were strong enough to help him.

Erec rested his hand on the box. He was ready to see his future now. With the Awen of Knowledge, the quest might actually work okay. He pulled the silky cord hanging between the two windows and their shades flew up.

There was peace in the immense, cold cavern. Hope, love, and joy echoed around them like the calls of long-lost friends. The Furies were relieved, grateful, and Erec was awestruck. All was well.

A reddish mist floated through the air, smelling of rosebuds. Erec held the boar vial around his neck — what was left of the Twrch Trwyth — with the red glass ball broken off.

"Thank you, again." Alecto smiled upon him. "You have done us a great service."

Tisiphone laughed in delight, then sucked in. . . . The room swirled. . . .

Erec's soul was leaving him. Pulling out into the air.

Everything was going black. He could feel himself drop.

"Take this," a voice whispered. "And remember me." Something fell into his hand.

The last points of light faded.

Dying.

Gone.

Static filled the windows. After watching a while to make sure, Erec pulled the shades. He climbed slowly out of the dark rooms in his head and back out to his dark room in Aunt Salsa's apartment.

What had happened? He had died. But he had not broken the yellow Awen ball to give him all the knowledge he needed. He had broken the red one—the Awen of Harmony. Why did he do that? It didn't make sense. Wouldn't the Awen of Harmony ball make everyone else miserable and insane with rage, and make Erec peaceful when he broke it? But it looked like the Awen's powers spread out to include the Furies, making them all peaceful and happy.

So, the Furies felt great. Wonderful. He would still die if he broke the red Awen ball. That was now clear. Okay, no problem, then. He would just break the yellow one. That would give him a chance to live and to save everyone.

It was five in the morning. Erec took the bee encased in amber out of his backpack and put it into his pocket. Maybe he would return it to Megaera when he arrived. Why not? he thought. He wouldn't need it, anyway, and it was probably hers. With a sigh, he wondered how long it would take to find the entrance to Tartarus, and then how much time would be involved in getting there. Erec had no idea where to start looking for it. He should have checked when he was at the library, he thought.

A bolt of fear flashed through him. What if he couldn't find it? Had he not looked for its location when he was at the library for a reason? Was he subconsciously afraid to go, and had he sabotaged his own plans?

But then again, it probably did not matter. There was a saving grace for him—the Hermit. Erec could always count on him to show up when he started a new quest, and make sure he was headed the right way. Why should this time be any different?

He debated waiting another few hours and saying good-bye to everyone, but realized that they would try to stop him from leaving. No, he would say his farewells now, while they still slept. That would give him more time to find the Furies before Baskania brought Spartacus Kilroy to them.

His stomach tightened into a knot as he made his way through their rooms a final time. A last glance, a hug, a kiss on the forehead. He reached Bethany last, wiping a few tears from his cheek. As he bent over her, one dripped and fell onto her face. She stirred, but did not wake. Erec put a hand on top of her head and closed his eyes, thinking of the bright future she would now have ahead of her.

Then he turned and walked out the door. Aunt Salsa's Port-O-Door stood open, and the Hermit was inside waiting for him.

CHAPTER THIRTY-SIX

Tartarus

THERE WAS A chill in the air of the Port-O-Door vestibule, and it was not from the temperature itself. The Hermit seemed completely different from any other time Erec had seen him. He wasn't smiling, no jokes or winks. In fact, he seemed as somber as if somebody had just died.

A white sheet was wrapped around him like a burial shroud, with a hood that stretched so far over his face he looked like a ghostly Grim Reaper. He did not say a word as he pushed spots on the map of Otherness so fast that Erec could not follow where they were going. The map resembled that of Aorth, but only because it lay deep in the earth. Erec had not seen a map like it before.

Soon the map showed a place that was aboveground, then underground, and then aboveground again. The Hermit pointed at a river running near the base of the Nether Volcano. "These are the Waters of Oblivion. They are shallow. You can walk through them. But I cannot cross with you."

Erec could hardly speak because his teeth were chattering. "Why not?" He did not want to hear the answer. He did not want to cross the Waters of Oblivion either.

"Anyone crossing them will soon die."

Erec gulped. "Can't we just put the Port-O-Door past the river, so we don't have to cross?"

The Hermit looked at Erec with mournful eyes. "I wish, Prince Erec, prince of light. I wish."

Erec felt himself gasping, as though he was removed from his own body. None of this seemed real. "What about B-Baskania? Will he cross the waters? How will he g-get out alive?"

"He has an agreement with the Furies. They signed an oath that he will live, as a reward for his help."

"H . . . h-how did he get his first message through to them?" Erec clutched his sides. "Maybe I could—"

"No, Erec Rex. You cannot. Baskania sent people across to the Furies carrying the messages that he would help them if they promised he could cross in safety. You could not do that—you have nothing to offer them."

Erec was shaking now. Why couldn't he appreciate his last breaths like he had in Aunt Salsa's apartment? Gone was the joyful feeling of life. Instead he felt only an ice-cold dread.

The door shrank to fit into a large rock by the river. The Hermit opened it, since Erec's hands were trembling too much. Erec felt the Hermit's hand land on his back and then push. . . .

When he looked behind him, the door was gone.

For a moment he stumbled around desperately in search of the door, or any way out of here. Jagged cliffs surrounded him, and the air was filled with an eerie flickering light, as though he were indoors. When he looked up, he saw no sun, only Earth far above him. Where was the light coming from? Was there a fake sun, like in Aorth?

A dancing reddish glow came from cracks in the nearby mountain bases, as if fires were lit behind them. Erec wondered if fire was burning in the base of the volcano. How would he get out of here? There had to be a way. . . .

He closed his eyes and calmed himself down. *Come on, Erec, why are you here?* He had to complete his sixth quest. *Give yourself to the three Furies.* There was no choice. He had to make a sacrifice to save everyone else. People he loved, and those he never met.

That idea gave him focus and strength. He fingered the Twrch Trwyth vial around his neck. All the knowledge of the world sat there inside the yellow glass ball. If he broke it now, he would know just what to do.

But how long would that knowledge last? It would no doubt tell him to cross the water now. What else could he do? The Fates had sent him here for that reason. He might as well do what he had to first, and wait until he needed the Awen of Knowledge before using it up. A small ray of hope welled up in him. Maybe when he knew everything, he would find a way to escape, after all. Baskania had made an agreement with the Furies. Maybe he could too.

After a few long minutes of staring into the shallow, rippling water, Erec waded in. He cried out in pain from its unexpected deathly cold. Was this it, then? His life would be over soon. He had stepped into the Waters of Oblivion.

Another step forward, and then another. The stream was shallow—the Hermit had been right—but the water raced around his shoes so fast that he almost fell over twice. Each pace felt final, fatal, as he continued. And then he stepped onto a dusty shore. Not far away, a dark slit at the foot of a steep cliff looked like an arched crevice in the rock. It probably was the base of the Nether Volcano, he thought. He set forward toward it.

Erec had never felt so alone. That's why he nearly jumped with surprise when a small figure darted out of the crevice and raced toward him. It took a moment before he recognized it was a cat. Soon, several more cats followed it out from the opening in the rock, running around through the dirt in circles. Erec was not sure if they were playing or if they were chasing something.

A scrawny cat sauntered up to him and rubbed itself on his ankles as if it knew him. Even though it was only a small comfort, Erec was glad to have the company. Plus it cheered him to see something here that was alive. If the cats had crossed the Waters of Oblivion, they had not died from it yet. So maybe he had a little time.

As he grew closer to the towering rock face, he could see that the crevice opened into a cavern. He approached it from the side. Most of its entrance faced away from him, so his view into it was obstructed. Still, he became more and more sure that this was the Furies' lair. A blue lizardlike creature bounced nimbly out of the cavern on its twelve legs, scuttling between Erec's feet before darting to the water for a drink. The odd thing ran away from a few cats, then back inside the cave.

While Erec walked closer, dragging his feet, a dozen blackbirds plunged from the sky into the cave. Erec wondered how they had gotten this far underground. They must have found a passageway somewhere. What was attracting them here? It was interesting, he thought. The birds were able to go straight to the cave without touching the deadly river that he crossed through. Even the cats strode through the waters, but the birds seemed to have a free pass.

A strange noise, like roars of vicious animals, came from the cave, growing louder as he approached. Snarls and screams echoed off the nearby cliff faces. It was hard to keep walking toward it. Whatever was in there did not sound human enough to reason with.

He forced one foot in front of the next until he finally rounded a corner. There, facing the cave entrance, stood Thanatos Argus Baskania, his black cape whipping behind him from the wind that rushed out of the cave. His face was molding and reshaping. Multiple eyes as well as his nose sank into deep pits in his skin, and were then swallowed completely into his head. The hideous gaps began to fill in until a smooth surface of flesh covered his entire face—except for a gaping mouth with a wicked grin. Then eyes sprouted everywhere, looking in all directions, both fearful and full of glee, depending on who their prior owners were.

Erec heard a whimper from not far away on his other side. He had been so overwhelmed with Baskania and the noise in the cave that he had not noticed the figure pressed against the rock. A pale, trembling Spartacus Kilroy sat on his feet, gripping his knees to his chest. His eyes were squeezed tightly shut and his lips moved silently. Neither he nor Baskania noticed Erec.

Baskania rubbed his hands together, facing into the winds blowing from the cave. He laughed with delight. "I have him here now, with me. I know you can sense him. How does it feel, my three lovely ladies, to be so close to freedom? You know all that you have to do if you want to get this last human soul, don't you? It's such a small price to pay."

A wicked hiss resounded from the cave, and something was

spat out at Baskania. A shrill voice cried, "Let us see this human, then. Prove to us that he is here before we discuss it."

Baskania chuckled. "Do you think you can fool me that easily? Once you see him you will put a Draw on him, and he will be yours. No, this human is nicely hidden at the moment, but *so* close at hand. Can you *feel* him nearby? Your freedom is so close. Ah, it must be tempting for you. Such a small promise you would have to make in exchange for this gift. I would be such an easy master. You could create all the ruckus you wanted, do anything at all, as long as you served my occasional commands. But if you'd rather wait another few years ..."

The snarling in the cave grew, as did the wind, forcing Baskania back a few steps. He turned toward Erec, and suddenly shock and confusion registered in his many eyes. His mouth sneered as he stepped toward Erec. "What are *you* doing here, boy? You'd be a nice gift at any other time, but you're in the way now. I'll deal with you later." He pointed at Erec and a rope spun out of his finger. It snaked through the air, but instead of wrapping around Erec, as it had in the past, it was swallowed whole by the Amulet of Virtues that hung around Erec's neck.

Baskania growled. "It's too bad I didn't have the chance to kill you before that thing got more powerful. But I'll take care of that now." He pointed again and a blast of black smoke shot toward Erec's face. About a foot away, it dove down and spun into the amulet, just as the rope had.

Anger flushed Baskania's features. "I've had enough of you, boy. Why don't you try a taste of what I gave to your old dragon friend? What was his name again? Aoquesth?" Something shiny flashed from his finger, and a silver black dagger sailed through the air toward Erec's heart. Erec froze, arms out, unable to move. The smoking blade brought him back to the day Aoquesth had died. Not even a powerful dragon could withstand the Death Blade. Now it was his turn.

But the Death Blade dipped in its course. Instead of slicing into Erec's chest, it struck the Amulet of Virtues hard, knocking him back a few steps, and then clattered to the ground.

Baskania glowered, staring at the blade. "Don't worry, boy. Killing you won't be a problem once I have a little more time on my hands. But I have something more important to do now. So take care of your dragon eyes for me. I'll want them in good shape once I'm ready to pluck them out of your head." He turned back to the Furies. "Well, ladies, have we reached a decision yet?"

Erec took another step forward and then froze. If he went farther, he would be able to look into the mouth of the cave. He was terrified of what was waiting for him. And they would see him. They would put a Draw on him, and he would not be able to turn back.

But, then again, there already was no turning back. He had crossed the Waters of Oblivion. There was no place to go.

"Who is out there?" a high-pitched voice screamed.

"Nobody important, I assure you," Baskania said. "Think about my offer, please. I am growing impatient."

Their rancorous screeches and screams rebounded through the open valley. Erec was shaking so hard that his muscles felt frozen. But he had to move now. Once the three Furies had agreed to Baskania's terms, it would be too late. He had a quest to do, and now was the time.

Before he could stop himself, Erec ran straight to where Baskania stood. What he saw in the entrance to the cavern made him gasp. Tartarus was well lit, much brighter than the valley where Erec stood. The opening was large enough for him to see far into its depths. Birds and bats filled the air, swarms soaring in flocks and solo. Harpies hopped and flew among them, shrieking and shouting out orders.

But the three beings whose eyes focused on him were something else altogether. Breathtaking, horrifying . . . there was no question in Erec's mind that these were the three Furies.

Each was about seven feet tall, but most of that height was occupied by their incredibly large faces. They were all heads, and tremendous batlike wings that shot out behind them, at first glance. It took him a moment to register anything past their faces, which radiated a soft glowing light, with expressions so ferocious and hateful that Erec became lost in a whirl of sorrow. Their hair—one with silken black locks, one with white, and one red—flowed behind them, curling into the air and sprouting from their jointed wings. Looking more carefully, Erec spotted feather-covered, human-shaped bodies stretching back from their heads. The three beings seemed so much greater than human, so full of energy and larger than life. It was as if they had been stuffed into their small forms just like compressed stars before a supernova.

Luckily, the three Furies took just as long to react to his unexpected appearance. "Well"—the black-haired Fury's mouth twisted into a wicked smile—"this changes the picture a bit, doesn't it?"

It occurred to Erec that everyone present, from the three Furies to Baskania, had probably read his mind by now. They knew exactly what he was up to. He didn't need to speak at all. So he just shrugged and started walking toward his horrid fate.

The shrieking of the Furies, and the resulting wind, stopped dead. They watched him approach greedily, hungrily, waiting until he crossed the border into Tartarus to give them the freedom they had longed for since the Earth was young. Erec felt like something tiny— a meatball, maybe, or more like a raisin—an insignificant thing to be digested for the greater good.

An anguished cry behind Erec startled him. He turned to see Baskania reaching toward him as if he were losing a son. He must have known it was too late. The Furies had already seen Erec, so they could put a Draw on him. Funny, though. Erec did not feel any Draw pulling him to them. Maybe they knew he was coming anyway.

Baskania was pathetic, Erec thought. The sorcerer had let greed and hunger for power shred his soul until losing his own real son, Balor, seemed to mean nothing to him. But losing Erec's dragon eyes, and also his bargain with the Furies, was too much for him. It was ironic, Erec thought, that nobody wanted to save his life right now more than Baskania did.

Which made walking straight to his death that much easier for Erec. He was stopping Baskania from having ultimate power. Maybe this really would save his family, the whole world. His life was a small price to pay.

So Erec straightened his back, ignored his desire to run as far and as fast as he could, and marched toward the three Furies. He clutched his arms so tightly that his hands went numb. His teeth chattered loud and hard. Each step seemed to take forever, yet, at the same time, sped by so fast that his last moments drained through his grasp like water.

Everyone watched him, fascinated. Even a few Harpies flew out of the cave and hung above him in the air, spellbound. Well, this is it, Erec thought. It's been a great life. I'm sure Bethany will go on to do amazing things. He smiled a bit, thinking of that, his last and best gift to her.

One more step. One more step. His end was close now. Would they kill him the moment he crossed onto the white rock of the cavern? There wasn't much room for him—but they were moving back now so he could enter. Step. Step. Step.

An odd noise came from one and then another of the Furies. The tense burbling sounded like excitement. Finally Erec stood before the distinct line where the dirt under his feet ended and the cave floor began. This was it. He had to step over it. No choice left. It was so hard to do, though. To knowingly give up his life, even for the best of reasons—to save everyone else.

He took a breath and held it, trying to savor the feeling of his last. Then, fighting every impulse, he pushed a foot ahead . . . and . . . stepped. . . .

The Furies' high-pitched whining built in tension and excitement until his foot was firmly planted on the cavern floor. Then the three exploded with cries of exhilaration. A force behind Erec pushed him, hard and fast, into the middle of the immense, brightly lit cavern of white stone.

Birds and bats sailed everywhere around him, darting over his head and between his legs. He shooed them away from his face, amazed by all the swarms of flying things. A lizard scuttled under his feet, and a few cats hurried by. The scrawny cat he had seen outside again rubbed against his leg.

Surprisingly, he was still breathing. Why hadn't the Furies destroyed him and disappeared already?

"A few reasons." The white-haired Fury's voice creaked like a rusty hinge. She sneered, pinched and bitter, eyes full of hate. "We are *interested* in you. This is a first, you see—having a person walk in of their own accord and donate their soul to us. And for our benefit, no less."

"And a prince!" the red-haired Fury screeched. "What a lovely gift."

The white-haired one continued. "We do know that you wanted to stop Baskania from controlling us. Thank you for that. You are an interesting specimen, and I would like to study you a bit before ending your life." She sighed. "What a shame that you are the only human here. If there was just one more, we could use *that* soul for our release and I could drop you into some nice hot amber and keep you like this forever."

So, that must be Megaera, Erec thought.

The black-haired one boomed, "Personally, I don't care much for studying you. I'll leave that to my sister's misguided tastes. But I plan on taking my time and savoring this moment. This is history for us, sisters! Next up, vengeance on the Fates for locking us in here for nearly an eternity!"

Erec fished in his pocket for the bee in the small amber block and pulled it out. His voice did not sound like his own, more like a small shaky imitation. "I-is this yours?" He held the encased bee toward Megaera. "I b-brought it for y-you."

A sharp wind gusted, knocking the amber block from his outstretched palm. Erec thought he felt something soft brush his hand in the stream of air.

A gleeful whoop resounded, and Megaera's voice was softer. "Look! This was one of my favorite bees. Such lovely creatures. And their numbers are shrinking, so this is even more valuable to me. Why . . . thank you."

"Yes," the red-haired one screamed. She sounded furious, although her tone did not seem to match her words. "Thank you, boy. You've helped us immensely. How it would have lowered us to *serve* a human, although the trade would have been a small one in exchange for our escape. Of course, after we did his bidding a few times, he would likely have found himself dead. But we would rather do things our way, and make up for lost time by warring with our Fate sisters and ransacking the world."

"Everyone will pay," the black-haired one screeched, a smirk on her lips. Her black jointed wings flapped behind her. "Are we ready, girls?"

"Wait!" Erec's hand shot to his neck and found the Twrch Trwyth vial. All he had to do was break it open and he would know everything—maybe even how to escape, if that was possible.

"Silly boy," Megaera said. "There is no escape from here. You already know that."

And he did know that. All of a sudden it was perfectly clear to him. He was in Tartarus, from which nobody escapes. He had walked through the Waters of Oblivion. Before him were three beings more powerful than any human could imagine, almost as much as the Fates themselves. They had been here since the dawn of time. They hadn't even bothered putting a Draw on him, because they didn't need to. He could not possibly escape, or live.

He had done all he could. That thought made him smile. Suddenly he understood what he had seen through his dragon eyes when he looked into his future.

He did not leave much time left, and he was not going to waste his last move. Breaking the yellow glass ball, the Awen of Knowledge, was pointless now. What more did he need to know? A moment of ultimate understanding before his death was nice, but there was something better that he could do.

He would break open the red ball. The Awen of Harmony. That would help things. It had to. Even if just for a moment, the three Furies would feel better. They deserved it, he thought, after being locked in here for so long. Whatever they had done to be locked up here must have been bad, but this had been an awful punishment.

Would it calm the Furies down enough that they would forgive the Fates, and also the people of the world above them? Or would it just give them a moment of happiness? Erec did not know. But he twisted the tiny red glass dodecahedron attached to the tail of the boar-shaped vial. Its tiny stem cracked, and a red mist slithered from it into the air.

Erec threw the tiny ball toward the three Furies. A shower of red glitter rained down on them and Erec, as well as the small creatures on the floor. Everyone looked around in wonder.

A new feeling settled in Erec's heart. He understood what life had been like for the Furies. His heart expanded with compassion for these immense and lovely creatures that had been so filled with poisonous hate and jealousy. An air of camaraderie filled the room, and they all exchanged heartfelt glances and smiles.

"Megaera." He reached a hand toward her. "Alecto." The red-haired one tilted her head and he smiled at her. "Tisiphone." He looked at the dark-haired one with appreciation. "I cannot imagine what you three have suffered here for all of these years. It is no wonder you feel as tortured as you do. You must! I hope you realize that any human, anyone lesser than you, would have gone mad."

Alecto's face registered shock mixed with delight. She no longer screamed, but spoke with a rich and resounding multitoned voice. "You did this for us. You offered your life to save us. And then, before we killed you, you gave us a moment of comfort with your Awen of Harmony, because you felt for what we were going through." She looked at her sisters with wonder. "This small, insignificant human has given us more than anyone ever has. It feels so good to have all that anger lifted. I can feel the other parts of me working now. They were hidden all of this time. So much of me has been . . . hurting." She sighed, clasping her heart. "My rage was weighing on me so heavily. . . ."

All three of the sisters were growing larger, occupying more of the cave. It made sense, Erec thought. They were not going to be confined much longer. Soon they would be able to expand into their true selves. He was amazed at how well he understood them now . . . how connected they all were under the influence of the Awen of Harmony.

Tisiphone scooped Erec up in a windy hand, and he toppled back so he was sitting on her palm. "And I have been so vengeful—all action, all malice. This boy understands why. I know that. But I agree. How wonderful to feel this harmony now! Is this how others live all of the time?" She sounded hurt. "Why would our *other* sisters treat us so badly?"

Erec said, "I've talked to your sisters, the three Fates. They don't want to hurt you, I'm sure. I can't say I know exactly what happened with you and them all that time ago. But from what I do understand about the Fates, they just try to help things and make them fair for everybody. Don't you think they locked you here because they wanted to protect us humans? Maybe they didn't know what else to do."

Protecting humans sounded insignificant when talking to these timeless beings. But he hoped they would understand.

Alecto laughed, her red hair waving around her face. "Normally I would have bitten your head off for suggesting such a notion. But it's odd. I actually agree with you. Looking back to what happened, I can't say they acted maliciously toward us."

"They gave us warnings," Tisiphone agreed, setting Erec down again.

The three continued to grow until they reached the cavern roof, twenty feet over Erec's head. He could sense that they were ready. It would just be moments now.

"Please!" he called out. "Consider this, before I die. Could you honor me, and this moment, by sparing the lives of the rest of the humans on Earth? I would appreciate it so much. And also, think hard before waging a war on your sisters. What if you set the example for them, and showed them how good things can be . . . just how they are right now with us? They could learn from you, and the rest of your eternity would be spent in harmony instead of hate and fear."

Tisiphone lowered her eyes. "I would be the last one to say this, normally. But this human has a point. I'd love to feel good like this all the time. Do you think it's possible to let go of what's been done to us, sisters? Can we let this travesty of justice pass without retribution? Should we forgive?" She shook her head. "I've never spoken that word before."

Alecto's eyes blazed. "Can we let our anger go? I don't know."

Megaera regarded the small ambered bee in her hand. "Can we stop being jealous? Look what I've done to living things out of jealousy."

There were no answers. The wind inside the cave picked up, tossing a few of the smaller creatures around.

Megaera smiled upon Erec. "Thank you, young prince. You have shown us true kindness and given us wisdom as well. I, for one, will promise, as a tribute to your rescue of us, not to harm humans once I escape. As for my sisters, the Fates . . . I will try my best. Reconciliation with them may be too hard to promise, as an eternity stretches before us. But I want to live happily, for once. You have reminded me how good that feels."

"Well said." Alecto nodded. "I agree to the same."

"As do I," Tisiphone said.

A spirit of peace filled the immense, cold cavern. Hope, love, and joy echoed around them like the calls of long-lost friends. The Furies were relieved, grateful, and Erec was awestruck. All was well.

A reddish mist floated through the air, smelling of rosebuds. Erec held the boar vial around his neck—what was left of the Twrch Trwyth—with the red glass ball broken off.

"Thank you, again." Alecto smiled upon him. "You have done us a great service."

Tisiphone laughed in delight, then sucked in. . . . The room swirled. . . .

Erec's soul was leaving him. Pulling out into the air.

Everything was going black. He could feel himself drop.

"Take this," a voice whispered. "And remember me." Something fell into his hand.

The last points of light faded.

Dying.

Gone.

CHAPTER THIRTY-SEVEN

CHAPTER THIRTY-EIGHT

The Boy

THE CAT *(FELIS catus)* is a simple creature. Commonly known as house cats or domestic cats, these animals like to cuddle, rub against things, eat fresh fish, and play games with smaller creatures like mice.

But cats possess other qualities that people generally don't know. For one, they have amazing communication skills. At least, among each other. Some people believe that cats have nine lives, which is far from true. Cats actually have no less than ninety lives, although they notoriously lose count close to the end and get a nasty surprise when they run out. Having ninety lives is a big plus for cats, considering how clumsy and daring they are, and how often they chase and get into fights with dogs and other animals much larger and stronger than themselves. Some have been known to die as many as ten times in one day. This fortunate trick enables cats, as long as they are careful to keep count (which most, unfortunately, do not), to cross the Waters of Oblivion a good many times before having serious problems.

And there is one more thing about cats that you might not know: They are very loyal.

A particularly scrawny version of *Felis catus* had watched the events in the vast cavern of Tartarus with great interest. He saw the three huge bird people who had lived there forever grow bigger and bigger until finally the top of the rock cave burst outward and shattered into the open air. Their wings stretched out into what looked like infinity, at least to a cat, and then they had soared away.

Of course, not even a scrawny cat would be afraid of a bird. Even very big birds like these.

The boy who had entered the cavern had fallen, though, and didn't look right. His coloring was all wrong, and there was no breathing happening. He had died, the cat was sure, but the boy was not returning to life as a cat would have. What was wrong with humans, anyway, having only one measly life to live?

Well, he wasn't going to just let the boy sit here. Not *this* boy, anyway. This particular boy had saved him once. And not just one of his lives. No, the boy had saved all of them.

The cat had been trapped under a garbage can once, outside of a house. It was all a collision of mistakes and failures. Before he knew it, what had started as a simple evening meal had become deadly. The garbage can was so heavy that it pinned him once it tipped over. And it would not stop crushing him. He died, of course, came back to life, then died again, came back again, and kept on dying so many times that it was clear he would run through all of his lives before the next morning came.

But then this very boy appeared out of nowhere in his pajamas and lifted the can off him. Not only did he save him, but the boy dusted him off, petted him a bit, and offered him some of the very tuna the cat had been after in the first place. At last the boy walked away, grumbling about "cloudy thoughts."

One good turn deserved another, the cat thought, even if it *was* too late. He bit into the boy's sleeve and tugged, but the boy did not budge. Humans were far too heavy for their own good.

So he sent a silent message out into the room. The birds were all leaving through the hole in the roof, no longer interested in staying without those three big bird people who used to live here. And without the birds, what interest would this place hold for a cat? It was time for them to go. And, if they didn't mind lending a hand, could they please help drag this boy out of here on their way?

Cats slithered across the white floor, surrounding the boy. Biting into cloth, they pushed against his weight with their heads and paws. Soon he was slowly sliding across the cave and out of the door. Pulling, shifting, the cats dragged him straight into the shallow Waters of Oblivion. At many points the boy's face was underwater, but he wasn't breathing anyhow. The cats were able to keep their heads above water for the most part. The rapids were fast, which helped in spots and made the crossing harder in others. They ended crossing the shallow river a good thirty feet downstream from where they started.

The scrawny cat had noticed another man who was slumped

against the cliff base when they had passed near to the cave entrance. For a moment he debated making another trip back again, not sure exactly how many lives he had left. Crossing the waters was sure to take another one away. But it seemed wrong to leave the man alone in such a desolate place, especially after they had done so well taking this one through.

He broadcast another call for help. The cats traveled back through the river again and found the man, who had not moved one bit. By the time they had dragged him across, though, the boy was gone.

CHAPTER THIRTY-NINE

Cookies and a Charm

ORDS . . . FLASHES OF LIGHT . . . music . . . laughter . . . memories . . . flickers of thought . . . Gone. Then back again. Then dark. How much time passed since that last bright spot?

Time played tricks. Was this real? What was he seeing? Was this his life playing back? Was it heaven? Then out again.

When brightness returned as two long slits in his eyes he gasped. He was breathing. But how?

Where was he? *Who* was he? And *how?*

He felt something soft against his face. A hand. And a voice—just as soft. "You need to drink more of this, Erec. Look, it's working!"

A warm taste of liquid metal and hot peppers spread through his mouth. When it hit the back of his throat he swallowed reflexively, and instantly felt better. Strength surged through his body, letting him lift his head slightly. He could see now as well. People gathered over him. Bethany was holding a glass of purple liquid. And a dragon looked over her shoulder. Was that Little Erec?

Another mouthful of the purple stuff went in and Erec almost choked. But then he started breathing well, and looking around, eyes open. "Where . . . am I? I must be dreaming. Or . . ." His face clenched. His whole family was with him. Were they dead too? Were they all in heaven together?

June appeared. "We're in a safe house in Smoolie, Otherness. Well, we're outside now, so Patchouli and Little Erec could be with you. King Derby and Queen Shalimar are keeping an eye on us. Your friend Rosco showed up early this morning at Aunt Salsa's house. He had tracked us down to tell us the news that we needed to get somewhere safe right away, and the Furies would be released soon. But you were gone. Bethany figured out where you went, and told us about your quest." She shuddered.

"We couldn't find the Hermit," Bethany said. Her eyes looked misty. "And none of us had any idea how to get to you and stop you." She sniffed, and a tear ran down her cheek.

Jack poked his head over Trevor's shoulder. "I told Oscar—I mean Rosco—about Kyron, Artie, and Griffin over at Spartacus's ranch, so he went there to get them. Spartacus was already gone by then. Baskania took him to give to the Furies."

Zoey snuck through the crowd and cuddled on Erec's chest. "I was worried about you," she said.

Erec tried to answer, but he did not have the strength. Bethany saw his lips moving, and reached over with more of the purple liquid. "Your turn to drink this stuff, Erec. It's dragon blood, and it's really working on you."

The burning metallic-tasting liquid felt good going down. With each sip more energy returned to him. Now he could speak. "Did Patchouli . . . ?"

"No." Patchouli looked down from what seemed like high in the sky. "Little Erec insisted. You saved him with your blood once."

Erec's voice was a hoarse whisper. "I think we're more than even. You know, I was sure I had died." He rested for a few breaths, and nobody answered him. "I don't know how I made it out of there."

A few people looked at each other, unsure what to say. Then Bethany brushed his hair from his face. "Erec, you *did* die. I don't know what happened, if the Furies saw you or not.

"But the Hermit was waiting for you on the other side of that river. He said a huge crowd of cats started coming across the water. A lot of them were together in one spot, going really slowly, like they were carrying something. When he saw it was you . . . Well, you know the Hermit. He shouted something like, 'Look what the cats dragged in!' A bunch more brought Spartacus Kilroy across the water, and he pulled you both into the Port-O-Door. Luckily, he took you here first, and then went to get us. That way he had time to warn us. If I had just seen you lying there dead . . ."

June's face wrinkled in pain and she hugged him. "All I know is you're back. The Hermit wasn't sure he could do it. I was so scared." She cried into his shoulder, Zoey patting his hair.

"I still don't get it," he said. "The dragon blood gave me my life back?"

"No," June said. She held up a cracked piece of gleaming yellow crystal. "It was this."

Erec had no idea what it was. "Huh?"

Bethany forced another sip of dragon blood into Erec's mouth, and then he found himself able to sit up. He took the cracked yellow rock from his mother. "What is it?"

"Amber," Bethany said. "It had a bee in it. The Hermit found it clutched in your fist. It had been preserved alive from one of the three Furies—probably that one we read about in the library that collected living specimens. I remember you said you found this in Baskania's fortress, right? Well, the Hermit told us that each of these things held a small breath of life inside. This one had only a tiny bit—just enough life to support a bee. It couldn't have brought a normal person back." She bit her lip. "But you are part dragon now, with Aoquesth's eyes. So you only needed a tiny jump start."

Jack said, "The Hermit cracked the amber open with a little marble statue of Anubis—this man with a jackal head. He said the ancient Egyptians believed Anubis took care of the dead. But the Hermit didn't know if it would work. We were all really upset, Erec. I mean, there you were. And the Hermit was saying that maybe too much time had gone by, or there might not be enough life in the amber to spark anything."

Erec sat up, rubbing his arms. How amazing it was to feel his arms! "But it *did* work. That and the dragon blood. But I thought the Furies took my soul. . . ."

June looked concerned. "I suppose they did use it to escape, but it looks like you got it back, kiddo."

Jack was petting and talking to a scrawny cat.

"Hey!" Erec did a double-take. "That cat was with me in Tartarus."

"Yeah." Jack nodded. "He said you saved his life once, and he paid you back."

The cat blinked at Erec, then darted into the woods. "Wait!" Erec called. "Come back!"

"I already asked if he wanted to stay with us," Jack said. "He likes to wander, though."

Erec shook his head. "That's crazy. I don't remember saving his life." He shrugged. "Well, I won't argue, I guess. I'm alive."

Bethany joined June and Zoey giving Erec a hug, and he thought he might die again. But this time of happiness.

Not until Erec had been up and walking around for a while did he think about Spartacus Kilroy. Smoolie was so spectacular, and Erec appreciated everything a hundred times more now that he had almost lost it all, so he found himself staring in awe at leaves and blades of grass for minutes at a time.

He took a walk alone to clear his mind, and bits of what he had gone through filtered back to him. He remembered that Spartacus had been dragged by cats across the Waters of Oblivion as well. Was he okay? Had he made it across that river and still lived?

Erec sat by a brook in the woods. Water bounded over some rocks and splashed into others, causing little white waves to break up the sparkles from the sun. It was so beautiful. But was Spartacus able to enjoy it anymore? It was strange that nobody had mentioned him. . . .

Who was it, anyway, that said that anyone crossing the Waters of Oblivion would die soon after? They could have been wrong. Maybe Spartacus had not been across it long enough, and he still could be saved. Erec had died because of the Furies—Spartacus had not even gone into Tartarus. He might be fine, Erec told himself. . . .

A shadow loomed silently by his side. Erec turned, then jumped with surprise. Spartacus Kilroy, looking perfectly fine, although a bit pale, sat next to him on a rock.

Erec almost fell over with relief. "You're okay! I was just thinking about you. What happened over there? Did those cats save you? I heard a bunch of them pulled both of us across the river."

Spartacus did not answer. Instead he picked up a rock and skipped it across the water. The small stone bounced perfectly on the stream surface, then hit a rock and catapulted to the dirt on the other side. He looked around him in wonder, just as Erec had. "It's all so . . . spectacular."

"Yeah, I know. I guess I never really *looked* at everything before." He laughed. "But Smoolie is extra pretty, anyway."

Spartacus nodded, and they sat in silence awhile. "I see your amulet has another slice lit up now. Guess that means you finished your sixth quest? Not bad—half done."

Erec looked down at his chest. His Amulet of Virtues was now half lit with glowing colors. The newest segment was sky blue, with a black symbol in the middle. "I can't imagine what this virtue will be. Complete stupidity? That seems to best describe what I did." He spun his dragon eyes forward so he could read what it said. "*Compassion.* Hmm. I think stupidity makes more sense."

Erec understood, however. He had felt compassionate toward the three Furies, even though they were using him like a pawn and taking his life away. That was the only reason he had chosen to use the red ball—the Awen of Harmony—for their benefit. And it had done a lot of good.

"So, are you planning to take a break now?"

Erec laughed. He hadn't thought there were any other options. "A break? That implies I'm going to start doing quests again someday. I don't know, that last one kind of knocked me out."

"That's an understatement." Humor twinkled in Spartacus's eyes. "But I bet you will do more. I get that feeling."

"I don't have that feeling. You know, I have a missing brother and sister out there. My triplet sibs. I think I'm going to find them first before even coming close to doing another quest. Those things are awful! I mean, the Fates sent me to my death. Nobody was even sure I could be revived. If I hadn't found that amber bee . . ." He felt sick thinking about how close he came.

Spartacus shrugged. "Maybe the Fates did know you would have that bee. Or maybe they just thought it was worth the risk. You did save everyone on Earth, you know."

Erec had not thought about that since he had returned to life. He really had stopped the Furies from destroying the world . . . and from becoming Baskania's servants. The thought overwhelmed him, and he lay back onto the grass. Above him, white clouds floated through a too-blue sky, intricate branches with sparkling green leaves creating patterns in front of them. It was all okay now. His mother . . . Bethany . . . his siblings—he would even be able to enjoy it with them. And Spartacus too.

"I can still enjoy this, you know," Spartacus said, as if he could tell what Erec was thinking. It seemed an odd thing to say, though. He picked up another stone and skipped it across the stream.

"How could you not? Listen to that." Erec pointed at two blue-birds perched on a branch nearby. They shouted at each other in high-pitched, speedy twitters. One of them seemed to be saying, "Truly, truly, truly." But the other warbled musical chatter over his call.

Spartacus smiled at the birds. "You'll find those siblings of yours. I'm sure of it."

"I hope so. I'm going to look for my birth mother, too. Not that she could ever replace June. But I would like to get to know her again."

"Good luck with that."

"What about you? I guess you'll go back to your farm again? Was Artie helping you out there?"

"He was. Before I left, Artie took over the morning feeding schedule. He's really good with animals, that guy." He pursed his lips. "We had a little bit of a surprise with Wolfboy when the full moon rose. Luckily Kyron still had some wolfsbane on him."

"Oops. Sorry." Erec cringed. "I forgot to tell you about that."

"Don't worry. Everything's fine. I will be going back to my farm, but I'm not sure how long I'll stay. I have some unfinished business. Too many things there now that I'm responsible for. It's a funny thing about me, when I take something on, I'm committed. Totally focused." He laughed. "I guess you can tell. But one of these days soon I'll be done."

Erec was confused. "Done? And then what? Is there something else you're going to do?"

Spartacus stared at him awhile, then said, "You have a caterpillar in your hair." He reached out to brush it off, but his hand stopped a few inches from Erec's head. Spartacus tried to get to the bug from different angles, then finally gave up. "That's funny. I had no problem shaking hands with Jack this morning. And Bethany gave me a kiss."

Both of them watched the brook race by, lost in their own thoughts. Everything was so peaceful. Erec wondered what the Furies were up to now, if they had talked to their sisters yet. It was nice knowing that they weren't locked away anymore.

"Are you going to forgive your father soon?"

Erec was surprised. He didn't remember talking to Spartacus about his dad. "I don't know. I guess it all ended up okay. And Bethany was right. He really thought he had it under control. It wasn't like he handed Bethany over to Baskania or anything."

Spartacus nodded. "I bet he felt even worse about her being captured than you did, if that's possible."

"So, what's that unfinished business on your farm? Just taking care of all the animals?"

"And people. Do you know how many completely dependent people are living there now?"

Erec was confused.

Spartacus grinned. "And how many of them look like you?"

"Oh, yeah!" Erec had forgotten the hundreds of Erecs, Bethanys, and Baskanias they had left on the farm. "Are they getting into trouble? Are the Baskanias . . . evil?"

"Not really." He laughed. "They're all quite tame. But they've formed little camps, and they have no clue how to support themselves. I mean, they try to help out, but they get confused. What they have no problem doing, though, is idolizing you . . . or whoever it is that they look like. At first they managed to paint pictures of you and post them up on sticks to admire, some made little statues of you, Bethany, or Baskania. All they really want to do is follow you, you know, and imitate everything that you do."

"That sounds *awful*. I'll have to stay away from them. Unless . . . do you think they'll find me?"

"They're not the type to wander around. Don't worry. I'll get them all settled, and I'm pretty sure I can teach them to do little bits to help run the farm. If Artie and Kyron still want to stay on and help, we can get all those folks squared away. Then I guess I'll be off."

"Off? Where are you going?"

Spartacus stared at him again. "You really don't know, do you?"

A strange thought crept into Erec's head, but he pushed it away. "No, I don't."

Spartacus picked up a rock as if to skim it on the water, but he just looked at it and put it down. "I didn't make it, Erec. They weren't able to bring me back."

Erec swung toward him in shock. *"What?"*

"I think you know what I'm saying. Do you really want me to spell it all out for you?"

"You . . . you're not . . ." This was why Spartacus could not touch him. "I . . ." This was why he knew what Erec was thinking, before he said anything.

Spartacus sighed. "Crossing the Waters of Oblivion did me in. I was fated, one way or another, from that."

Erec squeezed his eyes shut. He didn't want to hear this. "Baskania killed you. He used up your life for his own sick reasons, just so he could have more power." Suddenly he was sick with anger. Words churned in his throat, but they could not find their way out.

"It's not so bad, this." Spartacus studied his hand. "Doesn't feel like being alive. I will miss that. But there are some advantages."

"Are you a ghost?"

Spartacus shot him a mocking glance. "Don't tell me it's taken you this long to figure that out."

"But you look so . . . real. Perfectly alive. I thought maybe I was just dreaming this conversation. So . . . other people can see you too?"

"Sure. That's the way it is with ghosts. Nobody would know by looking at me unless I told them. Of course, I'll be open about it. But some other people aren't like that. They'll keep it a big secret, and try to make everyone think they're still alive. A few signs give them away though."

"Really?" Erec was curious. "Like what?"

"Not aging. Knowing or seeing more than one normally would. Oh, and not touching you, I guess." He laughed. "Is that some strange quirk you have?"

"Yeah. Ghosts can't touch me. I still can't get over that you . . . Why couldn't they bring you back?" He suddenly felt terrible. "I only had one of the amber bees. And they decided to use it on me instead of you. . . ."

"It wouldn't have worked on me. That tiny bit of life wouldn't have been enough to bring me back. You're the one with the dragon eyes, remember?"

Erec nodded. He felt a deep loss, even though Spartacus sat at his side.

Then, as if on cue with Erec's feelings, Spartacus stood and drifted away, noiselessly, across the grass.

Erec wandered back and was finally able to say a proper hello to everyone. Griffin raised a saber in salute, frightening June and Zoey, who stood nearby, but not disturbing Kilroy in the least. "Where's Rosco?" Erec looked around. "Did he have to go back?"

Jack pointed a thumb toward the log cabin they were staying in. "He's inside. Rosco's been acting kinda weird. I think he feels bad that you went to Tartarus and . . . you know. Like he could have stopped you."

Erec wandered through the rooms of the cabin and found Rosco sitting on the floor in the corner of a bedroom. "Hey, are you okay?"

Rosco shrugged. "I've been better."

"You better not be feeling guilty for me going to Tartarus. I mean, there was nothing you could have done. All right?"

Rosco looked at Erec like he was crazy. "I know that. I don't feel guilty. Well, not about that, anyway. Which is good, because I feel guilty for pretty much everything else in my whole life." He sighed. "I don't know, Erec. I think all of this"—he waved around the room—". . . you know, it's all been too much for me. Maybe that time travel from all those years ago is catching up." He shrugged.

"You just tired out, then?"

He sighed. "Nah. I'm . . . Never mind. It's stupid."

"What? Like I've never done stupid things?"

"Well, this is a little embarrassing." Rosco rubbed his forehead. "I don't know . . ."

"Come on. We're friends, right? Just—out with it."

Rosco looked at him sheepishly. "My mind is going. I started seeing things, which is the first sign that you're losing your marbles. It happened when I was picking up your friends Kyron, Artie, and Griffin from Spartacus Kilroy's ranch." He laughed. "Those are some weird but cool friends you found. Anyway, I saw . . . well, something really strange. Nobody else even said anything about it, so it was definitely all in my head. Well, of course."

Erec started to smile. "You didn't happen to see me there, did you?"

"Ugh." Rosco dropped his head into his hands. "I guess it's obvious that you, Bethany, and Baskania have been on my mind lately. So yeah, I did see you. But a lot of you. And them, too."

Erec was laughing now. He covered his mouth and hit the floor to stop himself, but it only poured out harder.

"That's right. Laugh at the weirdo. Story of my life."

"No," Erec spit out. "They were real. The versions of me, Bethany, and Baskania, I mean." He swallowed his chuckles and told Oscar the story.

"Wow, it must be nice to have a hundred followers who would do anything for you."

"Not at all. If they were here right now, all of them would be sitting against the wall and talking to you, saying just what I was saying after they heard it. It would be chaos."

"Yeah, chaos, I guess. But fun chaos. Well, maybe for a little while, anyway."

Erec thought that maybe Oscar was right. One of these days he would pay a visit to his look-alikes and see how they were getting on. "Want to go outside? My mom's grilling hamburgers."

"Yeah, sure. They say there is nothing like the stars at night in Smoolie."

Erec was not so sure about that. There was nothing like stars at night anywhere, he thought. Anywhere at all.

* * *

Enjoying his fifth hamburger, Artie was listening to Kyron retell how they smuggled themselves into Baskania's fortress in Jakarta. He wandered over to Erec. "Can I have youse charm now? Youse said I could keep it when you were back again. It was a pretty one. Shiny, too."

A warm breeze blew the hair from Erec's face as he bit into a juicy hamburger, loaded with ketchup, tomato, and lettuce. The sun was just beginning to set. "What charm do you mean, Artie?"

"That one, hanging on the pretty ribbon there." He jabbed Erec's chest. "I likes ribbons, too."

Erec picked up the Doubler charm. It had really come in handy. But he had promised it to Artie, so he slipped it off his neck and handed it to him.

Bethany slipped close to them, carrying the Serving Tray and munching on a fresh chocolate chip cookie.

"That looks yummy." Artie watched Bethany take another bite of her cookie. "Can I have one?"

"Of course, Artie," she said. "Do you want it now, or after you're done with your hamburgers?"

Artie disregarded her question. "Can I have *two* cookies?"

"I don't see why not."

"Can I have *three*?"

"Of course!"

Artie leaned forward, eyes wild with excitement. "How many cookies can I eat?"

Bethany closed her eyes and did some rapid calculations. "Given your probable age, appetite, love of cookies, lifespan, waking hours in a day, and percentage of free time, I'd say that you could eat about one million, eight hundred and twenty-five thousand."

In a flash of hunger and anticipation, Artie whipped the contents in his hand through the air and into his open mouth, gulping, then reached for the tray in Bethany's hands.

Erec watched, stunned. Artie had no idea, he realized, that he had not finished his hamburger, which had now fallen to the floor. Instead he had gulped down the Doubler charm.

A wind whipped by, almost knocking Erec over with a loud swish. Everyone turned to see what was happening . . . but then it died down.

For a moment Erec thought the Doubler charm was activating. But there was no lightning bolt shot into the air.

Artie opened his mouth as if to speak, but instead he burped—and a flash of light erupted through his lips into the darkening air. "Excuse me." He covered his mouth, embarrassed.

"What was that?" Bethany asked Erec, stunned.

"He just swallowed the Doubler charm that Wandabelle gave me. You know, the one that takes any magic that has just been performed and makes it work on two other things. Like when Baskania made a hundred of you, and I used it to make a hundred of me and him, too?"

"How could I forget?" she said, lips twisted. "But no magic happened here."

Erec shrugged.

"If I may," Artie said. "I do think if that is how the Doubler charm works, that magic may indeed have been done."

Bethany and Erec looked at him in shock. It sounded like somebody else had infiltrated Artie's body and was speaking through him.

"You see," Artie continued, "my memory is perfectly intact, even after the charm has worked its spell. I remember the fantastic calculation you just performed about my eating"—he cleared his throat, obviously embarrassed—"cookies. My dear, are your math skills, by chance, magical?"

"I don't know. They *are* my inborn gift. . . ."

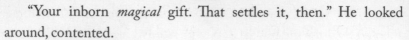

"Your inborn *magical* gift. That settles it, then." He looked around, contented.

"Settles . . . what?" Erec said.

"Oh, I'm terribly sorry. The charm picked up on Bethany's magic, which was her special intelligence in math. And when I swallowed it—how dreadful of me to do, but quite fortunate—I must have waved it in the air first. The charm obviously picked up her recent use of her power, and then sent it out again to two different locations. Only, they were both inside me."

"You do sound . . . completely different now," Erec agreed. "Like you're . . ." He hesitated putting it into words.

"It's all right, Erec. You are correct. I believe I have my old self back again. This seems to have reversed the repercussions from that Death Spell that Baskania had once tried to use on me. I was lucky that it didn't kill me. I believe Kyron told you that I held a glass dish in front of me, and it weakened the spell when it passed through so that I could live. But it took away my mind, I am afraid." He smiled. "Your Doubler charm was just what I needed, it turns out."

Kyron was watching, spellbound. He approached slowly, as if afraid he might wake up from a dream. "Dad? Is that really you?"

Artie held his arms open for his son. "It is, Kyron. I'm back, I'm afraid. Come here, boy."

Kyron ran over and gave his father a giant hug. "I can't believe it, Dad. I can't believe . . . Thank you, Erec. Again. Thank you so much."

Bethany's jaw hung open. "What two things did the charm work on? Your mind—your intellect is back. What else?"

"I'm not quite sure yet. Luckily it worked on the correct part of my brain. But I do have a feeling that something else about me is also more intelligent now." He pointed at the Serving Tray. "Do you mind?"

"Of course." Bethany handed it to him.

Artie asked for a chocolate-chip cookie, then he took a bite. "Umm. Oh, ahhh. Ohhh. Yes." He nodded vigorously, and a grin spread across his face. "Just as I thought. My tastebuds. Another cookie, please."

Erec and Bethany left Artie with Kyron and the Serving Tray. The Smoolie stars were starting to come out now. They were more beautiful than he had even imagined.

"Want to go for a walk?" Erec said.

"I thought you'd never ask."

Three Days Later

THE SCRAWNY CAT sauntered along a dark street. The smell of tuna beckoned him ahead. How many lives did he have left? he mused. Despite warnings, he had lost count. There were at least ten, he was sure. It was time to start being more careful.

By the time he had sniffed out the tuna, it had nearly disappeared into a fluffy pink cat. She watched him, grudgingly, and then pushed the remainder of the can toward him.

Thank you.

No problem. I have all of this I want at home, and more. Go ahead.

Well then, why are you out here? You could run into a dog and lose a life.

I'm not going home until I find my owner. She's been captured. I just don't know where she is.

What is her name? What does she look like?

Bethany Cleary. She is beautiful, with long dark hair that curls, and she loves to pet me and give me treats.

I've seen a girl with that name in Smoolie. Let me trace a map for you in the dirt.

But the pink kitten did not wait for the scrawny cat to make a tracing. She raced off, disappearing into the night.

Two Weeks Later

EVEN THOUGH DUMPLING Smith and her friends would no longer be breaking windows, and all looked clear and safe in their apartment in New Jersey, June had traced around the building again with the special chalk that King Piter had given her. That should keep them hidden safely, she thought. Never bad to be too careful.

It was calm and quiet at home, and the windows had been replaced. Erec was glad to take a break—although this time if

Bethany needed him, or even sent a letter, he would rush back in a heartbeat to her side in Ashona, where she was spending time with King Piter.

Days passed before Erec thought to unpack the backpack that he had been carrying around. A large white sheet was stuffed inside, and wrapped in it was a little alarm clock with a bow on its head and metallic arms and legs. He laughed when he set it down, watching it run around on the carpet and do a few handsprings. It was glad to be free.

Then a thought occurred to him. He picked the thing up and brought it to his room, setting it next to his similar alarm clock, the male version, on his desk.

The two devices froze, facing each other. He had not noticed before that the desk was wet, but pools of water sat below the clocks, dripping onto the floor. He realized they were crying.

His clock jumped high, flipping in the air, and landed on its knees before the other. Soon, the two of them were gallivanting, hand-in-hand, through the whole apartment.

Hmm. Was this perhaps who his clock had been seeing, and missing, through the Seeing Eyeglasses?

Erec smiled. The clocks had it right. There was a lot to live for.

Five Hundred Years Earlier

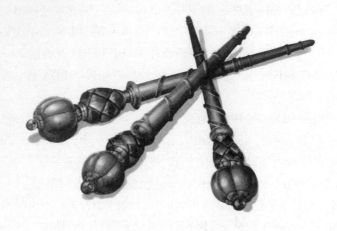

IT WAS MARCH thirteenth. Everything was set. Thanatos Argus Baskania was on top of the world. Literally. And why shouldn't he be? He had worked long and hard for this day. Next month, on April eleventh, it would be official. He would rule the entire human race.

It had not been easy, of course. But nobody else would ever have been able to do what he did. Any of it. Things had been so dreary before he had his way with the Substance this time. It was his gift: to see it, hear it, use it as he pleased, and make its magic follow along the pathways he chose. They called him "ultra absorbent," but he knew he wasn't absorbing the Substance; he was bending it to his own needs.

The Substance had been so useless before he changed it. And he himself had been pathetic too. He had thought it was his friend—a cute, silly notion. Well, he had grown up since then. Those stupid feelings it had given him, its cries and pleas . . . those only were there to weaken him. Of course he would not let himself become weak.

Nobody could use the Substance like he could. Especially before he changed it, which also let others use it better. That had been his greatest decision, his coup de grace. For so long he had kept its powers to himself. It felt good to be the only one to work its "magic." But then he realized: If others could do what he could—to a lesser extent, of course—he could control teams of powerful sorcerers. What was better, acting alone, or having an army of magic under you?

So he had done the unimaginable. He changed the Substance completely, changed the way the whole world worked, to make it possible for his underlings to use the Substance as well.

Once only very "absorbent" people like shamans, witches, and druids used to be able to perform magic, and only when they quieted their minds and focused. They'd had amulets, talismans, some spells that worked with practice, but nothing like there was now. He had made the Substance usable. It did his bidding. He had actually kinked the Aitherplanes with his own mind, to keep it from flowing freely, and made it more accessible, more workable.

The change had not been easy. The Substance had protested the whole way. He had ignored its cries, of course. Useless whimpering. The only problem now was that a few others were growing a little too strong for his liking, all from the changes he himself had made. Some were serving under him, but others were against him. They were leaching the power that he had created. That would not do. He would have to keep a tight thumb on them all.

So this, what he was doing today, at this moment, was a stroke of genius. The Kingdoms of the Keepers. He had created magic, the way it worked now, so he should decide who got to use it and who did not. Simple. Only those he deemed worthy would have a place in his kingdoms. Everyone else in the world would lose all of their magic—and even their memory of it.

Twisting and pulling the Substance into the dominions of Alypium, Aorth, Ashona, and Otherness was like scaling the steepest slope of Kilimanjaro bare-handed, but Baskania had loved every minute of it. Wrestling the forces, dominating his will over the motions of the world, was pure glory. He could not remove Substance entirely from Upper Earth without killing everyone there, but enough to sharply limit what they could do.

The Substance did not go happily, though. Its wailing was driving him mad. After his coronation next month he would spend a few years in Upper Earth just to get away from its noise.

It was snowing terribly today in the mountains. He had not expected it—it had been so sunny for the last few weeks. This sort of change would not do in his new kingdom. There should be something to protect it from the elements. A shield . . . a dome of golden haze over his prized city of magic. He walked out of the castle that had been built for him and gazed at the skies.

It would be a big job, but that only made it more enjoyable. He raised his hands and called to the Substance around him, making it move, create, change . . .

He felt it form, and suddenly the snow stopped falling around him. He could not see the dome he had just created, but he knew every particle of it in his mind. The weather in his Alypium would always be beautiful now.

One of his blind followers leaned out through the front castle doors on his cane. "Shadow Prince! Come quickly! There is a seer in the throne room. She is causing a stir."

Baskania shoved by him. The seer's face was hidden under the makeshift hood of her sackcloth coat, which reached to the floor. But a swatch of cloth near her feet glowed in a shocking red. Crowds gathered around her, shouting questions.

"Here he is!" someone shouted. "The Shadow Prince is here. Ask him if it's true!"

One of his followers looked at Baskania, trembling. "Did you ... *do* something to fix our weather today, my prince?" He bowed nervously.

Baskania frowned. "Yes. I did, in fact. Just now. To protect all of us here from the elements, I created a dome around Alypium."

Shouts and screams rang through the room. "She was right!"

"She predicted it!"

"She knows everything!"

People were begging the seer, each wanting her to help them, tell their futures. But her voice rang clear. "I came for one reason today. I have a prophesy for you, and gifts. Listen carefully to what I shall foretell.

"King Philibert and Queen Yolande, the rulers of Cyprus, Jerusalem, and Armenia, are coming here to live. Their lands will soon be taken over by the Venetians."

Baskania sneered. So, this was just a feeble attempt of someone he had left in Upper Earth to sneak in here. Clever, he thought, sending a "seer" to announce it, so it would be harder for him to turn them away.

Her voice rang out again. "They will have babies eight days from now, on March twenty-first. The children of this royal couple will be triplets, named Piter, Posey, and Pluto. These three babies are the next rightful rulers of these new Kingdoms of the Keepers."

What nerve! Baskania was not sure if he was more angry or amused. The seer pulled a few items out of her sack. Baskania could not see what they were. "These are gifts for your kingdom. They will show you who your true rulers are. This stone comes from the edges of the Earth, where the strongest magic exists. It is called the Lia Fail. You will hear it scream during any coronation when your rightful rulers are near to it. And these are the scepters of your next rulers. They will work only for those destined to be kings and queens. Keep them here until your coronation ceremony next month."

Baskania could not believe his ears. A tide of rage raced through him. How *dare* she? Who was this person, and how did she have the audacity to say such things. Triplet babies destined to rule the kingdoms that *he* created? Did she really think she could sway his own people against him? He pointed a finger at her to stop her in her tracks. But she seemed aware of him, dodging and darting behind the crowd until she disappeared.

His eyes narrowed. Someday, if he found her, she would pay. In the meantime, no real harm was done. Scepters, a screaming stone. All hogwash.

The more he thought about it, she was quite amusing. In fact, he would not stop this King Philibert and Queen Yolande from coming here if they chose to. No, not at all. A few pathetic Upper Earth rulers could do nothing to frighten him. Better to see what they were planning, and make them pay, slowly and painfully.

So, if three babies showed up at his coronation expecting to take over, well . . . it would not hurt to show his graciousness toward them. And if an accident happened to befall them all one day, then so be it.